Watcher

Rebel Wayfarers MC
Book #9

MariaLisa deMora

Edited by Hot Tree Editing

Cover image by Charles Thomas Rogers Photography

Cover model: Anthony Varrecchia

Cover design: Debera Kuntz

First Published 2016

ISBN 13: 978-0-9967486-8-1

DEDICATION

This book is for every person who skirts the fine line between citizen and outlaw. Those who are driven by circumstance and events to walk through shadows. Who by way of loyalty and love—with integrity and personal courage—strive to make a difference. There are more of us than you think.

Contents

ACKNOWLEDGMENTS

For any given book, there are scores more people involved in bringing it to publication than you might imagine. Of course, there are those who actively assist in every endeavor—photographers, editors, alpha and beta readers, graphic artists, and distributors. These people are important, and their roles are key. But frequently it is the behind the scenes folks who play just as critical a role, often without thanks.

People who provide inspiration through their actions, usually without realizing how they've impacted others. Individuals who become the conscience of the characters, and help shape the actions within the pages. This book is one of those, where the list of thank you notices could far outstrip the page count of the story.

Thank you to the gal at the concert who told me I looked amazeballs. That helped lead to Juanita accepting herself in ways that might surprise folks.

Thank you to the biker at the Veterans' ride who complimented my riding. That helped give Carmela self-confidence to best her situation.

Thank you to the elderly veteran outside the southern Louisiana gas station. The pride you had in your service shone through our conversation, and I carried that with me all year.

Thank you to the co-worker who gave me a gigantic beer mug. It helps to know there are good people who have my back.

Every interaction helps build my world, and these in turn enrich the ones I've created in my mind. Thank you all.

I do have a few specific thanks to give. Bear with me, because these are important.

Thank you to all active military service personnel, and every veteran, man or woman, who served on home soil or overseas; to each hero who didn't make it home; to all the families of those who serve. Thank you. You have my unending gratitude. I am humbled at the gift of sacrifice you have presented to all Americans.

An enormous thank you to Charles Thomas Rogers for capturing the image on the cover of *Watcher*. His work with Anthony Varrecchia was brought to my attention by a dear friend, and the swiftness with which everything fell into place meant this cover was destined to be. Anthony is amazing, and is as sweet and gracious a being as you could ever ask to meet. Also, a big thank you to Debera Kuntz for your talented ability to clarify my muddled ideas and bring them to life.

Becky Johnson and the gals at Hot Tree Editing have done a fabulous job, as always. I appreciate your willingness to go the extra mile to help shine my babies. XOXO

To my critique partners, Kristen, MirandaPanda, Kori, Jamey, and Kelsi: Thank you. *Watcher* is the better for your feedback. Plus, you didn't kill me. So, bonus!

To the readers. You folks who vote with your wallet. The ones who read these stories and come back for more. Y'all rock hard. Miles of gratitude.

To my cadre of personal motorcycle men and women who have grown to be more family than friends, thank you. From the bottom of. Except Tinker. You're still an ass. No, that's neither a metaphor nor an allegory.

And, that's it. Like I said, if I keep going, I'll double the page count, and none of us want filler in front of this story. Y'all enjoy, yeah? Muuwah! <3

Woofully yours,

~ML

Kentucky backwoods

Fifteen-year-old Michael Otey stood at the top of the path, shoulders back, long arms relaxed at his sides. His ma promised he'd grow into his reach soon, said Mikey just had to be patient. From where he waited, right where the path doglegged sharply, he could see the pitch in the grade as the dirt track plunged down the steep mountainside towards the holler. He was watching his pa and one of their neighbors walk the trail that led towards the mine entrance. Not quite dawn, the early light streaming through the fog-filled air created odd shadows, making the men appear as dark silhouettes—featureless and eerie when glimpsed through the trees. His pa turned just before the path crooked at the bottom of the hill and waved, one long arm extending far over his head and holding there until Mikey waved back.

Next year Mikey would be pacing the same trail alongside them, taking his turn in the elevator to be deposited into the bowels of the earth. Not yet, though. His pa was adamant Mikey not take the burden on until he was at least sixteen.

Turning and jogging five long strides off the path and into the woods, Mikey oriented himself, then set off at a steady trot back home, staying off the path for this leg of the trip. Eyes down, he scanned the ground ahead and to either side, occasionally stopping to collect black morel mushrooms growing from the hillside. Practiced motions allowed him to leave the roots intact, the soft stems of the black and gray fungus falling to the pinching pressure of thumb meeting fingertip. Elbow tucked inside the bag slung over his shoulder, Mikey cradled the mushrooms in both hands as he opened the container and placed them inside. With a self-satisfied grin, he allowed himself a moment of pride at the haul he would be dropping on his mama's table in about five minutes. Morels were a cash crop on a good week and a stew-stretcher on a bad one. She would be well pleased because most of the 'shrooms were big and clean.

In the barn later that afternoon, he'd been working his way through the daily list of jobs, and was measuring out chicken feed. This was normally Tabby's chore, but at only six, she was too short to reach the bottom of the barrel, and was prone to lean over too far, tipping herself inside. So, when it was nearly empty, as it currently was, dipping out a scoop or two of grain on her behalf was far easier than retrieving an angry little sister from the depths of the round prison. It hadn't happened often, but for him even once was too much, so if he were in a place to do so, he would meet her in the barn of an evening and help fill her bucket. Mikey was head-and-chest inside the barrel, scraping down near the bottom, having tuned out her little voice ratchet-jawing away above him. Tabby was jabbering animatedly about a dolly she'd seen in the mail-order catalog and how her birthday was only four months away when he felt it come over him. A spine-tingling strangeness washing through the air like soot before a storm.

First was the stillness. It seemed like noises were caught on the wind like cottonwood seeds in a cobweb; the waves of sound suspended as if they were dust motes in a sunbeam.

Then Pa's old mare squealed. The normally sedate horse kicked out hard at the walls of her wooden stall, the sounds she made both sharp and dull at the same time.

The earth underneath his feet stretched, jolting everything in the barn. It set the tools hanging from the long wall jangling discordantly against each other. Thinner metallic pings of hay tongs fighting against deeper gongs from shovels and rakes. Rattling and tumbling off the wall, falling in an awkward heap along the edge of the floor. Tabby's voice, raised in a shout, quickly cut off. As fast as the ground had lifted, it seemed scarcely a breath later when it fell back into place, the shudder that accompanied it moving through Mikey's bones, setting his teeth to aching as it tumbled him into the barrel headfirst. He pressed his hands to the sides of the container, legs kicking, arms working to edge himself backwards.

Finally, sound re-entered the world with a rush, coming with the faraway shrill racket of the emergency whistle three hollers over. Tinny and high-pitched when heard from his location, he knew if he were closer—when he stood under the tower during one of their monthly tests—the sound would beat like a fist, threatening to split his head down the middle with its ferocity. Tabby's frightened questions echoed through the metal, words warped until they were unrecognizable. "Hold on," he told her, shoving again and feeling the barrel's metal lip bite into his waist. "Can't hear ya, Tabby. Hold on."

He had barely extracted himself from the barrel when Ma ran into view, coming to a halt in the barn doorway. Chest heaving from her sprint from the house, her eyes were wide and nearly as frightened as the mare's, showing whites all around. "Mikey," she half screamed, half yelled, "you see to Tabby. Imma goin' to the mine." She didn't even wait for his response. She simply whirled on her heel then raced away, long legs eating the distance, toes flying out in front of her to punch down into the ground. Then her knee lifted and she hit her stride, the kick of her muscles driving her on again. He stood and stared at the slowly swinging door for a long time. Long after she was out of sight. Long after Tabby had gone quiet—questions lodged in her throat as the seriousness of what happened settled onto her. Long enough for the siren to cut off, winding down to a silence more painful than the whistle had been.

Something bumped into his hip, and he looked down to see Tabby had her face buried in his side, arms wrapped around his waist. Her grabbing him hadn't registered, but the sight—her bucket, empty but still dangling from her arm, handle digging into her skin, swinging once again to tap lightly at his hip—broke him from the paralysis threatening to swallow him whole. Carefully peeling her off him, he took the bucket and dropped it into the barrel, then bent in and filled it. "Here you go, Tabs," he said gently, straightening and holding it out. A taste of normal would help settle them both. "Go take care of the hens."

She reached and took the bucket from his hands, her little arms strained with the weight. Still facing away from him, her words asked the empty doorway, "When's Ma gonna be home?"

"I don't know, Tabs." Gaze on the same doorway, bereft of movement, stripped of hope, he repeated himself, underscoring his feelings of helplessness at the moment. "I don't know."

For days, the acrid smell of the explosion wafted around the mountains, carried up the valleys and hollers, riding on the breeze through the trees to the homesteads. Stiff-spined coal widows sat in the front rooms of their houses, starched collars and unsmiling faces accepting visits from friends and family. Most, like the Otey family, without a body to view. Houses like theirs often were less attended, avoided and ostracized in grief, because no coal-mining family wanted to think of the worst outcome. Death happened, in and out of the mines, so a roughly framed wooden box laid on the dining room table was inevitable. Something that happened to everyone eventually. In those cases, at least there was closure. The community knew what had transpired; they and the family mourned the death, and those left to their lives found ways to move on.

With the miners for whom body recovery was impossible, their families lived with the unknown. Stories flew through the community of miners rescued after what seemed impossibly extended periods of time. Days, weeks, months—the tales recounted the survival of men in

4

America, Canada, Russia, China, and a dozen other countries. Wild and fantastic, or dark and gruesome by turns, the speculation quickly carried a sour note of raw desperation. For the children of those miners, the stories brought unearned hope. Any day might be the one where their pa walked back through the door. Or the next. Or the next. For the widows of those men—women who knew they were widows in truth whether the ones they called husband were dead yet, or slowly suffocating in a lightless, confined space as much like a coffin as anything—those stories carried unearned pain, dragging them out of sleep time and again, as their tongues held back screams beating against their clenched teeth.

One week after the cave-in, an exhausted Mikey walked towards the house from the barn, neck twisted so he could stare at a dust-covered automobile sitting in the large, barren front yard. Taking the two steps up the porch in one stride, he yanked the front door open and stumbled to a stop in the doorway. A man, short and stooped, dressed in a mismatched suit, stood in the center of the room, briefcase in hand. The gray jacket he wore had been made for a larger man, its fabric a shade lighter than the pants which looked to have been unevenly hemmed, showing the tops of his ankles. A hat, colored yet another slightly different gray, perched on his head, looked to be the only right-sized part of his outfit.

With a handkerchief pressed to his forehead, the man didn't turn at the sound of the door opening. Nor did he shift his focus from Mikey's mother who stood, arms folded across her waist. She was near the motionless wooden rocker, shoved back near the coal stove, cold and unneeded at this time of year. The man didn't stop talking either, and Mikey heard him say, "...gone within three weeks, Mrs. Otey, unless we can come to...another arrangement."

Her eyes stayed stuck on the company man, and Mikey watched as her spine straightened, giving her another three inches of advantage. That, on top of the two she held even when bowed by grief. Head high, his ma spoke words directed at the man, but aimed at her son. "Mikey, honey," she said this softly, carefully, and he watched as the fingers of each hand dug into the flesh of her arms just below her elbows, steadying herself as she thought of instructions for a made-up errand. "Run to the creek, go up near the spring. Take Tabitha with you, son. I need a dozen crawdads. No less, not one. Bring me a dozen. We'll do a boil tonight. I'll show you how my people cook mudbugs."

By her people, Mikey knew she meant her family down in Louisiana. Her sister had followed her up to Kentucky, found herself a mountain man three counties over, and stayed. So she did have a few folks in the area. But the bulk of her people were living in stilt houses perched on the edges of shallow bayous in an area near Baton Rouge. He'd always liked to go visit in the summer, the foreign sounds of their speech musical to his ears, their cooking spicy but good. Those visits introduced him to a whole different palate from what his ma had learned from Pa's sister, here in Kentucky. Mikey appreciated both sides of the spectrum but knew his mother liked making Pa's favorite dishes for the smile it brought to his face.

Something with this man, this company man, wasn't right. An uneasy feeling strummed Mikey's nerves. He couldn't put a finger to it, but more than the man's jumbled-together clothing jarred Mikey to the bone.

Other than taking care of chores, as he'd been doing that morning, Mikey hadn't been five feet from his mother's side since the cave-in happened. Not five feet all through the waiting. Pacing the floor, two steps to her one, because she was that tall. He stayed close when the newspaper men shouted questions, turning a scowl on them when they wouldn't stop. Stayed close during the memorial service, organized once the company decided they wouldn't risk more lives to retrieve bodies buried by the mountain. Been at her side the whole time. Now she was sending him away. For crawdads. *Ain't right*, he thought.

"Ma," he said slowly, drawing it out as a careful question. Her eyes slid sideways, and when her gaze hit him, he felt the burden of every emotion she'd tried to hide from him and Tabby. Dark. Heavy. Sad. Bleak grief swept across her features and Mikey knew in his gut that this very moment she was making a life-changing decision. Had already made it, or she wouldn't be sending him away. "Ma," he said again, his still-changing voice cracking as he forced out the sounds.

At his voice, her face softened. Beauty hidden by the mask of grief surfaced for a moment, and she gave him a small smile, cheeks lifting as her mouth moved, curving. "Go on, now." Voice quiet, she made a shooing motion with her hand. She turned back to the company man, so named in Mikey's mind because that had to be what he was. Mismatched suit or not, he had one, which meant money. Mikey knew the house and land didn't belong to them, but instead was part of a lease agreement between his pa and the mining company. Everything in the house had been purchased through the company store, credit taken out of his pa's envelope to pay.

Seated on nail barrels around the feed store stove, Mikey had spent many a Saturday morning listening to men in the community talk and scheme about ways to get ahead. Get astraddle of the dividing line that would let them give their families what they wanted to give them. Men like his pa, Burnett Otey; his uncle, Ezra Ledbetter; and their shift leader, Irving Mason.

Some of the men who worked in the mines were lucky enough to own land independent of the company, but not the Oteys. His pa had people up here in the hills, but Mikey's parents hadn't been settled for long. The Masons owned an entire mountain and had lived in the county long enough so their holler was known by name.

Davy, Irving's lone son, was a good friend of Mikey's. The boys had spent many long summer mornings laboring side-by-side in the fields, cultivating their small cash crop of tobacco. Hard work followed by lazy afternoons laying alongside the creek, fingers twitching set lines, watching for the dunking of red-and-white bobbers indicating a catfish had taken the bait, hooking itself on the boys' offerings.

If the company man was in their home, it could mean his words drew a line under their time in this house. This was what his "three weeks" threatened. The grace period following the death of Mikey's pa was over, time for the mine to put a productive man back into this house. A working man, one who would ride the box into the ground. Taking away their sanctuary. The only home Tabby had ever known. His sister's entire history was tied up in these walls; she had been born in his parents' bed. Without hesitation, Mikey spoke up, offering his life in exchange, "I'll work for the company. I'll ride your elevator tomorrow, you give me a shift."

All the soft fled his ma's face, rigid lines of anger falling into place so fast he almost couldn't mark the transformation, her mask settling. "No, you won't, boy."

The company man twisted oddly, feet planted with his toes pointed towards Mikey's ma, shoulders and face turning so he could look back at the door where Mikey stood. Halfway between what he clearly wanted, and what he thought he needed to deal with. "How old?" The barked question hadn't stopped sounding in the room before Mikey answered, eager to put an end to where he believed this encounter was headed.

"Fifteen."

Without another word the man untwisted himself, turning to face the silently raging woman across the room. "He's old enough."

"Not without my say-so, he isn't." Ma's lips and mouth scarcely moved with the words. Her teeth were clenched tight, jaw thrust forward, anger distorting her face so much Mikey hardly recognized it.

"But, he's old enough."

"Not without my say-so." Her chin lifted, and Mikey felt the weight of her gaze again, her eyes cutting to him over the man's shoulder. "Son." She drew a breath and he saw her chest rise and fall with it, saw the man's focus return to her in a way that sucked the air from Mikey's lungs with anger. Anger at his pa for dying. Anger at the company for making it so nobody ever had enough to hold back anything, for making it so the least trickle of bad turned into a flood of pain. He hated the man standing in the room because he held power over Mikey's family, his ma, and ultimately, over him. She continued, her voice steady and sure, confident in a way he hadn't heard from her since before Pa died. This was a path she could control, and he saw the difference in her stance, the way her shoulders arched back. "Take Tabby. Do as you're told. A dozen mudbugs, no less."

Mikey waited for more, but Ma didn't give him anything. She sucked in another hard breath, looked as if she were bracing for a hit then her arm lifted, pointing the way, aiming a stiffened finger towards the doorway leading to his parents' bedroom. Without another word, she walked across to the door and disappeared into the dimness inside, moving on nearly silent footsteps. The man's head swiveled to watch her go, and then he turned to look at Mikey. In a flat, emotionless voice he said, "You better get gone, boy." His uncaring tone was at odds with the greed glittering in his eyes.

"Don't," was all Mikey could think to say and the man blinked at him, a slow, lascivious movement of his eyelids, pupils even larger when his eyes opened again. Tabby's voice rang through the yard, and Mikey stood frozen, watching as the man followed his ma into the unlit bedroom. *Jeebus*, he thought, whirling and hitting the edge of the porch in a single stride, leaping over the steps and into the dust surrounding their house. Barren dirt spread in a broad swath separating the house from the forest, the yard a barrier to fire and bugs, any thriving blades of grass relentlessly hoed up and removed. Tabby stood outside the barn, looking at the car, the expression on her face probably the same one he had worn earlier—interested excitement at what appeared to be some small out of the ordinary happening. She had no idea the weight this day would carry in their lives.

"Tabby," he called, quickly covering the distance to her. "We gotta go crawdad hunting, baby girl. Ma wants some for supper."

"Oh, goodie," she shouted, clapping her hands, the mysterious midafternoon visitor forgotten in her excitement at the prospect of a trek to the creek with her adored older brother.

***

"Ma," Mikey called out as soon he and Tabby hit the front stoop, bags and baskets in hand holding the fruits of their afternoon spent along the creek. Their haul included blue catfish and crappie, already skinned, or scaled and filleted, innards flung over the fence to the hens. There were also wild strawberries found hiding in a drift of last year's leaves along the path, and two dozen crawdads, hard shelled but homeless, scuttling around in the bottom of the paper bag Tabby carefully carried. He scanned the yard, seeing no evidence of their earlier visitor.

"Ma?" His second call was a question because there had been no responding answer, which wasn't like her. She was a "meet you at the door" mama, ready to hear about whatever had been going on that day.

"Tabby, stay here," he cautioned his sister, turning to see her setting the bag on the porch. Her eyes remained pinned to the top of the bag as if the crawdads might come bursting out of the opening any moment.

"'Kay," she responded automatically, using the tip of one finger to thump against the side of the bag, giggling brightly at the resulting scrabble of claws from inside the paper prison.

Mikey opened the door, took two steps into the house and stopped, frozen in place. The room, so tidy and organized when he left, was that way no longer. Furniture upended, tables turned over, doilies scattered far and wide. Pictures were off the wall, and glass had exploded everywhere from where the frames had been thrown or dropped. "Ma," he called softly, and then he heard glass crunching from behind the overturned couch, some unseen movement grinding it into the wooden planks of the floor. "Ma?"

A guttural groan answered.

Heedless of his bare feet, Mikey ran across the open area, reached the couch and grappled with it. Flinging it back with one hand before he was once again turned to stone, he stared down at what he found. Bloody and mangled fingers scratched at the gore-slickened floor, two fingernails embedded in a sticky puddle a few inches from the feeble movements. He scanned side to side, trying to make sense out of the puzzle in front of him.

A sound from the front of the room drew his attention for a moment, fear clawing at his belly until he realized it had to be his little sister. *No. God, no*, he thought, *she cain't see this*. "Tabby," he yelled without turning, "stay outside."

"'Kay." Her feet scuffed the boards in a clumsy skip as she moved a short step back away from the open doorway.

Whispering, he squatted down, not trusting himself to go closer yet, still not coming to grips with what was in front of him, "Ma." Hair tangled, snarled and matted with blood, a grisly veil of it covered her face like a tortured bride. It looked like a whip had been taken to her back, strips of material from her dress embedded into the torn and bleeding flesh.

She moved and groaned, the sound rough and painful to hear. It scraped its way into his ears and rooted in his head, setting up a loud echo, drowning out any other noise as if he were back head-down inside the barrel, digging out chicken feed. Soft and bubbling, her breathing was slow, a perceptible delay with every intake and pause, then release and pause. Each breath was drawn out for an immeasurable count of seconds. In and pause. Out on a high whine and pause. The beat in his neck counting out the time, the blood safely contained in his veins marking its passage. Her breathing was flooded with softly painful, liquid-sounding choking noises. There was not enough air in her for a true cough, her airways clogged and filling. In and pause. Out and pause with a groan.

"Ma, what can I do?" Afraid to touch her, Mikey reached out a hand anyway, his palm hovering over her shoulder. "What can I do?" A movement to the side sent him into a panic, and he whirled, seeing Tabby standing there, jaw gaping in a face gone too-pale, her eyes as round as her mouth, shock etched across her features. "*Get out,*" he screamed, aware she had started making a high-pitched keening sound. "Get out, baby girl. I told you to stay out. *Get out.*"

Her eyes flicked up to his face, then back down to the bleeding pile of flesh and tattered fabric that was their mother, then back to his face. That movement was all Tabby seemed capable of. Even more color leeched out of her cheeks until she was white as a sheet. He stood, scooping her up and walking with great strides to the door, seeing the tiny, bloody footprints she had left on the floor as she'd approached, unaware he was leaving a similar trail behind him. "Tabby, I need your help," he murmured, feeling her face pressing into his shoulder and neck, tiny arms choking in a tight hold around his neck. "I need you to listen to me, baby girl." This was his pet name for her, had been since she was born. Tabby was his baby girl, loved and lovely, now squalling hard against his neck, her hot tears searing him. "I need your help."

He set her bottom on the porch railing and tried to squat to her level, but her hold was firm and unmoving, arms locked into place around him. He stood back up, and she latched on harder, wrapping her legs around his waist, holding on with everything in her. When he tried to pry her off his neck, she jerked, shaking her head and making a loud, fitful hiccupping noise, seeming to lose her words, only capable of guttural noises. "Uh. Huh. Huh. Uh. Huh."

"Tabby girl," he whispered, not sure if she could hear him over her own sounds. "Tabby, sweet baby girl, I need your help." *Ma might be dying in there*, he thought, but couldn't find it in himself to be angry at his baby sister. It was a sight no child should ever have to bear, something he wished he hadn't seen. "Sweet baby girl." Unconsciously he reverted to the familiar movements from when she was a baby, when, to spell Ma, he would crawl out of bed with Tabby. Offering a sugar-teat in place of a bottle sometimes, the sweet-sodden rag always bringing a grin to her dear face. "Precious baby girl." Rocking and twisting, he stood in place, soothing the both of them into a mindless place, bleeding feet sticking to the dusty porch. "Sweet baby. Sweet girl. My baby girl."

He didn't know how much time had passed, wasn't aware the sun had descended behind the woods until he saw lights coming up the lane. The glow growing from faint to blinding, aimed at the house like a floodlight used for frog gigging. He felt pinned in place again, like his feet had grown roots and he couldn't get away. As if he were watching the spread metal jaws of the gig creep closer and closer, waiting for the plunging thrust that would lock those sharp teeth around his middle, pulling him out of the mire of his mind. The lights went out, and darkness flooded back in, as blinding in its own way as the light had been.

"Mikey?" That was Darren's voice. The presence of the oldest Otey sibling was unexpected because he had gone to Louisville for the construction season and hadn't even been able to come home for Pa's service. *Why would he be here now?*

"Mikey? What's wrong, bud?"

Darrie will know what to do, his brain supplied, and he nodded at the thought, suddenly feeling the slackness of Tabby's muscles. She had cried herself to sleep in his arms, no telling how long ago. He could have put her down and tended to Ma, should have kept better track of what was going on, but the thought made him remember what was waiting for him in the sitting room, and his arms tightened around Tabby involuntarily. Now he was the one holding on; now he couldn't let go, couldn't set her down, couldn't fail her more.

"Mikey, you're hurt. What happened?"

Glancing down, he considered the dried puddle of blood surrounding his feet. As if freed by the motion, an instant later Mikey felt the pounding of his heart through the glass splinters that had pierced his soles, the sticky blood dried to a thick, tacky cake between his toes. "Ma," he started, and Tabby stirred in his arms, so he took a step towards his brother, stopping when the pain blinded him. Whispering, he held out his arms, offering his baby girl up to someone who could take better care of her, telling Darrie, "Put her in your car. She cain't see again. She shouldn't have seen in the first place, but she didn't listen." He repeated himself, making sure Darrie heard what he needed to communicate, "She *cain't* see again. Not again."

Darrie's face was white, but he took Tabby and strode to his car, opening the door one-handed and carefully laying Tabby in the back seat. After surrendering her, Mikey's arms felt empty, light and disconnected, as if they were about to drop off his body, like the tail of a chameleon, falling to the ground and wriggling around. Darrie looked at her feet for a moment, flashlight taken from his belt giving a soft spotlight, halo shining around his head from where Mikey stood. *He's saving us both*, Mikey thought, and turned towards the door. Standing there, it felt as if a thousand horror stories were waiting just inside, and the last place he wanted to be was standing there. *There's just us*, he thought. *She's depending on me.* As he moved to open the door, he felt Darrie's hand on his arm, the pull demanding, so he turned to face his brother.

Before Darrie could ask his question, Mikey said, "Ma's in there. It's bad, Darrie. If she ain't dead, I don't know why." He sucked in a breath, trying to fortify himself. "Company man was here today. Ma was tryin' to keep the house. He gave us three weeks, but she was tryin' to keep the house."

"I enlisted," Darrie blurted, and Mikey's chest hitched as if with a blow. His first thought was, *You cain't leave us*, but then he pushed past

14

what he knew was a selfish child's reaction. This was good; it meant Darrie wouldn't ever work the mine. That hole that ate dreams and people, and broke families apart.

"That's good," Mikey said, because it was good manners to congratulate someone. Then, he couldn't stop the flow of words, had to repeat his pain, needing Darrie to understand what wrongness had laid in wait for him this afternoon. "Mm…mm…" He swallowed the stutter tripping his tongue. *"Ma's hurt in there."*

"Your feet?" Mikey frowned. What he could see of Darrie's face surprised him, an unfamiliar expression of uncertainty on an older person; older meaning Darrie was twenty-four. There were nine years between each of the kids. Ma had made more than one joke about only having another baby when the current one was old enough to help out. Tabby didn't know Darrie, not really; she wasn't his baby girl like she was Mikey's. Darrie had been gone from the house nearly all her life, only coming back on holidays when the house would already be overflowing with family, one more face in the crowd to her.

"I'll live." He waited, but Darrie didn't move, didn't say anything. Frustrated, Mikey shook his head. "Ma's in there," he reminded Darrie, then took it farther, feeling like he needed to prepare his brother for what he would see. "Her back looked like old man Toller's mule that time it decided to sit down instead of pullin' logs." Toller had whipped the hide and muscle off the mule's back; killed it where it had sat. Hitched to a too-large log, the mule had been smart enough to know he couldn't pull it out of the muddy woods. Too smart for his own good, because if he had only tried, Toller wouldn't have gotten so pissed, and the mule would have probably lived. *If the mule had only tried*, Mike thought. *At least Ma tried.* "I didn't get to…I couldn't…Tabby came in…" He trailed off, forgetting what he wanted to say. "It's bad."

"You wanna stay here?" Mikey frowned again, because this wasn't Darrie protecting him like Mikey had tried to protect Tabby. This didn't look like care so much as fear, and he wondered for a moment if he shouted "Boo," loud like Pa used to do when he told a ghost story, whether Darrie would up and run for the hills, doing his best imitation of a spooked horse.

Mikey shook his head and turned back to the door. Reaching out to pull the handle, he heard the squeak of the spring as it stretched, making a muted "sproing" sound when his grip slipped slightly, letting the door close by a couple inches. He had stopped the swing before it slammed shut, and then Darrie was behind him, arm reaching out to grab the edge of the door, his other hand flicking the switch on the flashlight still in his hand. The light faltered across the destruction of the sitting room, jerking here and there. "Holy fuck," Darrie said on a soft breath, sweeping the light back and forth again. The glitter of glass shining from the floor suddenly reminded Mikey of the company man's eyes just before he had followed Ma into the bedroom.

Gagging and choking down his scream at the memory, Mikey stepped inside, feeling the biting slice of glass on his soles. The light flicked and flashed, then settled on their mother, lying motionless on the floor where he had last seen her. He stared, seeing things he hadn't noticed before, the beam from Darrie's flashlight bleaching the scene of color, giving him a straight view of the damage done to her. From her shoulders to the curve of her buttocks, her back was flayed. The skin along his mother's spine had been laid open with a knife, and something had gripped each strip of pink and bloody flesh, pulling it back.

No more bubbling breaths came from the crumpled body. No moans or groans. No noises at all. No singing as she was accustomed to do every evening. After the meal was eaten, and the table cleared, her voice would sound sweetly through the gloaming as her children prepared for bed. No soft words of encouragement about homework, chiding him even if Mikey didn't see a need, knowing he wouldn't use any of it once he started riding the car into the ground.

She'd always pestered him to do his best, to continue until he solved every problem, carried him through the learning curve until he wasn't happy unless he had the best grade possible. Until he felt he had worked his hardest, given his all.

She led by example, her own high school diploma framed and in pride of place over the rolltop desk along one wall, the same desk where she sat to write weekly letters to her people. Where she sat to read the letters received in return, her laughter ringing through the house, voice calling out for them to come listen as she sounded out the voices carried to them in an envelope, interpreting the Louisiana patois for her Kentucky-raised children.

No noise. No sound. No life left in her body.

Flayed and destroyed, she had laid in her own blood and died while he'd stood on the porch, cradling a shocked and scared Tabby. He'd failed to protect either of the women in his life.

***

Mike sat on the edge of the porch, legs dangling, his feet pounding in time with the blood pooling in them. The pain had eased in this position with no pressure on the cuts. Slivers of glass had been extracted by long tweezers wielded by Davy's Aunt Barbra. Once done, she had drenched Mike's feet in kerosene, not warning him first so the pain hit like an out-of-the-dark sledgehammer. It had taken all his strength to not howl and scream. Instead, he'd flung his head back, his closed eyes streaming tears into the hair on the sides of his head. With clenched teeth, as they had been so often today, he'd waded through the waves of pain until at last, they'd shallowed and stilled like water in a river's wide bend.

Barbra had wrapped his clean feet in absorbent batting, tied into place with strips of kitchen towels, torn and destroyed for this use. Darrie had dug in their parents' dresser until he'd returned with a pair of Pa's socks, and Barbra had carefully threaded Mike's feet into the oversized tubes of cotton. She'd folded them on his calves until they'd threatened to cut off his circulation, declaring at that point, "Should hold 'em in place. You stay off those pegs, boy. Gonna need some healin' before you can do much walkin'."

From where he sat, he could see into Darrie's backseat. Mike used the angle to keep watch on Tabby, trying to make sure she didn't wake up alone. Darrie had herded him from the house, planting Mike where he sat before Darrie took off, running as fast as he could over the ridge and to the next house over, the Masons', where they had one communal phone for five houses. They were an odd family, with the older generation fixated on a particular version of God not everyone understood. But, at least his friend Davy was normal as far as Mike could tell.

Barbra had come back with Darrie, along with old man Mason. Sheriff department cars started showing up about twenty minutes later, their trip up the mountain telegraphed with glimpses of their whirling bubblegum lights. An ambulance had come up the vehicle-lined lane later, the driver parking off to one side, leaving plenty of room for even more cars to roll into the yard. Every lamp in the house had been lit, and each man entering the room carried a brilliant flashlight, those casting shadows across the yard through open windows and doors. Darkness moved and writhed as it shifted and changed, fleeing from the illumination carried in by men. Men who, at a glance, were so much like Mike's daddy had been, it freshened the pain of his loss, even more grief and agony tying themselves to what had happened.

Radio chatter from the cars scratched at his ears from a distance, updates on the scene rolling out to multiple departments across several counties. The company had no record of a man meeting the description Mike had provided and had no history of sending anyone up to evict the family of a man recently killed in their mine. The implication the company would never, ever think of doing something Mike knew to be their play at trying to keep the Otey family from reaching out to the papers with the story. Mike didn't believe for a moment the man wasn't who he'd claimed to be; he had the smell and feel of the company, rotten and greasy to the core.

The scuffing of shoe leather on the porch behind him shook him from his brown study, and he turned to see Darrie making his way towards Mike. The glass embedded in the soles of his brother's boots scratched the wood with every stride. Using the railing as a handhold, Darrie settled into place beside Mike, legs draping over the edge of the surface. "Newmill said it will be a few days before we can stay here again." James Newmill was the county deputy who had been here the longest, first to show, probably be the last to leave. His face showed more strain with every passing minute. Mike turned to look out across the yard again, surprised when he realized the glow in the distance was the false dawn of the rising sun.

Mike watched as the crew from the ambulance came towards the house, a long board held in one man's hands. Darrie said, "Mister Mason said we can stay with them for a spell. They've got an empty place in their compound." Glancing around, Mike realized the strobes on all the cars had been turned off, no longer washing the house and barn with undulating red and blue lights.

He sucked in a breath, focusing back on the car Darrie drove, determined to watch over Tabby as she slept. With a stretch of the spring, the door behind him opened, men's voices murmuring in the stillness of the breaking dawn, even the birds quiet for now. From the corner of his eye, he watched as the men carried a still, draped form strapped tightly to the board, now balanced between the pair.

"We should leave soon. Newmill said if there's anything you need from inside before we go, to just tell him and he'll get it for you. He's going to pack a bag for you and Tabby, but is there anything else you need, bud?"

The men handled the board with care, placing it gently on a gurney; the board, in turn, strapped into place much as the body was. When the wheels unlocked, the rolling stretcher hit the bumper of the ambulance, and the legs folded neatly underneath, the whole mechanism sliding into place with a click and a thud. A deputy closed the doors, slapping the back of the vehicle with one palm, the noise startling in the silence. Turning his head, Mike watched as the big vehicle rolled forwards, slowly navigating between the cars still scattered across the yard, gaining speed as it neared and entered the lane, headed down the mountain and back into town. The light bar on top of the rig dark, siren silenced. No need for urgency with their burden.

"Anything, Mikey?"

"Mike," he corrected his brother, his eyes traveling back to Tabby, finding her still sleeping. From beside the barn a chicken clucked, then the rooster cleared his throat with a squawk before letting loose with a loud crow. "Cock-a-doodle-doo," Mike echoed, then lifted both hands, putting them on the railing and resting his forehead against his arms. "Call me Mike, yeah?"

***

Cap in hand, Mike stood in the front waiting room of the company office, staring blindly out the window. He had been standing there a while, the scene in front of him seldom drawing his attention as it changed only slightly while men moved back and forth, working the coal elevator belts. Trucks trundled back and forth, a chaotic pattern to the movements.

A noise came from behind him, and he turned to see the pretty receptionist who'd let him into the office standing beside her desk. Leaning slightly to one side, she had the fingers of one hand resting on the flat surface, supporting her weight. He could see one foot moving, her ankle rolling and then she shifted her weight to the other foot, repeating the motions. The high heels of her shoes evidently not the most comfortable, but she had found a way to make it through. That was all he had to do now, find a way to survive, to cope with whatever was coming next. He had to make it so he and Tabby would have a place to stay. The cuts on his own feet gave him a kinship with the receptionist on a different level; stinging and throbbing from him standing on them so long, they were another thing to be endured. *Just gotta make it through.*

"Mr. Dixon can see you now, Mike." She hesitated, and then continued, her soft voice filled with compassion as she said, "I'm so sorry for your loss."

Ma's funeral had been three days ago. Her murder a week ago. His birthday a day ago.

He knew it chapped the company's butt when the local police couldn't label Ma's death anything other than murder. When the company representative had been bold enough to ask for proof, the coroner said there was no way she had split herself open, hips to sternum, especially after somehow miraculously managing to lay no fewer than forty-five cuts up her back, and none of those angled to fit her reach. Not knowing Mike was within earshot, the old man, elected and not appointed to his office of coroner, went on to tell the rep in a scathing tone, "And Mrs. Otey certainly did not rape and sodomize herself in such a way to cause significant internal trauma." At the thought, an image of Ma lying on the sitting room floor slashed through Mike's mind, and he knew he'd flinched in a way the receptionist saw because she made a sympathetic noise.

Mike moved first one foot then the other, legs stiff from being locked in place so long. He headed to the back of the room, towards the door that led into further recesses of the building. While the door stood open, the gaping entry wasn't inviting. Knuckles to the wooden frame, he asked for permission to enter. Darkness past the threshold seeming denser than it should be, layers of shadows trailing across the floor. "Come in," was called from beyond the door. Gravel-filled and hard, the voice was a man's, rough with years of sucking down coal dust.

Stepping into the room, Mike saw who he assumed must be Dixon. A tall man dressed in a thick, dark blue shirt, a darker section of fabric on his left breast showing where a name patch had been removed not long ago. Mike's gaze fell to Dixon's hands, one of them extended for a handshake, ready to grip and squeeze hard. He hadn't always been a manager, the mountain's blood still inked into the knuckles of his fingers, callouses visible even before Mike's palm met his to feel them. Dixon squeezed, not gentle, but not intending to cause harm. A man's greeting.

"Otey." A greeting of another kind, this one passing through lips that barely moved. Dixon seemed to be a man like his pa had been, holding words and trust close to his chest. Mike nodded, waiting. Dixon had called for him, asked him here and set the time. The entire show was his, so Mike was biding his time, waiting to see what this was about, praying it wasn't his worst fears. Dixon didn't leave him wondering long. He immediately turned to the subject, proving he knew exactly how dire Mike's situation had become with the death of both parents. "You turned sixteen. An adult now. Got a mouth to feed in addition to your own. You need a job, I got a job for you."

"Done." He didn't have to think about this even a second, because if the company was offering him a job, it meant he could keep Tabby in the bedroom their ma painted, and sleeping in the bed their pa made for her with his own two hands. Keep her surrounded by as much of their parents as possible, for as long as he breathed. Remind her with every waking moment how loved she was, how precious they had held the life of their baby girl.

"You don't know the job." This was an observation, made not in surprise, but more like resignation. Dixon knew Mike had to take it, didn't have any options other than this, and without any other words, he efficiently communicated his displeasure at the pressure applied.

"Don't matter," Mike spoke the truth. Tabby was all that mattered, and Darrie had only two more days before he shipped out for Basic. Two more days for Mike to sort out a life for himself and their sister, putting something into place to allow Darrie to go ahead with his plans and leave without worry weighing him down. Mike would do anything to make things better for them. Family. "Need it. Seems you're offering it." He shook his head, sweeping his arms out to the side for a moment before they dropped back down. He chewed the inside of his cheek a minute. "We got a done deal."

Dixon looked at Mike for a moment, then his head tilted to one side, the corner of his mouth pulling down. Thoughtfully, if a shout could be called thoughtful, he shouted, "Tina, bring me the blue folder."

From the front room of the company office, Mike heard surprise in her voice as the receptionist shouted back, "The blue one?"

"Yeah," Dixon called, confidence now infusing his voice, "the blue one."

Appearing in the doorway, she held two folders in her grip, pressed against her chest, arms folded across them. One a dull brown, the edges of a dozen papers showing along one side, angled in untidily. It was a folder that had seen a lot of use. The top edge discolored, slick with oily nervousness that had bled into the material from sweaty palms, owners anxious about handling the lightweight cardboard. The other was a dark blue, thicker, stiff with newness. The accordion bottom expanded and swelled by the contents. A flap tied in place with a thick red string wound around a large, flat button held it closed.

Dixon reached out and took the blue folder from her, then nodded at the door. Wordlessly, she turned and exited the room, carrying the rejected one away. Mike wondered at the contents of the brown folder, but only for a second because Dixon twisted his head to look at Mike. Dixon stared without saying anything, fingers moving to the string as if they'd completed the motion hundreds of times, capable of solving the folder opening puzzle without Dixon's conscious assistance.

Two papers retrieved from its depths, Dixon discarded the folder on the office chair, then walked forward and around the desk. He angled at the hips to lean back against the desk. Neither sitting nor standing, it was a simple lean for a casual conversation, as if Mike and Tabby's lives didn't ride on the outcome of this talk. "Need a trainee. Pay to start is not as good as shift work, but give me three months, and I'll have you there. Have you there, and more, and when you check your paystub, you'll remember this talk and see what I mean. It's a good job. Has benefits you don't know you need, but you do. Your sister needs you? Say she's having a bad day, or gets sick? This gives you more flexibility, a chance to be there for her. Keeps you out of the hole, Otey." His mouth closed, twisting to the side as he scrutinized Mike hard. "That's important to me, because I counted your daddy as a friend, and I know it wasn't a life he wanted for you."

Mike nodded slowly, not yet certain if he was agreeing to something, or asking the man to continue talking. Whichever it was, it worked, because Dixon kept speaking.

"You take this job, it means keeping your mouth shut. About everything. Anything. Nothing you see or hear leaves your head."

Like I'd snitch on the man signing my paychecks.

Dixon shrugged, gaze fixed on Mike's face, and apparently reading his impatience with this proclamation, decided to lay it out. "Might seem like a little thing, but it is what it is. You see shit and talk about it, we got a problem. It becomes my problem? That problem ends with you in the hole." Dixon shook his head. "But not takin' a shift. And then where's your sister?" Dixon paused a moment. "No, it'll be good. Keep you where your family needs you to be. Give you what you need so you can do what you have to. But a big part of this is knowing you'll keep your mouth shut, do as you're told."

The words didn't surprise Mike. He'd heard stories about how dissenters were dealt with, the crunching of bones coming to a sudden halt at the bottom of a stone slide down a narrow shaft. "Company business. Not mine." He didn't shrug, didn't shake his head, didn't give Dixon anything other than his words, but he knew they had been accepted at face value when the man held the papers out to him.

"Go up front, get these filled out. Tina will need an ID if you have one..." He paused at Mike's headshake, and then continued, "We'll sort it out, see what you have, what your momma might have had in the Bible at home." Then, exhibiting he had an extremely thorough knowledge of everything in Mike's life, he said, "You and Tabitha can stay in the house, Darren gets to head down to Fort Hood as he needs to, and everything settles down. Your life goes back to as normal as it can be, under the circumstances."

Turning away, Dixon moved to the desk, giving Mike his back. Taking this as the hint it was intended to be, Mike went to the door and did as he was told, handing over what he had on him and taking a list of what was acceptable to bring back. Tina worked efficiently, making notes and copies of everything as she told him to show up on Wednesday, two days away, at eight o'clock to begin his first day. He listened intently, fingers working to put papers back into place in his wallet.

Focused on the task, because the wallet was new, a Christmas gift from two years ago, unused until that morning when he'd decided he was a man and knew every man carried a wallet, Mike nearly missed what she said. Nearly, but didn't, so he caught her whisper, "Dixon is a good person, real good. But you need to watch yourself, Mike. No one, and I mean no one, is going to have your back in this. Tread water for as long as you can, but you get yourself to shore before you drown. You hear me?"

His eyes flew up to lock on her, but she was studiously not looking at him, hands working to tidy an already tidy desk. He waited, but she said no more, and eventually he grunted, then turned to walk out.

New games

"You get me?" From his position nearby, Mike listened as Dixon hissed the question between hard pants of air. The expression on Dixon's face didn't match the exertion, his features a mask of disconnected blankness. One hand was wrapped around the throat of a man, held by that grip against the wall of the alley behind a bar. The man's answer was to turn his head with a wheezing breath, followed by the distinctive sound of a mute disagreement, the echo of ejected spittle hitting the wall and slapping down the alley.

"Right." Dixon said this single word with a growl and Mike saw his face was no longer disconnected nor blank. "You'll get this." Dixon snarled. Pulling back a closed fist, he powered forward with a punch, which took the man's neck from Dixon's hand. The blow flattened the man against the wall, and much like the spit trailing down the bricks, his body slipped down the wall, back to the surface, head lolling forward.

"Drag him to the truck," Dixon said, shaking his hand out as he stared down at the man. Without a word, Mike moved to do as he was told. Scooping his hands underneath the man's armpits, he pulled him away from the wall, and slid him on his back down the cobblestone alley to the truck. Dixon met him there, and between them, they hefted the man, deadweight in his unconscious state, over the tailgate. "Lose yourself for a couple of hours," Dixon spoke as he folded into the driver seat, his gaze cutting to Mike. "I'll be back. You be here."

"But, don't you—"

Whatever else his protest would have held, Dixon cut him off quickly. "Lose yourself. Be back in two." The engine roared, exhaust echoing down the open tunnel created by brick walls, and Mike stepped away from the truck, turning to watch as it rolled steadily away.

It wasn't the first time he had assisted Dixon. Tonight was a union man the company needed to shut down. Last week it had been the shift worker who drank away his paycheck, leaving his wife and two babies in nappies to fend for themselves. The week before it had been a man forging checks, trying to cash in fake for real. It was the first time Dixon had left him behind, however.

Mike looked left and right, not seeing anything, but he knew with as deep as the shadows were along the walls of the alley, there could easily be folks who saw. Saw Mike's role in the events, even if his part was mostly watching.

At least the union guy wasn't local so there wouldn't be any kinfolk to deal with come tomorrow when the man turned up at the hospital.

Mike turned and jogged quickly up the alley, took a left at the end and shifted to a smooth running stride, one he could keep up for miles. With sure steps, he followed the upward winding road to where it changed to gravel, then trailed that to a bend, turning off onto a weed-covered lane, tree branches crowding it from both sides.

At the end of that lane was an opening where the moon shone down, filtering through the leaves and branches of the trees dotting the open meadow, lights from the town visible below. He moved in, counting rows until he came to the right one, then turned to trot up between the markers, footsteps slowing as he neared his destination.

Dropping to his knees, he rocked backwards to land on his butt and put his back to the solid marble headstone. "Hey there, old man Gregor," he said conversationally, reaching behind him to pat the stone. "Just came by to see Ma and Pa." He turned, looking at the plot next to where he sat, the ground still raised into two long, low mounds. The minuscule metal marker the funeral home had thrust into the dirt showed the head of the graves. Names written in small letters. Laverne Badet Otey. Burnett Samson Otey.

He didn't have to see the information to be reminded. Mike knew their birthdays were only days apart. He'd grown up listening to Pa pretend to complain about how hard a month February was for him because it came with both birthdays, their wedding anniversary, and Valentine's Day. He'd always played up how expensive Ma's tastes were when the least person around her knew the truth. She didn't want gold or diamonds, didn't care about a new stove or car to drive. She was happiest with simple pleasures. Her family around, songs in the air, and good food on the table. And, without looking, Mike knew their going home days were only days apart, too, offset by only a week. A week without Pa, then the nightmare which was Ma's murder.

Sitting there, he glanced at the moon, marking where it was in the sky so he could keep track of the time. Wouldn't do for Dixon to come back only to find Mike not there. Then, for the next hour and a half, he talked to his mother and father. Spoke to them about what his day held, what was going on with Darrie and Tabby, explained how important his job was and how it meant Tabby could stay where she needed to be. Where their parents had brought her into the world, a place Mike prayed she could grow and thrive, surrounded by the things they held dear.

What he didn't do was tell them about the specifics of his job, because he knew it wasn't anything they would want for him. One of the lessons he had learned from his father was how you measured the worth of a man. You wanted people around you who were straight talkers, not liars. Folks who were faithful, right, and good, not twisted

28

and evil. And, more than anything, you wanted people around you with honor.

***

A noise came through the open window from the front porch and Mike sat straight up in bed, suddenly awake and wide-eyed, staring at the square of darkness. He waited, and then it came again, the sliding of something across the wooden planks of the stoop, a pause, then another slow slide with a hitch in it this time, the slide interrupted with small stuttering movements. He couldn't place the noise, it didn't sound like a hound. It wasn't a raccoon, either.

He was alone in the house. Tabby had gone to an overnight lock-in at a local church camp. Their Uncle Ezra had picked her up long before dark and driven her and a herd of other kids up the mountain past where the Mason compound was.

Darrie had been gone for months. Mike and Tabby had gotten a letter from him last week telling them after he finished up in Oklahoma, he'd be headed to Fort Lee in Virginia for more training. Darrie said he expected another eight weeks to pass before he would be able to take a few days and come home. After that, since he would be in the business of feeding the supply train for troops, which was needed for nearly everywhere, it would be anyone's guess where he would be stationed.

Shaking his head, Mike swung his legs from the bed, standing in his skivvies. He shivered in the breeze wafting through the window, bringing with it the sound of that stuttering slide again. Making his way to the sitting room and then to the front of the house where, almost as an afterthought, he grabbed the baseball bat propped in the corner. Then, hand on the knob, he yanked the door open, bat in one hand, hovering over his shoulder, ready to swing.

Nothing was there. No shadowy figures stood on the porch. No boogie man ready to jump out at him. With a relieved sigh Mike looked around, seeing nothing there, nor in the yard. He made a scoffing noise far back in his throat, ducking his head to look up past the eaves, judging the time by the moon hanging in the sky over the trees.

The noise came again right at his feet, and with a jolt he looked down to where the sound was, seeing a dark puddle on the porch.

Reaching out a hand, he flipped on the light and then stood in place, frozen in shock. Tipping sideways, his hand opened to catch his fall against the doorframe and the bat fell to the floor, the crashing boom as it landed and bounced not even registering. Mike dropped like a stone, starch gone from his knees, his legs giving way. The pain didn't hit him as he went down hard, hands out in front of him in a warding off position, but not against the fear of falling, they were warding him from something much more damaging. His eyes stayed focused on the figure lying on the porch.

This time when the ambulance pulled out of the yard headed down the mountain, he was riding in the back, lights reflecting from the trees as the leaves absorbed the screams of the siren. Arm stretched out as far as he could reach, Mike's hand was gently wrapped around a tiny one, cold in his grip. A hand that held onto him so tightly it cut all the circulation in his fingers, until he couldn't feel their tips. All that night, and the ones which followed, one thought continued to pound in his head: *Not my Tabby. Please, Jesus. Not my Tabby.*

An honorable man

Mike's gut trembled as he stood, legs stiffened against the shaking threatening to take him to his knees, sick to his stomach while he waited for permission to sit back down. *Please, God*, he prayed, not even sure what he needed. Leaning forward slightly, he pressed his palms to the tabletop in front of him, tenting both hands so his fingertips went pale and bloodless under the strain, white circles showing at the base of his red-stained nails.

The door at the back of the room opened with a murmured "All rise," and in swept a stately, tall, white-haired man, back straight, robes swirling around his legs as he strode purposefully up the two steps leading to his chair. Pride of place, front of the room, the judge's seat at the bench put him head and shoulders over anyone else. He stopped and swept the room with eyes piercing and hard, and Mike flinched when the brows over those eyes snapped together in a scowl.

As he sat, Judge Zonder stared straight at Mike and barked a question. "Mr. Otey, did you not understand my instructions the last time you were before my court?"

Glancing at his lawyer, Mike swallowed nervously when he saw the little man's eyes were as round as he knew his own had to be. Looking back up at the judge, Mike sucked in a breath, then, still standing because the bailiff hadn't spoken and no one except Zonder had sat, Mike said, "No, sir. You made yourself clear."

"Then why..." Zonder paused a moment to sweep his hands out to the sides, indicating the entirety of the room. "...are you back in here today, Mr. Otey?"

Mike glanced at the lawyer again, a man to whom he had spoken exactly once. Mike was hoping for some instruction, any indication of what he should do. The man was useless, his face red and sweaty, mouth gaping like a marionette, panic curving the corners of his lips down. Looking back up at the judge, Mike paused a moment trying to gather his thoughts, but when Zonder made a "hurry up" motion with his hands, Mike bowed his head in submission. No help, no end in sight, no way for him to get out of this mess. *I'm sorry, Tabby. So sorry, baby girl.*

Without him meaning to, from that pose of defeat, his mouth started moving, and Mike talked. Gaze not wavering from the narrow strip of wood in front of him as sounds poured from his mouth. Eyes tracing back and forth along the grain in the tabletop, he spoke for several minutes, his words falling into the growing stillness of the courtroom. Each statement exploding in him, damage spreading with every word. In agony, flayed from the inside, he had no idea his body was jerking in place, physically flinching with every revelation. Mike's eyes slid closed partway through his recitation, so he didn't see the judge's head slowly sinking to rest on his hand, Zonder's fingers cupping his forehead, the position hiding his reactions from the gallery of observers there to see the show. Didn't hear the soft thumps as people's rear ends found the bench seats around him, any ability to withstand the story exhausted.

When he was talked out, after all the words had escaped him, Mike stood there a moment and then sucked in a hard, hiccupping breath.

Holding it for a second, then two, then three, before his body expelled it in a series of sobs so violent they shook the table where he leaned. Head swinging back and forth, forth and back, Mike's neck straightened, lifting so he could see the judge looking down at him with sorrow, tears running down Zonder's face, his expression agonized.

In the courtroom, the only audible sounds were women's soft cries and clearing of throats from hardened men. The bailiff murmured quietly to Zonder, asking if he needed to take a break, then the old man's voice responded, softly rejecting the idea.

Lifting his gaze to Mike, the judge locked eyes with him, the stare lasting a long time, well past when Mike's breathing evened out. He hadn't meant to say what had happened, hadn't intended to tell the whole of his family's troubles. The words had just burst out of him, and now he didn't know what to expect. Now everything was known, the extent of the damage dealt to someone he loved more than life itself. Someone he would protect to the death if only granted the chance. *Tabby.*

"Son," Zonder's voice went ragged and low when he spoke, the pain on his face made audible. "I wish I could make this all go away. Wish like anything...*Christ*, son, I wish I could turn back the clock." He paused, swallowing hard before continuing. "But I can't." He paused and a stillness filled the room. "Facts laid before this court are clear. You were taken into custody with the blood of the man you nearly beat to death still on your hands, and you haven't contested that evidence. In fact, you admitted to the assault as you spoke to the court just now."

The judge drew in a breath, lips pressing into a thin line for a second. "This is the second time you've appeared here in front of me, the first scarcely a week ago when you broke into the offices of a church and rifled through private records. We took into account your age and circumstances as they were known *at the time*." Zonder paused and swallowed, the clicking of his dry throat audible in the quiet courtroom. "We also warned you what would happen if we saw you again."

Zonder shook his head, fingers of one hand lifting to press hard against his lips, and then he bowed his head for a moment. Looking back up, his hand dropped as he again locked gazes with Mike. "I can't set any of that aside, son. It's my sworn duty to uphold the law, to interpret it as needed. You did this thing, and I can see on your face that you understand you have to pay."

Mike interrupted, knowing he shouldn't, but he couldn't keep his mouth from opening. "I'd do it again, Mr. Judge, sir. Mr. Zonder. I'd do it again. And again. And again. As many times as I could, as long as I have breath in my body. The man deserved every blow, every stroke from my fists. Tabby's my sister, sir. I was the first one to hold her, outside of the midwife. I'm all she's got left since everything's happened. All her little life, she's had me to lean on. Now, I'm all she's got, and I'd do it again. She's my responsibility and"—he leaned forward, fingers tented on the table again, supporting his weight—"*I failed her*. It's all I can do, sir. I'd do it again. Preacher or not, he needed to *pay*."

Softly, gently, Zonder, his tone flooded with compassion, said, "Mr. Throndell, you should counsel your client that statements such as these are not in his best interests." Mike's lawyer jerked his head up and then down, and he leaned over as if to speak to Mike, but Zonder kept talking. "Mr. Otey...Mike. I can't set aside what the court knows, can't change the laws as they are written. What I can do is interpret the judgment, mitigate the punishment in a way I think allows us to find a path out of this."

Zonder leaned forward, one elbow on the stand in front of him, gaze still intent on Mike. "I understand from what you've said today honor is important to you. Is that right?"

"Yes, sir. An honorable man is one you trust with your life. My pa taught me that."

Zonder smiled briefly, but no gleam of humor touched his eyes. "Your pa sounds like a smart man."

Mike said, "Yes, sir, Mr. Judge, sir. He was."

"Mike, I have leeway in cases such as this. Your age, the crime which occasioned your response, your clear and strong sense of integrity, all of these things provide me with a great deal of leeway. I can make you two offers for punishment, and you should think about them long and hard before you pick either one. Take your time and talk to Mr. Throndell. Let him counsel you. It's what the state pays him to do. You need to speak to your aunt and uncle, call your brother for guidance if you can. Decide what direction works and then we'll set things in motion. I can't hold this offer open indefinitely, but I can give you at least the night."

He leaned back and his hands disappeared below the top of the bench, the material of his robe bunching at his waist. "Fifteen months in county prison. No picnic, but it's not federal. County is a better situation than federal by a long shot, son. Fifteen months in county, less than two years from your life. Fifteen months. The day you turn eighteen, you're released."

Zonder nodded, took a moment, seeming to consider everything he had said, and then nodded again. "Or, you can join the army. Sign up for a four-year stint, and this goes away entirely. No marks on your record, no need to deal with the fallout from being in prison. I can promise that. I know the local recruiter, and we can emancipate you today, get you signed up and he'll make it right for us, son. County or army, those are the options available to you." Zonder leaned forward, continuing, "Think about it, and we'll meet back here—"

Mike didn't wait. He again interrupted the judge's words with a half shouted, "Army. Sir. The army."

Frowning, Zonder said, "That was not a considered response, son. I'd like you to take the night—"

"With all due respect, sir," Mike broke in quietly but firmly, "army is where my brother is, and to hear him talk about it, the way they challenge you and push you to be better, the army is where I need to be. So I can learn, sir, not sit around twiddling my thumbs and wait for my sentence to be finished."

***

Mike cupped the back of Tabby's neck, feeling her slump into him, resting her head against his thigh. He looked up at Aunt Loretta. They were standing outside the bus station in Lexington. "I'm gonna send money. Much as the army'll let me. She won't go without, ain't gonna be a drain on you." He sifted his fingers through his little sister's silky hair. "She gets what she needs, from me."

"Mikey." The corners of Loretta's lips curved slightly. "She's gonna be okay."

No, she wasn't. How could she, after everything. After he let horrors into her world. *Look after Tabby*, one of the last directives from their mother, and he failed on all counts. He didn't tell Loretta any of this, just moved away on the sidewalk so he had room to crouch next to Tabby.

She leaned into him, cheek to his shoulder. He circled her with his arms, seeking comfort for himself, pulling her close. Things had moved so fast, it didn't seem like he'd had a chance to breathe for months, running full tilt against enemies he couldn't see or put a name to. "Baby girl, I love you." He fingered the hem of the shirt she wore. One of his hand-me-downs, too large, but the only thing she was willing to suffer on her body. "My little raggedy girl. I gotta go, Tabs. The bus is leavin' in a minute." She pressed tighter, and he felt her hand on his back, fingers twisted into his shirt, holding him in place. "I'm comin' back, soon as I can. Me and Darrie both, we'll be back so much you're gonna be kickin' us out the door, ready for us to get gone again." Her head shook back-and-forth. "Oh, yeah, you know it. Be so tired of us."

God, what he wouldn't give to hear her happy giggle again. Her sweet voice, something he used to tune out, thinking she droned on and on, and now she was so quiet. He gave her a squeeze with his arms, and asked, "You gonna miss me, baby girl?" Her head moved up and down, a silent nod. "Love me, Tabby?" Another nod.

"I love you more," he promised and squeezed again, hearing the bus driver calling names. "It's time. I gotta go. You be good for Aunt Loretta, you hear?" The nod came slower this time. "I'll see you real soon, Tabs. Love you."

"Love you." Scratchy and quiet, her voice was gravelly with disuse. Nearly two months, and these her first words. *Praise Jesus*, he thought, standing with her in his arms, holding her tight for just a moment more.

Target is clear

"Jeebus," Mike muttered, hitching his rucksack higher on his shoulder, marching in place three measured paces after the shouted instruction to halt came.

"Yeah, boy," a voice murmured from behind him, laughter thickening it considerably. "Italy is hot. North Africa is even hotter."

"Ain't that," he whispered out of the corner of his mouth, eyes on their commander who stood near the front of the rank. "It stanks."

"Tannery," the voice said, this time a chuckle breaking free.

"Jeebus," Mike said again. "Really stanks."

"Price of beauty." This came from his left. Mike cut his eyes to the side in time to see a grin on his friend's face. Grant Williamson had been in boot camp alongside Mike, and they came out of it with both of them headed to Fort Leonard Wood for their training as something the army called an "elite combat engineer" but the men, and everyone else, called sappers. To wear the sapper tab gave a soldier instant respect, only one of four specialties to have the honor. Their entire cohort hadn't been able to stay together, but Mike counted himself lucky he and Grant had been side-by-side since. *Luck of the draw*, he thought, knowing he was fortunate to have this man at his back. "Leather shoes and bags from here are the shit." Grant chuckled. "All beauty comes with a cost, and Eye-talian leather is the real shit, man."

"Quiet." Shouted from the front of the rank, the irritation in their commander's voice had them standing still and silent, arms at their sides as they waited for instructions.

Seated on the side of his bunk that night, Mike asked Grant, "You think Gaddafi wears Eye-talian leather boots?"

"Fuck no," came the immediate response. "Gaddafi's boots are made from the skin of German babies."

"Sheeit," Mike said, making a face. "That's gross, man."

From his greater age of twenty, Grant looked and acted like he lived in a different world from the one where Mike had come. He had an answer for everything, was steady and hard to anger, and even though they hadn't yet been in a combat situation, all the training he had done alongside his friend with both dud and live ordnance had proven to him that Grant had a steady head as well as hands. He looked up to him, not quite hero-worship, but Grant was who he wanted to be in three years. Confident and competent. Good and honorable.

***

"Say again," Mike shouted into the radio handset, covering his other ear with a flattened palm. "Did not copy. Say again."

Static greeted him, and he scanned the men squatted in a half circle around him. He gave it thirty seconds, counting down slowly like Pa had taught him about thunder back in the mountains of Kentucky. One-one thousand, two-one thousand, three-one thousand...

"Command, this is Echo Bravo Golf Niner Two Two and I did not copy. Say again." One-one thousand, two-one thousand, three-one thousand...this cycle had gone around two more times before he shoved the handset into the side pocket of a pack sitting on the red sand. Looking up at the men, he saw fear or hopeless resignation on every face except one, so he focused there when he spoke. "Second Armored seems to be non-responsive at the moment," he drawled, and Deke laughed while Mike grinned back at him like a loon. "Not the first time we've been here," he said, glancing around at the rest of the men. He then finished fastening the straps on his bag before hefting it over one shoulder, shrugging into the harness.

"We set our charges, then head back out, easy does it. Target is clear. The only question we had was about any changes. If we're out of communication, then the expectation is there are no changes. OPORD rules, no frags, no changes. If there were, brass would have gotten them to us." He pulled one of the pockets on his pants open, the quiet sound of the zipper louder than it should have been in the silence.

Flattening the map on his thigh, he held it in place with his palm for a minute, looking again at the men. "Corky," he called, and the youngest member of their unit startled, then froze in place as he realized his movement telegraphed nervousness. "We got this, son."

"Yeah, Watcher, I get that. You're on it. No worries, old man."

Mike shared a rueful glance with Grant, the two of them acknowledging that to these kids they were old men. Old and seasoned, because individually they had been deployed for more than the rest of them combined, and had multiple successful missions under their belts. Mike, now called Watcher, because the FNGs—or fucking new grunts—were of the opinion he saw everything. Grant, with a call name of Deke, because he could weasel his way out of nearly any punishment, deking around it like he was on the ice in Michigan where he came from. Definitely the old guys here.

"Okay, then. Let's go blow our bridge." He stood and scanned the horizon. "Eighty-second will be there when we need them, I have confidence. Those boys are faithful to a fault, never failed me yet."

Forty-eight hours later, Mike and Grant were sitting in the makeshift gym back on base, tepid water in hand. Tipping the top of his canteen in a toast, Mike said, "Another successful run, my friend."

Grant reached out and bumped his against the offered rim, responding, "Hell, yeah. We crisped that shit, man. Cheers to our fine asses."

"Cheers." Mike lifted his water, took a long swallow, and then dropped his hand back to rest on his thigh. "Could have gone badly, man. You did a great job keeping the guys together."

"Fuck that," Grant laughed, shaking his head. "I didn't do shit except back you up when you needed it, man. You're the glue, and you fucking know it." He reached out, thumping the back of his hand against Watcher's shoulder. "You're a good man, Otey."

"Yeah, back atcha, brother." Mike grinned at him, then he frowned, seeing a somber expression roll across Grant's features. "What's up, man?"

"Not sure how to tell you, Mike." Grant held his gaze, regret and sincerity in his voice as he said, "Not re-upping. Four does it for me. Time for me to head back, get my ass stateside, find me some pretty pussy to play with."

At his blunt talk, Mike winced, then focused on the news in the speech. "I'm losing you?"

Nodding, Grant reached out and put his hand on top of Mike's shoulder. He gripped tightly for a moment before he made a fist and pounded hard. "I'm here another ninety, then I'm out and about, brother. We need to find you a wingman before I go, preferably one who's better at the damn job than me, since I haven't gotten you laid yet."

Shaking his head, Mike said, "What'll you do?"

"Dunno, just know the army ain't the be-all, end-all for me. I'm looking for something else." He shrugged, then said, "I don't regret the experience, the chance to travel like this, and I sure as fuck don't regret the opportunity to meet you, brother."

"Same here, man. Won't feel right without your ugly mug watching over my butt." Mike drank the last of his water, balancing the empty canteen in one hand. "But, I still got you. I still got you today." He sucked in a breath, blowing it back out slowly. "My belly's ringing the dinner bell, you ready?"

"Sure. Let's go get some chow, and then we'll troll the zone, see if we can get you laid tonight. Target is clear."

***

Mike took a step back and felt his shoulders smack into the plaster-covered wall running alongside the road. He shook his head vehemently, trying to push away from the person in front of him. There were hoots and laughter from along the wall, and softer noises of clothing being discarded or moved, adjusted to make room for the activities of the evening.

In his head, he heard a stuttering slide, smelled decaying metal, rust, saw the glow of a false dawn growing bright around the peak of a mountain in a Kentucky skyline. "No," he muttered, squeezing his eyes closed as he felt a hand groping across his belly, angling downward. "Huh uh, no. No, ma'am." Fast as a thought, he reached out, clasping tight around the wrist attached to the hand, only easing up when he heard a soft grunt of pain.

Looking down, he saw a girl standing close, pulled there by his grip on her arm. Her other hand was trying futilely to peel back his fingers from her arm as she stared up at him, her mouth twisted in pain. Shocked, he released her and grasped her shoulders, setting her back and away from him. "No," he said again, firmly, "no more."

"Damn, Watcher." Grant was nearby, leaning his forearm against the wall. His stance was wide, with feet planted firmly and he was angled in, hips moving powerfully. His body was big; so big, if you didn't know to look, you would never see the girl on her knees in front of him, accepting him into her mouth. "You need to get you some, brother. I'm only here another week." He grunted, then groaned, mouth gaping open as he tipped his head back, cords standing out on his neck. "*Fuck. Yeah, baby.*" The fabric of his shirt rippled with movement then stilled as he groaned again, hips rocking forward a final time.

After a few moments, Grant stepped back, adjusted himself and turned to face Mike who still had his hands on the girl's shoulders, keeping her away from him. "Seriously, man. You need to pop that fucking cherry. It's a burden no man needs." He indicated the girl, saying, "She's right here, man. I already paid her for you. Let her jerk you off, at least."

"Grant," Mike said, his voice low and intense. "I cain't. I just cain't."

"Why the fuck not, Watch?"

Mike shook his head. "She's just a kid."

"So are you! It evens out." Grant laughed, reaching out to steady himself against the wall as he refastened his belt one-handed. "Makes it okay."

"She's just a kid. I'm twenty." Mike pushed her away a final time and she slunk away to run along the street, turning and disappearing into the first alley. "Girl wasn't much older than Tabby is, Deke. Just a kid."

"How's your sis doin' with school starting back up? I saw you got a letter from your aunt at mail call." With ease born of long practice, the two ignored the rest of the men populating the whores' wall and turned to walk back the way they'd come.

"Doin' good. Tabby's doin' real good. Hard to believe my little girl started junior high this year. I need to ask to rotate home for a visit soon. Maybe before Christmas." He grinned, thinking of the most recent picture their Aunt Loretta sent him. It was taken outside, a not quite teenaged Tabby sitting astride a four-wheeler, helmet in place, a grin wider than her face showing nearly every tooth in the girl's head. "Darrie's supposed to have leave for Christmas. Would be real good to see both of them."

"You should go," Grant told him.

At a noise behind them, both men whirled, dropping into defensive crouches. Unfolding and laughing, they looked down at the young girl Mike had refused. She was standing with her body as far away as possible, arm stretched out, fingers fisted around the money Grant had given her.

"*Laa*," Mike said, shaking his head. "*Laa*, child. No." She took a step backwards, then bent far forward and shook the money. He waved a hand at her, frowning when she flinched at his movement. Then he told her no again, "*Laa*." One skipping step backwards turned into two, and then with a flick of her hair, she whipped around and was running, pelting down the street back to the wall.

"Bah. Your loss. If we ain't taking the money back from the kid, means you're gonna pay me back." Grant reached out, wrapped his elbow around Mike's neck and tugged hard. Pulling Mike against his side, Grant scrubbed bent knuckles fiercely across the top of Mike's head. "Your fucking loss, in so many ways, brother."

Drink me out of the country

Watcher stood in one corner of the briefing room, narrowed eyes flicking back and forth, looking at the map on the board. He lifted a steaming mug of coffee to his lips, sipped, swallowed, and then blew across the top of the liquid before he sipped again. To his right stood the commander, silently waiting. Watcher sighed, and then took another sip before he said, "It's gonna be a bitch to get through with so many men. You want us to remove impediments to troop movements, or have a running fight?" Twisting his neck, he looked at the commander, as usual trying hard not to wince when he saw the kid.

At twenty-four, with nearly seven years of solid deployment, Watcher was the seasoned vet in the room. The only person who had more years than him was their local liaison, and that man was someone's grandpa. The idea on the board had merit, but he wanted all things to be taken into consideration. This meant he would be walking the thin line of encouraging while discouraging, once a-fucking-gain.

"Rolling with only half the guys gives us greater mobility. We can calculate the needs for the blow you want, take that, and enough to also take down bridges as needed, but if we split the group—" He walked towards the map, finger pointing at a location. "—then we can remove this route, too." Without turning around, he said, "Gives the hostiles only one corridor to move everything, which will keep things nicely contained. As long as they have at least one bridge to use, they won't reallocate construction units to rebuild for at least a while, so we leave them one. By leavin' one to give us a pinch point, and taking out these two"—he lifted his other hand, still holding his cup, pointing to the pin on the map indicating the original target—"we make our boys' lives easier."

"How do you see this shit?" The question from the kid in the greens didn't surprise him, but still drew a rough laugh.

"I'm a watcher. It's what I do." He shrugged, then smiled. "You know the code. Sappers, we live for this, sir. When it absolutely positively has to be blown up, breached, or destroyed overnight, we're there. Because, sir, there is no situation that a small amount of properly placed explosives cannot handle." The commander laughed, and Watcher grinned.

"Hey, Watch." He turned to find the signal officer standing in the door and nodded, giving him full attention, eyes focused on the paper in the man's hand as it was waved up and down. "I have an urgent personal for you."

There was more movement outside, and Watcher saw a figure approach, then the unit chaplain's head peered over the kid's shoulder, eclipsing him. Watcher's stomach gave a lurch and then dropped into his boots. Only one reason for an urgent personal message to coincide with a visit from the preacher, and he took a second to try to compose himself, putting an impassive mask into place before acknowledging the man. "Preach."

"Watch, my friend," the chaplain said, his voice quiet and sympathetic, rich with shared pain. "Let's walk." Preacher reached over to pluck the paper from the signal officer's hand, tucking it into the front pocket on his shirt. "Come on, brother."

That night Watcher lay in his bunk, eyes open, staring sightlessly up at the shadowed rafters holding up the flat metal roof. In his mind, he kept rolling the information Preach had for him, which was more than what was on the paper. The message said to call his aunt. Lots of room for wiggle there. Interpretation of disaster was implied, but it could have been his uncle or even Darrie. Anything. Nothing to point towards the story Preach had.

"Why?" He hadn't been aware he was about to speak, and the sound of his voice, raw and anguished, shocked him. He jerked and closed his eyes, then squeezed them tightly, hands fisting into the blanket underneath him as he shouted, "*WHY?*"

In his mind he saw her, grin wide as her cheeks could stretch, sitting behind the wheel of the beat-up old farm truck he'd bought from the used lot in town. Arm leaning against the top of the steering wheel, Tabby's head tilted slightly, close-cropped hair curling all over her head.

She was always like that. Always careful with how she dressed and looked. After what had happened to her, Watcher felt it was understandable, but it worried him. Worried him so much he asked Tabby's talking doc about it once and the woman gave him some lame explanation of why his sister seemed determined to look as masculine as possible, but still loved to dress her dollies in frills. She looked cute, was cute, but she hid it behind baggy clothes, unattractive haircuts, language to make a sailor blush, and an attitude of indifference about nearly everything.

She loved that truck, though. Called it a classic. Spent every dime she earned working at the local drive-in on things to dress it up. Seat covers, floor mats, even a brand new sound system. Since the day he drove it into the yard with a little three-inch yellow bow taped to the hood, she had loved that truck. Hardship license since she wasn't old enough for a regular one, but she was a good driver. She had learned in their uncle's old jeep, careening all over the meadow for days, grinding the gears down to nothing until she got the hang of it.

"Watch, they said it might not be an accident." Preach's voice was in his head, and Watcher's neck twisted, pulling his ear down to his shoulder, instinctively trying to block sound that wasn't there. Words existing only in his memories. *"Weather was good, early morning clear skies. No reason for her to run off the side of the mountain."* There hadn't been any images to go with the story, just the words burned into his brain. *"Nearly a hundred feet, brother. I talked to the sheriff's men. There's no guardrail there, just a sheer drop. Took them hours to recover her."*

He opened his eyes, turning to where his pictures were taped to the wall. One was from Easter Sunday this year, Tabby standing between their aunt and uncle in her store-bought yellow dress, their cousins scattered in front and around, two of the little ones clinging to Tabby's legs. A close family, from the looks of things, Tabby favoring their aunt enough so most folks didn't question. Appearances matter in a small town. Everything always looked better from the outside. This was a holiday picture taken outside the church, sunshine streaming down making everyone squint as they looked at the camera, grownups smiling in spite of the glare. As ever, when forced into what the doc called gender-appropriate clothing, Tabby looked uncomfortable as anything, Aunt Loretta's arm around her shoulder pulling Tabby tight to her side. A protective hold.

There was noise from outside his quarters, footsteps of several men moving between the rows of containers that were masquerading as living space. A tap at his door had him swinging his legs off the bunk as he called, "Enter," poised on the edge of the metal cot which took up one whole side of the room.

The door pulled back and five men filed in, one after the other, crowding the space inside, the smell of sweat and dust rolling off them. Watcher stayed seated, looking up into the faces shrouded by darkness. He asked, "Need a light?"

"Naw," came the response from the man on the end and he swung his head that way.

"Rawlins." He greeted the soldier, and then observed, "Unusual location for a debriefing." They would have barely returned from the ops he and the commander had been planning earlier today. After talking with Preacher, Watcher had bowed out of the boots on the ground portion, knowing his head wasn't in the right space, but had painstakingly gone over the plan with the leaders of the two teams, needing to know they had all the tools to make it back alive.

"Not a debrief, Watch. We were silk tonight." That was good to hear, meant the mission had gone smoothly, everything working out as planned.

"So then what's the occasion?" If they weren't here to talk about the ops, then he didn't have a clue what they wanted.

"Heard about what happened." Rawlins thrust a hand forward, the unmistakable shape of a whiskey bottle dangling from his fingers. "Wanted to toast you before you go stateside." He removed the lid, lifting the bottle towards Watcher by the neck. "You're the man who watches our back, makes sure we're good. Makes it so when we sleep tight at night, we do it with no worries. Makes it so our folks back home sleep the same way. We wanted you to know we'll do the same for you, brother. Anything you need, we'll bleed."

He sat there for a moment longer, elbows to his knees, then he slowly unfolded. In the small space, he stood nearly chest-to-chest with men who trusted him with their lives, men he trusted in the same way. He reached out and took the bottle, lifting it to his lips and taking a long, hard pull at the contents, feeling the burn as it moved into his still-unsettled gut. Standing with the bottle still lifted, he swallowed convulsively a time or two until he was convinced the whiskey wouldn't be making an immediate reappearance, then leaned over and passed the bottle back to Rawlins. "Hooah," he said softly, close enough to feel the outrush of breath as each man standing before him echoed the sound. "Thank you."

"Anything for you, Watch," one of the other men said, and he looked in that direction, the corners of his mouth lifting on one side.

"Opie." So named because his ears hung off the sides of his blonde head like cab doors, but the man's hillbilly looks were deceiving. He was one of the smartest men Watcher knew. Reaching out to tap his fist on the man's shoulder, Watcher nodded. "Thank you, brother." He received a return tap on the shoulder from Opie, and then down the line, one from every man as the bottle was transferred from hand to hand, each of them lifting it in salute before drinking and passing it along. "Means a lot, brothers."

Tucking his chin to his chest, he took in a hard breath, pushing down the pain as he had been doing for hours. In a voice thick with unshed tears, he forced out words that bound them together as a unit, using the creed to let them know their message was received. He knew what it meant for them to come to him like this, dust still on their boots from the ops. "I am a sapper leader, the cutting edge..."

Each man joined in with the words memorized back at Fort Leonard Wood, the oath every army combat engineer gave, their voices ringing loud in the enclosed space until the door opened and there were even more men joining in. Selfless, honorable, a promise to each man who stood beside him, the creed was how he lived, how he had lived for the past eight years. With a shout, each man within hearing distance ended the recitation of the promise, "...sappers lead the way."

In between the shouts of "hooah" filling the air, Watcher recognized the voice of one of the medics and grinned, this one more heartfelt than any other today. Danielson—the Aussie they all called Bulldog because once he got it in his head to save a man, even God himself couldn't pull him away—had joined the men standing in between the container units and was shouting, his distinctive accent mixed in with the American drawls and clipped consonants. "Bloody hell, you noisy lot are a pain in my arse."

"Sorry, Bulldog," Watcher called, and the men standing in front of him shifted, letting the man through. He reached out, taking the bottle from where it had made it back down to Rawlins, and then offered it to the medic. "Drink me out of the country, yeah?"

"Too right, I will. You shoulda gone out yonks ago." Bulldog lifted the bottle and set it to his lips, then pulled it back, wiping the rim with the hem of his shirt. "Fair enough." He took a drink, brought it down and gestured with it, setting it swinging from his fingertips. "You cashed up or need me to kick it in for ya?"

"I'm set for home," Watcher responded, shaking his head as Bulldog swigged at the whiskey again. He heard the men outside moving away, headed back to their own bunk assignments. "Thank you," he said, retrieving the bottle just as Bulldog was about to drink again, handing it back to Rawlins. "Thank you all."

***

Standing in the windswept cemetery, Watcher frowned as he looked across to where his aunt and uncle sat in chairs underneath the funeral home's awning. Something didn't add up. Aunt Loretta was genuinely grief-stricken, her eyes nearly swollen shut with the crying she had been doing. She was suffering, having loved Tabby like a daughter, raising her these past years alongside her own kids. When he got home last night, her hands had trembled as she'd reached out to him, folding herself into his arms like she was the one returning home after a long time away.

His gaze swung left, and he stared. Gabriel, his oldest cousin, stood at the end of the row of chairs, boots to the dirt instead of on the fake grass carpet the funeral director had laid, topping the raw ground beside the open grave. Bright red hair like his momma, Gabriel was staring at his own father with open dislike.

This was one of the things bugging Watcher most about this scene. None of the family wanted anything to do with Uncle Ezra. And Ezra looked as if the entire proceedings had been conceived to interrupt something of dire importance that he needed to get on with. This event, Tabby's funeral, was clearly an inconvenience to him.

Cutting his eyes right, Watcher saw the local pastor approaching, Bible in hand. As the man opened the Book, preparing to begin the service, Ezra stood and said, "Hold on, preacher. We're waiting on the Masons." The pastor nodded, folding his hands over the Bible as he pressed it to his chest, taking two respectful steps back from the grave.

Watcher's chest compressed. He never wanted anything to do with the Masons after their associate pastor had hurt Tabby. Davy was different; he'd already been gone when everything happened. Watcher wouldn't have minded seeing him today, but for Ezra to put a pause on this service, a moment so painful for family and the ones who loved Tabby more than breath, so others of that clan could attend—it didn't make sense.

Before Watcher could ask anything, Loretta spoke up, drawing his attention back to her. "Bethy was her best friend, Mikey. It don't seem right to do this without her here." He stared at her a moment then dipped his gaze to the toes of his boots, deliberately setting aside the emotions evoked by her words. Tabby never mentioned being friends with Davy's little sister. He thought she told him everything. *Might not be—*

Watcher swallowed, staring at his boots, somberly considering the shine and noting it was already dulled with the splatter of red clay. His dress greens fit well, comfortable but hot, and he reached up to adjust the beret he wore, tipping it a centimeter forward. Isolating silence spread through the small group until a few minutes later when a pickup pulled into the parking lot of the church. Watcher looked up from his study of the ground to see Irving Mason and a slip of a brunette girl climb out.

As they approached, he saw the girl's face looked a lot like Loretta's. All the pain she felt worn on the surface, her expression reflecting a devastating grief. His aunt opened her arms and the girl—he assumed it was Bethy—threw herself into them, landing half on Loretta's lap. The two women held each other, sobs breaking through and filling the air, creating a space around them as people, including his uncle, moved away, uncomfortable with the show of emotion.

The sound of a throat clearing drew his attention, and Watcher turned to see the pastor had stepped back up to the head of the grave, the scuffed toes of his thrift store shoes sticking out over the hole. Watcher glanced down, eyes tracing the shape of the casket already partway lowered into the opening, the spray of yellow flowers draping over the curved sides. Yellow, Tabby's favorite color. "If we can begin?" The question was directed at Ezra who nodded impatiently.

Watcher drew in a hard breath, holding it for a couple of seconds before he allowed it to trickle out through his nostrils. Then he took another one, deliberately blocking out the words of the preacher, words he was sure were intended to be comforting, but hearing someone who didn't know Tabby saying anything about her seemed wrong. Just wrong.

Glancing around, he again felt a sense of isolation. Darrie hadn't been able to make it home in time for the funeral. He would be here in a couple of days, but once the coroner's office released Tabby's body, the funeral home pushed for a fast burial. They weren't set up to hold a body for long, and as soon as they got the go-ahead to plant her, they wanted to make it happen. Watcher and Darrie would have their own memorial for her, a jar of clear moonshine already in place in the back of the truck he'd borrowed from Judge Zonder.

Over the years he had stayed in touch with the judge, who was present, seated two rows behind Loretta and Ezra. He didn't know why, but there was bad blood between Zonder and Ezra, so it was no surprise the look Zonder turned on the back of Ezra's head was thick with something like disgust. But as Watcher saw Zonder's gaze swing to the man who stood at the foot of the grave, the look turned to something darker, more like hatred, and *that* caught his attention in a big way. *What the hell?*

Mason, the patriarch of the clan that lived up the mountain, was a fire and brimstone preacher and had his own captive congregation living in their extended family compound. Word was he had turned off bitter with age, driving off first his woman and then his boy, Davy, leaving him with only his daughter at home, but a plethora of family on the land.

Watcher looked at the girl, taking in how her thin body leaned into Loretta. Dark head to the older woman's shoulder, Bethy had her cheek pressed to Loretta's breast. Arm around her stomach, holding tightly just as Loretta's arm was around her back, securing her in place. She had been Tabby's best friend, according to Loretta, but Tabby hadn't mentioned her to Watcher. Not once.

Something flashed to the side of where he stood, and Watcher spun, his attention jerked back to the preacher. He saw the man bend over, coming up with a fistful of wet red clay, and Watcher dialed back in on what he was saying, "...and we commit Tabitha's body to the ground; earth to earth, ashes to ashes, dust to dust. Blessed are the dead who die in the Lord. They will rest from their labors, for their deeds will follow them."

Watcher looked back to the grave to find the coffin had been lowered while he was distracted with his thoughts. As he stood there, unable to do anything to make things right, he saw a clump of clay fall into the hole near the head of the coffin, but off to the side. Respectful. Keeping the shining surface free from marks for a moment longer.

Staring into the hole, he saw another small clump fall to the side, knowing it came from Loretta. Another small one came to rest at the base of the casket, and he glanced up, seeing Bethy staring at her own hand, smears of red marring her palm.

Then there was a loud thud, and Watcher looked back down, seeing a large clot of dirt that hadn't been tossed, it had been thrown. Thrown hard if the splatter all around where it lay was any indication. To see where it rested pushed all the air out of his lungs, and Watcher nearly lost his balance, staggering sideways with the punch that hit him to see the yellow of the roses marred in such a way. Petals knocked from the stem were scattered everywhere with the force of the blow, the entire arrangement askew in a way which made him want to jump down into the hole and fix it, make it right for Tabby.

When he could tear his eyes away from the obscenity he looked up, expecting to see Ezra wiping his hand, but his uncle still clutched his clod, head angled towards the end of the grave and Watcher's head turned, too. He stared at the tall man standing there, chin lifted high. Mason was proud of his accomplishment, red bandana calmly moving over his palm, between his fingers, cleaning off any trace he had touched dirt, that it had been him to violate Tabby in this way. "Daddy!" a shocked female voice whispered, and Watcher glanced at the girl still standing in the circle of Loretta's arms.

"Get in the truck, daughter," Mason said, his voice low with threatening meaning but the girl didn't move, she just stood there looking at him. She was studying him, like Watcher studied maps and plans, trying to plot out the safest routes for himself and his men. Safe, but still accomplishing the mission. Achieve the assignment. Target is clear.

You could see the moment she made her decision, when she came to a choice. And for her, Watcher hoped it was the right one, because from where he stood, he knew her life's road just took as abrupt a turn as any dogleg on a wooded path. It would be up to her to decide if it was good or bad. "No," she said, and with this statement, her back went straight. Resolute. Firm.

"Go get yer ass in the truck, daughter." Mason's voice vibrated with anger and menace, and Watcher saw the color leech from the girl's face as she shook her head.

Then she said something which didn't make sense, but from his reaction, Mason must have known exactly what she was talking about. "No more." Two words, spoken softly, made her father draw back and then push forward with one shoulder and hip, his posture so aggressive it could not be mistaken as anything other than a threat. "You've done your worst, Daddy," she whispered, soft voice still ringing loud through the pall of silence gathered over their small group. Watcher fancied it rang past where they stood beside an open grave in a cold, windswept graveyard situated on the side of a mountain in eastern Kentucky, echoing through towns and into nearby mine shafts. "Done your worst, took her from me. You've taken everything." She shook her head violently, the movement pulling her bare inches from Loretta's side, but even as Bethy moved, hair flying all around her head, Loretta's arms tightened, bringing her back, holding tight.

Bethy whirled, looking at Zonder, and her next words were even more nonsensical than the previous ones, even as things began to make sense to Watcher. "I'm sixteen. You've been a judge here my whole life. You know how that man is, sir." She paused, and Watcher saw her throat work as she swallowed. "You know what he is. Emancipate me. Make it so I don't have to deal with him anymore. Ever again. He made me marry a man last year, Taylor. Mr. Zonder, Taylor's worse. Please. Make it so I feel safe."

Watcher saw her hands tremble as she moved her hair, reaching to tug at the collar of her dress, showing the judge something hidden from where Watcher stood, but it couldn't be good because Zonder's features got hard in a way that Watcher knew it had to be bad. "Emancipate me." Her demand was breathy now, because she also had seen the change sweep across Zonder's face. "Don't make me go back."

Twenty minutes later Watcher was in Zonder's truck, Bethany Mason on the seat as close to the passenger door as she could get with it still closed. They were driving down the mountain to Zonder's house, where the judge had decreed all parties should retire so the proceedings would have at least the veneer of normalcy.

Watcher's mind wasn't on the girl in the truck but stuck in the hole in the ground he had just driven away from. His gaze staying on the rearview mirror until he lost sight of the three men, bent over, shovels working methodically to shift the dirt from the mound beside where the pastor had stood. They were shoving it back into the hole a scoop at a time. Watcher knew there would be too much dirt, so there was sure to be a pile remaining after they were done. Even after they packed it down with boots and the backs of the shovel blades. Even after the rains came, settling the dirt and packing it more. For a long, long time there would be a body-sized pile of dirt placed on top of the filled grave, mounded up as if it hid the child resting inside the box deep in the hole.

Since he was focused on his own pain, it surprised him when Bethany spoke, shocked him so his hands jerked the wheel, the truck swaying on the rutted dirt for a moment. "She was my best friend. My very best friend." Without saying anything in response, he nodded, still coming to grips with Tabby having a friend she didn't talk about. "I heard what they said happened. I don't believe it, Mike. She'd want you to know she fought it back. She tried hard, and fought for a long time." These words stole his breath, made darkness flood his vision so he could hardly see the road. They pointed to the truth of the clear weather calamity being less accidental than he could stomach. "She'd want you to know, Mike. That she fought it back. She loved you, hated what she'd done to you—"

"What she did to me? She didn't do anything to me. What are you talkin' about?" He interrupted her, knowing his tone was dark and dangerous, cutting off her words with the question, which she answered immediately.

"Tab knew she was the reason you had to go away. Hated that she drove you away from everything you loved." Her words sliced at him, making the constricted feeling around his chest return, silencing him as well as brutalizing him bloodlessly. "Hated it, but she loved you so much. Loved hearing about what you were doing, all the different people you'd meet. Things you saw. She loved everything you sent her. Read me every letter a dozen times. You'd call, and she'd be giddy over the moon for days. Helped her beat it back."

"She didn't do anything to me. Not a thing. Nothing to deserve feelin' like that." He could hardly force the words through his throat, tight to the point of pain. He knew Bethy's words and voice would be haunting his dreams for a long time, because he didn't write home often, and called Tabby only infrequently. Discovering how much those things meant to his sister, knowing he could have made it better forever if he had only known—he would have to live with the knowledge, and that living wouldn't be easy. "Nothing. Ever. Her whole life."

"I was there the night it happened, you know." At her quietly spoken confession, his head whipped so he could see her, and he instinctively steered the truck to the right as it slid and shuddered to a stop, his feet stamping hard on the brake pedal and clutch, controlling the vehicle automatically. "She didn't do anything to deserve that, either. None of them did." Her already soft voice dropped to a barely audible whisper. "Not one of us."

Bethy was the same age as Tabby. Same age, same place, and now, he knew she shared the same ghosts. Each stared at the other, eyes locked and at that moment he knew...*knew* it had happened to her, too. Happened and she didn't have anyone to help; no talking doctor, no one to lean on except his damaged sister, because her pa had run everyone off who would give a shit.

"You beatin' it back?" Watcher hadn't meant to ask the question, didn't know where it came from, but it was on the air between them, and he waited.

Bethany swallowed, a hard, painful sound as her throat worked. Her head made one sweep, left to right, right to left, and she froze in place, staring at him.

"I got a friend in Nashville," he said, shocked he got the words out, but there were more to come, restitution for a hard life where Bethany'd done what she could to make his sister well, now needing someone to stand at her back. "He'll put you up. Find you a job. I can help with expenses. I've got it, yeah? Whatever you need, Bethy. I'm there for you. I couldn't...can't change things for Tabby, but I can do this for you, sweetheart."

***

Two days later he and Darrie drove Bethy to Nashville, to where one of the men from his unit had moved after separating from the military. She and Tyrell, his guy, hit it off right away. Ty teasing her like she was his long lost little sister, while Bethy dished it right back at him. Sass and attitude, but a fast growing affection between them smoothed the way. A day later, convinced she was settled and safe, Watcher and Darrie headed home. Watcher had set up a bank account for her and dropped some money in it, calling the noncom who handled payroll for his company and making it so the money that had been going to Loretta would go into the new account every month instead.

Since she had been married at fifteen with her pa's permission, it actually made things easier. Zonder had begun the process of a divorce but being as she was already emancipated, in the eyes of the state of Kentucky, she was an adult. This meant she was able to make her own decisions and if one of those decisions involved leaving the family holler and moving to Tennessee, no one, not a single person—not even her father—could tell her no.

On the way home the two brothers took a turn through Lexington, checked into a motel, and it was then they mourned the loss of their little sister, toasting a being they loved more than life, whose existence on this earth was cut far too short.

Beat it back

"No, sir. I will not be reenlisting, sir." Watcher's eyes remained focused on the wall behind his commander's head, refusing to look at the kid. Hands folded into the small of his back, at ease, Watcher could hold this pose for hours. He had already told the men, taken all the guff he intended to take, and was ready to hand ownership of everything back for someone else to deal with. Someone's responsibility, but not his. He'd been in charge for so long, even thinking about having a space in time where he could simply *be* was seriously fucking attractive.

"This is the army's loss, soldier." *He doesn't even know me enough to know my name*, he thought, then wondered, confused, *What the hell am I doing following his orders when he don't even know my name?*

"Yes, sir." Gaze still on the wall, he didn't notice the kid moving until he had invaded Watcher's space in a way that made his skin itch to get away. He barely covered his instinctive flinch when a hand fell on his shoulder and squeezed.

"Mike, every man in this unit will miss you."

At hearing his name, he cut his eyes to the kid's face and saw real regret there, maybe tinged with a hint of fear. *Was I ever that young?* "I'll miss the men, sir," he said respectfully, but firmly, "but it's time."

The kid turned loose of him with a nod and walked back to his desk.

***

"Naw, brother." Rubbing his forehead, trying to stave off a headache earned from reading close-spaced newspaper reports, Watcher spoke quietly into his cell phone. "Nashville ain't my speed these days." He was talking to Tyrell, who was trying to convince Watcher he needed to come stay with Ty and Bethy until he got his feet underneath him. "Gonna hang with my aunt and uncle for a bit, see what I can come up with."

This statement wasn't exactly true. Actually, Watcher was still unsettled by whatever it was had bugged him at Tabby's funeral six months earlier. Bothered and disconcerted, he was pissed off at everyone for assuming they knew the reason for the wreck, and found himself needing better information. He'd stopped in Louisville for only a couple of nights, and wanted to head back home to get a read on his blood. Watcher was convinced if it wasn't an accident, he'd be able to see if there was anything else that could have been done to help Tabby get past the things that had happened to her on that mountain so long ago. One way or the other, he needed answers.

"That little girl doing okay?" Irritably, he pushed back from the table, scanning the library for anyone he knew. If he didn't give her a name, maybe he could get over his fear on her behalf, some of the nightmares that woke him sweating, imagining she wasn't dealing with her change in circumstances well. Dreams that left Watcher trembling with fear she'd wind up taking a sail off a switchback on a high mountainside, too. He had a recurring one where he was the first person present at an accident scene, first one to clamber over the lip of the cliff, and always...always first to the truck. Any help trailing so far behind him that he was alone when he saw Bethy's face, her body crushed and bleeding. A face that always swam and changed, until finally the shock of seeing an image of Tabby would bring him out of sleep with a shout.

"Oh, hell yeah," came Tyrell's laughing response. "She's runnin' the show at a local radio station now."

"What in the hell?" The question yanked out of Watcher in surprise. "She's working at a radio station?"

"Started as the coffee and donut intern. Two days 'a that and Bethy'd talked her way into one of the engineer rooms. Three days after *that* she was laughing and cuttin' up on the air, and the station got hundreds more call-ins than usual. Every single one 'a them wanting a little piece of the sunshine she was spreading around. Worked her way up from there, brother."

Watcher found himself grinning, the muscles of his face stretching uncomfortably, cheeks quickly aching with the unfamiliar movement. "About time that girl caught a lucky bounce." *Beating it back, one day at a time.*

Outrider years

"Otey." The shout of his last name got Watcher's attention, and he lifted his head to twist around, looking down. Pausing, he held the nail gun steady and leaned towards the peak of the roof he was working on. Two stories down stood Miguel Orland, owner of the construction company where Watcher had been employed for the past year. "Come on down." That kind of summons couldn't be ignored, so with a sigh, he found an anchor and secured the gun, then padded carefully across the roof, rubber soles gripping the felted material firmly as he made his way to the ladder and descended.

"Yo, boss," he said when both feet were firmly on the ground. "'Sup?"

"Got a request for a bid. Need you to go take a look, tell me why the client can't find a contractor to take the job on." Orland thrust a packet of papers towards Watcher, holding them extended until Watcher reluctantly reached out to take them. "They've been through three companies before coming to me. Go see what the deal is."

"Okay." His answer was short, and he hoped conveyed annoyance at having to leave a job unfinished to go scope out something they might or might not take on. Walking to his truck, he unbuckled his tool belt with one hand, studying the name and address. Frowning, he considered the information as he folded into the driver seat, slinging his belt down into the passenger floorboard and changing into his boots. Outriders was an odd business name for this area, where most were named after the family that founded them.

Pulling up into the parking lot, he double-checked the address on the papers against the numbers on the side of the building. They were a match, which meant he was at the right place, but this was not a business. Not by a long shot.

The parking area nearer the building was marked off in narrow slants, each about half the size of a standard space. A number of these were filled, motorcycles backed up to the building, the front wheels angled to the side, handlebars twisted. He saw a dozen different types of bikes, but only one American manufacturer and Watcher stood in the door of his truck for a minute, staring at the machines. "Beautiful," he murmured, tearing his eyes away and leaning back into the cab of the truck to grab the paperwork and tools needed to work up the proposal.

When he straightened, Watcher was surprised to find half a dozen men standing close to the vehicle, arranged in a half circle, arcing out from the truck's bumpers. "Hey," he said, his gaze sweeping along the line, unsuccessfully trying to determine the head honcho. "I work for Orland. He sent me to check out the stuff y'all want a bid on." Upon closer inspection, each man wore a vest, similar in that all were black leather, some covered nearly entirely on each front panel by small patches, some of them with only a few. They each had at least two, placement similar to military units so he ran his gaze across all of them, finding what looked to be the highest ranking man standing in the bend of the line, smack in the middle of everything.

With a nod, Watcher indicated the man he had selected, and the guy's face split into a wide grin, white teeth shining in a full, dark beard. "I'm Killer," the man said, confirming Watcher's thoughts on which patch indicated a name and which a title, "President of the Cynthiana Outriders. We've got a lot of work needs doin' to the clubhouse. I'll walk you through. Me and Painter—" He pointed to the man to his right, whose title patch read Lieutenant. "—can tell you what we want." Killer made a gesture and the remaining men silently turned and walked away, some heading towards a cluster of bikes near an outbuilding, and some headed to the door set into one side of the long, flat building.

Watcher nodded, and then as the remaining men stayed in place, staring at him, he offered his name, "I'm Mike Otey, folks call me Watcher."

Killer's eyes narrowed, gaze sweeping him from boots to cap. After a moment he tipped his head, and then astutely asked, "Which branch?"

With a grin, Watcher answered, "Army." He sucked in a breath, and then quietly called, "Hooah," not surprised when it was echoed by both men. A sense of belonging swept through his belly. "Fort Leonard Wood, Sapper. Only been out a few months."

Killer nodded, and then said, "Medic, overseas for far too fucking long. Painter was my partner. My brother's still in, too. Glad me an' Paint could settle here. Bein' out, like this, after bein' in so long? We found it's nice to have folks you trust at your back."

"Know what you mean there," Watcher said, turning to follow the men across the lot. "My brother's in, too, he'll be out in a couple months. Counting the days."

"I feel ya." Painter spoke for the first time. His posture and movement was giving off an uneasy vibe, attentive gaze sweeping the area around the building, not seeming to miss anything. "Hard to breathe free, 'less you got someone watchin' your six."

"Yeah," Watcher responded, twisting his neck to sweep his gaze across the front of the building, cataloging the location of the men out of habit. "I know that's right."

Two hours later, he had everything needed to write up the quote and stood in the great room on the ground floor of the building. Glancing around, he saw the space had partially filled up with men, each dressed similarly to Killer and Painter. Motorcycle boots, jeans, T-shirt, and one of those damned leather vests. Standing not far from him, his two guides huddled with a couple of men for a moment before walking to him.

He glanced at the bar, where there was a flag pinned to the wall with the word Outriders across the top in an arc. The symbol underneath matched the one on each vest. In fact, every element was recreated on the flag, including the diamond shape with 1% inside, and the small square enclosing the letters MC.

One of the questions he had about the bid would help lay to rest some of his curiosity about their group. "Any organization information I need to put on the bid other than Outriders?"

"Naw, that'll do it. I'll get the info to my guy in SoCal. He'll deal with the bills. Way folks around here don't want our money, you actually turn in a bid, I can almost guarantee you got the job, man." Killer snorted a laugh. "Don't mean we won't haggle, you come in high."

"My bids are fair. Fair but competitive." He grinned as he spoke, to show there wasn't any offense at the insinuation he might jack up the bid with Killer's admission they were the only show in town when it came to the construction modifications wanted. "We're not cheap, but neither are the materials we use." He laughed, knowing he wasn't able to keep the pained tone out of his voice completely when he saw both Killer and Painter flinch. "My crew does good work, too. In and out, focused on the job. Not my friends, but they don't have to be to do what we do. They just have to do what I tell 'em."

Silence fell between them, and Killer's gaze hit him for a moment before skidding up and over his shoulder. It took some doing, but Watcher forced down the itch between his shoulder blades at not knowing what was behind him, trusting the man to give a heads-up if there was something to be worried about. A few seconds later, his gaze returned to Watcher's face, and then Killer grinned, holding out his hand.

Palm to palm, Watcher gripped and lifted once, twice, before releasing the grip, getting ready to leave.

"Come by tomorrow night," Painter put in, and Watcher turned his head, looking at him, wondering at the abruptness of the invitation. "'Bout eleven o'clock. We got a half a dozen military guys who'll be in town for the night. Come have a beer with us, give us a new audience for our stories."

Nodding slowly, Watcher said, "Well, all right. I will. I'll take you up on that. Thanks."

***

15 months later

"Goddamn right, brother. Best day for this chapter, you walked through that fucking door." Painter staggered sideways, caught himself on the edge of the bar and straightened, looking Watcher in the eye. "Killer said it, more'n once. 'Never met a man more born to the life than Watch.' Swear, brother. Love you, man. Love and respect, brother."

Patches leaned on Painter's shoulder, lifted a fist and thudded it against the patch now affixed underneath the name on Watcher's chest. "Fucking President. Own that shit, Watch. Killer'd be proud."

They were at Killer's wake, held in the main room of the Outriders' clubhouse, and the officers had just announced voting Watcher in as president. He didn't understand Painter's glee, because this fucking bizarre decision meant they passed over the man, who had held the lieutenant position within the chapter for nearly three years, while Watcher had only been a fully patched member for eight months. With being so new to the club, and never having held any officer title, this was entirely jacked. It was unheard of for a short-term member to be voted into the top role in the chapter. Not nearly unheard of, but according to each man who came to congratulate him, this had never happened before in any club any of them knew about.

Watcher stood with his shoulders against the wall at the end of the bar, looking out over the crowd of men. There were members from a half a dozen chapters, and not only were there national officers present but Morgan, the club's founder, was here. He'd showed up not two hours after they'd got the news about Killer's wreck, and had organized everything. Morgan had a knowledge of the county, which surprised Watcher since he had never heard of the man before joining the club. But, with the amount of info Morgan had on the political and official ins and outs, he'd evidently been around a lot, and for a while.

Watcher's gaze swept the room again, looking for trouble, wanting to stay ahead of it. He knew it'd come eventually, couldn't help but know from the angry shouts that had accompanied the announcement as Morgan walked over holding out an open palm, without words demanding Watcher accept the patch balanced there. Watcher looked down, seeing that same piece of fabric held in place with a safety pin for now, not even having time to take a sewing kit in hand before Morgan pulled him into the first of many quiet conversations.

Words flowed from the man's lips like water, and Watcher found himself nodding in agreement, because as if he were going down a list, Morgan had acknowledged every misgiving Watcher was feeling. Watcher didn't know high protocol, not at all. Of course, he knew a little of the day-to-day things because you had to learn fast as a prospect. Pure self-preservation, so you didn't fuck up every time you turned around, but Watcher had no knowledge of the deeper points, the things which touched the core of the outlaw biker life. No idea what to do if he found himself in another club's territory. No idea what went on in church, those closed-door meetings the officers held in the room behind the bar. No idea what some of the roles in the club were supposed to be as opposed to what their little chapter used them for. Felt like he didn't have any idea, and he *seriously* wanted to buy a fucking clue. He would settle for a damn vowel at this point. *Any fucking thing.*

Morgan promised someone to help him along, a mentor, was offering up his own son in fact. John, a man who had made a study of clubs and the differences in them, having observed several organizations from the inside. Temporarily patching in with approval from his old man and the receiving club's officers, getting a feel for what made a good club, as well as what made a good officer. John had a few years on Watcher but seemed to be decent, and levelheaded, someone he could learn from. Especially if he was anything like his old man. Watcher found he liked what he was learning about Morgan. Liked the man nearly as much as he had Killer.

At the thought, a wave of sadness washed over him, and he twisted to see the picture tacked to the wall next to the office door. Taken at a recent hog roast, it showed Killer with his arms slung around Watcher and Painter's shoulders, their inside arms crossed over his back, outside ones linking the three men to the line of club members standing and staring at the camera.

Killer was grinning, his smile splitting his beard, white teeth shining through, eyes crinkled with laughter just trailing off. Watcher couldn't remember what Painter had said, but Killer had found it hilarious, as he often did, and had cackled like a madman for so long the bitch taking the picture got impatient, snapping the shutter before his features had settled down into the scowl he typically affected for the camera.

Lifting the beer in his hand, Watcher tilted the top of the bottle towards the picture, thinking, *Never met a better man.*

"He was a good brother." Morgan's voice came from beside him, and Watcher jolted, not having seen him walk up. "Good dad. Good man." Leaning back so his shoulders rested against the wall beside Watcher,

Morgan sighed. "You can tell the measure of a man by how he treats his kids, don't you think?"

That was a loaded question if he ever heard one. Everyone knew John, Morgan's son, hadn't done right by his families for a long time. Families, as in plural, because he had an official old lady and a daughter, then had taken on a side piece, who wound up pregnant with his son. The man had fucked up so bad his old lady took a runner, had been gone for months now with his girl, Eddie.

All John could do was sit and spin, because she'd hid so well no one could find her. It had gotten to the point few people even believed the two were still alive. Meant Morgan hadn't seen his granddaughter for any of those months, and you could see the lines of anger and pain struck into his skin when he talked about Eddie. The side piece had given up her boy to John, and Luke was living with Morgan for now.

Knowing all this, instead of responding to Morgan's question, Watcher grunted, lifting his beer to conclude his silent toast to his friend.

Loyal to a fault

Fuck, Watcher thought, eyeing the now-closed door leading from his office into the main room of the clubhouse. Not twenty minutes ago, there had been a crying, screaming woman cowering on the floor, and he had watched in fascination as a man had visibly restrained himself from dealing out a well-deserved and entirely justified retribution. Davy Mason, one of his best friends growing up. The man had gotten out of the holler and made his own way in the world, and they'd both settled into the life. Different clubs, but same love of bikes and brotherhood. Mason had been dealt blow after blow all his life, had become a master at locking his shit down, and today Watcher had seen him force control back into place piece by bloody piece. "Fuck."

Tipping the desk chair back, Watcher leaned to grab his beer. Not giving that first shit it was warm. The motherfucker was wet, and after what he had witnessed, each sip would be the start of his own lockdown, building a wall between the pain he had observed and what he needed to do next. Three beers later, he felt close enough to normal he was ready to pick up the phone, preparing to pull the trigger on what would be another life-altering change. Pausing for a moment, he dialed a number from memory, not the one he originally intended, but this one needed to be first.

"Darrie." He greeted his brother when the call connected. He gave the usual pleasantries a minute, then cut off his big brother's questions with a brusque, "I've made a decision."

Two years as president of this chapter had pulled the shades from his eyes. The Outriders. Watcher now knew he'd been coddled as a prospect and new member, shown a picture far from the reality of what the club actually was. He had known about the drug and gun trade, of course he had, a blind man couldn't miss it. The shit was everywhere in Kentucky. Seemed like every sixth driveway led to a lab, and few people were walking the streets without some kind of monkey on their back.

Dealers had gotten smart, setting up what amounted to drive-through clinics treating chronic pain. Using doctors who worshiped greenbacks as gods, oath be damned; ones who didn't give their own first shit about what they did to the people or the families behind the addicts. Morgan's talk about how the family was most important was thin, and when push came to shove, every promise broke in pieces the first time the club had gotten wind of how much money could be made. Runners brought the shit in from Canada or from Mexico, depending on which direction proved most profitable. This meant bringing in people to work, covering shipments, storage, and distribution—the entire dirty business. A lot of men, none of whom had loyalty to anything, most certainly not the Outrider patch.

What Watcher hadn't known about were the other trade routes they ran, all of them bloody. Flesh trade, transporting girls in from foreign countries and parking them in a stable, branding each of them on the face with the club's mark. Making it so these girls, some of them only just out of childhood, could never go home. People would take one look at the scar, much more permanent than a fucking letter on their chest, and know what the girls had been forced to do to survive. It only took one exposure to that and Watcher had flat refused to have the shit run through his territory, and Morgan agreed, knowing the history, and rightly judging that it would be a breaking point for Watcher.

Protection and enforcement were another path the club walked. This one bloody, too, with enforcement sometimes stretching thin to include elimination. Bodies stacked like cordwood in the back of a pickup, territory cleared for one of their other trades on an as-needed basis. Mine shafts reopened, lined with lime and death.

This last bit of shit that had landed in his lap tonight was the final straw. Mason—a man he had always trusted to be at his back, someone he knew without a doubt would take his six—had been royally fucked over, and hard. By family, of all the shit. Over time, Watcher found out Morgan knew the county so well because he had dipped in and out of here for years. Heard through the grapevine Morgan had fucked Mason's mother. They had one child together, but Morgan had, in essence, gained three kids from that unhappy union. John, now called Shooter, and Mason were half brothers, raised apart...and Shooter hated Mason with a passion which was uncomfortable to witness.

Since being voted in as chapter president, Watcher had necessarily spent a lot of time with Shooter, learning the lay of the land and how to handle dozens of situations in the way Morgan wanted. They had gotten friendly but would likely never be friends because the more comfortable the man became in their association, the more open Shooter got and let down his guard. And what Watcher had found behind the wall was not pretty.

The story told by folks who had known Shooter a long time was that before his old lady left, he was good. Or at least better than he was these days. He worked hard to keep the club out of trouble, tried to find ways to mitigate damage caused by Morgan's orders. However, since he lost his old lady he had gone sideways in a bad way, using club product of any kind, services too, and the man did not get off easy. His kinks were so fucking twisted Watcher would see the Cynthiana party dolls flinch at the sound of Shooter's voice. When he stayed a while at a chapter where they ran flesh, more than one woman had to be permanently retired after he was done with her.

It was entirely fucked up, and knowing he was part of this in even a small way turned Watcher's stomach.

So, two months ago when Darrie called and said he had started a club out west, Watcher listened. The Southern Soldiers sounded very different from the Outriders—a club designed around the idea of honor and populated with combat vets who all had the same mindset. Ones who believed the oath to serve and protect didn't end with separation from the military, but only upon death. When Darrie called and explained what he was doing, he turned around and asked the impossible, wanting Watcher to jump ship and wade up the creek to where his brother would be waiting. Watcher had asked for some time. He knew he would have to make his play carefully because it wasn't a done deal Morgan would be cool with him leaving the club, and Watcher didn't want to bring heat down on Darrie or his men. He also kinda wanted to stay breathing, and knew that wasn't a done deal, either.

"And?" his brother prompted, and Watcher recognized the tone of tense anticipation in his voice.

Watcher took a moment, his mind racing back over the scene he just witnessed, where a woman had been forced to serve a man she hated, possibly tying herself to another one who now detested her. Forced because if she didn't, then—the man she hated, one who was crazy and not like a fox—would kill her without any hesitation. None. Shooter would take his fists to her, or if he weren't in a mood to go slow, he'd use his knife. Watcher knew this because it had happened before. When it happened again—and it would happen again—Watcher knew he would be the one finding a shaft deep enough to bury the stench of betrayal. Because that was what the Outriders demanded, so it was what he gave.

Loyal, to a fault.

Time to dig out from under, to try and find some way to peel off the shit which had become buried so deeply in his skin. Get away from the weight of pain and blood, and knowing his part in it all. Time to atone, regardless of the cost.

"I'm in."

My grave

Jarred from sleep when rough hands clamped tight around her upper arms, Juanita was disoriented for a second, and after a frozen moment of reaction, she tried to pull away. Utter darkness shrouded her room, the lack of any light was confusing and frightening. Dazed, she twisted, struggling to break free from her unseen attacker, legs snarled in the quilt her *abuela* had given her. Hauled from the bed, she fell to her hands and knees, tangled hair around her head. Clawing futilely at the floorboards, pain ripped through her fingers as nail heads and splinters tore at her skin.

Thinking of nothing except escape from whatever nightmare monster was in her room, she'd made it halfway underneath the bed when one of her ankles was seized in an iron grip, dragging her backwards. A weight landed on her spine, the pain from impact paralyzing. All the air was knocked from her body, leaving her unable to take a single breath. Damp fabric slapped across her nose and mouth, and as she fell into a bottomless tunnel, she belatedly realized she should have screamed.

Consciousness returned in stages. First was pain. Unbearable and overwhelming, it pierced Juanita's skull as if it were a pickax, like the one her father used to carve the family garden from the mountainside. Second was sound, loud and echoing through her head. Men bellowed nearby, and she flinched. Their unfamiliar voices overrode any other noise, the weight of anger carried in their shouts terrifying. In time, the pain in her head subsided, and she became aware of her body. That was the third stage, awareness. Every inch ached. It felt like her bones had been crushed, the sharp edges slicing through her skin. "Mama," she whispered, feeling a sharp stinging as her dry lips cracked with the movement, blood a welcome liquid pooling in her parched mouth. "Papa." Her eyes felt too large, sore and swollen in their sockets, and with the desiccated membranes in her mouth, she knew dehydration was part of what she needed to fear.

Legs splayed wide apart, her hips ached from the unfamiliar angle. Her feet were weighted down somehow, made so she could only move them an inch or two in any direction, a tight constriction around her ankles. It hurt when she tugged, and the ache made her remember the tight hold of the hand around her leg.

Carefully, she opened her eyelids a slit, shocked when she was unable to see anything. Darkness surrounded her. A darkness so total, she lifted her hand in front of her face and could still see nothing. *I'm blind*, she thought, heart tripping over itself in her chest, the swirl of bile in her belly threatening to wash up her numb throat. She was bending forwards to explore the restraints on her legs when footsteps sounded near her, but not anything she'd expected. Instead of on the floor where she lay, they were above her head. Not far, but not close either. Scuffing across a wooden floor, each footfall was followed by the jingle of a spur rowel, dragging across the boards in a slow but somehow threatening manner.

The surface on which she sat was damp, and she pressed her palm to it, finding it wasn't a floor at all, but dirt. The wall she leaned on, also soil. *A grave.* Ropes around her ankles led to anchors out of reach, crusted liquids sticking the fibers together, making them impossible to untie by feel. With her dry tongue to her drier lips, Juanita tried to make a sound, but couldn't. Absolute fear had stolen her voice. The footsteps began retreating, and she was suddenly more terrified of being alone than she was of whoever wore those boots. "*Hola. Hola! Hay alguien ahi?*"

The footsteps stopped retreating and instead, returned in a rush to directly over her head, boot soles slapping against the wood, spurs jingling brightly. She turned her face up, eyes stretched as wide as she could make them, hoping to see something, anything.

Nothing.

A stomp, then another, as particles of dirt and dust disturbed and drifted down to lodge in her eyes. Blinking the pain away, she saw a sliver of light appear about eight feet away. It grew and grew, and then a head appeared. *Not blind.* Haloed by the light, features cast in darkness, she couldn't determine anything other than it was a man. Then the trap door over her head was flung open fully, thudding as it landed and she saw him. It was then she knew this was indeed a grave, and as he leaped the three feet from the floor to land on the dirt between her shackled legs, she hoped she would die quickly.

Lost and found in Mexico

Watcher rested against the fence running the length of his brother's backyard, elbows to the wooden rails. Beer in hand, he idly watched as Darrie's latest girlfriend swam to the edge of the pool closest to where he stood. His mind wasn't on the woman. Hell, Watcher couldn't even remember this one's name, Darrie churned through them so fast. He wasn't thinking about the pool, an in-ground luxury which would have been unthinkable in eastern Kentucky but a seeming necessity in the arid and dry New Mexico desert.

No, he was thinking of the upcoming run the Southern Soldiers had on tap. Club business took precedence, as always. Still, his gaze tracked her as the woman stood on the shallow lip ringing the pool, one hand gripping the edge of the cement. She reached behind her with the other, and he saw the fabric of her top relax and loosen. She lifted it over her head and then carried it with her hand into the water where she wiggled, that hand coming back out in a moment and dropping a sodden pile of fabric to the walkway around the pool. Both parts of her two-piece bikini, no doubt. *Shit.*

Leaning back into the water, she pushed off the outer wall with both feet, gliding smoothly to the center of the pool on her back. Legs opening and closing in lazy motion, each swing of her thighs revealing dark flashes of her pussy. Pebbled nipples on her breasts proudly breaking the surface of the water, each breath offering more of a show. She lifted her head and looked straight at him, winked wickedly and licked her lips with an open-mouthed smile before relaxing back into the water, floating effortlessly.

"Fuck, Caroline, get your goddamned suit back on," Darrie yelled as he walked out of the barn where they stored their bikes and tools. "That's my goddamned baby brother."

"Relax, bro," Watcher muttered. "Ain't like there's anything there I ain't seen before."

"Might be so, but she don't have to put herself out there like that. Fuck. *Shit*. What if one of the other members was here?" Darrie leaned on the other side of the rail fence and shook his head, watching as she swam to the edge of the pool. His face tightened as she hefted herself out of the water, sitting naked on the edge before she rose to her feet, gathering up the wet swimsuit as she straightened. Reaching up, she twisted her long hair into a dark rope, tugging it over her shoulder so the ends lay alongside one breast. "Fuck. *Shit*, Caroline—"

That was all he got out before she twisted and snapped, "I know my own name, Darren." She dropped the suit and bent, giving them both a clear shot of her pussy before knifing through the water of the pool in a shallow dive.

The sound of an approaching bike interrupted whatever Darrie was about to say, and both men turned to look up the long drive, seeing a distinctive bike approaching. "Spider," Watcher said and twisted to look at the pool, seeing Caroline backing towards the end by the steps, more of her body exposed with each stride. Eager eyes fixed on the approaching man and bike, her dark skin looked sleek and soft, drops of water trailing down her body. "See to your woman, brother."

"Fuck. Shit. Caroline, you do *not* want to piss me off, woman." Long, angry strides carried Darrie around the end of the fence and took him to the edge of the pool where he picked up her wet swimsuit. Balling it in one fist, he threw it at her where she stood, the water lapping around her hips. The fabric hit the water right in front of her, and she didn't even flinch, just reached out and snagged the fabric pieces, redressing herself with casual movements. Watcher turned his attention back to the Southern Soldiers' member, the bike engine dying as Spider stood, straddling his bike. Watcher motioned a question with one hand towards the barn and received a nod in response.

"You need to ditch the bitch, bro," Watcher said quietly as he walked side-by-side with Darrie towards Spider, already standing in the barn's doorway, eyes to the pool behind them. "You deserve respect, and a good woman who respects you wouldn't be pulling that kind of shit."

"I know." Darrie sighed, and his steps slowed so Watcher shortened stride to match him. "She's history, as of today. I'll deal with her when we see what Spidey needs." Watcher heard him give a heavy sigh. "Caroline was hot, brother."

"Yeah, hotheaded. She also brings drama and stupid with her ass. Tits and ass can be had nearly anywhere, bro, and pussy comes with it. You need sweet and clean along with that, with a serving of smarts." He lifted his chin, acknowledging Spider's greeting. "Pussy ain't anything without smarts."

"Yeah, yeah. Like you'd know," Darrie said in a long-suffering tone, and then called out, "Spidey, man. Whatcha got for me?"

"Debrief inside," Spider said, jerking his head to the darkness inside the barn, waiting in the doorway until they stepped through. Then, he gave a visible scan of the yard, pausing with his eyes towards the pool as he yanked the door closed, shrouding them in dimness until Darrie hit a switch, flipping the lights on over the workbench.

Darrie had sent Spider to scope out the Machos, a rival club that had recently started encroaching on their territory. Previously content with their own power base, isolated across the river in Mexico where they worked hand in hand with the cartel to control trade and bring in *dinero*, things had recently changed. Now, the club was reaching across the bridge, tagging business and deals out of the hands of the Soldiers. Spider had connections in the cartel from a series of events in his past he referred to as his "shit days," and the hope was he would be able to leverage those contacts to move this club off the Soldiers' territory in a permanent way.

"Machos are restless, blaming us for a variety of ills assailing their sick-as-fuck carcass of a club." Spider launched into his report without any preliminaries. "Me and Opie had a convo with the second in command. According to their looey, the Machos are hugely solvent, highly organized, and significantly motivated to keep things the way they are." He shook his head, leaning one hip against the workbench. "I don't buy it. They're tagging our bang-bangs because on their own they can't locate the same or better merch, which means they are all over our shit, because we have the hot-as-shit good shit. But, brother—" His neck twisted, and he sucked in air through his nose, face twisting with anger and disgust. "—one thing they have in ample supply is pussy. All ages, all kinds. They got Thai pussy, Mexican pussy, Canadian pussy. I ain't never been offered so much pussy in my life. It was enough to—"

He stopped talking as their heads all turned towards the barn door, hearing engine noise from another bike coming up the drive. "Boss?" Spider's one word was a question, and Darrie grunted a negative response. They were not expecting anyone else tonight.

Watcher whistled a soft single note, and once he had Spider's attention, he jerked his head towards the back of the barn, waiting for an acknowledging nod before he moved in that direction. Fading into the shadows at the wall, he took up position beside the back door, waiting, listening to the quiet settle around the house and barn after the bike engine cut off. Spider moved to the front door, reaching out to kill the inside lights before throwing it open. Immediately his posture changed, relaxing as he must have recognized friend, not foe. "Devil," he called the name of another member and Watcher relaxed, too. Extending his arm, Spider twitched his finger to flick the light back on and stepped to one side, letting a big man walk through the doorway.

When Watcher had first rolled into town, the Southern Soldiers had numbered four plus his brother, all of them working day jobs, and the club didn't run any businesses. Out of necessity, riding was more of a hobby than a life for them because there wasn't a line of income to support the club other than the token dues the few members paid. No clubhouse, they had no gathering spot other than a local bar, and no financial cushion to fall back on if anything went sideways with any of the members.

After Watcher had joined, Darrie's little band grew significantly, and the Soldiers soon boasted nearly three dozen members. They also had three businesses with paper in various men's names, giving them a decent flow of green coming into the joint coffers. Seeing those accounts grow gave everyone confidence, building a solid foundation for the kind of club they all wanted...needed.

That kind of shift was good for morale in the club, but unfortunately, the profitability they found brought more than just good feelings. It had swung eyes and attention their direction the club hadn't experienced previously, and while Watcher had expected the challenge, it wasn't long before he knew he hadn't prepared Darrie for it well enough.

As hot as Watcher's head ran, Darrie's temper was much worse. So, the first time one of their runs got hit and Watcher wasn't close enough to talk Darrie down, it meant his brother's reaction was extreme. The Soldiers hit back, and hard, torching two buildings full of cartel product. This meant the club's subsequent lesson was painful.

In the normal world, the Soldiers' response would have been expected; tit for tat, you take my shit, I torch yours. But, the cartel didn't appreciate taking a hit from a group they saw as upstarts. Men the cartel didn't have one lick of respect for. From the cartel's perspective, the Soldiers were a little snot-nosed club, playing out of their depth in the big boys' games. Just another club needing a lesson in the way the world worked, a la cartel. So when the mob responded, they rained pain down on the club. This cost the Soldiers members...and blood. A man to one ambush, then two more to another. In the process, the Soldiers took down a dozen of the cartel's men, but that was no consolation when their own wounds gaped wide.

With Watcher's influence, Darrie began to strategize and plan, developing more long-term goals. That's when Watch went to work in earnest, taking on the veep role in the club as he took on more men. He put in time talking to people he knew through his Outriders associations, through his stint in the army, and through the family he had built around himself over the years. He recruited, always with an eye towards getting ready for a conflict he couldn't even begin to effectively predict. Looking for and finding men tired of the bullshit found in many clubs, they'd built a cohesive one filled with men who would be ready to go the distance for a worthy club.

He had picked up individuals from a dozen different clubs; long-time members who voluntarily dropped their center and walked out in good standing, or as good a standing as they could, given they had surrendered their patch. It killed, but he had also picked up men from Mason's club in Chicago, one he knew was struggling against dying.

Rebel Fiends had so many men patch out and go gypsy, they could hardly roll any strength. After the most recent conversation between Watcher and Mason, when Mason had once again loyally opted to remain a Fiend, Watch knew seeing the club die had to be stripping Mason's soul. The man desperately wanted what Darrie and Watcher were building, and Watch knew every conversation with his friend thrust the knife deeper, twisted it further, and ripped the wound open a little more.

Through all this, Watcher and Darrie had differed in their approach and strategy. Out of respect, Watcher had continued to publicly bow to his president, but in private, the brothers far too often argued viciously. Every encounter meant Darrie wanted to go in guns blazing and take down what he saw as the source of the problem, the President of the Machos, Carlos Estavez. Watcher tried to keep the Soldiers working the edges of things, cutting one after the other of the cartel's supply routes for the Machos. His intent to starve them, but not to the point of collapse. He wanted to leave them with a limited base, something the Soldiers could police and control, because he believed the Machos as a controlled influence would be better than whatever unknown factors might fill the void. Since the brothers didn't...couldn't agree, the club was tracing the path Darrie routed for them, but Watch reserved the right to argue as often as he could find space and breath.

Spider was the club's road captain and one of Darrie's originals, proudly wearing a founder's patch on his vest. Devil was one of Watcher's, had moved up to an officer fast, now their sergeant at arms, so for this conversation, whatever it was, the two factions within their club would be evenly matched.

"Prez," Devil said in greeting. He shut the door firmly behind him, gaze sweeping across the men standing in the barn, coming to rest on Watcher. That gaze didn't move when Devil spoke, and it wasn't lost on Watcher that Devil may have given token respect to Darrie, but expected the decision to come from the veep instead of the president. *Fuck*, he thought, then jolted as what Devil said registered. "Machos are rolling 200 across the bridge right the fuck now."

"Fuck. Shit," Darrie breathed, and then, tellingly, *his* gaze swung to Watcher.

Fuck.

Watcher took in a hard breath, blew it out, rolling his muscles and deliberately releasing tension in his shoulders, feeling them lower and move back so the next breath wasn't as hard. And the next after that, easier still. "Any chatter?" He frowned, tipping his head to one side, waiting. "Any contact at all?"

"No chatter, no contact. Just got a call from one of my men in immigration. He said the bridge detail was panicking." Devil shook his head. "Bad mojo, brother."

"No doubt," Watcher said, leaning to one side and spitting into the dirt of the barn floor. Deliberate confidence would help everyone maintain their control. "Don't fucking care. We got firepower and the high ground. We're way past ready for this shit. You already roll our brothers?"

"Nope. Your call, man." Devil stepped closer, hand out at waist level, palm extended to Watcher. Devil's hand was shaking, pupils wide. He was riding the edge of freaked out. "What do you want me to do?"

Watcher knew it didn't matter which direction they jumped; men would die. The win was choosing the leap that had the least cost in lives. *Please, God, let me get it right.* "We unass and fuckin' move. Make the call, get every man here at Soldiers' base. Put the families at NHF," he said, referencing a church compound in town. "It's near the mall, embedded in a dense population, and we got friends there. Tell them to talk to Terri. She'll handle everything." Terri was an old lady to one of their members. She would make sure the families had a place to hole up while things were coming down on the club. She was solid, organized and steady, precisely the kind of thing nervous wives and mothers needed to see.

Watcher reached out, gripping Devil's forearm hard, pulling him close, mouth to his ear. "Settle yourself, brother. We're in time. We got this covered."

If Machos were rolling across the bridge between Mexico and the US, it meant they were still in El Paso. Watcher wasn't lying to Devil. There was time. El Paso was far enough away the Soldiers could get everything placed just how Watcher saw it in his head, as long as they remained focused and fucking *moved*. Devil nodded, the movement jerky but it was there. Watcher was stepping back when a noise came from the front of the barn. Twisting in place, he looked to see Caroline coming into the barn, and what he focused on was what she carried.

"Caroline, what the fu—" That was all Darrie got out before the rattle of semi-automatic rifle fire filled the barn. Watcher, Devil, and Spider dived to the side, rolling behind the workbench and boxes near the walls.

From where he lay, Watcher saw Darrie still stood in the center of the barn, staring dumbstruck at the nearly naked woman staggering sideways from the recoil of the gun in her hands.

Watcher stared as red began to roll down his brother's arm, blood covering the skin and tattoos. Caroline had righted herself, holding the gun with both hands, carefully angling it away from her body. He could see her mouth moving, but with ears still deafened from the gunfire, any words were lost to him. Darrie still stood in the open, unguarded in his shock. Unlike the rest of the club, he had never been in combat, serving instead as a liaison between forward troops and the supply camps, so his gut reactions were different, more civilized. "Darrie, get the fuck down," Watcher shouted and saw Darren's head turn and dip, knew his gaze was on the wound in his shoulder where one of her bullets had grazed across his skin. "Get the fuck down."

Caroline's face was distorted by a grimace, bitter with anger, and Watcher saw the gun was lining up on her target. He twisted, looking at Spider and Devil. They stared wordlessly at him. "Machos," he heard through the ringing in his ears and jolted, swinging back to look at Caroline. Spanish phrases flowed from her mouth like velvet, and with that, his mind settled, bringing instincts forth with the threat.

Pushing to his feet, he drew his gun from the waistband of his jeans and in a single smooth motion, brought the weapon up and fired, seeing the small hole appear as if by magic in Caroline's forehead. A spray of blood and bone erupted behind her, fanning out over the oil-darkened dirt of the barn. Her knees gave way, joints unhinged as she crumpled to the ground, upper torso flung back by the velocity of the bullet that ended her life. The firearm fell beside her, an inert object no longer posing a threat.

"You shot her." That thin shout came from Darrie, and Watcher dragged his gaze from where she lay—a fallen soldier, because that was her role, in truth—to look at his brother. Darrie had clamped a hand over his shoulder, blood trickling between his fingers. "You fucking shot Caroline."

"Uh...yeah, brother." Watcher slipped the gun into the back waistband of his pants. "She shot you." Footsteps from behind him, then Devil and Spider strode into view, headed towards the body. "With a semi, Darrie." Watcher shook his head, not believing he had to explain his actions. "Shot at all of us." Devil glanced back at him then bent over, avoiding the messy dirt as he slid his hands into Caroline's armpits. "You were standin' there, target on your chest. Just...standin'." Backing towards the door, Devil dragged the limp body across the floor, the heels of her bare feet making the slightest furrows in the dirt. "I'm partial to ya. So yeah, I fuckin' shot her."

Spider picked up the gun, cleared and ejected the magazine, glancing at it before slapping it back into place. "Not one of ours," he snapped, turning to stare at Darrie. "Means she got it elsewhere, Prez." His eyes cut to Watcher on an angry glare, then back to Darrie. "Machos, brother."

Darrie's mouth opened and closed, then his chin dipped to his chest, and Watcher saw his fingers clamp tightly on the still bleeding wound. He muttered something, but with his mouth aimed at his feet, Watcher didn't catch what he said. Any confusion was erased a moment later when Darrie's head tipped backwards, and he howled at the rafters, "*In my bed.*"

***

Opie called a soft "Clear," from down the hallway and Watcher's gaze swept the room he had entered. So far today they'd found precisely nothing at any of the properties where the Machos were known to store product. After being informed the Soldiers were ready and waiting for them in Las Cruces, the other club had pulled back into Mexico, impotent fury swirling in their wake. No meeting, no fighting, no war. In fact, the only casualty that entire day had been Caroline, and it had taken a week of digging to find out where she had come from. Sister to one of the Machos' women, they still weren't sure what her motivation was, but at least her body had been returned to her family.

Now deep into Mexico, Darrie, Watcher, and two dozen of the Soldiers had embarked on a campaign to clear away some of the support Machos had in place. With diesel fuel and some well-placed explosives, they'd utilized the diverse skills they'd learned in the military to blow the Machos' way the fuck off-kilter. Day four, they were on the tail end of the op, and today's efforts were looking like a big fat goose egg.

Backing out of the empty room one quiet footstep at a time, Watcher paused at a noise. *What the hell?* Tilting his head, he tried to separate what was going on outside from the sound he'd heard in the room. There had been a cry, or at least he thought he had heard something. Sweeping the room again, he paused, his gaze halting on the rug in the middle of the floor. It was an anomaly. The room held no furniture, except old, broken slat chairs, and those were tossed along the walls. Why would they leave a rug in the middle of the space? Whistling a single tone, low, he called one of his team members back as he took a careful step forward, squatting down to grip the edge of the material.

Watcher eyeballed the circumference, tracing it with his eyes. No threads, no strings, no wires. No lumps along the perimeter, but near the midpoint, off to one side, there was a slight rise in the surface. Not much, only a fraction of an inch. If he hadn't been studying the floor covering so closely, he would have never seen it. Fingers under the rug, he slipped them first one direction, then the other, encountering no resistance. Nothing holding it down, no traps so far.

Rolling the rug backwards, he duckwalked sideways, pulling the braided fabric back and over itself, folding it in half when he saw the side of the trapdoor hidden underneath. From the door came Opie's soft voice. "What you got there, Watch?"

Focused on what he was doing, Watcher answered with a shrug as hands came into view at the other side of the rug and together, he and Opie pulled it all the way off the hinged door, set flush with the level of the floorboards. They lifted the rug carefully, silently setting it to one side. Another soft sob came from the space beneath their feet, no longer muffled by the layer of fabric, and Watcher gained certainty there was at least one female in the hidey-hole.

Chin up, he stared at Opie, then pointed at the ring embedded in the door's wood. Holding up three fingers, he waited for a nod, then flattened himself to the floor beside the edge of the trapdoor. Gun in hand, he rolled silently to his back, eyes on Opie who had one hand outstretched to grip the iron ring, one hand lifted in front of him, three fingers raised. Mouthing the words, Opie locked eyes with him and, lowering one finger with each count, measured out the seconds. Three. Two. *One.*

Yanking back on the ring, Opie flung open the door, releasing a chorus of screams. Watcher rolled, elbows locked, gun in hand angling down into the opening to see a packed mass of bodies. With them writhing and shifting, it was hard to make out details, but what he did recognize made him lift the gun to a neutral position, resting his forefinger outside the trigger guard. Long hair, short hair, dark brown and pale pink skin, the few faces raised to see the invaders were as diverse as any army classroom, except for gender.

His gaze locked on one woman, lips pulled taut in fear, bottomless brown eyes staring up at him. Hair drawn back into a loosely woven braid, he saw she had an oozing wound, what looked like a burn in the shape of a crown embossed in the skin of her neck, directly behind her ear. A brand. Opie's voice rose over the din coming from the hole in the floor, calling their men to the room, but the woman's eyes never left Watcher's face. In them he saw what looked like hope, the lines radiating from the corners lessening. Then shots rang from the yard surrounding the house, a sharp cry of pain coming from the hallway, floorboards beneath him shaking with the feet running through the house.

Opie reached to close the door, but Watcher lifted a hand, staying the action. The fear in the woman's face was palpable, and he would not lock her in darkness again. Then he and Opie were up and moving out, sweeping left and right as they came into the hallway, seeing bodies downed on the floor.

An hour later, Watcher stood staring at the back of a truck as Devil slammed the tailgate shut, slapping the metal in an unspoken command to move out. Watcher stayed there as the vehicle disappeared, driving away from the house behind him with the blood-covered floors. In the bed of that truck were three blanket-wrapped bodies, cocooned respectfully in coarsely woven wool, red already seeping into the fabric.

"Watch...brother," Opie spoke from behind him, and Watcher's sharp gesture cut him off, not wanting to talk, not wanting to listen, just needing silence and space. *Just for a fuckin' minute.* Lifting a hand, he scrubbed across his forehead, feeling grit scouring his skin. The plume of dust trailed off and around a butte, shifting red and ochre sand whirling in the wind. Heavier grains fell back to the earth, no options of fighting against the implacable force of gravity. Smaller, finer grains held their place longer, the wind pushing them this way and that, taking them far from where they had previously lain at rest, eventually settling them nestled against new neighbors. Different, but the same. *Jesus.*

Tipping his chin down finally, Watcher felt the tendons in his neck creak and pull, complaining against being held too long in one position. Looking down, he stared at the leather and fabric clenched tight in his hand. His fingers gone white, except where the red from the garment stained them. Two patches on the front of the vest caught his eye, and Watcher sucked in a breath in response to the intense pain that tore through his chest. Small rectangles of fabric, held in place with closely placed stitches. He remembered watching the needle stabbing up and down, passing through the layers of material, laughing when the sharp steel pierced the tip of a finger, chuckling at the first blood seen by the vest. President was stitched on one patch, the other held six letters. One word, *Danger*. Darrie's road name.

***

Juanita

She watched as the man vanished into the distance, dust swirling up between the back of the van in which she rode and where he stood. Feet planted wide, hands on his hips, he stared at her until the vehicle turned, breaking their joined gaze. The moment he was out of sight, fear swept over her. Surrounded on all sides by silent women, she closed her eyes and swallowed, trying to force the panic that infested her back into the tiny hole she'd long ago dug for it to live. As they traveled the rough backcountry road, she bounced and moved with the van, bare breasts rubbing against the shirt given her. Fingertips chilled, she looked down at the bottle gripped tightly in her fist. From his hand to hers, offered with an intense stare that remained locked on her until she broke the lid's seal and lifted, drinking deeply of the water.

Watcher.

She'd heard the men call him that name, read it on the front of his vest. Held that vest for him as she stood next to the van, shivering in the heat. He was the leader, but his men seemed to respect him, not held vassals by fear. He'd then shed his shirt, and tugged his undershirt off, handing that to her as well. Confused but accustomed to obedience, she'd stood quietly, holding heavy leather in one hand, and a sweaty cotton in the other. Eyes downcast, she'd been humiliatingly aware of her exposed skin, covered only in dirt and bruises. Once he got his shirt back on and buttoned, he reached and retrieved the vest, slinging it around his shoulders, arms shoved through the large holes, settling it into place with an impatient shrug. She looked up when he took the undershirt from her, watched him gather it oddly in his hands, felt his gaze searching her face.

It wasn't until he lifted it towards her head that she understood his intent. Ducking, she had felt the stretched neck glance along her nose, passing over her hair and like a child, she'd raised first one arm, then the other, allowing him to work them into the sleeves. The backs of his fingers skimmed her sides as he settled the shirt over her torso, covering her nakedness. The greatest act of kindness she had ever received, and just the memory was enough to flood her eyes, nose stinging with unshed tears.

Large enough that it covered her to midthigh, she smoothed the fabric against her skin. It was his shirt, stripped from his body to cover hers. Soft and warm. Chin dipping to her shoulder, she breathed deeply, a jumble of odors reaching her nose. Sweat, but she smelled so much worse, having been inside the hole for three weeks as punishment. It didn't pay to refuse the men, not smart to fight the things they forced upon the women, but the weight of giving in was sometimes too much, and when one of the girls came back—her mind shied away from the bloody memory. Sometimes all you could do was fight.

She breathed deeply again. Oil and grease, gasoline, and underlying everything was a fresh woodsy scent. Like the woods on top of a mountain. Like the Sierra Madres, seen on a family vacation, her upturned nose childishly pressed to the window of her papa's car, watching as scrub gave way to true trees. Her muscles relaxing at the memory, she breathed deeply again. A forest of springy evergreens. Clean, musky. Free.

Watcher.

Outside looking in

Watcher

"*Señor.*" Watcher heard the soft voice of a woman and turned to look that direction, seeing one of the nearly thirty rescued from the hole under the house three days ago. This was the doe-eyed beauty who had first caught his attention. The woman who, mired in the filth covering the floor of the dirt-walled room in which she had been imprisoned, had stared up at him, hope in her eyes. Her mouth moved, lips clamped together, then she breathed out, "*Señor, por favor.*"

Turning away, staring at the mess of papers on the desk in front of him, he responded with a question. "Yes?" He knew his tone was brusque, but he didn't have time for niceties. Darrie's funeral would be back in Kentucky, and he needed to already be in the wind, not dealing with some fucking Mexican bitch who cost his brother's life to rescue from whatever it was the Machos originally planned for that abandoned payload of flesh. He had too much bullshit to deal with already, without layering on anything else.

Getting the bodies home had taken a day. Getting the women out of Mexico and installed in the basement of the church had taken another. Then even more time to parcel the women out to various members' homes. Today, Darrie was flying home. Watcher had come back from the airport only a few minutes ago, seeing his brother's casket loaded into the cargo hold of a commercial jet. In four days Watcher would be standing in the graveyard watching the last of his blood be laid to rest in the family plot. The space beside Darrie forever empty, designated for a wife his brother never found.

"Señor." The woman began again, and Watcher propped his elbows on the desktop, dropping his head into his hands. *Gonna lose my shit if she don't pull it together*, he thought, grinding his teeth. If she didn't get to the point, he knew he would blow up at her, and decided to hurry things along.

His testy, "Do you speak English?" was brusque, but they would have a better chance of communicating if she did because his Spanish was poor. *Piss poor*, he thought, *another item on the list of shit I need to get better at.*

"*Si*…yes." She stumbled over her response, but at least it was forward movement, albeit slow paced.

"What do you need, honey?" Sighing, he deliberately gentled his tone, dipping down to soften the edge of his soldier's tongue demanding information. "I'm finishing up a few things, then I have to leave." Twisting in the chair, he turned and studied her for a minute. Her hair was clean and shiny, the dark strands looked soft as silk, drifting unbound over her shoulder. He saw she had pulled up the collar of her shirt, and held her head tipped slightly to one side, reminding him of the wound he had seen on all the women rescued from the hole. A brand. Symbol of the cartel's ownership, it marked them as property.

"I am…" She paused, eyelashes drifting down to rest on her cheeks. Eyes closed, she continued, "Sorry *tu hermano*, your brother, he died."

Watcher grunted in response, gaze fixed on the part in her hair. With her head tipped down, it was all he could see. Musing, he noted the thin strip of skin looked pink compared to her dark hands, twisting against each other where they wound themselves into knots in the hem of her shirt. When she didn't speak for several seconds, he urged her again, hoping to draw this awkward encounter to an end. "Thank you." After pausing for a moment, reminding himself to go gentle, he asked, "Honey, was there anything else?"

She didn't move. *Jesus.*

Some of the former captives were staying here in Darrie's house, the woman in front of him one of nearly a dozen. If they all approached him to express gratitude this way, it would be a week before he was able to leave. *Fuck.* "Honey, there's no need, but I appreciate your sympathy. Darren would have been glad to know his sacrifice bought your freedom." *Shit, I didn't mean it to sound like she owed me anything for us getting them free.* "What I mean to say is, he would be happy to know you don't have to worry about the cartel now."

"I would...I want." Her neck twisted, tipping her chin towards one shoulder and she hissed, whether in frustration or pain, he wasn't sure. "My respects...*gah.*" She made an angry sound, then rattled off a sentence in Spanish, the only word of which he caught was English. "*Ingles es tan dificil.*"

"Honey," he said in what he hoped was a soothing tone. "It's okay. Take your time." Impatiently rushing her had added to the layers of her anxiety, and Watcher hated thinking he'd caused even more distress.

Lifting her chin, she opened her eyes, whiskey-brown pools staring at him. After a moment she said, "I would go with you. To pay respects. With your brother. For him." Breaking her words down into halting individual phrases seemed to undam her tongue, allowing her to finally communicate what she needed. "*Por favor, señor. Quiero honrarlo.*"

"No need for that." Head shaking back and forth, he pushed the chair away from the desk, intending to create space to stand before he recognized the flood of tension in her muscles at his movements. *Scared as fuck, and still standing here with an ask she won't back down from.* He admired her fortitude, having come through what she had, and still had the guts to push past her fear. She'd shown the same courage at the site in Mexico, when she'd allowed him to dress her in his shirt. *Scared as fuck, yeah. But she's strong as fuck, too.*

Halting his movements, he mapped her reactions, watching a slow easing of her muscles when he remained seated. "What I mean to say is it's nice you want to go to the funeral and all, but I'm not driving over. I'm going on my bike."

None of the women had ridden back on members' bikes. Not only weren't they steady enough on their feet to balance on the back of a motorcycle, but it was the Soldiers' way to not put unpatched pussy on their bikes. Instead, they had confiscated three of the cartel's cargo vans abandoned at the location, loading the women into the vehicles and bringing them home.

The firefight at the house in Mexico had been unique in his experience. The Soldiers had actually stumbled into what looked like a cartel-on-cartel fight, two distinct groups of men converging on the house at the same time. Each gang had telltale signs meant to quickly identify friendlies from the enemy. While the Soldiers lost three men, each of the cartel factions had nearly a dozen dead.

At his words, she lowered her gaze to the floor for a moment, then lifted her chin again, even as her eyes remained averted. "I would go."

Shaking his head, he forgot her nervousness and pushed to his feet, freezing as she took two quick steps backwards, her shoulders slamming against the wall with a bone-rattling thud. She squeezed her eyes shut and shook her head fiercely back and forth, hair whipping around her face. The motion ended with strands draped across her cheeks, caught in the web of her lashes. Lips barely moving, she whispered to herself, "*Muy estupida. Odio esto.*"

"Honey, you aren't stupid." Watcher took a careful step in her direction, hating to see how she cringed into the wall at the sound of his feet moving. "Not stupid at all. You've been through a whole hell of a lot, and what you've lived through would spook anyone. Make it hard to think in one language, much less try to communicate in two of 'em. You're overwhelmed, and out of your element. I see a woman who's making her way the best she knows how. I respect that, honey. Not stupid. Don't say that." *So fucking strong.*

Her eyes flew wide open. Those dark pools latched onto him and he felt like he was drowning in her. Thumping solidly against the wall, her head fell back and he read sorrow on her features. A devastated helplessness. This mattered to her. "I want. Please. I would." Drawing in a shuddering breath, she breathed the single word on repeat, "*Please.*"

"Okay." Her plea broke his resolve, and Watcher surprised himself with his immediate agreement, following it up with what he expected to be a show stopper. "But I'm leaving now. Right now. So, I don't have time for you to pack." He knew the old ladies of the club had brought the women clothes, and expected this one wouldn't want to leave behind the few belongings she had.

He was surprised when her trembling lips spread in what should have been a smile. She made the effort, but missed the mark by a fair amount. With movements controlled and careful, she leaned through the doorway and pulled a small duffle from the hall. "*Gracias, señor.*"

***

Deja vu, Watcher thought, staring across the open hole scarring the red clay to where his aunt and uncle sat. Uncle Ezra lounged back in the chair, one ankle propped high on top of a skinny knee while Aunt Loretta perched on the edge of her seat. He felt someone approach right before Juanita slipped one warm hand into his, her other arm wrapping tightly around his waist, holding him up as much as holding on.

They'd been on the road for hours, sitting in a rest area outside Oklahoma City before he asked her name, and then been taken aback when she stared at him for a long minute before declining to disclose it, her only response a whispered, "Señor."

By then he knew her too well to allow that kind of shit. Had seen her naked the day they'd rescued the women. Been riding with her legs wrapped around his hips for nearly 700 miles at that point, and there she was, thinking hard about holding back on something as simple as a name. He had reached out and cupped her tiny chin in his hand. Ignoring the blinking flinch telling him there was an instinctive expectation of pain to accompany the touch, Watcher told her, "You're safe with me, honey. You should get that by now, and if you don't—" He shook his head. "—then you probably won't ever."

He poked a finger at the patch on his vest, then up at his own face, "I'm Watcher, not señor. Got it?" He knew the women were required to call their...benefactors by titles of respect, prefacing any communication with don, el patrón, or señor. He wanted to draw a clear line in her head separating him from the kind of men who had been forced on her in the past. Wanted her to see him.

He'd felt the tiniest of tugs against his fingers when her head moved up and down, and waited a moment before asking again. "You got it? Call me Watcher, not señor."

"Yes," she said immediately, muscles in her jaw tensing under his fingers as she spoke. "You are Watcher."

"And your name is...?"

"Juanita." She blinked and cut her gaze to one side, quickly spitting out the rest without urging. "Juanita Teresa Consuela los Carmen del Estavez."

In the musical flood of Spanish, he heard a name that caught his attention. Her last name snagged his focus and didn't let it go: del Estavez. It was attention-worthy because the president of the Machos was Carlos Estavez.

Standing with her arm wrapped around his waist, her warmth pressed against his side, he reminded himself for the two-dozenth time he needed to ask her about that.

Glancing down, he saw Juanita's attention was directed towards the rose granite headstone he and Darrie had gotten installed not two years ago. It took decades, but their parents and sister finally had a lasting memorial. He cut his gaze to the turf-covered pile of dirt standing at the head of Darrie's grave. One more thing for the to-do list: contact the same company, get them to do another one. He sighed, lifting his eyes to look across the grave again.

This time, Watcher's brows drew together in a sharp frown, because Ezra was no longer comfortably lounging, but had edged to the front of the folding chair, bewildered attention firmly on the road down the mountain. That was when Juanita began to shake, not a tremble but a full-fledged palsy born throughout her body, transferring through to his. Then he heard it, felt it through his boots. From the earth herself and up into his legs, his body. A growing roar, a distant rumble that could only have come from a hundred metal throats.

Twisting to look down the road leading up the mountain, he instinctively pushed Juanita behind him. Holding her in place with one hand firm around her upper arm, he made sure she stayed close but protected. He tensed when he saw them, the first ranks three wide as they swept around the curve and into the straightaway leading to the cemetery gates, two staggered columns farther down the lines. Relief washed through him as he recognized the man on the lead bike. Head up, sitting straight, confident and proud: Mason.

That relief was short lived when Spider stepped around the grave to place himself into a protective position beside Watcher and stare at the bikes coming up the road. Spider's mutter wasn't quiet when he asked, "What's that motherfucker doin' here?"

A slow-boiling rage started in Watcher's gut, and he growled, "Watch your lip, brother. We're standing at my brother's grave, and you will watch your fuckin' lip. Shoulda known Mason'd come and pay his respects. Known him all my life."

"Fuckin club killer." Watcher turned to face Spider and saw his sneer was no less cutting than his words. "You heard what he did in Chicago, right? Traitor. Fuckin' hell, brother. Bastard put his own brothers to ground. Tore up the club that took him in. Killed it. They say he's torqued up a new set of rags, but the bastard fuckin' killed a club we'd all known for years."

Rage no longer building but now burning through him, Watcher knew he couldn't say everything he wanted. In this life, if you had to explain what you'd done, you did so from a position of weakness. He knew Mason was still struggling to keep things together after wrestling control of his club from the previous president and officers. Picking carefully along what was publicly known and the background info he had from phone calls, Watcher walked a fine line that he hoped would be enough to shut Spider down.

"His actions were backed by a bunch of his club members and officers, Spider. You got no idea what he was dealing with. From the outside-in is one story, but if you get a chance to learn what the view was from inside lookin' out, you'd sing a different tune." Watcher shook his head. "We might never know the full details. It's not our club, and even though I count Mason a brother, it's not my place. What it is, very definitely, is his, meanin' it just as definitely ain't yours. What I do know is it was long fuckin' overdue. Long time comin', man. You don't know that, I get it. Still got no call to say shit about this man. Won't stand for it, Spider." Watcher's anger was evident in his tone, and he watched as the weight of his words struck Spider, saw him decide to stand down and accepted the chin lift in mute apology before the man stepped backwards.

Back straight, heat where Juanita stood close baking into his side, Watcher faced Mason, studying how the bikes with him pulled up in ranks and parked. Legs swung over the backs of bikes and once the last bike's engine died, the silence in the mountain meadow was eerie. Chilling.

***

Standing on the front porch of the house where Mason grew up, Watcher listened to the laughter and conversation filtering in from all sides. Mason had brought a portion of his rebirthed club with him to pay respects to the fallen Southern Soldiers' president, and leadership from two other clubs had accompanied him. Combine those three groups with the Soldiers in attendance, and all told there were more than a hundred and thirty bikes parked around the big open area of the Mason compound.

A diverse mass of humanity, each individual had interesting stories to tell spanning the past three months. While Watcher and the Soldiers had been mired in a running war with the Machos, Mason had waged his own internal war, seizing control of the Rebel Fiends from the old president, Deacon, renaming the club Rebel Wayfarers.

Lights had been wending their way up the mountain for several minutes, their progress through the switchbacks heading upward easily tracked from where he stood, the headlights illuminating the trees on either side of the narrow drive. "You expectin' more company?" Mason spoke from behind him, and Watcher shook his head.

"Saw the lawyer in town today before the service. Saw all the family I care to see at the service. Not sure who this would be." He shrugged, gaze tracking the vehicle as it rolled through the last ring of trees and into the open space. "It's your place. Might be for you."

"Doubt it," Mason said, and Watcher felt something bump his shoulder, looking down to see a bottle of beer dangling from Mason's fingers. Parked, the truck's headlights extinguished, leaving the clearing in the low light from before. "Ran everyone off the 'top when the old man finally kicked the kettle. Pissed off everyone when I did, got nothing here for me other than the land now."

Accepting the beer, Watcher nodded his thanks, bringing the bottle, dewy with condensation, to his lips and taking a long drink. "Truck looks familiar," he observed, then saw the light inside come on as the driver door opened. "Fucking shit," he muttered, stooped and placed his bottle on the edge of the porch before he took one long step off the edge, bending his knees to take the force of the controlled three-foot fall.

"What the hell?" Mason's mutter came from behind him, and he heard a thump that meant his friend had taken the same route off the porch, eschewing the stairs on the end that made an easier path down.

By the time Watcher had taken two steps, the small figure was out of the truck, the slam of the door loud in the silence beating in from all sides. "Mike," she called, and then her arms were wrapped around his neck, holding on tightly, body pressed against him. "I'm so sorry. Ty just found out today and called me at work. It took a while to figure out where you were. Oh, Mike. I came as soon as I could." She pulled back to stare up at him, then leaned in, pressing her cheek to his. "I'm so sorry."

"No sorries, doll face. No sorries, okay?" Eyes closed, he held her slight form, his mind turning back the years, again seeing her white face staring at him across the bench seat of Zonder's truck, the same truck she'd just parked in the compound. "Good to see you, Bethy."

***

Mason

Mason held his tongue for the minutes it took his little sister to greet his friend and convey her condolences, not wanting to intrude. *How best to handle this?* He scrambled for a path in his head. Cutting a look around at the groups of men standing at the entrance to every building on the place, he saw there were gatherings of friends and a few enemies surrounding campfires set near to tents or trucks turned into makeshift beds. Only a few knew he had blood living, and most of those he counted as enemies.

Cautiously not saying her name, he quietly told Watcher, "Bring her inside when you're ready." Turning so Bethy couldn't see his face, he stalked towards the house, one springing stride taking him from the ground to the porch. Scooping up his beer, he yanked open the screen, telling the men inside, "Got company. Lose yourselves." Pointing to Tugboat, one of his most trusted and one of the only friends who knew about Bethy, Mason said, "Stay," receiving a chin lift in response. The men scattered without complaint, but he knew that one action had marked Bethy as someone to note. *Nothing to be done about it*, he thought, stepping to place his back against a wall.

"What's goin' on?" Tugboat asked, and Mason tipped his head towards the door, hearing footsteps making their way up the stairs to the porch. Bethy came through first, followed by Watcher.

She walked into the room, head swinging left and right, likely cataloging the changes in their childhood home. He had gutted the whole house, lifting it four feet in the air and put a proper floor under their feet. This was always the first thing he noticed, the solid wood underfoot where there had been shifting dirt growing up. She turned to look over her shoulder at Watcher and her gaze crossed him. Crossed, and then came back and he watched as anger flashed across her face before it settled into blankness.

"Hello," she said, her tone cool. Watcher's head swung from Mason to Bethy, and he took a step towards her, halting in place when she held up her hand. Without looking away from Mason, she said, "I only came to pay respects, Mike. I won't stay." Turning towards the door, she called over her shoulder, "Ty says to call him sometime."

"Bethany." Tone harsh, Mason whipped out her name, and she rocked to a stop, an arm lifted, hand outstretched towards the screen. He didn't know what to say. It had been twelve years since he had seen her, twelve years of following her through the shadows, working to protect her every step of the way. Watcher had long since shared what had happened at his little sister's funeral. Shared what Bethy had confessed that day, Mason's tightly held belief of her safety falling away with his words.

She stopped but didn't turn, and Mason called her name again, "Bethany," and watched as her body shuddered through a flinch that caused a wave of fear to churn in his belly. *Why won't she look at me?* Her arm settled back at her side, and at the slow movement, he called her again, "Bethy."

"Davy." Her voice was plaintive and filled with pain. Her shoulders slumped, head tilting forwards as she spoke again. "What do you want?"

"Want?" He echoed her word, not sure what was going on here. For the first few years after he had left home things had been so unsettled in Chicago, all he could do was send money home to help take care of her. Even now, three months into rolling his own club, things were still shaky. That was why when Bones, President of the Skeptics, and Hawk, President of the Dominos, offered to ride down to pay their respects to Watcher's brother, he'd jumped at the chance. "I want for you to look at me, Bethy."

She sucked in a breath that sounded clogged, tipping her chin towards the point of her shoulder. He could see her eyes were squeezed shut, brows drawn down to force her lids closed. Her body shuddered again as she took another gasp of air that hitched a half a dozen times on the way in. Lifting her head, she twisted her neck a little farther, looking at him out of the corners of her eyes. Stormy grey, her eyes were exactly like the ones he saw in the mirror every day, and his face relaxed into a smile.

Holding her gaze, locking her in place so she couldn't retreat, Mason slowly opened his arms wide, giving her a clear invitation. It would be up to her if she accepted or not. If she walked out that door, from his side of things, nothing would change. She would forever be his baby sister, and he would continue to protect her from the shadows. Keep her safe. Always.

Bethy held the pose for one second, then two, and took in another of those hitching breaths before turning on her toes. An instant later she hit Mason full force, arms flung around him, hands clutching at the shirt beneath his cut, her face burrowing into his chest like she couldn't get close enough. Shoulders jerking and jolting, her whole being seemed to vibrate like a tuning fork. He felt her tears before the first audible sob, and the entire front of his tee was soaked within a minute as she wept out a lifetime of sadness in the arms of her big brother.

She's damaged, brother

"So there's this thing I want to do," Bethy said, flipping her shoes off at the door and hurrying across the room to where Mason and Watcher sat, talking to Tyrell. She had barely walked in the door from work, still buzzing with energy.

Juanita sat nearby, legs folded underneath her in an upholstered chair, eyes fixed out the window. Watcher noticed she had once again found a seat where she could easily hide the brand she bore. He frowned, muscles pulling into a scowl as he scanned the other people in the room, knowing even before he did that none of them were looking at her, much less the brand. When with friends, she shouldn't have to worry about their reactions, and Watcher made a note to talk to her about that. *Yeah, like you've talked to her about the other hundred things you've fucking thought about*, he silently scoffed.

He had enjoyed the heat and softness of her pressed up against his back for so many days. Been pleased she sought him out for comfort when things overwhelmed her, her tiny hand creeping into his, holding on like he was her lifeline. Conversations in English flying around with such a mishmash of club jargon and Kentucky slang it would have been hard for most people to decipher, much less someone for whom English wasn't their first language. Watcher liked how she settled each time they stayed in place for more than a few hours, finding places to sit where she could keep her warm brown eyes on him. He knew she tracked him as he moved because if he were out of sight for too long, she would come looking for him, pressing herself against his side if the occasion allowed. Comfort in that physical connection went both ways, even if she'd never know what the soft touches did to him. What it meant to him.

Tipping his head back, Ty groaned at the ceiling. "Oh, Lordy, here it comes."

Bethy giggled, moving behind Mason and draping herself across his shoulders, kissing the top of his head. After the scene in the homestead at the Mason compound two days earlier, she had dropped any misgivings or hesitation where her brother was concerned. She and Mason had talked through the night, the rest of the crowd giving them space and privacy. Next morning Watcher said his good-byes to the Skeptics and Dominos, as well as many of the Rebels, watching as they rolled out of the compound and down the mountain, two by two, headed back to Chicago.

Mason had kept three Rebels with him. Tugboat, an old Outrider Watcher knew from their shared time in that club, and two other members, Red and Tats. Watcher had kept Opie, Devil, and Spider, sending the rest of the men back home. The Southern Soldiers would be holding a memorial for Darrie in two weeks, once everyone had made it back to Las Cruces.

"There's this band I want to promote, but they don't have a label." Bethy swung past Mason, pulling a chair out from the table and over so she could perch right next to her brother. She'd been staying close, and Watcher knew from Mason's affectionately amused expression he was enjoying seeing and talking to his sister for the first time in so long.

Twelve years, he marveled, still surprised by the information Mason divulged over coffee that morning. Twelve years since Mason had last seen his little sister up close, twelve years of her thinking she was on her own, never knowing Watcher and Mason had long been co-conspirators for her safety.

Watcher reached out and grabbed a handful of cookies from the open package on the table, the entire surface of which was littered with junk food. Popping a couple in his mouth, he mumbled around the mouthful, "So, promote them. You run the schedule, you make the rules." She did, too. Since beginning as a coffee and donut intern at the radio station, she had worked her way up to station manager. No small feat for a mountain girl whose formal schooling ended at ninth grade.

"Not like this," Bethy demurred, shaking her head. "Can't promote or play more than a set percentage unless the band has representation. Dem's de rules. This band doesn't have a label. Can't do it. Want to." She made a face. "Can't." She shook her finger at him, "And stop talking with your mouth full. That's gross."

"So, get them a label." He tossed another cookie in his mouth, chewed for a few seconds, and then stuck his tongue out at her, drawing loud laughter from all sides. Glancing over to where Juanita sat, he saw a smile drifting off her face as she turned back to look out the window. He swallowed. "You know enough folks in the industry now, you probably know someone who'd take them on." He laughed, saying with an affected accent, "Represent, sistah."

"Sure, I know folks. Good ones, but they won't do right by these kids. The machine will chew them up and spit them out, and all that talent will be flippin' burgers instead of filling arenas. They deserve more." She shook her head, then leaned across to turn a bag of snacks her direction. She picked through the contents, pulling out two large potato chips. Fitting them to her mouth, she turned to look at Ty and uttered a muffled, "Quack, quack," around her improvised duck lips.

Mason shouted with laughter at her antics, and the sudden noise seemed to shock Juanita. Watcher stared, helpless to calm her fears as she scrambled to her feet, clumsily wedging herself back into the corner nearest the chair. Half hidden by the window drapes, she was already cowering with her head down before he could react. Moving as fast as he could, Watcher was all the way in front of her before he saw how she was shaking. Like she had done when the bikers first rolled up the mountain, her body visibly quaked.

"Hey, hey," he whispered, pitching his voice for her ears only. Stopping his advance only when he was in her space, he made it so he blocked out the rest of the world for her. "Look at me, honey. Hey, now, Juanita. Come on, look at me. Honey." He was trying to draw her out, bring her back to herself, away from the terror consuming her. Her eyes had squeezed shut, tears gathering on her lashes, those oversize droplets swimming with shame and fear. Pain lanced through his chest, knowing the panic she had to be feeling. "Shhh. It's okay, honey. Hey, hey, it's okay."

Her head thrashed back and forth, braided hair flying like a whip, thumping solidly against the wall. "No, no. *Por favor.* No." The tears flung from her lashes to land on her cheeks, tiny trails glinting in the overhead light.

"Juanita." He took another step towards her, leaning even closer. "Honey, look at me. Swear to you, you're safe. I'm here. Right here with you. You're safe, honey. Never again," he vowed, the intensity of his emotions vibrating through his voice and her eyes flew open, staring at him. "Swear. You never have to be afraid again."

Raising his hand slowly, not wanting to spook her any further, he gently settled it on her jaw, using the pad of his thumb to sweep the moisture from her cheek. Lifting his other hand, he cradled her face between his palms, pulling her closer, seeing something flare to life in her eyes he didn't expect.

"Never again," he repeated, staring into her dark brown eyes, drowning in the passion he saw there, feeling the reflection of his own desire in his chest, his throat, his cock. With a gruff voice, he whispered, "Never be afraid. Not when I'm here, honey." Tugging gently, he drew her forward, feeling how she trustingly tottered on the balls of her feet. Tilting his head, he dipped his chin and brushed his lips across hers, the soft pull of air across his tongue evidence of a surprised gasp. "I'm gonna make it okay for you. Always."

***

Juanita

She stared up at Watcher, the heat from his hands baking into her skin, frozen like a mouse underneath the shadow of a hawk. He had kissed her. The barest of touches against her lips, but it had been there. His last words spoken so close to her lips that puffs of breath from his mouth seared her. Scented with beer and sweet cookies, a mixed flavor Juanita knew she would find pleasant if taken from his tongue. Something she wanted to have the right to demand. A promise.

When she had panicked at the loud male laughter echoing around the room, he had come to her immediately. It had only taken an instant, and she had been lost in her head, the barest of breaths before she'd fallen into the black hole of awful memories. Heat from the lights, the crack of the whip, smell of spilled blood. Everything overwhelmed her senses.

The lurid sound of amusement similar to what she had heard so many times coming from observers. People standing on the sidelines of the scenes she had been forced to participate in, uncaring of the agony their mockery inflicted. Startled and frightened, the sound had forced out all conscious thought. With her heart racing, her instinct to try to find an escape drove her from the chair only to find herself trapped in a corner, helplessly hiding behind the decorative window coverings.

Watcher had effortlessly brought her back, made her fears recede. In his hands, she felt safe, secure. Then in another breath, he had stirred her soul in a way she'd thought impossible.

Footsteps came towards where she and Watcher stood, his hands still cupping her face, eyes boring into hers. The soft feminine voice of Bethany came from across the room, which marked the person approaching as one of the other men. That knowledge caused her to tense again. Watcher made it clear he saw because, with a brush of his thumbs across her cheeks, he let the touch of his hands and sound of his voice anchor her, speaking over Bethany's words of concern to order, "Look at me, Juanita. Only at me. You're safe. Always safe with me."

She believed him, her trust having been born in a remote shack in Chihuahua. From the first glimpse of him, the look of unvarnished shock on his face at finding women in the mud- and filth-covered hole, telegraphed his dismay. From that instant, she'd known he would never behave the way the men who stole her from her father's house did. Every moment since had built on the foundation laid that day, so much so the mere sound of his voice was steadying. Only days away from the end of her worst nightmare, and she would never have believed it possible, but she trusted him. The scent of his body, and even as innocent as their contact had been—the way he felt underneath her hands or between her legs on the motorcycle—he had still managed to imprint on her a belief in his words and actions. In him as an honorable man.

"Watch, man. Sorry." Mason's voice came from right behind Watcher, and she tensed again. Trying to get away, she found herself struggling ineffectually against his grip.

Effortlessly Watcher controlled her, thumbs sweeping in a constant arc over her cheeks, not relinquishing his hold. He stared at her as he directed his words to the man standing just out of sight behind his shoulders, "It's okay, Mason. My Juanita got spooked. But she's good now. Yeah?" The question was for her, and she held her breath, pressing her lips together. His eyes flicked to her mouth, and his face softened. The caress of his fingers paused a moment, then he dipped his head down, eyes locked on hers as he kissed her again. Gentle, soft, tender, the feel of his lips moving against hers became her whole world for a moment, then he pulled back, asking again, "Yeah?"

"Yes," she whispered, rewarded by the return of his smile.

***

Watcher

"She's damaged, brother," Mason said, face twisting in anger as he stabbed his spent cigarette at the ashtray on the patio table. "That scar on her neck? That crown...I've seen this mark before, Watch."

"Yeah, I have too. I know where it comes from, know the kind of filth that thinks humans are worth only what they bring on the block," Watcher said from where he leaned his elbows against the balcony railing. "One of the cartels uses it to brand their property. Humiliation tactic. Makes it so the women can't ever go home. People know what it means, they know what happened, and in a community of uptight assholes, that mark equals pariah. Exile." He shook his head, reaching up to pull a toothpick from the corner of his mouth. After her fright, Juanita had stuck tight to him until Bethy asked for her help to prepare dinner. Soft words and clasped hands leading the woman away, it fractured his heart to see her look over her shoulder to verify he remained where she'd left him. Between the two women, they had made a delicious meal, and it had torn at him how relieved Juanita seemed when he praised their efforts. So much to rebuild.

After-dinner cleanup was in progress, and he and Mason had escaped to the balcony to have a private chat, something they hadn't found much time for.

"Been so mired in my own shit," Mason said, looking up from underneath his brows, "nearly missed finding out about Darrie in time, brother. I know I said it at the service, but fuck, man, hated to hear he bought it like that."

"Yeah," Watcher said, his throat tight as he forced the words through. "It's been one shit play after another by the Machos. We've contained them for now, but I know they'll be back. Fucking roaches die easier than Estavez." Folding the toothpick over one finger, he broke it, then broke the pieces again, and again. Irreparably destroying the piece of wood.

"Was a wrong place, wrong time thing, man. From the looks of the dead left behind, we got caught up in some internal action of theirs. Two sides, marked by equipment and footwear." When they'd sorted the fallen after everything went down in Mexico, the warring cartel factions were easily distinguished from the other. Commonplace tactics to sort friendlies from foes, the dead soldiers from each gang wore matching shoes and carried identically modified firearms and equipment. White versus black for the shoes, silver tape against black on the gun stocks. "Every year they're more organized, Mason. Harder to beat back."

"Keep on it. That's what you gotta do. Keep on it, and keep shit contained. You got people who look to you to make their lives better, so you keep at it." Mason paused, then asked a delicate question which— coming from anyone other than Mason—could have been offensive. "Soldiers have enough weight to stay viable with this shit? You sticking with them?" Mason flicked the box of smokes open, plucking one out and tucking it in between his lips. The scrape and flare of the match head illuminated his face for a moment, glowing end of the lit cigarette adding to the shadows and turning a known form into a stranger. With a snap of his wrist, he snuffed out the flame, leaned forward and tossed the spent match into the ashtray. Leaning back, Mason tilted his head, blowing smoke towards the floor of the balcony above. Seen like this, completely unguarded and at ease, Watcher could almost forget Mason was the president of a massive motorcycle club. Seen like this, he just looked like a man, kicking back and chatting with a friend.

The sound of motorcycles came from the street below, and Watcher tossed a glance over his shoulder, seeing six bikes pull up in front of the corner bar. The men backed their bikes to the curb, lining up at an angle. Coordinated. Comfortable. Like what he had in New Mexico.

"Yeah. We've got the membership to survive. And yeah, I'm sticking. Fuck, man, they handed me this," Watcher gestured at the president patch on his vest. "Darrie…he wanted the club. Loved it. Lived it. He'd want it to survive him, prove he made something that mattered." Mason nodded, drawing on his cigarette. Watcher told him, "He wouldn't be pissed about dying for something that mattered, either." He motioned towards the sliding doors, into the apartment where Juanita sat next to Bethy, heads bent together over a magazine. "Rescued a lot of women that day. Mothers, sisters, daughters."

Mason cleared his throat. "Damaged, brother," he repeated, staring up at Watcher. What he had to say acknowledged something Watcher hadn't yet settled into, that she would be his. "Woman's a beauty, for sure. But you're going to have a fuckton of work to get her past this."

"Was her idea to ride with me, did you know?" Watcher asked, knowing Mason couldn't have known. He didn't wait for the headshake, simply kept talking. "Pay her respects. Body abused, mind abused, I can't tell you the misery we pulled them out of, brother. So fucking sick and wrong, humans…women kept like breeding animals in a cramped, dark space. Naked. Limited food and water. They were doling it out, making sure the weakest got the lion's share. Keeping everybody alive, hoping for a miracle." A glance over his shoulder showed the bikes still parked, but the riders weren't headed into the nearby bar, they were moving down the street as a unit. Organized. Carefully coordinated.

"Uh, Mason?" He tensed, wondering why he'd ever ask the question, yet he still did. "You expecting company?"

"Fuck no," Mason returned, rising to his feet. "Why?"

"Six headed towards this building." They weren't trying to hide their movements, striding down the street as if they had every right. His hand reached for an empty holster at the back of his waistband. *Fuck.* He'd left his piece under his jacket lying on the floor near the front door. "Can't see the patch."

Mason leaned over the balcony railing, tracking the men with a twist of his neck. "*Jesus.*" He clipped out the single word, pulled out his phone and dialed without looking at the device, thumb moving across the buttons. One of the men halted, raising a hand. Mason spoke into the phone, "Bones, brother. Wanna tell me what the hell you're doin' in Nashville? Thought you were headed back to Chicago?"

The man turned on the sidewalk and Watcher could tell he was scanning the building's face. His head tilted back, motionless, facing their direction, and after a moment he lowered his hand from beside his head as Mason did the same. Mason turned and looked at Watcher, then threw back his head and laughed at the expression Watcher knew he wore on his face. "Friends, brother. Chill."

***

Voices woke Watcher the next morning. He was still tired, not having slept well. It felt early, and from the light seeping into the room, he knew the sun had barely risen. He lay motionless on top of the sleeping bag he had spread along one wall of the living room, eyes barely open, scanning the room. The blankets Bones had flopped down on last night were rumpled and empty. *Where was he?* Watcher could see two figures in the kitchen, seated at the table, backs to the windows. Silhouettes framed in the scant light.

Their voices were quiet, pitched for privacy and politeness. One, melodic and sweet, countered by the other, much rougher...more intense. Spanish phrases flowing and tripping, Watcher listened and stared at the shapes seated so close to one another. Juanita's voice rising and falling, agony threading through the sound and quiet tremors testified to how close her tears were to the surface. An emotion he couldn't put a name to swept through him, and Watcher gritted his teeth, fighting through the impulse to stand up and shout at Bones to get away from her. *She's not for you. She's gonna be mine.*

Mason's words floated through his head, *She's damaged, brother.* Watcher fucking knew she was damaged. He saw it every time she cowered at a man's voice or cringed when attention swung her way. One of the Soldiers' old ladies had gotten Juanita and some of the other women to talk the first night out of Mexico, supplying them with whiskey until they could speak without fear choking their words. He hadn't been there, had still been in Mexico sorting a halt to the aggression, or he would have put a stop to the prying, but even if he hated the method, he couldn't deny the intel was important. All the women rescued had been used hard in one way or another, and Juanita, beautiful and petite, mature and protective, had found herself a favorite of several of the cartel's regular customers. She'd put herself out there time and again to save the youngest ones. Coming forward in a way which probably appeared eager, had taunted the limits of what the men could do. The worst of the worst had destroyed what was precious and dear.

In far more detail than he wanted, Devil's old lady had told him about the things Juanita admitted she had been forced to do. Things that turned his stomach to hear and he could only imagine what it was like to live inside her head, reliving those moments. It was one of the reasons Watcher had tried to wear a gentleman's hat the whole trip, adopting a hands-off policy from the get-go. He'd dreamed of her, of taking her, of things never experienced but now desired with a fierceness which surprised him, and then struggled upon waking to find it only a dream. Stubbornly he'd kept the same hat on, even when it grew more complicated by the day. Only tossing it aside for a brief moment last night. In those seconds, he'd found the reality of Juanita cradled in his hands outstripped the promise of his imagination by a far measure, but her fear was like a living thing standing between them.

Now, she was seated companionably close, no...intimately close to a man who spoke her native language, who could understand the cultural implications of everything that happened to her. As he looked on, Watcher saw the man lift his hand, and flinched as Bones' shape merged with that of the woman. Watcher's lips twisted with resentment at seeing Juanita sag into Bones, seethed as the man pulled her closer. With a scowl, he prepared to look away as he anticipated the moment when their heads came together. But, it never happened.

Instead, he heard her soft sobs, the muffled sounds heart-wrenchingly miserable and without realizing he had moved, Watcher found himself on his feet, striding quickly to where the two people sat, side-by-side but separate. Wordlessly, he squatted next to Juanita. When he reached up to rest his hand on her thigh, she lunged towards him, pulling away from Bones' grip and burying her face against Watcher's neck. One small hand curled around his shoulder, holding on as she stammered in Spanish, sobbing. *She came to me.* Pressing the side of his head against hers, he gathered her into his arms and lifted. Turning to walk away, he carried her to where she had slept, the small guest room down the hallway. Settling on the bed, back to the headboard, he held her in his lap as she cried.

She's damaged. He again heard Mason's voice, and this time, he countered it with his own silent vow: *I can make it better.*

Everything I have

Juanita

Even without opening them, Juanita knew her eyes were swollen and tender, raw from crying for so long. At some point, she had fallen asleep, and just now woken, held in the same position by Watcher's strong arms. A quiet voice sounded in the room, words indistinguishable but the tone scathing. Then a terse, rumbling response appeared from underneath her cheek where she lay against Watcher's chest.

Bones, she thought, pressing her lips together. Remembering. She had risen from bed early. Since being kidnapped, the nightmares and fear meant she'd often found herself unable to sleep more than one or two hours at a time. The insomnia had lessened since her release from captivity, but even without dreaming, the horror was still so close it seemed there had only been a few breaths between then and now. Intending to make coffee for the group, she had been quietly exploring the kitchen when she had heard the soft words from the doorway leading to the living room.

"Si Dios fuera lo suficientemente amable para permitir qué tome está carga de usted querida, lo haria." *The man's voice was quiet, but he allowed the ache from inside him to be heard through the vibrato and tone, letting his sorrow on her behalf throb through the air and around her, wrapping her in his warmth without a touch.* "Si pudiera hacer qué se vaya...hacerlo desaparecer, lo haría querida."

As he spoke, Juanita's hands lifted to cover her cheeks, even though she wasn't facing him and the man had no idea the heat that had risen to bring color to her face. With his words, he gave her knowledge that what happened to her wasn't hidden. By offering to ask God to remove her burden, by telling her he would take it from her, make it go away if he could, he communicated he knew how she was broken, damaged in a way which meant an honorable life would be forever out of her grasp. "Señor, por favor—"

Interrupting her, speaking English, the scolding tone tore at her confidence, "No, Juanita. You call me by my name. Nothing less between us than honesty. I will not allow less." *Back still turned to him, she listened as his feet moved across the flat kitchen floor, bare soles making scant noise.* "Bones es mi nombre. Mi mamá me dio el nombre de Salvador Emilio del Villa Ramos, pero hoy en dia voy por Bones." *From nearer, he continued, again in English,* "Call me Bones, Juanita. I want to be a friend to you. I have the sense you do not have many of those. I would like to be the someone you can call on...in what and how you need."

Another cautious footstep signaled him moving closer. He said, "I watched you last night." *Juanita pressed the tips of her fingers into her cheeks, digging deep, drawing unconscious furrows through her flesh.* "I saw how it is with you." *A pause filled by clothes rustling, a sound she had become intimately familiar with over the past months and at the remembered images and pain, her stomach revolted. Retching, she staggered towards the sink, pitching forward with a bend at her waist, hands splayed to either side, hair hanging past her face.*

Heat came from beside her, a grip tangled in her hair as it was gathered up, pulled out of the way and over her shoulder. She waited for the wrenching pull, waited for the pain, but it never came. Gaze flickering over the tattooed skin of his hands, the dark lines trailing up his arms, she tried to make sense of what she saw. Remembering even his face held emblems and words, some phrases she recognized and some she did not. Sneaking glances when the men were busy talking to each other last night, she had nervously studied him and knew he wore a mix of Spanish, Spanglish, and English. There were even two visible tattoos she was certain were in German.

Hard shell covering. Camouflage for a man who felt so deeply he believed it a weakness. A man who could look past what had happened to her? Not likely, Juanita knew, not if he spoke so easily of his mother. His life would have been surrounded by strong women: su madre, una abuela dulce, hermanas. Women who would frown down their noses on her in disgust, destroy what was left of her with a sharp word or a pitying look. He would see the comparison at a glance, folly to think otherwise. He was not a man like her Watcher.

Beside her head, the faucet came on. Sweet, cold water flowed as easily from the spout as lies would from this man's lips. His inked and colored hand appeared, cupping to contain a portion of the flow, lifting to her mouth with a commanding, "Bebe esto. Bebe por favor." Unable to ignore him, she dipped her chin, drinking from his hand. "Querida, por qué te haces esto?"

Eyes stinging, Juanita shook her head, denying his words. It wasn't her doing this to herself, it was him. His lean body pressed to the counter beside her, one arm resting on her shoulder, blazing a path across her skin. Tresses held casually in his fingers, one demanding hand bringing another offering of water to her lips. Touching her in familiar ways, insultingly so, as if he already—

Her brain stuttered, breaking the thought off in the middle as she squeezed her eyes closed. He could have. She didn't look at every man who visited her. Couldn't always see their faces, but was given no reprieve from feeling their bodies, their hands twisting and pulling at her. *Their sucking mouths on her breasts, raising maroon welts ringed round with tiny black bruises, proof of embedded teeth.*

Not able to resist, her torso had been forced down as men entered her with ripping pain, bent double so anything they wanted was available to them. They knew her unwilling, those men. Hands always bagged to blunt the attack of her nails, or arms awkwardly bound behind her back so she couldn't fight. Standing upright, tied to a hook embedded in the wall so she couldn't escape. Hours upon hours, until her shoulders were screaming from the angle, wrists held together ending in impotent fists over her head. Red wet running down the insides of her thighs.

Wedges in her mouth to hold it open, or a filth-encrusted towel thrown over her face so she couldn't bite once she had proven herself unafraid to use her teeth. Her traitorous mind held onto memories of tearing flesh and the nauseating burn of hot and salty blood running down her throat. She felt again their stained fingers pinching her nose shut until she was drowning in flesh, throat blocked as ropes of saliva dripped from her chin, chest heaving weakly for release. Everything ending in pain. Reliving it forever, pain and chains. Blackness and hunger, and the terrifying sounds of her sisters in slavery crying in the darkness around her.

"No, no." Bones' voice came from nearby, and Juanita jerked back until there was a ripping tear of roots from her scalp as his fingers snarled helplessly in her hair. Her hand flailed, passing underneath the water, spraying the window with droplets that trailed down like tears. An ocean of pain. She had wept herself dry after the first week.

Mouth closed, jaw clenched so tight her teeth were aching in her head, Juanita stumbled over Bones' feet and fell backwards. Fell, but never hit the floor because his arms, wiry and strong, caught her. Supporting her, holding her, his face close as he leaned in, mouth moving. She twisted and flung herself back and forth, trying futilely to tear free from his grasp. This was when the tears came in earnest, wide rivers of them escaping her eyes. Silently she cried, weeping for everything stolen from her. Salt on her tongue; the bright taste competing with dark copper and bitterest bile.

"No, no. Estate quieta, querida." Locking his gaze with hers, he gripped her head with one hand, the other like an iron bar across her back. Folding her against him, he crooned soft words to her, holding her as she cried. Quieting her, easing the pain with his care. Somehow she found herself seated at the table with a handful of paper napkins clutched in her fingers. Watching as he bustled around the kitchen, making coffee, bringing her a filled-to-the-brim cup heavily dosed with sugar and enough milk to swirl through the darkness, creating a beautiful roiling cloud of caramel-colored liquid.

Carefully avoiding serious conversation, he had sat with her and talked. He allowed the silence she needed, not requiring anything from her. Permitted her time to recover. Amusing and witty, he told her about his friends in Chicago, and she learned his life had not been as sweet as she imagined. Sadness suffused his face when he spoke of losing his sister young, his mother soon after.

In her privileged life from before, English was a requirement and often spoken at home. Her captivity had stolen some of that from her, her fears stealing more. With Bones, as he seamlessly transitioned from English to Spanish and back again, he showed her how the things could be blended to make something more than it was before, like the milk in her coffee, taking something worthy to an abundant goodness. Raised in a Spanish-speaking household in Midwest Norte Americanos, his accent was unique and choice of words sometimes entertaining, but as he exposed more of himself with each story, she came to believe this man could be her friend. He would never be her Watcher, never make her tremble with a touch, but Bones could be a friend.

That was when she lost it for the second time that morning because she had nearly thrown all of this away without knowing the treasure behind his mask, reacting in a panic to imagined demons. If he were less *of a man, he would have cast her down, stepped across her prone body to whatever it was he wanted. Staring up at him, leaning into his touch, she tried to explain, tried to make him understand, but even as she stammered her regrets, his eyes left her, locking on something across the room.*

Weight and heat came to rest against her leg and recognizing it, she did not pull away. Instead, she went to it. To him. She knew this pressure, had felt it a hundred times while riding behind Watcher, measured it in the fingers trailing up her knee to the outside of her thigh to gain her attention so he could point out the beauty all around them.

Watcher had shown her a horse running free in a field, mane breaking like a wave in the wind. Tail held high, it had flagged the beast's drumming retreat from the noise of the machine they rode.

He'd drawn her attention to the beauty of a rainbow tumbling free from the clouds overhead, brilliant colors scattering and reflecting across the road ahead of them. Gems drawn down from the sky by the hand of God.

Together they'd grinned at a child, face plastered to a sheet of glass, staring at them from inside a car, nose held upturned like a piglet. The absurdity emphasized by the soft mocking grunts and squeals coming from deep in Watcher's chest. Laughter chasing them down the highway, his heavy gravel broken by her light belling.

Those were times she loved. When he shared the things that made him smile.

Now, Watcher touched her, and she twisted in her chair to find him kneeling close, right beside her, eyes only for her. Flinging herself into his arms, she curled up against his chest, and the flow of tears was unceasing because this was something she wanted. Wanted him, more than life.

Sitting on the mattress, draped across Watcher's legs, cradled to his body, she let these memories flow through her and away, releasing the pain they held. Bones was talking again, his accent pronounced because he was...upset?

"...do not handle her with anything other than utmost care, my friend, then will we have words. Juanita, beautiful, sweet Juanita, she deserves to only have goodness in her life. If you cannot give her this, if you cannot promise me now this is what you will have for her in your heart, then lift your arms and allow me to take her from you." Watcher's arms tightened, not releasing her in any way and Juanita's heart jumped into her throat at his silent rejection of Bones' words. "Can you give me your oath?"

"Not sure how this became your business, Bones." Watcher's voice rumbled underneath her cheek, muscles all over his body tensed as the possession in his words shocked her. "She's mine, and I won't be handing her over to anyone, much less someone like you."

Bones' voice carried a thin edge holding blood and danger as he asked, "Someone like me?"

"Slick player. I saw you last night. Saw how you watched her. Saw how her getting spooked by you and your boys coming in registered with you. Saw how you eyed me. Didn't take you ten minutes before you decided to ignore my claim." He leaned forward slightly, taking her body with his as he hissed, "And I have a fucking claim, do not mistake that."

Leaning back, he took a moment to settle them against the headboard before continuing, "Dismissed what I have with her. You saw what you thought was your chance this morning, took a shot, but missed the fuckin' mark so far you can't even see how you hurt her more." Watcher smoothed a gentle hand down her back, then up, broad palm cupping her shoulder to press her closer. "Someone like you, a user…a *player*, who don't give a fuck the destruction you leave in your wake."

"I will leave you with your misjudgments, Watcher. Miscalculating seems to be a trait the Otey brothers shared. Danger showed his poor judgment in a bloody way with the Machos"—Watcher tensed, seeming about to say something, but Bones bulled through—"and everyone knows you counseled him differently. He should have listened to you. Everyone knows you are methodical and patient, but today you have made a grave mistake."

"What mistake?"

Hatred dripped from Bones' voice as he said, "Mistaking me for one of the men who would take joy from hurting the beauty you hold in your arms. *Preciosa*, such a wealth of beauty inside her even evil could not defeat." He paused. "I offered her my friendship, and"—voice softening and lowering in register, he spoke directly to her, causing her to jolt in response because he knew her to be awake while Watcher, holding her, did not—"Juanita, my friendship is no lie. *Mi bella amiga*, you can come to me with any need, and I will see it fulfilled."

"Baby?" Watcher's arms tightened around her again, and she angled her head up at his question. Soft, caring face, worried eyes, lines at the corners. The edges of his mouth tipped down, teeth worrying at his bottom lip. "Honey? You okay?"

Juanita searched inside herself for the fear. The terror that engulfed her when Bones touched her, when Mason filled the room with his laughter. The paralyzing revulsion of being surrounded by hateful, faceless men, hard fingers pinching and twisting with pain drawn into her body with every breath. It was still there, she knew, perhaps closed away for now, barricaded behind a door deep inside. But in Watcher's arms, every emotion other than joy was held at bay. She was safe, could even be brave. Tipping her chin higher, she looked at him until her vision blurred, his face swimming.

"Honey," he called, even though his mouth was only inches from hers. Called Juanita as if he needed to bring her back from miles away, as if she were separate from him. "Talk to me."

"*Si*," she said, and then shook her head, feeling the tears welling in her eyes escaping, slipping down the sides of her face. She wanted him to understand, wanted no lies or confusions between them. "Yes, I am okay. With you here, I am okay."

***

Watcher

Watcher pressed his trembling lips to the skin of her forehead, holding there, a sense of peace sweeping over him. The whole scene this morning, from waking and seeing her seated near Bones at the kitchen table, to just now, with Bones stalking out after she made her verbal choice, telling the world she was safe in his arms, had been brutal. Watcher knew what he wanted, but until a moment ago, he hadn't been sure if she felt anything in return.

How the hell do I do this? His thoughts circled the same knowledge they had for the past week, every time he fought against the urge to take Juanita to his bed. Not fall in love with her, because that was a done deal, his fate sealed the first time she'd lifted her chin and braved her own fears. No, his worry was much more fundamental.

I'm like a fucking joke, he thought, *a walking, talking cliché*.

His dick thickened, thudding against the zipper of his jeans. *No fucking idea what I'm doing.* He slipped one hand behind her head, threading his fingers through her hair. Leaning down, he nibbled his way down her cheek, leaving little kisses in his wake. Her hand gripped his arm, and she shifted in his lap, soft ass grazing and then cradling his cock so he groaned, pressing his face into her neck.

At my age, and I'm still a fucking virgin.

Watcher thought back to all of Deke's laughing jokes about needing experience and closed his eyes. He would willingly pay for some confidence about now. He didn't count the half a dozen fumbling attempts ending with him soaking his pants or the gal's hands. He had used his hands on women, too, loved touching their bodies, feeling them react to him. But he'd never sealed the deal, so to speak, the specter of what happened to Tabby and Bethy never far, and he'd wanted the act to mean something, and none of those women had.

The mechanics of the process weren't a mystery. Watcher had been at enough club parties and seen more than one live show by party dolls, but those women didn't draw him in. Nearly every one of them had an agenda. He had never found someone who wanted him just for himself. Never found anything that was right, special enough.

Trailing his nose up Juanita's neck, he nuzzled against her cheek, dragging his lips across hers, feeling her fingers tighten around his arm. He twisted in the bed, settling her on her back, his elbow to the mattress. "Talk to me," he urged her, stroking across her belly with his palm. Looking down at her face, he was astonished to see what he thought was evidence of arousal in her parted lips, heavy lids covering half her dilated pupils. *Surely it's too soon for her. Not even a day in trade for each month she spent a slave*, he thought, deciding to let her drive this thing between them ahead only at her pace. "What do you want, honey?"

The tip of her chin angled towards her shoulder, and she shrugged, her eyes dipping to his throat. Avoiding his eyes, whether in fear or reluctance, he couldn't guess. "Honey," he whispered, anchoring his hand to her waist, holding on and holding her to him. Fingers of his other hand drifted through her hair, loose for once, sheets of inky beauty spread across the pillows. Soft as silk running across his fingers. His cock throbbed, and he shifted his hips away, not wanting her to feel pressured if she noticed his erection.

Still, she lay silent at his side, and he dipped his head, pressing his cheek to her temple, wishing for access to intelligence like he'd had back in the military. Without it, he was floundering like a fish out of water. *I missed the boat on that one*, he thought, filled with aching need, but unwilling to go forwards in any way if she didn't initiate the play. If she couldn't talk to him, couldn't express her desire, then she sure wasn't ready for anything more. *I can wait.* Time to slow down.

"You should sleep. You had a restless night." He drew in a lungful of her scent, preparing himself to pull away when he felt her fingers circle the wrist of the hand he had at her waist. Gentle pressure tugged upwards, and when he ceased resisting, she drew his hand up her chest, until his palm settled on her breast. Their gasps sounded together, and his fingers involuntarily curled around the soft mound pressed into his palm. *Yes. God, yes.*

"Honey?" Caressing her, he asked for confirmation even as his hand was lifting and plumping, feeling the shiver when he grazed across her nipple with the pad of his thumb. Mouth to her ear, he whispered, "Juanita, honey. *Jesus.* Tell me what you want."

Her answering whisper was delayed, voice breathy when she replied, giving him a verbal go order. "Anything with you, Watcher." His other hand moved, touching the back of her neck as he gave another thumb swipe across her nipple. She arched, head tipping back into the pillow, but not to get away. This was her lifting upwards into him, seeking more touch, more sensation. "*Dios*, Watcher."

"Yeah?" Seeking affirmation again, he pressed his lips to her cheek, gliding down to the point of her jaw, that delicate angle needing attention from him in the form of tongue and teeth. He slipped down on the bed, giving himself more room to discover every inch of skin on her neck. Mouthing and nibbling, he traveled up the column of her throat, feeling her nervous swallow.

He took her mouth an instant later, hand back to her waist to hold her close, other hand winding up her hair, feeling the silk sliding through his fingers. The kiss grew heated, starting out as a soft exploration and quickly changing to a gasping embrace. Juanita dueled with him for control, telling him without words she was exactly where he was in this; hot and bothered, ready for more. More he didn't know how to initiate, not really, his few experiences not preparing him for this.

Tongues sliding and probing, she captured his bottom lip between her teeth, the tiny pricks of painful pressure shooting straight to his dick, making him jerk in his pants. The heaviness there grew in direct relation to the length of the kiss, the press of her teeth in his flesh.

"Jesus," he whispered, then his cock jerked again, this time in response to the intense heat from her hand covering his crotch. "*Jesus,*" this drawn from deep in his throat, his voice gravelly even to his own ears. She cupped the head of his cock, fingers wrapping partway around him, molding the fabric of his pants to his erection.

"Juanita," he began, then lost his train of thought as her hand stroked him. Her mouth moved against his, and he remembered to kiss her, feeling her tongue spear between his lips. He sucked firmly, dragging a moan from her, then kissed her hard, her head angling to accommodate. "Honey," he started again, pulling back. *Need to tell her. Explain.* She stroked him again, and he lost the thought, his hips instinctively moving with her caress.

She seemed to recognize the urgency that gripped him, slipping out of his hands and down the bed. Hot fingers worked at his belt, then the fastening of his jeans, and he felt the chill of air on his dick for only a moment before heat like he'd never experienced before engulfed him. Still on his side, he tried to freeze every muscle, not wanting to move and make a mistake, not wanting to fuck things up and hurt her.

"Juanita, I've never..." He trailed off as she moved on him, hot and wet. Scorching heat, sucking hard on his dick. Sizzling through his veins, drawing his balls up tight to his body. "Honey..." At this point, he didn't even know what he wanted to say, losing himself in the sensation. Pressure around the head of his cock, different pressure around the base, and he opened his eyes to see she'd taken all of him into her mouth, lips wrapped around his shaft. "I've never done this..." The pressure around his cockhead increased, and he watched as she swallowed.

His head fell to the side, and he pressed his forehead into the pillow. *Jesus.* Her hand settled on his hip, pulling and pushing, urging him to a movement he didn't know he needed until he denied it. Her head slipped back and forth, the sliding ring of pressure and heat better than his hand ever thought to be.

Juanita moved faster, seeming to become frantic, and he didn't know what to give her, scared out of his mind he'd hurt her, locking down his body. After a few moments, she allowed him to slip out of her mouth, pressing her cheek to his belly and immediately he missed everything she'd been doing so much it felt like a slicing blade in his gut. "Watcher," she said, the heat of her breath driving away the air's chill on the head of his cock where it angled in front of her. "What did I do wrong?"

"What?" Surprise ripped the word from him, and he saw her eyes clench shut. "You didn't do anything wrong, honey." She'd gifted him with something he'd wanted, but been afraid of, and now he'd made her feel she'd done wrong. *Fucking it up.* "I'm just..."

She finished his sentence with an understanding so wrong, so far off base, it would have been laughable if it hadn't hurt her so, "Not interested." A breath, then she whispered, "*Dios*, I'm sorry."

At her words, he reached down, hooked his hand under her arm and pulled. She helped, pushing with her feet, and he rolled, positioning her partly under him again. Leaning up on his elbow, he threaded his fingers through her hair, trying and failing to direct her face so he could see her. "No, sweetheart. Nothing to be sorry for. That was incredible." Amazing enough his cock was still thumping and thudding, blood rushing through, each jerking movement causing it to brush up against her thigh.

"But you didn't like it. I did it wrong." With her chin to the side, she avoided his eyes, staring at a point over his shoulder.

"Juanita." Scary as it was, humiliating as it might be, he needed to tell her. Couldn't let her hold any shame for what she'd been doing, or not understanding how very much he liked it. "I have a secret to tell you. Can I trust you?"

Her eyes darted to his, then away and she nodded. "Of course, *señor*. I would tell no one."

"Watcher," he reminded her, and she bit her lip at her slip back to a title, her nose wrinkling as she nodded again. "I know you won't. I do trust you." *How to introduce it?* Best simply barrel ahead, get everything behind him and see how she felt about him after she knew. "I've never had that before." Her eyes widened in disbelief, and he nodded. "Yeah, my first time." He leaned in so she couldn't miss his sincerity, exposing his own uncertainty and fear of failure. "I've never done that. Never had it done to me. I liked it, honey, but I didn't...don't know what you want me to do. Enjoyed it...a lot." His voice dipped on the last word, stretching the sound out, and he got a different eye flare in response.

"I know the basics, but I'm afraid of what I don't know. Most guys...they had different lives than me. I just never...so here I am, in bed with a beautiful woman who I want to make love to, but without the first idea how to do it so I don't fuck it up for you. I'm the one who's sorry, honey, because I want to erase every bad thing with good, but my fumbling fingers won't let me figure things out. Normally I have steady hands, but not with you. You strip my control, make me question everything with how beautiful you are, how you touch me, how you make me feel."

"Never?" Her voice filled with shock, she probed the truth of his statements. "Not ever?" Wordlessly, he shook his head back-and-forth, staring down into her face. He watched as a change swept over her features, a growing self-assurance which looked so good on her it stole the breath from his throat. Surety suffused her expression, and then a tiny smirk hit her lips. "Mine to introduce to pleasure?" He nodded, and she fucking *purred*. His cock, which had been deflating during their conversation, rushed back to life, blood pounding through in a rapidly increasing flood.

***

Juanita

Dios, she thought, staring up at him. Untouched, and as handsome as he was, a miracle in her hands. *I have enough experience for the both of us*. With that thought, she had a plan and put it into motion. With growing confidence, she asked, "You liked my mouth?" Since Juanita understood what held Watcher back before, she wouldn't rush into it, would take the time to watch his reactions, see what he liked best. Confidently bring him with her mouth, give him a release so when she worked him up again, he would have staying power. He wasn't a teen, but if it was really his first time, she thought he'd be able to manage two fairly quickly. This way she could make the sex good for him, make it last, so he wouldn't question his own abilities. *Or mine.*

Green eyes darkening with desire, he nodded in response, thick fingers tightening in her hair, tugging at her scalp without knowing he was doing it. Watcher was so tightly wound, his body intent on forging forwards. His beard scratched her face, tickling her lips as she lifted to press to his mouth. Immediately he took control of the kiss, angling and slanting his head so his mouth moved across hers, tongue dipping deep to tangle with hers. Not shy about where he'd been before, only where they were forging new ground. *Good.* Hand to his hip, Juanita slipped her fingers under the hem of his shirt, skating across his back and up, dragging her shirt out of the way with her other hand, the bare skin of their bellies grazing and then settling into contact.

Bringing her knee up, she planted a foot on the mattress and slowly rolled, so Watcher was on his back, never breaking their kiss, not breaking the contact in any way. She reached out, her hand unerringly finding his cock, taking his sudden groan into her mouth. Stroking slowly, up and down, she brushed and slid her fingers along his shaft. *I'm in control*, she thought, marveling how destiny had brought this man to her. A man perfect for her, possibly the only one who could most benefit from the fate befallen her. With a last smooth glide of her tongue against his, Juanita broke the kiss. Staring down at him, she smiled slowly as she bent close again. Mouth to his chin, she kissed through his beard, nibbling on his neck, watching avidly as his head tipped backwards, the muscles of his neck bulging, calling for their own caress.

Skipping his chest, mostly covered by his shirt still, Juanita liked what she saw. Mouth to his skin again, she glided fingertips across his belly, engrossed in an instant by how his muscles jerked and quivered at her touch. Hand steadily stroking up and down, she tightened her fingers rhythmically around the shaft, rolling up and over the crest of the engorged head, then back down. Opening her eyes, she marveled at how beautiful his cock was, a bead of glistening liquid at the tip and her tongue darted out to lap at it, curling around the crown.

Sucking him into her mouth, Juanita felt the pebbled surface of the head against her tongue and palate. Swollen and aroused, he filled her and then some, she felt the stretch as her lips took in his girth. Up and down, steady movements began and she adjusted to cover the shaft she wasn't yet taking in. She would be, having already proved to herself she could, swallowing the salt and musk that was Watcher. *My Watcher*, the words flashed through her mind as he spoke, his voice rich with awe. "What do I do?"

Pulling him deep, she reached up and gripped one of his hands, bringing it to the back of her head. Fingers threaded with his, she clenched their grip around a hank of her hair, applying pressure he could feel and she could respond to, taking him even deeper, the vibration of his groan rising through his cock. In moments she felt his muscles tighten and relax, then tighten again, his hand cupping the back of her head as his hips lifted. Opening her throat, she took him deep, deeper, swallowing around him in a way she knew he liked, because that firm grip on her hair tightened and Watcher ground out, "Fuck, *Juanita*," gifting her with clear recognition of who was giving him pleasure. Leaned across him as she was, she felt when the muscles in his thighs turned to stone underneath her and knew he was trying to fight it off, holding back because he was unsure. Wet between her legs from giving this to him, she pressed close, wanting something for the first time in what seemed forever.

Hand firmly wrapped around his cock, she jacked him fast, focusing her mouth and tongue on the head, urging him to climax. Watcher's warning came, as she knew it would. Him being the gentleman he was, he'd give her the option of backing off, willing to spill on his belly if she couldn't take things through to their conclusion. "Juanita, I'm going to..." A groan broke from deep in his throat, and his hands fell away from her head to grip the sheets at either hip. She increased her speed, needing to own his pleasure in a way she'd never owned a man. Lips locked around his shaft, she sucked hard and then pushed down fast, swallowing, forcing him deep, feeling the heat as he gave in, coming hard, spurts of semen flowing down her throat.

Groans and grunts filled the air around her, painting a picture of Watcher's passion with resonating sounds. Body stiff with an intense orgasm, it seemed to go on for a long time. Juanita held tight throughout it all. Tongue working up and down his shaft, her fingers squeezed rhythmically until he was done. He groaned a final time, muscles previously wound tight relaxing into slackness, his cock losing its rock-hard firmness in her mouth. Juanita licked and sucked him clean, allowing his still half-hard cock to drop to the hollow of one hip. Settling her head onto his belly, she didn't want to look into his face, filled with a sudden and intense fear he hadn't really liked it.

The sex ring hadn't been her first introduction to intimacy, that having been courtesy of her boyfriend. Julio had been experienced, and interested in arousing her passions, claiming Juanita was a natural at everything she did, claiming to love what she did both to, and with him. Julio had also been sleeping with two other girls, something she'd found out when she'd stumbled in on him in the backroom of the local market where he'd worked. But during their time together, she'd found a healthy desire for sex was part of who she was, and she'd enjoyed exploring things with him. Kidnapped not long after they'd broken up, her next months had been a discovery far different from what he had managed, and by the end, she'd found ways to lock herself inside her head when a man had approached. Giving him her body, but not her mind. Not *her*.

Watcher was different. The idea of him being so inexperienced was intoxicating, and she hoped he'd enjoyed himself enough to want more with her. She breathed a sigh of relief when his fingers returned to her scalp, trailing and twisting through strands of her hair, stroking and easing her nerves. "Honey," he whispered, his voice thick and heavy with emotion. "That was unbelievable." She smiled, tipping her head and kissing his belly, seeing he was still half hard. She trailed a fingertip up the underside of his cock, watching as it moved with her touch. Juanita smiled again when she saw it thicken, starting up the path back to hardness.

"Watcher," she spoke quietly, fingertips still working slowly up and down his shaft. "Do you have a condom?" His fingers tightened briefly in her hair and then relaxed, stroking and pushing through to her scalp again.

"Yeah, honey. In my wallet." Attached by a chain to his belt loop, his wallet was still in the rear pocket of his only partially discarded jeans. She abandoned his cock, reaching across him to tug the wallet out of his pants. Offering it to him, she sat on the bed nearby, taking in all that was Watcher as he opened the leather rectangle, fishing out a wrapped condom. His body was tall and broad; thick, dark hair manageably short, beard the same. Tanned by the wind and sun, he was strong, arms perfect for holding her. She focused on his face. Green eyes filled with curiosity, it looked like he was studying her and she realized she'd frozen into place next to him.

He's seen me naked, she thought, swept back to the hell hole for a moment, then forcibly jerked herself away and back into the moment. "Juanita, you don't have—"

He's seen me naked and wasn't disappointed. With that, she gained the courage to grab the hem of her shirt and lift, closing her eyes as she dragged it over her head, not looking at him when she tossed it aside. Reaching behind her, she worked to unfasten the still unfamiliar clasp on the bra one of the Soldiers' women had provided. *Everything I have, I owe to him*. She knew instinctively he would hate knowing she'd given even a second's consideration to the thought, so she pushed it away. *Not why I'm doing this*, she reminded herself, peeling the straps down her arms, putting herself on display.

Lifting to her knees, she pushed at the too-big jeans, also given to her by the woman of one of his friends. *Nothing I have is mine, except me. I can give him me*. Everything else was only surface, and he was the one person she wouldn't be afraid to have know her, inside and out. His hand reached, fingers digging into her hip and he tugged. She fell onto him, kicking the pants from her legs as he found her mouth with his and kissed her deeply, not shying away from delving into her mouth so recently on his cock, so recently swallowing down everything he offered.

Juanita shifted to her side, then to her back, silently urging him to roll with her, pulling him so he partially covered her, pinning her to the mattress with his weight. Mouth to his, she kissed him, hands roaming, pulling and pushing at the fabric of his shirt, his jeans, wanting…needing the skin-to-skin only he could give her. A moment later, his clothing joined hers on the floor, condom rolled down his already stiff cock. She tipped one knee to the side, opening her legs for him as she tugged on his hips, encouraging him to move over her.

He did, and she took his weight as he adjusted, elbow to the mattress on either side of her head. She reached between them and took the length of his cock in her hand. Swiping the head through the wetness there once, twice, she positioned him between her lips, stroking slowly up and down the length of his cock. "Please," Juanita whispered, and he kissed her again. Rocking her hips, lifting up, she took him inside a fraction of an inch. Thick, so thick it took her breath, and the heat of him was scorching.

Watcher lay on top of her, and with a quiet groan that shuddered through her chest, he pushed and, with a stuttering in-and-out motion, he glided inside her. She felt the controlled power behind each movement, deeper on every stroke, taking up residence there, rooting himself and burying his face in her neck on another groan. *I'm his in this moment*, she thought, praying it would be more than this, wrapping her arm around his back. Then he gave her reassurances she didn't know she needed. "Mine, Juanita. Mine." He gritted out the words like a vow, and she believed them.

Rocking, she moved, helping set a rhythm to give them both pleasure. Listening for cues, she worked to sustain the motion, keep things going even when he lost it. He panted grunts into her ear when he dove deep between her legs, too far gone to stop, hips working instinctively to bring him to climax. Arms around his shoulders, she thrust one hand up into his hair, holding on tight, the other splayed across his upper back, pulling him to her. "God, Juanita. Yes, honey." Her legs lifted, curling around his hips, giving him room to move deep. "Ahh, baby." She closed her eyes when his teeth buried into her shoulder, when his groan vibrated through her again as he set himself deep inside her and trembled in her arms. Satisfaction rolled through her when he growled his possessive, "Mine."

My Queen
Watcher

Watcher sat at the kitchen table with Bones and Mason, his gaze fixed on Juanita as she stood at the counter beside Bethy. Ty and the other men were in the living room, their conversation centering around whatever game was on TV. Mason and Bones talked quietly, giving him space he desperately needed to come to grips with all that had happened. *I made love to Juanita, someone I've vowed to protect, but failed to protect from me.*

The only consolation? A confidence he hadn't realized she lacked was echoing from her now, new light beaming from her face with every smile she turned his way. *Well, not the only consolation.* He'd made love to her. She'd helped him through every wave of nerves that swept over him as they'd laid in bed, and he'd made love to her. And now, she was acting as if he'd handed her the world. As if in her giving everything to him, including the best two orgasms he'd ever had, he'd given her diamonds in return. *I didn't even make her come,* he thought with disgust, then immediately wondered with concern if pleasure might be something blocked for her. It wouldn't be surprising, given what had happened to her, but God, he wanted to give her back everything she'd given him. Jewels of sweetness, waves of confidence, and bright moments of loving untainted by fear.

She hadn't been shy, not once they'd started, her surety helping him move through things. Certain he'd mess up, he'd nearly frozen a dozen times, but her signals helped him remain focused. At least until his eyes rolled back in his head. When she'd swallowed him down her throat, the heat and pressure so intense, he wasn't sure he'd survive the explosion boiling out of his balls. Then after, when she'd effortlessly transitioned them into the next phase, he'd been amazed again. Being inside her had shattered him. Experiencing for the first time having a woman be all around him, her body enveloping his dick in sleek muscle, the feeling took his breath away. The knowledge that she wanted *him*. Finding a rhythm between them, having her pumping up into him, fingernails digging into his back...exquisite. Her accepting the hard slapping of his hips against hers, mouth to his shoulder, darting nips from her teeth pushing him harder, faster, until he emptied himself inside the condom, hot splashes of his own climax nothing next to the satisfying trust she gave him.

Amazing. Juanita glanced at Watcher over her shoulder, and the expression of joy faltered on her face at whatever she saw on his. He gave her a grin, tipping his chin up, trying to show her the desire she'd roused in him hadn't flagged. Wasn't gone. *I could take her again, now*, and the moment the idea crossed his mind, his cock began to uncoil and fatten. Trying to capture her scent, he sucked a deep breath, and then watched as heat rose in her eyes, matching his. *Need her*. Without thinking, without giving a damn who else was in the room, he stood, holding out his hand and—*fuck him*—she came to him without question. He waited until her palm rested against his, joy threading through his heart as her fingers laced between his knuckles and he led her from the room.

As soon as the bedroom door closed behind them, Watcher turned and lifted her, pressed her against the wall and pushed between her thighs until her legs fell open and wrapped around his hips. He rocked against her, the pressure and heat feeling unbelievably good, his dick so sensitive he could feel the seams in their jeans creasing his skin. He kissed her hard until they were both panting for air, desperate for more. "Show me." He breathed the words, lips grazing across her jaw. "God, Juanita, show me what you want," he whispered, mouth to her throat.

Her fingers tangled in his hair, and her lips lightly brushed his ear when she said, "Anything." With thoughts of scenes he'd witnessed, exaggerated emotions of porn, knowledge of what the women he'd had his hands on liked, he walked to the bed, kissing her, working her mouth over until she moaned sweetly. Stretching them out on the mattress, one hand threaded underneath her shirt, he found and cupped her breast, fingers slipping into her bra and tweaking her nipple. "God," he breathed, as mouth to her neck, he nibbled and sucked his way down, then back up, kissing her hard again.

One hand flattened between her legs, he pushed against her core, pressing hard with his thumb, feeling her arch up into his hold. *Make her feel good.* Rubbing and stroking, Watcher fondled her, knew it was good from the tension that built in her limbs as she pressed her thighs together. "Want you to come, honey." Mouth to hers, he took in every panted breath, heard and felt the high, keening whine as it built in her chest. He pushed his hand into her pants, happy for once they were baggy and not form fitting. They gave him room to maneuver, and he took advantage, curling his fingers into and underneath her panties, slipping through the wetness he found there. Rolling and sliding, he delicately stroked across her clit, dipping a finger inside her, listening with pride when the sounds from her mouth grew louder as he pushed deep. A second finger and she twisted her head, pressing into his neck, burying her face against him, arms folded around him, holding tight. "For me, Juanita. Come for me."

He took his cues from her, matching his careful thrusting to her hips lifting into his touch. Timed everything with his mouth on her neck, on her cheek, back to her shoulder through her shirt, biting and grazing her with his teeth. Fingers inside her, curling and twisting, thumb pressing and circling on her clit. Press and circle, press hard, circle again. He felt her pussy clamp down on his fingers, knowing she was climbing to inescapable heights when she whined again, every muscle in her body tightening. His name escaping her mouth on a short-lived wail, *"Watcher,"* cut off when she burrowed under his beard, face pressed tightly to his neck while she came hard on his fingers.

"So beautiful, honey. Everything you do." He dropped a kiss on the side of her head, hearing her breathing fast and hard. "Make me feel like I know what I'm doing." Cupping his palm over her sex, he cradled her into his side. "I've never asked for easy, never expected to find perfection. God—" He kissed her again, feeling her arms squeeze him. "—top of the world. You make this all effortless, and I'm one hell of a lucky guy."

***

"Time to roll," he told Spider, looking away as his brother walked to the rest of the men, passing the message. Seated on his bike, Watcher kept his eyes on Juanita where she stood next to Bethy, sides of their heads pressed together, Bethy's mouth moving as she spoke quietly into Juanita's ear. They stood like that for another minute, arms wrapped tightly around the other. The moment was broken when Mason called to his sister, pulling her away and into his arms. Juanita's eyes found Watcher's, and when he held out his hand, she came to him without hesitation, giving him her trust as she had from the beginning.

He twisted his wrist, holding her steady as she swung her leg across the bike behind him. Snuggling up tight against him, his cock hardened. *Fucking hell*, he thought, feeling the softness of her breasts pressing into his back. He heard a noise and looked up, seeing Bones watching from across the parking lot. They'd be rolling together for a while, the clubs all wanting to have miles of bonding to build on for future encounters, and this gave them an opportunity to ride through neutral territory, none of them owning any part of this countryside. As he stared, Bones lips curled into a devilish grin, and he nodded then fucking winked, apparently approving where Watcher's relationship with Juanita had gone.

Twenty minutes later, Watcher had settled the speeding bike into place behind Mason, Juanita's arms wrapped tight around his middle, going there after she'd finished waving good-bye to Bethy and Ty. Cheek to his back, she curled deeper into him, and he sighed in contentment. *If Darrie knew what his death bought, he'd be happy*, Watcher thought, knowing it for truth. Darrie'd tried as hard as Deke to get Watcher laid, and he'd never given up on the attempts. One of his brother's hardest burdens was bearing the weight of everything that happened to their little family through the years, and the toll of what happened to Tabby had torn through both of them, wearing them down.

Feeling the sweetness pressed up against him, Watcher found he'd never been happier to disappoint his brother. Holding out hadn't been a conscious decision to wait for a woman he could love, but it didn't suck knowing she'd been his first. Special, and good, and everything he could have hoped for.

***

"I'll be right here," Watcher murmured into Juanita's neck as he glided deep and stayed rooted, feeling the last tight pulses of her climax slowly decreasing. Filled again with the profound awe he felt every time she gave herself to him, he touched her reverently, palm stroking up her side, thumb brushing across the bottom swell of her breast. "Promise."

Her unease was palpable, defeating his attempts to soothe her fears. Muscles still tense, arms wrapped around him, she shivered. "What if they don't like me?" There was a Soldiers' party planned for the following night. It was their memorial for Darrie, and meant a dozen different clubs from the region were invited. Juanita had been worried since he'd mentioned it back when they were leaving Nashville. Not about the strangers, or at least he didn't think they factored in her anxiety. It was about the men he called brother and their women.

143

"They're going to love you, honey." He pulled out slowly, then pushed back deep, feeling himself beginning to soften but wanting a few more minutes of closeness. "You got nary a thing to worry about."

"Things are never that easy," she whispered.

His return whisper was just as soft. "Easy as I can make it, rest of your life. Promise." This time, when she shivered, it was for a different reason as he pulled out and slowly traveled down her body until his chin rested right above her pussy. "Easy as I can make you come right now," he whispered, moving to drag his tongue across her lips, flicking across her clit. "Easy as this."

The next morning, she darted around the house, a house that was empty and echoing without Darrie's presence, but she helped make it less lonely. Room-by-room she went, cleaning and straightening, tidying things away. Then she disappeared, and after twenty minutes of silence, Watcher went looking for her, finding her in the bathroom. From the doorway he watched her for a moment as she appeared to study her reflection, making minute adjustments to her hair. When the tears began trailing down her cheeks, he realized she was attempting to hide the brand on her neck.

"Honey," he called softly, hating how she still cowered momentarily, "no one will say a thing to you about what went before. I get that what you're trying to hide feels like a huge flashing sign to you, but no one will notice. And if they do, they won't care. That life wasn't something you chose, not an experience you sought out. They're not gonna give a fuck about it."

She stared at him through the mirror for a long moment, then dropped her eyes, breaking the connection before nodding. He knew she wasn't convinced, so he moved in behind her and wrapped her up, bending his head to place a soft kiss on the brand. With emphasis, he told her, "I don't give a fuck about it. So they won't, either. And if they do, well, I don't give a fuck about *that*. Or them." He pressed a second and then a third kiss to the mark. "Love my honey. Love my Juanita."

At those words, she relaxed in his arms, finally, just as the first roar of bikes sounded in the distance.

An hour later, he'd been proven right and knew it, watching as she tentatively settled onto the grass next to one of the women. Greeting Juanita with a smile, Spider's old lady reached out and gave her hand a reassuring squeeze. Daena and Juanita had begun to chat when Opie spoke up from behind him.

"Good turnout, boss. Danger woulda been pleased." Turning to look over his shoulder, Watcher nodded. Opie's lips pressed together, and Watcher stiffened, sensing this would be the precursor to something he didn't want to hear. "Need to talk about what we're doin' with the rest of the rescues. We need to find 'em shelter, permanent like, or get them back home if they want to go."

"We're going to do whatever it takes to make sure those women have what they need." Watcher hadn't known what he was going to say when his mouth opened, but his words didn't surprise him. Neither did the emotion that swelled inside him, a determination to see this through. "And you mind my words, brother. We're going hunting soon."

Tilting his head towards Juanita, Opie asked him, "How much of this is for Danger, and how much for her?"

"Don't fuckin' matter, brother. Same outcome gonna hit the horizon. We need to, we'll end Machos entirely." Looking at Juanita, he let the sight of her smile warm him. "Estavez needs to die."

"Brothers will care, Watch. You know they will. They'll be all-in for revenging Danger's death. Gonna be less so for a bitch they don't know. It's asking a lot." Shaking his head, Opie cautioned, "Not sayin' it to be a dick, just makin' sure you're lookin' at all angles, brother."

Opie grimaced and Watcher cut off the argument he knew was coming. So soon after losing three men, no one wanted to think about crossing the river again. Not yet. "Now's not the time, Opie. Tonight's for Danger, not for strategy. I ain't gonna back down, though. So don't think this is me takin' back anything I said."

With a nod, Opie acknowledged his words, making it clear he would comply even if he might not agree with the directive. Watcher found he didn't really give a fuck because Machos needed to pay for what happened. Not only with Darrie but because of Juanita. Because of all the women. "Shit can't go unanswered, Opie. We can't let them continue to do whatever the fuck they want and expect to keep any authority. We make our own way, and we force our authority down their fuckin' throats if need be. Slit 'em if we need to make room."

Watcher saw the boy in Daena's lap reach out, fingers aiming for Juanita's neck and without pausing, Watcher was on his way to Juanita's side, long strides taking him there as the boy's fingers touched her skin. He dropped to his knees behind her, an arm firm around her chest, lips pressed to the side of her head as little Dean told his mother, "She a qween, Mama. Gots a cwown."

Juanita was trembling, but Daena smiled down at her son and didn't see. Watcher felt Juanita tensing and knew she was preparing to retreat, something he couldn't let her do. He instinctively knew if she left the party, not only would Daena feel guilty, but Juanita would never be able to face the group again. Brushing his mouth deliberately across the brand, he caught Dean's awe-struck gaze and grinned. "She's my queen, Dean-boy. This tells the world she's mine." Another kiss to the brand earned a soft hitch in Juanita's breathing when he repeated, "She's my queen."

Time of miracles and wonder

Watcher stood in the doorway and looked towards the house from the barn, one ear listening to the rumbling talk from behind him. He might be giving about half his attention to his brothers, but his real focus was on Juanita, watching as she hung sheets on the line. Bending over, standing and stretching up, bending over again. He smirked, thinking, *Love the view*. In the desert's arid climate, the laundry would be dry within half an hour, and then he'd get to see her gathering them in, arms spread wide to capture the billowing fabric, breasts straining against her shirt. Watching and knowing that when he laid his head down on fresh, clean sheets tonight, it would be with her by his side. *Best part of my day*.

Since coming together the first night in a borrowed bed in Nashville, they hadn't slept apart. For nearly three months, everything had developed into exactly what he had hoped and prayed for. She was all he needed, and he tried his damnedest to be the same for her. Learning what she liked, giving it to her every chance he had. Loving her had turned into a favorite song, one that played in his head all day long. She loved him, too, and he knew it, even if she didn't say the words.

There had been struggles along the way. He'd been terrified the first night she woke fighting and ran from him, fucking beat feet as fast as she could. Bolted from his bed to disappear in the closet. He went to her, and in silence, she'd fought him with every breath. Pulling away to dart back into the closet, again and again, pushing her way behind the clothes on the racks, struggling to stay concealed as best she could. She'd scored deep grooves into his flesh with her nails before he could get her under control. That was also the first time she'd tried to run away, ashamed of what she'd been driven to do by the demons in her sleep. His mistake was thinking everything had settled down, so once Watcher had gone back to bed with her in his arms, he'd slipped into sleep beside her without understanding how deeply her terrors ran.

An hour later the alarms around the periphery of the property had woken him, and when he looked at the screens, it had been just in time to see a black and white image of a sobbing Juanita staggering out into the desert. He'd been afraid an ATV would frighten her and worried he'd lose her if he pursued on foot, so he'd gotten on the bike and set watch on a road about a mile out. Thank God she'd stumbled into the road right on top of him. After freezing in place for a few moments, her chin dropped to her chest before she accepted his outstretched hand, climbing onto the bike behind him. Minutes later they were back at home, and he tried to reassure her with both words and actions.

Now, however, something wasn't right. They'd had more episodes, of course they had. A person didn't get over the kind of things she'd lived through without scars. But, unless she was keeping the dreams from him, she hadn't suffered through one for weeks now. Something else was up, and it was bugging him to no end. She wasn't sick, wasn't stressed, but she'd seemed abnormally tired over the past couple of weeks.

Opie spoke again, and Watcher changed position, twisting to look back at him. Without any idea what his brother had said, he owned up to the fact he hadn't been listening with a quick, "Didn't catch that, sorry."

"No doubt, eyes only for your woman. Like seeing you wearin' this kinda happiness, Watch. She's gonna make a beautiful mama." Watcher's face must have given away his surprise, because Opie laughed gleefully, shaking his head. Choking on his laughter, Opie said, "Jesus, Watch. Did you seriously not know? Look at her little belly."

Focus again on Juanita, Watcher now saw the signs he'd missed. She was rounder, only a little, but it was there. Her rack was bigger, too, and not by a little. He'd even joked about it in bed, playing with her breasts until she'd been moaning for his cock. Sensitive, so fucking sensitive, and he hadn't a clue. "Shit."

"Oh, man. That word does not shout joy." Opie's voice was quiet, but anything else he had to say was lost, trailing to silence behind him because Watcher was already on the move, striding towards the house. Opie didn't have it right, because if she were pregnant, then Watcher would be the happiest guy in the world...but only if *she* was.

"Juanita," he called softly, seeing the smile fade from her face as she turned his direction, paling at whatever look was on his face. He wondered, *How do you ask a lady if she's preggers?* Then felt his heart clench when her lips trembled right before she looked to the side and down, avoiding his eyes. "Honey, is everything okay?" Time to ease her back into a situation where she'd be comfortable, and he set about trying to do that, taking a towel out of the basket and folding it in half before dropping it across the line stretched between them. "Thought I'd help a bit." *Shit.* This would be guaranteed to make her more nervous because it wasn't something he'd ever done before. "Thought we might talk." *Sure, that'll make her comfy, asshat.*

Her voice trembled when she said, "Watcher?" The question evident in the uplifting tone at the end of his name. "What...?"

"You pregnant?" *Fucking shit, my mouth doesn't have a damned filter.* He rolled his eyes at himself, reaching for another towel while studiously not looking at her. *I want this.* He could see her from the corner of his eye but refused to look straight on. In the two minutes since Opie dropped the bombshell on him, he'd already become invested in this kid, if she indeed was pregnant. "Just...seemed the thing to ask. We had a condom break and all." They had, on the trip back from Kentucky, something he'd put aside in his head since she didn't talk about missing her cycle. He hadn't paid attention, though, so he didn't know if she'd skipped or not. "Thought I'd ask."

"*Si, Papi,*" her pet name for him slipped out, and the single word gave him hope. He held his breath, but she didn't say anything further, her simple yes still enough to nearly unhinge his knees.

With shaking hands, he tossed the towel in his hands towards the basket, not paying attention to the fact it fell half to the ground. Staring at the basket, he asked quietly, "You sure?"

"*Papi,*" her voice faltered, and stopped.

"Juanita, are you pregnant or not?" Now his words sounded stern, not something he wanted, so he intentionally tried to moderate his tone. "Honey, do you know for sure?"

From the corner of his eye, he watched as her shoulders moved up and down in a shrug. "I think, but not for certain, no." She paused, then continued, her voice so soft he nearly lost it in the sound of the wind moving the fabric around them. "I didn't want...I don't know."

"You don't want it?" Sickness rolled through his belly as he snapped the words, voice back to stern, and Watcher turned his head to the side so she didn't have to look at the pain he knew was stamped on his features. "Don't want my kid?" *God, what if it isn't mine? Maybe that's what's got her spooked.* "Is it mine?"

"If I am, then yes, it is...yours." She hesitated before finishing her sentence, and he wasn't sure why until she corrected herself. "Ours." *She wouldn't be claiming it if she didn't want it*, he thought with a thrill of excitement. "And..." She paused again, and he waited, giving her time to find the words she needed to say. "I do. I would want...yes." Her voice was soft again, hesitant when she asked, "Would you?"

"Fuck yeah, honey." Voice firm, there'd be no mistaking his pleasure now, and he turned to see tears standing in her eyes. "You havin' my kid?" He nodded, planting his feet because it had to be her to come to him this time. "Fuck yeah, I want all of that."

With a quiet sob, she turned her head away and down. "Juanita, honey. Come here." At his soft encouragement, she took one step, then another, and then she was pressed to him, arms around his waist. Lips to the top of her head, he took her weight as she sagged, sobbing in clear relief.

***

Watcher lay in bed next to Juanita, propped on one elbow, using the end of her braid to tickle her nose, grinning to see the faces she made in her sleep. He'd wake her properly in a minute, kiss her up from sleep and then listen to her cute grumbling. That shit would stop as soon as he got his mouth on her, but he knew from experience she'd put up a good front for a bit.

They'd bedded down last night before he'd got a chance to go to town and hit the pharmacy, and Watcher made a mental note to do that errand first thing this morning. Palm to her breast, he grazed his thumb across her nipple, watching through the fabric of the tee she wore to bed as it firmed, bunching up and poking a tiny tent in her shirt. He'd made a good start last night, exploring the myriad of ways she was more sensitive and responsive, and from his very thorough investigations, at this point in his thought process, he started smiling, confident of the result from the pee stick she'd be using today.

Leaning in, he brushed her jaw with his lips, dusting soft kisses up the apple of her cheek to her temple, nuzzling into her hair just so he could smell her. *God*, he thought, *I love her*. A buzzing startled him, and he twisted his torso so he could reach his phone where it lay on the nightstand. One eye to the display and he saw it was barely coming on six in the morning, way out of character for Pops to be making a call. Thinking he was prepared for anything, he put the phone to his ear and grunted a brusque, "Yeah?"

"Prez, man, need you." Chaos in the background. There were snapping crack and crash noises of something wooden being destroyed, the slamming of what sounded like a sledgehammer against a wall. "Gotta lock Spider down, man. Need you. LCPD, brother."

Mixed with the rhythmic pounding, an anguished howl rose and rose, drilling into his head with torturous precision. After a moment, he could make out the single word repeated again and again in a continuous denial. *"No."*

"The fuck is goin' on?" He clipped this question while on the move, swinging out of bed and striding to where his jeans lay on the floor. If they were at the police station and Spider was this out of control, Watcher needed to already be there. No time to waste. Pulling up his jeans, one hand to tuck things in comfortably, one to hold the phone to his ear.

"Daena." Pops' voice broke on the name, and he froze, waiting. "Single car accident, she didn't make it."

"Papi?" That was Juanita, reacting to his mood and his physical actions as Watcher tipped his head up, remembering words much like those which had ripped his world apart. Through the phone, came the sound of another crash, another shrill and wavering, *"No!"* He now realized the noise was Spider, losing his shit because his old lady was gone.

Watcher headed straight back to the bed, lips to Juanita's for a hard, quick kiss, eyes open and on her face, seeing anxiety and fear circling each other there. "I gotta go, honey. Club." He stole a second kiss, softer, then heard another ringing *"No!"* from the phone, the pain in Spider's voice clamping his throat around his words. Juanita held up a hand, and he clasped at it, fingers wrapping around tightly. She did the same, giving him silent reassurance she would be here, be thinking of him...be waiting for him. *Single car accident.*

He heard Preacher's voice in his head for the first time in a long while as the words slithered through his mind, sand gritting underneath his boots as he stalked to his bike. "*Watch, they said it might not be an accident.*" The whole way to the station those words circled the others, and he futilely tried to push them away. If it was a genuine accident, then it was bad, but the brothers would circle the wagons, try to support Spider in the best ways they knew. He couldn't get away from the memory of other words, *They said it might not be an accident.* Not that he thought Daena would be down to take her own life, knowing how she loved Spider and their three kids, but if it weren't an accident, then this could mean war.

By the time he got to the station, the cops had called medics in, and Spider had been sedated for his own safety. The accident report passed to Watcher in the hallway said she'd driven straight into an electric pole, the long wooden spear breaking in half and crashing down on top of her car. The wreck shouldn't have killed her, the car's airbag had deployed and she'd been saved from eating the steering wheel, but the heavy length hadn't wavered as it fell, crushing her as it crumpled the roof. It had been hours before the firefighters were able to extract her body, no need to rush. By then they all knew it was a recovery, not a rescue.

Three days later, a black ribbon pinned to his breast, standing straight, Watcher lifted in unison with five other men, taking Daena's body on her last trip. One ending in a dark, sharp-edged hole. Standing to one side of the casket, from behind his shades he stared at Spider who cradled his youngest in his lap. A beauty, she looked very much like Daena. The two boys who made up the remainder of Spider's blood family stood close, pressed to either side of their father. The oldest, four-year-old Dean, stared at Watcher, his gaze never wavering, not even when Spider's arm curved around him. Fear took hold of Watcher in those moments, because he knew nothing Spider could do would make it better for the boy, and with a child of his own coming, the terror of losing Juanita sank deep inside him.

Taking a shuddering breath in, he turned away from the boy's gaze and faced Preacher, standing at the head of the void carved from the earth, shadowy depths waiting for its burden.

***

"Dad, wanna come down here with me a minute?" Watcher turned his head to look at the doc, hoping his disbelief was plain on his face because he found himself voiceless. "Hold out your hands, Dad." Juanita's fingers squeezed his and released, her features at peace for the first time in hours. A nurse draped a cloth over his outstretched arms and then the doc was putting their baby into his arms. "It's a girl." Cradling the small body, he focused on her face with its little features, mouth working soundlessly. *My daughter*, he thought and turned so Juanita would be able to see her, but couldn't take his gaze off the tiny, perfect, beautiful baby girl he was holding. *My miracle.*

Hands entered his field of vision, wiping and swiping at the baby's face, at her arms, pulling the covering back for reasons he ignored. *My daughter*. A voice nearby urged him to the bed, and he took the three steps to Juanita's side, watching as her trembling fingers shakily peeled back a corner of the blanket. "*Hermosa, ella es mi corazón.*" Lifting her exhausted eyes to meet his gaze, Juanita smiled radiantly. "Thank you, my love."

Gently he placed their daughter in Juanita's arms and together they discovered the perfection hidden by the warming blanket. Ten fingers, ten toes, lips curving in a bow as she suckled her mother's little finger. Fussy rooting led to being offered a true nipple, and he loved seeing the joy on Juanita's face as she mastered that mother's skill, feeling their daughter latch on for the first time.

"What's her name?" After laughing softly when Watcher refused to cut the cord, the doc had settled back into his role and was currently—

"knitting things back together from what our sweet girl did in her rush into the world"—his words as he worked with forceps and needle.

Watcher smiled at Juanita, this was something which had taken weeks to settle. They had two names picked out, one for a boy, Darren Gael, honoring his brother and her father. For a girl, it was more complicated, as Juanita described the traits of saints and relatives, but they had finally come to an agreement. "Isabella, but we're gonna call her Bella." Juanita's name was now Juanita Teresa Consuela los Carmen del Otey, she had dropped her mother's name of Estavez when they'd married. But, it meant the name became part of his baby girl's name, "Isabella Delfina Christina del Estavez los Otey."

* * *

Head back and resting on the wooden panel behind him, heel angled firmly against the floor, he pushed and flexed the muscles in his leg, gently gliding the rocker in a back and forth arc. Watcher sat with a swaddled Bella curved into his shoulder, face nestled in his neck. *Sweet baby mine*, he thought, listening to the soft noises from the house. Just him and his two girls, finally.

Not saying he hadn't been glad for the company over the past couple of weeks, but it was good to have things settling back to their new normal. Bethany had come out to stay and help with Bella, instinctively knowing Juanita would need emotional support. Juanita's mother would normally have been the one to descend on their household, reorganizing and directing how things would go with her granddaughter. Not with what had happened, though. Watcher wasn't certain Juanita had even contacted her parents after her rescue and knew from gently questioning her that she held tight to a deep fear of their rejection of her. The family's disgrace from having a daughter used as she had been was an insurmountable barrier in her mind. In her head it was better to not know than be confronted by what could be a painful rebuff. As long as she didn't contact them, they couldn't turn her away. Bethany's presence helped distract Juanita from all of that, keeping her focused on the beauty in their lives now.

With Bethany came Mason, his stay much briefer, but no less sweet. It was never bad to see a man he considered a true brother, always a good time to get a chance to visit with someone who mattered. Their clubs were bonded as close as the two men could make it, and it comforted Watcher to know he had at least one strong and loyal ally in his war with the Machos.

Turning things over in his head, he picked at the edges of the most recent problem, the flood of drugs crossing the bridge in El Paso. Machos had help and backing from Central America, and paired with Estavez' corruption of the authorities on the Mexican side of the border, meant he was nearly unstoppable. *Nearly*, Watcher thought with satisfaction. Soldiers had found and torched a warehouse and tunnel complex last week, and it had been good for Mason to see how well the club worked together, no man standing down until the last body fell. No one backing off the bloody work needed to take back and protect their territory.

Mason's only comment had been an observation of how the actual leadership of the club had gotten tied up tightly in only two men, him and Pops. Once Watcher got past thinking it was a criticism, they'd laughed together, because it was true. Not something he wanted, creating what amounted to a single point of failure, but finding soldiers was the easy part, digging to find out who could be leaders took time. Mentoring and building their brotherhood, making sure there were ample opportunities to foster the fellowship and trust needed, took even more time. *Worth it*, he thought. Bella squirmed and cooed, her movements slow and sleepy; he glanced at the clock on the wall. Nearly feeding time, which would mean he could curl in bed beside his Juanita as she nursed their daughter. *Important things in life*, he thought, *worth any work it takes to get there.*

Give me what I need

Six years later

Watcher stared at the red and white Indian motorcycle parked behind the bar he and his brothers were in the process of purchasing. With an overhead gesture, he kept them moving up the alley and out into the front lot, backing his pipes to the building. Scarcely a second after he'd killed his engine, Spider was standing close, his mouth running. "Did you see that Indian? Who the fuck is in our town? In our fuckin' bar? Man's gotta have balls, rolling into Soldiers' territory and not declaring himself. Doesn't matter who it is, shoulda held enough respect to fuckin' front his visit."

"Easy, brother," Opie cautioned, and Watcher caught the weighty glance passing between Opie and Devil. All of them well aware Spider had not dealt with the death of his old lady well, spiraling nearly out of control over the first year. He'd come back, some, but wasn't stable, not by a long shot. Daena's death had been ruled an accident by the cops, but Spider had a conspiracy theory and suspicions about who he felt was behind it. He'd talked it up again and again, but there wasn't any evidence. Without that proof, Watcher couldn't authorize any action because it would have opened the door on a war which might have no

157

end. As it was, the skirmishes the two clubs engaged in still left dead behind. *Too many*, Watcher thought, standing up off the bike.

The Soldiers hadn't grown much since Darrie's death, something Watcher had consciously done at first, keeping a lid on their membership numbers. He tried to keep his core focused on cycling between buildups of their businesses for financial support, and training the members they had. Mentoring them, teaching as he had been taught about protocol and what the brotherhood was supposed to mean. Not what the jumped-up clubs thought it was about, that being bitches and booze, blow and weed, parties and rolling a cage if you didn't have a bike. No, he wanted them to understand what had gone before, so they'd cherish what they had. Respect the patch and look up to the old guys, no matter from what era they hailed.

"Hold, brothers," Watcher called as Pops neared the door. Pulling his phone from the pocket of his vest, Watcher dialed and waited. "Be home late, baby." He spoke softly, as if his voice through the phone would disturb the sleep of his daughter, safely in her bed miles away. Juanita laughed, the music pouring through the call and into him, filling Watcher up with love. The beauty his life had become amazed him every day.

"Okay, *Papi*," she told him. "Be safe, bring yourself home to me soon. Our Bella loves her papa."

He smiled as he disconnected the call, turning to see a grin on every face, including Spider. Cutting off any razzing, he uttered a preemptive, "Fuck you," pushing through the door past them and into the bar. Once inside, he paused, taking in how few tables seated customers, none of which looked to be the owner of the motorcycle they'd seen. The bartender, now, he looked the part. Dark hair, wiry build, confident movements, and it seemed even the entrance of half a dozen badasses didn't make him nervous. With a casual motion, Watcher indicated the bar, and seated himself, watching in the mirror as his men took stations on either side of him. Watcher was their president, and they would protect him with their lives. The knowledge swelled in his chest, giving him a fierce, puffed-up pride to know the brotherhood they'd built was unbreakable.

Some brief banter with the bartender and a definite declaration of ownership of the bike out back finally brought them to a lull in the conversation. Asking for permission to be in their territory in a way-the-fuck roundabout way, the guy seemed laidback and without divulging they would soon be his boss, Watcher assured him the Soldiers wouldn't have a problem with him working and riding in their town.

Then, the moment the man's back was turned Watcher heard Spider mutter, "Fuck this shit. Ain't right." At those words, Watcher tensed, knowing they were about to have trouble. A minute later, he was proven right, Spider launching himself at the bartender. Between Watcher and Opie, with Devil's assistance, they disarmed Spider—at least of his drawn piece, the man was known to carry more than one. Watcher casually tucked the gun into the small of his back. Fingers wound tightly in Spider's shirt underneath his vest, he stared at the man behind the bar and grinned, feeling a trickle of anticipation curl through his gut when the guy didn't look tweaked.

"Looks like Spider *thought* he had a problem with that, but he was wrong," Watcher said, sitting back, dragging Spider away from the bar and seating the man's ass firmly on his own stool.

Spider snarled, "Ain't right and you know it, Watcher. We don't need a nomad gettin' in our business."

"Shut up, Spider." Opie's sighed, telling everyone he was running shorter than normal on patience with their brother today.

"You shut up, Opie. You know it too." Spider was still snarling, but Watcher had stopped paying attention to him. The bartender was rapidly cycling through shades of pale and looked like he might pass out. *Fucking hell, dude's just a kid*, he thought, seeing the expression he'd taken as age fell away, revealing itself to be bluster and maybe a bit of hard experience instead.

"You might want to sit down a minute, kid. You look a little green." As if Watcher's words cut the threads holding him up, he immediately flopped on top of a short cooler, moving away from where they were seated along the bar. The guy's next thoughts were telegraphed as loudly as if Watcher had a window into his head, as the kid shot a glance up under the bar to where Watcher already knew the resident shotgun hung from a rack. *Dammit, this could go any direction. If we get into a shootout here, we'll never clear the paperwork to buy this bar.* They needed it, needed to shore up the funds in the club more, wanted to be sure they could take care of their members because Watcher was about ready to launch a campaign to bolster their ranks. It was time, and he and Pops had both agreed to it during the officers' last church.

"Awww, naw, kid. Don't do that." Watcher clucked his tongue and gave his head a shake, only taking a breath when his words pulled the kid's attention back to him. Speaking to one of the members who had come with him today, he said, "Pops, grab that scatter gun, wouldja?" Weapon handled, now he needed to keep the kid upright so he could keep thinking straight. People who were threatened and got their heads crooked, could and did do anything. Running on instinct, still trying to control the situation, he said, "Devil, why doncha give your Jack to the kid."

Pops and Devil moved in unison, and Watcher stared in surprise when the kid didn't move, didn't even flinch as they neared him, coming from two directions. After a momentary stare down with Devil, the kid took the proffered shot glass and downed the drink, never breaking the glare he directed Devil's way. With a laugh, Devil scuffed his fingers through the hair on top of the kid's head, a gesture which could have been taken different ways, but Watcher knew from this man it was affectionate. Something you'd do to a little brother. Devil said, "He's a keeper, Watcher. Look at this fucker; he's not even sweating."

Before Watcher could respond, the bartender was on his feet trying to shrug the whole drama off, announcing last call as if they were regulars at the bar on his shift and shit like this happened every day. *SNAFU.* Watcher remembered Deke's assessment of more than one mission gone sideways and couldn't help it. His laughter spilled over, triggering his men's amusement, too. A pounding on his back from the side stopped abruptly, and he could only watch as, after they'd made it through to the other side of this shit, Spider still showed his ass and tried to take the kid down, diving across the bar from his stool.

Too old, or too slow, it didn't matter which factored because the kid deflected the attack and knocked Spider to the floor behind the bar. *Like with everything else we got goin' on, every time we take a step forwards, Spider's pulling us two back.* Pissed and powerless to stop the drama unfolding in front of him, Watcher eased his hand to the gun in his waistband. He was ready to respond, ready for the kid to take this where Watcher knew any of the men looking over the bar at their brother on the floor would take it, if the same happened to them. Blood, because they would defend their patch brother to the end, didn't matter if he was in the right or wrong, the club came first. Club. Family. Honor.

Watcher found himself surprised and relieved when the barkeep offered a one-sided grin, looking up and joking, "You dropped something, Watcher." *Jesus, no end to the surprises from the dude. Not a man, but not a boy, not for a long time.*

"Let the fucker up, kid," Watcher said slowly, staring hard into Spider's face to communicate his rage. *Coulda fucked everything.* "He's done." Spider blanched as he realized the insult he'd offered Watcher. Overstepping in a big way, and Spider knew the penalty for what he'd done. Knew he'd be due retribution for disobeying his president's orders. *Enough, time to let it go, for now,* Watcher thought, following with a spoken order. "Let's have one more round." He wanted to get to know this man better and cast about for an idea, grinning when he thought of a way to manage this and also give Spider a chance for reconciliation. "Let Spider serve, and you come sit. Got a name, kid?"

"Name's Andy, and I got this." The man introduced himself by a government name as he reached out to flip up the pass through for Spider, allowing him an easy return to the group, but Andy never gave them his back. No trust there, not anymore, and Watcher's anger at Spider swelled again when he realized Andy remained watchful and tense in order to approach and finish serving their orders. *Ballsy guy, carrying through with regular business after all the shit.*

Watcher caught Opie's eye, tipping his head towards Andy and communicating he'd like the man engaged again. They didn't have enough info on him yet. A new rider in their town wasn't something to worry about, but a skilled fighter who was cool under pressure working at the bar might be. With a nod, Opie said, "Well, that's a shit road name, Andy. We should call you Ice Man."

Great opening, Watcher thought, and seamlessly picked up the laughing banter. "Yeah, Ice Man, because you are cool under pressure. Pour yourself a shot, Ice Man. Drink with the Southern Soldiers before you close up." He flipped another bill to the bar, pointing to the whiskey bottle still standing nearby. It had taken a moment before Andy moved, and there was no grin on his face as he went through the motions to pour and toss back a drink, tapping the empty shot glass on the bar in front of Watcher in thanks. Placing the change back on the growing pile on the bar in front of Watcher, Andy pushed through to closing, and as Watcher and his men walked out the door twenty minutes later, the lock clicked into place behind them with finality.

"Devil, you and me gonna slide to the back, have a chat with Andy soon as he's off duty." Watcher pointed to Spider. "You, fucktard, are gonna get your ass back to the fuckin' clubhouse and stay there. I'll deal with you later." Without him having to assign them the duty, Pops and Opie bracketed the sullen Spider as they left. Watcher sighed. "Gonna have to deal with him," he told Devil, not taking his eyes off the rapidly dwindling figures of his men as they rode away. "Hate this fuckin' shit."

"'S why you got the patch, Prez. Because you'll deal, even hating it," Devil countered, kicking his bike's engine over, rolling the throttle, the ringing of his exhaust effectively ending their conversation. They moved their bikes and waited. Half an hour later, the back door of the bar opened, and Andy walked through, stopping in his tracks when he caught sight of them.

"Fuck me," Andy muttered under his breath, then did his best to ignore them while he readied his bike to ride. Before he started the Indian, he finally greeted them, demeanor as cool as the Ice Man Devil had dubbed him. Low, with no particular intonation, he simply said their names before he rode away, "Watcher, Devil."

Devil was grinning wide when Watcher heeled up his kickstand, pulling out behind Andy. Watcher let Andy take point, and he and Devil rode the left and right thirds of the lane as they trailed him to a diner up the street. Watcher chuckled to himself, he caught Andy's wide eyes in the mirrors a number of times as he nervously watched the Soldiers members ride behind him.

The three men sat in the diner parking lot for a minute, staring at each other. Watcher wanted to give Andy a chance to speak first, needing to see what his reaction would be. Something about this kid was intriguing, and he wanted to know the background which could develop this mix of self-confidence and nervous awareness. "Can I help you, gentlemen?" Andy finally asked, and Devil laughed at him.

"You gotta quit bein' so fucking funny, Ice Man." Andy tipped his head to one side, looking at Devil, plainly confused. "We ain't no fucking gentlemen. That's twice tonight you've made that joke."

Devil laughed again, and Watcher told the kid, "Just wanna have a chat, Ice Man. That's all. Public place is good for this." Without another word, he swung off his bike and stood, waiting, again giving Andy time to process and deal. He was pleased when hardly a moment later the kid dismounted, and followed him and Devil inside.

The waitress took one look at them and blinked in surprise. This wasn't a Soldiers hangout, but she'd heard of them, no doubt. "Anywhere's good, fellas." With a nod, Watcher took the corner booth, putting his back against the wall, sliding over so Devil could take a seat beside him. Spider's piece dug into the small of his back, and he grimaced.

"Coffee." Watcher quietly placed his order, then sat in silence, waiting for the other two to do the same, so the waitress could leave. Once she'd cleared earshot, he spoke. "Not here to give you grief, Ice Man. You aren't affiliated with anyone, owed me no notice when you rolled into town. That said, I admit I like to get to know folks on my piece of dirt, and wanna keep rollin' with you. So tell me, where does the Ice Man hail from?"

Andy snorted, then laughed. "Ice Man, really?"

Devil scoffed, then explained, "Dude, Spider is fucking nuts. The man is around the bend. Fuckin'. Nuts. You stared down one of the craziest nights we've seen from him in a while." Devil scoffed again. "Knocked him on his ass, then talked smack about him while you were holding him down. Knowing he'd been carryin' a heater, and havin' to know the rest of us was carryin', and still, you bullshitted and straight out dealt with his shit without hardly breakin' a sweat." He leaned back, angled towards the table. "You were chill as shit, dude. Doubt you'd like to be called Chilly Willy, but fuck man, ice water ain't any cooler than you were tonight." Devil leaned forwards, palm flat to the table. "Interesting to see a man like you behavin' like that. Not a big dude, not a hardass, and definitely not projecting badass, but delivering it just the same. All without blinking twice. Ice Man, definitely."

Watcher broke in, "Are you from around here?"

Andy shook his head, his expression guarded as he glanced between the two men. "Wyoming, originally. But I've been all over, working various jobs over the past while. Made it to Las Cruces recently, stopped in at the bar one night for a brew, saw a notice they were looking for a bartender." He shrugged. "Easy work, nice cash on a good night. I'm just..." He paused a minute, and Watcher got the sense he was searching for words. "...feeling my way through it, right now. Making enough money to send home and get me to the next town."

"What's back home in Wyoming?" A rolling stone. Not a surprise, a lot of men who adopted the life of a biker weren't big on being stuck in one place. They'd be wanting to be in the wind as often as possible, and working your way across the country was a good way to fund the itch. But saying he sent money home meant there was someone left behind.

"Baby brother, grandparents," Andy hesitated, then shrugged, hiding something. "That's it." Watcher decided to allow him the evasion, let him hold whatever secret lay in his past. For now.

The talk went back and forth across the table after that, the men sharing stories of riding and the road. Bonding over tales about people and the bullshit which always seemed to be washing around some folks. By the time they walked back outside to their bikes, Watcher had found even more of something he had liked in the kid, got a nod from Devil when he looked a question at him. Standing next to their bikes, he admired the Indian again, thinking to himself it looked a lot like one Mason had owned several years ago. "See you around, Ice Man," he said, sticking his arm out for a wrist grip.

In the clubhouse the next day, Devil and Opie approached Watcher, both partial to what they'd seen. Andy Jones, Ice Man, would be a member worth pursuing. Time to fill the ranks again, and he was a likely starting point.

***

"No, man, ain't going down that way," Watcher told Opie, his voice low and quiet. They were sitting around a bonfire in Watcher's backyard, this following a family barbecue for all members and possible recruits. Men who were hangarounds, not yet prospects, interested in what the life might offer them. Watcher's challenge was to figure out what they could offer to the club if the two paths intersected.

Juanita had taken Bella inside half an hour ago, but not before Watcher had gotten a tight hug from his little girl. He and his officers had gathered on the stumps and stools to one side of the fire, pulling in close, talking over a threat they'd heard about only that afternoon.

Machos continued to be a thorn in the Southern Soldiers' side, a pain seesawing from irritating to dangerous as their influence and strength in the region wavered dramatically over the past couple of years. Multiple sources told the tale of the Machos club suffering through bout after bout of internal discord. Not surprising since they remained tied tightly to the cartel, the only surprising thing was Estavez endured.

Watcher had a special hatred for the man.

Estavez was a distant cousin for Juanita, but private connections didn't matter to him. Not only had he known about her kidnapping, but the bastard had actively encouraged her captors to parade her out at one point, making sure all customers knew she was family. Saw how little he cared for her safety. His behavior, as well as the brand on her neck, ruled out any possible return to her home village after the rescue.

Not that Watcher would have let her go anywhere.

From the beginning of them, he'd seen with great clarity what he wanted. It wouldn't be enough to merely have Juanita in his bed, he wanted to tie her to him. The pregnancy had been the first catalyst to getting him off his ass and taking care of that detail. Then Daena had died, and things in his life shifted to fast forward, night terrors of losing her spring-boarding him into action.

So, only months after Darrie died, after rescuing her from underneath a cartel whorehouse, he had taken Juanita to Vegas, and with a fake ID, married her. Remembering the emotions swelling inside him when he slid the ring onto her finger there in the little chapel still made him choke up. A week after they found out for sure about Bella, and at that moment, looking at the plus sign on the plastic stick, he knew his life would be complete. Family built on a firm foundation, both of them knowing fate had a hand in bringing them together. The cost of their joined lives had been his brother, but fate turned a kindly eye towards the couple, filling their lives with a richness Watcher vowed to never take for granted.

Now, talking to Opie and Devil, he came to a decision. The Machos had been behind some cargo hijackings in recent months, and today Soldiers received word another large shipment of product had gone missing. Large, as in *large*. And this delivery was needed so they could turn the weapons into cash, and then invest that profit into the mission they supported. The supplier claimed no responsibility, and the courier wasn't talking. Couldn't talk, having been found facedown in a ditch off a backroad running out of El Paso.

If they could find out with certainty the "who," then Watcher would call the shot, and the Soldiers would move. He couldn't allow things like this to stand, or risk the cartel capitalizing on what they would see as a weakness. Time to start things moving.

"Devil, you're gonna call Estavez. Set a meet soon as you can, brother." The only way to know for certain if the bastard had his club involved was to take Estavez' measure, face-to-face. Once the order was issued, in Watcher's mind it was done, and with the topic put to bed, he moved to what he hoped would be a better one. "What'd y'all think about Ice Man?"

Andy had come to their party, and his behavior had been interesting enough for more than one member to note. Instead of hanging on the edges of conversations, hoping to be seen while he sucked back free beer, he had pitched in and worked whatever was needed from the start. And he hadn't kept his distance from the families at the party. Not Ice Man. Watcher had looked on in amazement as he wasted no time making fast friends with kids and old ladies. Pops had come over and dug his elbow into Watcher's ribs with a grin at one point, saying, "Lookit that shit." When he'd glanced over, Watcher had seen Andy turning his hand to being a playground for Pops' grandsons, the two boys hanging from Andy's outstretched arms with wide grins. One of the boy's feet firmly planted on the man's ribs as the kid dug in and shoved, swinging through the air while Andy laughed. This kind of behavior seemed the norm for the guy, and Watcher understood the family-starved emotions driving him.

Devil started it with a quick and loud, "You know where I stand. If Ice Man will patch in, he can be my prospect."

"Oh fuck, no." This was from Pops. "Mine. You ain't gonna ruin the man."

"Jesus, old man, you even gonna fuckin' be around long enough to teach the guy all the what-not-tos?" Opie pitched his hat into the ring. "I got this one. Ice Man's mine." Shaking his head, Opie turned to Devil, "Brother, you got two already. Take care of what you got before you try'n add to the pile."

Two additional members who hadn't met Andy at the bar piped in with their positive observations from the night's party. Scanning the faces around the circle, Watcher nodded to himself. He opened his mouth to say something when Spider interrupted, his approving tone at odds with his words. "He's a kid."

"So was I," Opie spoke up, irritation with their brother evident in his tone. "You were a dick to him, not once, but twice, in the man's place of business, him not trying to do anything other than serve you a fuckin' beer. He held his—"

"Not what I meant. Peace, brother." Spider's words were quietly intense, lines on his face strained. "You misunderstand, and I get I was havin' a shit day. I get it; I know it, you fuckin' know it. You don't gotta throw my shit in my face every fuckin' time I turn around. You're fuckin' worse than a ball 'n' chain, swear to fuckin' God." Spider shook his head, looking away from Opie, whose face looked like he'd gladly put his brother six feet under. "He's a kid. My ma had a sayin'. Now, granted she mostly said it about her boy toys, but I think it can apply here. 'Catch 'em young, train 'em right.' That's what I mean. He's young enough for us to show him what a club can be, have him become a brother, and stay a brother."

The statement stung. Nearly more than having Estavez crawling up his ass, Watcher hated what the war with the Machos had done to the makeup of the Soldiers membership. *I understand it's best to know the kind of balls a man has before things get hot,* he thought, *but still.* Every member they lost, every patch voluntarily dropped into a sponsor's hands meant loss. Lost time, working with and teaching through the prospect period onwards. Even worse was the lost knowledge when the member leaving was of longer term. Losses in the ranks were hard enough to take, and Watcher thanked God all his officers were lifers, because he didn't know what he'd do if one of his inner circle hiked out.

"Not a dig, Prez," Spider said, his response telling Watcher he had visibly reacted. "Fuck no. We all know every goddamned reason given over the past couple of years were bullshit." They weren't all, but he knew what Spider was getting at and nodded. Several of the defections had been because Watcher held the line on trafficking. Not every man knew the full breadth of Juanita's story, and he damned well didn't want them to, but he couldn't...wouldn't allow his Soldiers to be part of guarding flesh property or escorting groups of illegals brought into the country for any reason. But, especially not with the expectation they'd be making their living on their backs. So he carved the rule in stone without explanation and refused to back down. This meant some men saw the cash walking through the desert as enough of a reason to leave the club.

"I know. And you're right. Want and fear has weeded out the men who didn't understand what it meant to wear a Soldiers patch on their back." Watcher looked around the circle, nodding slowly. "What we have here though? Trust and love and respect. Each of us"—he shot a glance at Spider—"even when we're bein' dicks, have our brothers' backs. This"—he swept his arms out to the sides, looking at each man in turn—"is our brotherhood." Pointing to Pops, he said, "Old guard, Pops is an original in a lotta ways, and we respect it. All of it. We turn to him for wisdom." He paused a breath and smirked. "Even me. And that makes us stronger than 90 percent of the clubs who call themselves one-percenters." Jabbing a stiffened finger at the diamond sewn to the front of his vest, he said, "We are Southern Soldiers, we are proud one-percenters, and we are the strongest motherfuckers around."

A chorus of "hell yeah" and "fucking right" came from all sides and he grinned. "Don't mean we don't want the kid. I'd sure like to see Ice Man take up a place on our line. So if you think you can influence him"—he glanced at Opie—"then you should. Now, we're about to get into business in Mexico. Because sittin' here, I've come to a decision." Pushing to his feet, he watched the wave of stillness settle over his men. They were all staring up at him, waiting. "Keep it close. Need to know only." He took a breath because once done, this wasn't something he could retreat from. "Two days. Estavez has two days. My brothers, Sunday we cross the bridge."

***

"*Papi.*" Her voice rich and ragged, Juanita called out to him as he thrust deep, the heat and slide of flesh pulling a groan from him. He watched as her neck arched back, pushing her head into the pillow and she cried out again, this time wordless and vibrating with pleasure. Urgency pulled at him, but he kept the pace slow, bottoming out and grinding in with each stroke, stretching time for her. She reached up, threading her fingers through his hair and holding his head steady, staring into his eyes as she came.

In minutes, he followed her over the mountain, feeling the familiar electricity shooting up his spine as every muscle in his body stiffened. *"Mine,"* he ground out the word, ass clenching and driving him deep, deeper. Watcher and his brothers had talked far into the night, feeding the bonfire and drinking, telling stories to shouted laughter. It was hours before he followed her inside, waking her as he crawled at last into their bed, and she had eagerly met every caress.

"God, baby," he muttered into her neck, slipping his arms underneath her shoulders and holding her tightly. "Love you so much." He stayed planted, feeling the final pulsing of his orgasm leaving him, loving how Juanita quivered underneath him, coming down from her own mountain, sliding back into her body. A breath later, he realized the quivering wasn't her recovering from making love, but tears. "Hey, hey. Honey, are you okay?" He pushed up, trying to get a look at her but she avoided his gaze, shoving her face against his chest. "'Nita." He gave her a squeeze. "What is it, honey?"

She gave a hiccupping sob which had him on the move, slipping out of her body and to the side, gathering her into his arms. Turning to his back, he arranged her against him, head on his shoulder, giving her room to hide her face if she wanted. "Honey, tell me what's wrong." A head shake, not surprising, but frustrating all the same. "Juanita, I love you. Honey." Crooning in her ear, he stroked her back, slowly, hand moving up and down soothingly. "Take your time."

Moments passed, and Watcher kept stroking. Not pushing her, treating himself to the softness of her skin, over and over. Silent but for her occasional sob, the longer he held her, the more her muscles relaxed, letting her sag against him. He took her weight willingly, hoping she knew after all this time he'd take anything for her, from her. They didn't talk about it, but he'd thought she was long past the shit from Mexico, so maybe this was something else. Finally, she moved slightly,

171

rolling her head so she could press her lips to his chest, those actions releasing his voice again. "Honey, tell me."

Low and slow came the words. "One day you will want more." So softly he nearly missed the sound, she whispered, *"Te amo, mi corazón."*

I was wrong. This was Mexico. Watcher tightened his arms around her. "God, I wish I could make you believe, honey." No longer a constant companion, but when her fear reared its ugly head in the past, it still brutalized her. *Hate seeing her like this.* "Wish you could see what I see." He had a thought, and rolled, taking her with him to the edge of the bed. Standing, he scooped her up and carried her in his arms to the mirror on the front of the bathroom door. Chin to the top of her head, he stood with eyes closed for a minute, breathing her in, immersing himself in the woman he loved. Shampoo, citrus, a hint of musk from the sex. "Everything I want, right here in my arms. Look at you, honey." Lifting his head, he did as he told her to do, staring at their forms in the dim light.

"My life, my love." Dipping his chin, Watcher brushed his lips against her temple. *This is so damned important. I have to get it right. Every time, do it until I'm old and gray, glad for the chance to tell her.* "Look, Juanita. Look at us." *I love you, honey. Believe me, baby.* "Look at how we fit. Look at this, honey. Just look." The intensity in his voice brought her head up, and he caught her gaze in the mirror. "Don't look at me, baby. Just look." He shifted, letting her legs drift down, feet to the floor in front of him. Wrapping his arms around her, he bent over her shoulder, lips to her cheek. Whispering, he told her again, "Look at us."

Minutes ticked by as they stood there. Minutes where Watcher wasn't sure what the outcome would be. Juanita's doubts weren't rational and in the bright light of day, she knew it, but the demons she still bore had dug in deep. He worked every day to help peel back the layers of her uncertainty, to give her a safe place to feel any emotion and push past it. Another minute slid by before she relaxed minutely in his arms. Lips to the side of her head, he pressed a kiss to her skin. "*God*, I love you, Juanita. You are *everything* I need. You are all I need. I got everything I wanted, and then you gave me more. Gave me Bella. Made my world even richer. You will always be what I need." Another squeeze, and she sighed.

"Watcher." When she said his name, he turned her and crooked a finger under her chin, lifting her lips to meet his in a soft, slow, deep kiss. She leaned her forehead against his chest, murmuring, "I see. Thank you." Arms around his neck, she gave a hop when he lifted, wrapping her legs around his waist. "I see. *Mi amor*."

Back to their bed, he settled her next to him again. "Tell me what you saw, honey."

Her arm across his stomach tightened, and she lifted her chin to look up into his face. "Love." Her voice was hesitant, soft, and he waited, knowing she had more to say. "But you…we wanted more babies." It caught at his chest, a fishhook stuck deep, pulling free but leaving damage behind which could fester. He couldn't deny her statement; it was true. Both had wanted more children, especially after holding a sweet baby Bella. "I cannot give you that."

"Not your fault, honey." He cradled her head to his chest, letting the pain sweep through him. Estavez had stolen so much from Juanita. *Motherfucker needs to pay. And pay. And pay.* "We're blessed. *I'm* blessed. You and Bella in my life? Definitely blessed."

After Isabella had been born, they both wanted more, as fast as they could manage. Two years later, after having no luck, Watcher had gone to the doc, sure the fault lay with him, hoping a new wardrobe selection would free things. Two months after that, he took Juanita to a doctor where they found an infection suffered while enslaved made their Bella a miracle indeed. The doc didn't rule out another pregnancy because they'd proven they could beat the odds, even if they weren't known odds at the time. But he didn't offer them much hope.

"Can we be enough, Watcher?" Gentle and quiet, her question rose from the darkness, and he knew this was her deepest fear. That he would find her wanting, withdrawing his love and turning away from what she might forever see as damaged goods.

"You already are, honey." Lips to the top of her head, he pressed a soft kiss in her hair. "I can't imagine life without you. You and our Bella, and my brothers to have my back. Everything I need, honey. Always gonna be the same answer. You can ask the question a thousand different ways, and the answer won't change. Every day, you give me everything I need."

What's in your heart

Rolling to his feet in a smooth motion, Watcher crouched in place, taking shelter behind the rusting hulk of a car as he scanned the street. Echoes of gunfire still rolled through the air as he swept his gaze left, then right. Evaluating the scene, he took in the condition and position of each of his men and saw the tail end of a convertible as it carried the gunman away. Two down, Diamond and Opie, but both were moving in the dirt. Andy was down, too, a wide streak of dark discoloring his jeans. Watcher heard footsteps pounding away, retreating up a nearby track between the ramshackle houses. He studied the street again. No visible threat.

Knowing his Soldiers would have his back, he stood upright and stalked back into the hovel behind him. It was the residence of one sick fuck bastard who would know whose finger had been on the trigger today, and who would also know two additional things. Important things. One, where the money was for their missing shipment. Two—and this was arguably the most critical information, especially after this action in the street—where Watcher would find Estavez.

Groaning, the fat man in the room lay on his side; arms, legs, and chest strapped tightly to a wooden chair, toppled to the floor during his questioning. His face was bloody, already swelling, and mixed in the blood on the floor were portions of two teeth. "Motherfucker's gonna talk now." Watcher heard and turned to see Devil had come inside with him. Reaching down, Watcher gripped the arms of the chair and wrenched at it, rage helping him right the furniture with the mass of the man still attached. Once all four legs were back on the floor, he pulled his fist back, surprised when a hand on his elbow stayed the strike. Devil pushed his face close and hissed, "My turn."

Ten minutes later the man was back on the ground, this time not moving. Still breathing, but staying that way was definitely not a long-term thing. "Nothing," Devil gritted the word, pulling back his foot and launching a hard kick at the fat man, burying half his boot into the soft, flabby stomach. "Fat man didn't sing, boss." Unexpected motion from across the room caught Watcher's attention, and he was already headed in that direction when he saw Andy on his way inside.

"Watcher, got a dude hit out here," Andy called, and Watcher made a decision. Up to now, he hadn't been thinking of Andy as a brother, more of a potential acquisition, looking for a place where the guy would fit in the club. After today though, a day where Andy had willingly come along on what Watcher had been clear was expected to be a rough run, and then stood shoulder-to-shoulder with them facing fire? After he took a bullet for the club? Watcher owed him respect and would give it, endorsing the man in even unspoken ways.

"Saw you patching him up, Ice Man, thanks," Watcher said without stopping, continuing to stalk across the room. He saw the movement again, a small form darting backwards, but there was no escape from discovery. He reached through a doorway. *Woman?* He wondered at the slightness of the figure, and then feeling how thin the arm was, revised his estimate down to child. Then Watcher rewrote his thoughts again as he pulled her into the light, seeing a brand on her collarbone which turned his stomach. *Slave.*

She reached up to adjust her shirt, pulling and tugging it to try and hide her shame. *Oh darlin'*, Watcher thought, *we'll get you out of here.* In a whisper, her voice jagged with fear and pain, she begged, "*No me hagas. Por favor, señor. Por favor. El me va a matar. Por favor no. El lo hara. Por favor.*" She gestured to the man on the floor, breaths bubbling out through the blood in his mouth. "*Mi tío me dio a este hombre. Mi dueño.*" Her hand gripped his wrist with a fierce strength belying her frail stature, words pleading, "*Por favor. Por favor, señor.*"

With those words, he knew who she was, and it turned his stomach more. Estavez a blood relative, showing his stripes once again as he had with Juanita, family no barrier to his cruelty and greed. "*Donde está tu tío?*" Andy made a noise, and Watcher turned to see a shocked question on his face. The age of the girl and the circumstances in which they found her would be hard for the kid to witness, if he even understood what he was seeing. "Her uncle is the President of the Machos. He'll want her back. I need to know how to get in contact with him."

A fierce emotion swept across Andy's face, and the doubt Watcher read there pissed him off. No way he'd be sharing Juanita's story here. Maybe not ever with this dude, but for certain not while a girl in the same situation who may or may not speak English was listening. *Fuck him*, Watcher thought, *he doesn't know the road I've ridden.* Aloud, he growled, "Unharmed, I'm not a fucking monster." He glanced away, not wanting to see any more evidence Andy didn't trust him. The dark blood still wetting the fabric of Andy's jeans reminded Watcher he'd taken a bullet for the Soldiers today. Forcing respect into his tone, Watcher asked, "You okay, man? Looks like you were hit too."

Eyes still on the girl, Andy muttered, "Yeah, through and through, muscle only. It'll hurt like a bitch tomorrow." Evaluating the wound with a long look, from his experience Watcher knew Andy had it right. He'd used a bandana to tie off some of the blood flow, giving the wound time to form a clot. *Need to remind him to take the tourniquet off in a few*, Watcher thought, turning back to the girl as she spoke, "I speak English."

Thank you, Jesus. Her speaking English so well would make his life a hell of a lot easier. *And I could use a dose of easy*. "Thank fuck," he said. "I need to talk to your uncle, little one. We have some shit to get straight before I can leave."

The girl-child, because she wasn't a woman, no matter what had been done to her body, nodded and brought out a phone. She dialed and got out one word, *"Tio?"* before Watcher took the phone away. He was out the back door and away before he trusted himself to speak, putting as much distance between the girl-child and this conversation as possible.

Instead of questions, silence was all he got when he lifted the phone to his ear. Estavez probably had already heard about the street showdown and shootout and been expecting this call. "Your man was loyal."

"Give a man enough reasons and his loyalty will not waver." Estavez' voice was oily, twisting into Watcher's head, mixing with Juanita's stories about her cousin. "I gave him...just enough."

Rage washed over Watcher and in an instant, he knew the fate of this girl was in his hands. Her entire future, his to mold. His role as profound as the one he played in Juanita's life, from her first glance upwards out of the mud and muck and into his face. "Man's dead." He played his hand, not caring any longer about the response. Testing one last time, to see if Estavez was redeemable, he asked, "Your niece? What should I do with her?"

"Matters not to me. Fuck her if you want. Kill her if you don't. But, please, don't leave me a mess, yes?" Estavez' tone never wavered, his indifference regarding her continued existence not an act. He really didn't care about the girl. Sounding like he was musing over what to have on a menu, Estavez said, "If you do not kill Maria Luisa Carmela, I could find a use for her still." His tone changed, becoming brusque when he changed course, telling Watcher, "No, you should kill her. It would not be worth the effort to collect her. You killed my man, go ahead and take care of Maria. To save time, if needed, they can be buried together." Unable to speak, Watcher listened as Estavez continued, "Tell me if you will, how fares my lovely cousin? Is my Juanita well?"

With shaking hands, Watcher brought the phone down, resisting the urge to throw it to the ground, grind it to bits underfoot. *Motherfucker doesn't know what he bought with his play.* Disconnecting the call, he stood still as a statue for a minute, then two. Breathing deeply, sucking in breath after breath, he tried to pull his rage back under control. *Motherfucker,* circled around in his head, thoughts tangling, superimposing Juanita's face on the girl's. His Bella's face. *Gotta get the girl safe.* A noise had him turning and crouching in instinctive response, only straightening when he saw Devil exiting the structure. One look at his face must have told volumes because Devil growled low in his throat.

"Fucker's gotta die, Dev." There was a growing rumble from the side of the building, and one of his Soldiers appeared, driving a car. Watcher had a thought on how to deal with disposal, and got a nod in response to his question, "Car belong to the asshole?" He sucked in a breath before turning back to Devil. "Carmela"—instinctively he renamed the girl, afraid she would have bad associations with strange men using her given name—"comes with us," he continued, reading the lifted chin Devil had in reaction. "Brother, I can't leave her behind. Not like this." He pointed to the building behind him. "Her owner's dead, so what's she got here? Nothing waiting for her at home, either. We all know that's true from everything we've learned. Her family probably won't take her back, and in any case, her family is who dealt her this life. We bring her back with us, we buy her better. No matter what, it's gotta be better than what she's had." Watcher shook his head, thinking about the church they'd teamed up with to shelter rescues. "The mission gives her better odds."

Without waiting for a response, he turned and went back inside. It startled him to see Carmela had evidently bonded with Andy and was clinging to his side. She cringed in genuine fear whenever she looked at any of the other men, but trusted the kid. Quietly, Watcher issued orders to deal with the dead man and then approached Andy and the girl slowly. Wouldn't do to spook her now, not with the sick look on Andy's face which said she'd evidently shared some of what Watcher knew she had to have lived through.

He'd need to give her the illusion of choice, to gain her cooperation to get her across the river. "Little one, where do you go?" He squatted as he would with Bella, resting one knee on the floor, grounding himself and making it so she knew he couldn't move fast if she decided to evade. Giving her the power in their conversation.

Andy's hands rested lightly on her shoulders, and Carmela leaned back, letting him take her weight, using that connection to anchor herself before she answered. Softly, her voice quavering on the cusp of losing control, she said, "I have nowhere, *señor*." Her dark brown eyes swam with tears, but she bravely held his gaze. Steady. Waiting. Having been taught life wasn't fair by the same people who were supposed to protect you. *Like Juanita and Bethy*, he thought. *Like Tabby*.

Never again. Not for this one.

"Devil, I want you to put her on your bike, nice-like." Watcher held her gaze, willing her to trust him. Trust him and by extension trust these rough men who surrounded her. Trust them to be kinder, gentler, more human than the filth to which she'd been given. After a long minute, she twisted her torso, staring up at Andy who nodded. Without looking away, holding Andy's gaze, she reached out one trembling hand, and Watcher saw it swallowed up by Devil's gentle grip.

Andy then took away any ease Watcher had by showing *he* didn't have faith in them, not really. Not yet. "I promised her safety, Watch. Don't make me sorry I trusted you."

Do I give him this? Do I hand him the knowledge of what was done to her? What was done to my Juanita? Watcher gave it a minute, then stopped Andy when it looked like he was about to speak, deciding to ride the middle road, giving him a little honesty, but not more than he could handle. "It's not like that, fucker." Watcher shook his head, willing the man to understand. "Her uncle told me to bury her with her *patrón*, Ice Man. I can't do that. We'll get her safe, hear me?"

Without giving Andy time to respond, he walked out, yelling directions and instructions to his men. *My men*, he thought proudly. *My brother's legacy. Andy needs to understand how we are. Needs to believe in us. The club. Family. Kids and family, they're why we do it all. So fuckin' important he understands what it all means. Honor.* "Diamond," Watcher called, "you good, brother?" This started the process of cleanup and staging to roll. Between him and Opie, they sorted the men, waiting for the ones who had driven off to return, Watcher knowing whatever gully or ravine they found would serve here. Once everything was settled, it only left Andy to deal with, and Watcher found he'd grown impatient. Unwilling to wait any longer, he needed to know where the man stood. Andy's injury gave him an in, so Watcher walked over to where he sat on his Indian. "Are you sure you're okay to ride, Ice Man?"

"Yeah, it's good. I got this," Andy responded. Watcher nodded, looked down at his bloody left leg, and laughed at the lie. No way would the leg support him to stand and start the bike. Watcher kicked the Indian to life and gave him a chin lift. "You did good with Diamond, thanks." Watcher raised his fist to meet Andy's in a bump, then turned and mounted his own bike. A whirl of his finger in the air and they were off, headed home. *To Juanita*, he thought, *and my Bella*. Glancing in his rearview mirror, he saw Devil in line behind him, tiny Carmela wrapped around his torso, seated on the gas tank. *With our Mela.*

*** *** ***

"Papa," Bella called across the yard. Even without looking Watcher knew her shadow would be with her. Mela still hadn't opened up to any of them, but it had been only a couple of weeks. Not surprising she'd be keeping her own counsel, still. For the first few days, her smiles had been a rare commodity, but recently she'd loosened up, and every grin fed his joy. Each time he witnessed proof of her healing, he thanked God he'd brought her home. Straightening from where he had been crouched down next to his bike, Watcher wiped his hands on a rag, smiling as he saw the girls running pell-mell across the lawn towards him.

"Slow down," he called, warning Bella, but his princess didn't listen, running into his legs full force. He reached down, cupping the back of her head, keeping her from a rebound tumble as Mela rocked to a stop nearby, her approach significantly more sedate and controlled. "What are my girls doing?" In discussing how best to help Mela through what had happened to her, he and Juanita had decided to treat her as their own, including her in everything like family.

Bella's eyes turned up to him, love shining strongly from her tiny face and he basked in it for a moment before turning to Mela, thrilled to see a wary trust in her gaze. "Gone help joo." Bella's mouth curved, and he smiled in response at her gap-toothed grin. Her first bottom tooth had come out two weeks ago, its partner hanging on by only the narrowest of margins.

Growing up, he thought with an inward wince. *Dances and prom and learning to drive will be next.* Pushing those thoughts aside, he asked, "What are you helping me with?"

"You bike, siwwy." Bella's lisp was ridiculously cute, and he couldn't help himself, he bent over and picked her up, cuddling her close for a moment, her impossibly long legs wrapping around his waist.

Glancing back at Mela, he tipped his head to one side. "Do I get two helpers?" She nodded solemnly. *So old.* Age rested there in her eyes, in her distrust of everyone around her except Bella. Bella she had adopted immediately, and it wasn't uncommon for him or Juanita to find the girls sharing a bed, a bath, and on one hilarious day, one of his shirts. Both their heads had poked from the neck hole, each girl had an arm extended through a sleeve as they'd jumped out from behind the couch, shouting in unison, "Ta-dah!"

"Right. Bella—" He bent over, setting her feet back on the ground. "—I need a wrench from the blue toolbox. The wrench I need's got a green handle. Can you get it for me?" She nodded and turned, racing off on the errand he'd made up on the spot. Mela's head turned to watch her go, then she looked back up at him. Waiting. Wanting her own task. "I need a rag holder, too. Can you do that for me?" He extended the greasy rag, half expecting her to screech and pull back, but she simply took it from him, holding it without breaking their stare. "I'm adjusting my chain. Means I gotta sit on the ground." She was right beside the bike, nearly exactly where he needed to be, and he needed her to move, trying to find a way of sitting down without scaring her by getting too close.

From the first night, she'd watched his easy affection with Bella, but hadn't initiated anything with either him or Juanita yet. He still hoped it would come, but for now, he'd settle with just not frightening her. She nodded and took a step to the side, then surprised him by folding her legs to sit down. Patting the ground next to her. A clear invitation, he accepted and knelt, then sat. Tools still on the rag underneath the bike where he'd laid them when he first heard the girls, he picked up what he needed, and started to work.

A minute passed, and then, "Papa Watcher?" Mela's voice was soft, her interrogatory tone was unexpected, and his heart caught, jolting in his chest.

He didn't turn to look and tried hard to ignore the thrill he got from her name for him, one he hadn't heard before, steadying his voice so he could answer. "Yeah, my Mela?" He leaned back, elbow to the ground so he could reach up to poke at nothing with the wrench in his hand. He wanted to look busy, giving him a chance to focus on her without seeming to do so.

"Am I here forever?" She took in a sighing breath, and he forced himself to stay as he was. "Will you make me leave?" Another heavy breath in with a controlled exhale. "I'm happy." This last was said in a whisper, almost like a guilty confession, as if she didn't believe herself worth happiness.

"Mela, you're tearin' my heart out, honey." Without moving, he spoke, staring at the bike. "You deserve happy, honey. Deserve to be a kid. You can be my kid, if you want. Stay here forever." She made a noise, and he looked back to see her focused on his hands. Clenched tightly around the tools, they were discolored from the chain lube he'd been working in, stained by the work he'd done, but they'd wash clean, if he used the right kind of cleanser. "Look at my hands, Mela. See how dirty they are?" She nodded, and he dropped the tools, letting them clatter to the ground. "Hand me the rag, honey," he held out his hand. "Watch me." She did, and as he wiped his hands, she remained focused. Each stroke of the rag took a layer of dirt and grease away. Each pass left his hands cleaner. "Nothing is so bad it can't be wiped away. You let Juanita and me, we'll help you clean everything away, honey. Everything, until you're new again." *Not a lie*, he promised himself, *we'll get her there.*

"Papa, there's no gween wench." Bella flung herself on the grass next to the driveway. "I'm tired." She laid back, staring up into the sky. "Stayin' here forevah." Her words unconsciously mimicked the just-interrupted conversation, and he glanced to see a grin cross Mela's face right before she settled herself on the ground next to her friend.

"Me, too." Mela laughed, for the first time sounding like the child she was and he marveled at the way she so easily moved from a tough discussion to being silly with her best friend. Only six years separated the two girls in age, and his mind shied away from traveling down a path where he imagined his Bella in the same situation. Instead, he chose to drop to the ground next to his daughter, closing his eyes so he could listen to the beautiful music of children's laughter ringing through the air.

"I'm a fish," Bella declared, and he turned his head, smiling as he watched her sucking in her cheeks, trying to make fish lips, failing due to the gap in her bottom teeth. Mela hooked her thumbs together, folding her hands and then inverting them so they formed fish fins underneath her chin.

"Glub, glub." Mela sucked air as she tried to talk through pursed lips, laughing through it all. "I'm a fish, too." Grinning wide, she waggled her fingers. "Fishy, fishy."

"My favorite kinda fish," he laughed. "Tickle fish!" Fingers to Bella's sides, he started his campaign, falling to his back again when Mela came to Bella's defense. Moments later, both girls descended on him, fingers at the ready, drawing peal after peal of laughter from them all.

***

"Hand me the sugar, bebe." Juanita was trying to be quiet and knowing the effort she would put into it made Watcher grin. She knew better. Should know, anyway. Quiet would wake him every time. He could sleep through a mine detonating, but you let someone whisper, and he'd be upright and alert in an instant.

He stretched and sighed. It was Sunday, and from the slant of the sunshine coming through the blinds on the front windows of the house, it was late in the afternoon. After lunch he'd sat to watch the game for a minute, ankles propped and crossed on one arm of the couch, head to the other end, and he'd apparently fallen asleep.

Juanita would be in the kitchen rustling up supper. At least one and maybe both girls with her. A month since they'd brought Mela home, and she had finally been settling. Until yesterday, when Andy, who she'd begun calling *Tío*, had come out to say good-bye. A rolling stone to the bone. Devil had called it during church a week ago, said he'd seen signs in their friend that he would soon be moving on. Not destined to be a Soldier, after all.

From the time they returned from Old Mexico, Mela had locked onto Andy every time he was near, the bond created between the two seemingly unbreakable. Watcher had seen her chin quiver when Andy had sat her down to talk. Then she'd collected herself, bringing out the serene composure Watcher hated to see, that of a woman when she was still only a child.

A camera shutter clicked a dozen times, and he knew Mela was capturing another moment on film. She'd found an old 35mm camera in a box, and always kept it near to hand. She'd have him at the pharmacy every day developing rolls if she could, excited to see every image, discovering beauty in even the blurry ones. Making memories for herself, and he loved seeing her find something she could enjoy.

"Mama 'Nita, do you think my family misses me?" Watcher's breath clogged in his throat at the question. *God, what can Juanita say to that?* He didn't know how he would respond, and he wasn't a woman tortured and abandoned by her family, much less a child.

"Bebe, look in your heart. What does it say?" A chair scraped across the floor, then a thump as something heavy was placed on the counter. "When you think of your mama and papá, what do you hear in your heart?"

Thin and weak, Watcher still heard the response. "They do." Voice soft and quiet, Mela asked, "Could I call my papá sometime?"

Watcher and Juanita had discussed this. Multiple times. At length. They disagreed in a way which meant they'd never see the same side. He was in favor of looking for the girl's family, knowing in his soul he wouldn't rest if his Bella were missing. Wouldn't rest until she was back with him, whole or not. Juanita felt differently, and her strong reservations and objections were what had swayed him, ultimately. She believed the girl's family was better off believing her to be dead than find out what had happened.

Surprising him, Juanita didn't respond negatively. Instead, she asked a question, "You think your papá can see what's in your heart?" A pause, then Juanita continued carefully, "Instead of what's on your skin?" Another thing they disagreed about, and on this one he felt more vehemently against leaving things as they were. If he had his way, Juanita's brand would be history, taken away by a surgeon's knife, leaving her skin blemish free. She'd told him, carefully, but repeatedly, what was on her skin didn't matter, the surgeon couldn't excise her memories. They'd had a first consultation, and the doc said Mela would be a good candidate for removal of her brand.

Voice soft and quiet, Mela answered, "Mama 'Nita, Papá is a good man. He would...not..." A frustrated noise, then a burst of Spanish followed by Juanita's admonishing, "English, bebe." Bella would be bilingual because she'd been raised from birth in a home where language usage flowed smoothly back and forth. Mela had to work harder with English, so Juanita wanted her focusing on the foreign language until she was thinking in it, and no longer translating in her head. "Papá would want to know. Papa Watcher is like him, and Papa Watcher would want to know. I know, Mama 'Nita. I *know*."

"Then we'll call your papá, when Watcher wakes up." Juanita sounded calm, but Watcher knew it had to be a struggle for her to hold her composure. If Mela's family wanted her back, he and Juanita would lose their little girl. It would be a blow, because Mela had folded into their family and they both loved her. Not only that, but he knew Juanita would forever wonder if she'd done right by turning her back on her own family.

"I go see Papa's wake." That was his Bella, and her light footsteps raced towards him through the house. Closing his eyes, he rolled his head towards the back of the couch, feigning sleep. In a not-so-sneaky tiptoe, she approached the sofa, then called back towards the kitchen, voice far louder than she intended. "Nope, still seep—" Her words cut off in a squeal as he rolled and grabbed her, tossing her into the air and catching her, then bringing her down for a quick kiss to the tip of her nose. "Papa's wake, Mama!"

***

Watcher twitched the curtain back from the office window in the barn, phone to his ear, watching as his two girls played in the pool. Double ringing in his ear, signaling an international call, then a connection, and a woman's voice, *"Hola."* His Spanish wasn't up to the job of wading through staff to get to the man, but he suspected the information found out by Mason's boys about who Carmela's father was would mean they had multilingual staff.

"Hello, is Mr. Estavez available?" He paused, then when there was no response, reverted to a secondary position. *"Hablas Ingles?"*

"Si, un momento, por favor." Silence on the line, and then a heavily accented male voice spoke.

"Hello."

Watcher took a breath, all his patient scripting having flown from his head. He'd gone over what this conversation would be dozens of times, wanted to do it fast but thoughtfully, so as to cause the least pain. Unless this man was in cahoots with his brother, and the word was he was not, what Watcher had to say would be torture.

"Hello? *Hola?*"

"Mr. Estavez? Raul Estavez?" Best to make sure of which brother, because he wanted Raul, not Carlos. Carlos was the man he'd spoken to on Carmela's phone, the man who had earned a lifelong enmity with his words.

"*Si*. What do you want?" *Interesting*. Not conversational, this question seemed wary, like demands were expected.

"You have a daughter. Maria Luisa Carmela."

The threat, when it came, was quiet, but vibrating with hatred. "If you harm one hair on my daughter's head, I will kill you." *Shiiiiit*. This did not sound like a father who was down with what his brother did.

"No, man. No. Fuck no. It's not like that. I...my men, we rescued her. About a month ago. Today, she gave me your name and number. I called to—"

A shout and then the sound of something falling, crashing in the background, the voice on the phone changing as it shouted again, echoing as a tortured question rolled through and to Watcher. "*She is alive?*"

"Yeah, she's...she's alive."

Surging swells of Spanish, a woman's voice joined in, shouting and screaming, a babble of language which managed to communicate one thing clearly. *Joy*. Joy that Mela lived. Joy and a release from a terror so stark Watcher prayed he'd never know anything like it. Moments passed as the voices and sounds wound down, becoming quiet, and then the man's voice, "May we...can she...would she speak to us? My wife and I. Will she talk with us?"

Making a split second decision to not question them further, Watcher told him, "She's outside in the pool with my daughter." He wanted to give them the knowledge not only was she alive and safe, but she was also being treated well. "Let me step outside and call her."

"She's playing in a pool." The tone was quietly jubilant, and probably Estavez passing information to his wife, because it was followed by a quickly stifled female cry.

Watcher quickly covered the distance across the interior of the barn to the outside door. Once through the opening, he pulled the phone slightly away from his face and called, "Mela. I have someone on the phone for you."

Quiet in his ear, then a hoarse repetition, "Mela. Mama, he called our Maria, Mela."

Carmela's head lifted and she saw him with the phone. She had frozen for a second before a pleased expression flashed across her face and then she was clambering excitedly out of the pool, eschewing a towel as she raced through the grass and dust towards him, mouth open in a glad shout, "Papá!"

Twenty minutes later, her words and tears had slowed, and she uncurled from where she'd been sitting on Watcher's lap. He'd gone to his ass in the dirt outside the barn when her legs collapsed from under her, catching her and guiding her down as she talked and talked, the flow of words from her slow and pained at first, then transitioning to a swift and happy chatter. Over the past minute, he'd heard his name twice, and now her gaze drifted up to his face as she said, "*Si, Papá.* He's right here. *Si, Papá. Te amo muchissimo, Papá.*" She giggled, and nodded, "*Mucho.*"

Holding out the phone, she told Watcher, "*Papá* would like to speak with you, Papa Watcher." She stood, looking down at him with a sweet smile. "*Gracias*, Papa Watcher." Fingers to her lips, she smiled again and took two steps before she was running, her run ending with a shrill scream as she cannonballed back into the pool.

Watcher spoke into the phone, "Yeah?"

"I should like to meet you, *señor*. Maria…explained things. *Mi esposa* and I will be in El Paso in the morning. Before we…" The voice trailed off, then picked back up. "I would like to know if you could be persuaded to continue sheltering Maria, for a time." *Fuck.* Juanita was right.

"*Mela* is welcome to stay here for as long as *she* likes." He emphasized both the name and pronoun in that sentence, making it clear Estavez didn't factor as much as he might think. Not if he was going to throw away the precious gift of a daughter returned alive, when he'd clearly believed her dead.

"I have certain—" A frustrated huff of breath, then, "Perhaps speaking of these things in person would be best." Now Watcher was intrigued because it might mean the asshole Estavez brother might not be the only one with things in play. "Thanks are not...could never be enough, *señor*. This day you have performed a miracle, raised my daughter from death. To hear her voice, her words which speak of your care for her, how you have treated her as if she were your own child. Tomorrow is soon enough for business, right now I want to bask in the knowledge there is a God, and he has seen fit to return my daughter to me. *Thank you*."

A few words later and Watcher disconnected, staring across the yard as Mela lifted her arms in the air, whirling around in the water, shouting and laughing as she played with Bella.

Bikes are like livin'
Juanita

Juanita woke with a start and rolled over in an empty bed. Blinking and squinting against the dim nightstand light, she looked up at a figure standing next to the bed.

She relaxed, blowing out the breath that had locked in her lungs.

Her husband.

Watcher was staring down at her as he emptied his pockets, placing his phone on the nightstand. His wallet was next, followed by an object which gave her a chill, one of his pistols, drawn from the back waistband of his pants. He always carried a gun, but typically it remained in the pocket of his vest. Watcher's expression was tense and serious, and seeing this look on his face gave her another chill. "*Papi*," she whispered, shoving up to a sitting position. "What's happened?"

"Nothin', honey." Said soothingly, it was an obvious lie, but one he would stick to, which told her whatever had happened involved the club. A matter for the men, but not her, nor the other women of the

Soldiers. His posture told her he was weary, ready for relaxation and rest. "Girls sleepin'?"

"*Si*," she said, her lips curling into a quick smile. Both girls claimed to have scarcely survived the last days of the school year and had been excited this was the first long weekend of summer. "Mela is a demon on that bike." Before he left two days ago, he had brought home a small dirt bike for the girls, and Mela—no surprise—had taken to it immediately. She was older, true, but her experiences had matured her in painful ways.

Juanita worried because at times Mela's need to compensate for what she went through incited her to daredevil stunts. Adrenaline helped the girl push back the pain of what she'd endured. That and Mela constantly looked to find ways to bind Watcher to her even tighter. The girl knew embracing the smaller version of what he rode would make him happy. "She must have tipped the bike over a dozen times, but each spill only made her want to master it more. She is determined to have your approval when you first see her ride it."

This brought a sincere smile to his face, one which warmed his eyes and she basked in his approval at sharing part of their day, aware in this regard she and the girls were the same. "And our Bella?" He shrugged out of his cut, laying it aside. He discarded his clothing, and she froze at the bruising revealed on his body. He had been in a fight. A fight or an accident, but if he wasn't willing to speak of it, then she couldn't even acknowledge anything was amiss. "How'd she do? The girls were supposed to take turns."

"Bella would rather be the passenger, *Papi*. You know this." And he did, because he had carried her pillion behind him many times. Her tiny body balanced on the motorcycle, hands clutching tightly to his belt loops, helmet obscuring much of her face. She was terrified of bikes but rode with her papa because he loved having her with him. "Mela got some photos of her on the bike, but when our Bella took a turn around the field, she frightened herself, and handed it off to Mela."

He frowned. "What'd Bella do? She wreck?" Easing his body prone on the mattress next to her, he hissed through his teeth as he settled in.

"I think she hit some loose dirt. It frightened her." Juanita moved closer, stroking up his arm with her fingertips. Risking his dismissal of her concern, she quietly asked, "*Papi*, you need anything?"

"No, honey, I'm good. I took something before I left the church." She froze, knowing now why he didn't want to talk about whatever had happened tonight. Being at the church meant the club had refugees to drop off at the shelter there. Refugees might mean women. *Women like me*. His hand cupped her jaw, turning her for a soft kiss. "No, baby, nothin' like that. We needed to make a donation to the padre. Nothin' more."

She took in a shaky breath, despising the way her chin quivered. She loathed knowing he saw and felt her fear, and knew how he hated it, too. "Okay, *Papi*," she whispered.

"Sleep, honey," he ordered, brushing against her lips with his again. "It's all good."

In minutes he had followed his own advice, resting heavily against her side, arm draped across her chest to pin her in place. *Not that I'd ever want to leave*, she thought, feeling her lips curling at the idea. She stroked his arm. *Not that he'd allow me to.*

A donation. With the evidence of brutal combat on Watcher's body, Juanita knew what it meant. They'd found a coyote or group of the grasping human extortionists and stripped them of the money paid by men and women who longed for a better life. Things were so bad in Mexico. The cartels were fighting amongst themselves, and every day the news brought stories and pictures of fighting and death. Just yesterday the girls had been watching cartoons and a shout from Mela brought Juanita running into the room. Their program had been interrupted by a live news report of beheaded and dismembered bodies which had Bella crying in terror.

Mela had folded her sister close in her arms, cradling the back of her head to force the smaller girl's face into her neck. Television off, silence in the room finally, Juanita knelt next to the girls and wrapped them up in her arms and love, holding tight until their fear passed.

The first meeting with Mela's family had gone better than Juanita could have ever believed, nearly as well as she'd prayed for. On a hunch, Watcher had trusted Estavez with the address to their home, and the four of them had stood outside in a sea of black leather and his brothers as they watched a caravan of cars and trucks roll up the road towards the house. Even Watcher's strong hands couldn't restrain Mela when her father stepped out of the vehicle, and she had darted away, her long legs flashing underneath her dress as she raced towards her papá.

It had taken a long time, but the tiny family of three had finally gotten themselves under control enough to approach the house, Mela carried in the crook of her father's arm. Legs around his hips, she had her arms wrapped around his neck, head to his shoulder. Raul hadn't wiped the tears from his face when he greeted Watcher, proud to let the other man see his joy. Then he turned to Juanita and recognition flashed across his face followed by a quick shout of happiness. Her cousin swept her into a close embrace with him and his child, the tightness of his grip testimony to what the reunion meant to him.

She knew their connection had made Raul's request easier to make, because he needed Mela to remain in the United States for her own safety. The business part of the discussion was restricted to the men, as it should be, but he had told Juanita enough to make her understand this wasn't a casual appeal. Carlos was on the warpath and had long ago joined his fortunes to the wrong men, the fruit of his associations coming ripe, finally, and choking all around him with its poison.

She'd watched over the next weeks as Raul became a frequent visitor at their home. Rewarding to see how comfortable he was around them, around Watcher. His wife a different story, because after their first visit, she hadn't returned. Her initial horrified reaction to the markings Juanita and Mela shared had made Watcher angry, as well as Raul, but in the end, she had more than redeemed herself in Juanita's eyes.

Leaning forward to embrace Mela's mother in greeting, Juanita was startled when the woman pulled away without touching her, then saw the expression on her face. Lips pressed tightly together, her sad eyes were fixed on Juanita's neck, and she knew what the woman had seen. Unable to stop herself, Juanita turned to the side and buried her face in Watcher's back, shutting out the world and this gutting reminder she would never be what she once was.

"Does my Maria..." Her voice was trembling, but Raul cut her off, his words and tone firm and unyielding.

"Maria is alive, Consuela, and this is all that matters."

Trying to recover, Mela's mother murmured, "Of course, Raul. Of course. She's alive. My baby lives. We are so blessed."

Watcher's arms curved around Juanita and pulled her close. "Let's go out back. Mela can show you her prize-winning cannonball." Clearly communicating the topic was closed, he steered the conversation for the rest of the afternoon. Then the men retired to the barn to discuss business, leaving the women and children beside the pool.

"Will you have it removed?" The straightforward question surprised her, and she looked up to see Consuela staring at her. Since the initial clash, the woman had gone out of her way to try and put Juanita at ease, a laughable endeavor since Consuela was the reason for the anxiety. A good woman, a kind one, she hadn't known for certain about Mela's brand until the girls changed into their swimming suits. While she'd done a good job disguising her sorrow at the mark on her daughter's skin, Juanita had seen.

"No, I will not." Juanita paused, then decided to give her the argument she used most often on Watcher. "It's on my soul. That cannot be removed."

"Do you think..." When Consuela paused, Juanita looked at her, surprised to see her fighting with emotion. "Do you think I could assist, my cousin?" Claiming family connections, Consuela was doing more than mending a breach caused by her instinctive reactions. "I could approach your mother. She mourns, Juanita. The last I heard, she still lights candles every day."

"No, please no." Juanita shook her head, feeling her hair sweep across her shoulders, letting it drape across her neck, hiding her shame. Staring at the girls playing in the pool, she left the concealing cover in place, needing it for now. "Better she never knows."

"Would you have kept Maria from me, then? Made me weep every day for the daughter lost? Wondering every day if she were dead, or trapped in hell?" The fierceness of the whisper took Juanita by surprise, and she turned to stare at her cousin's wife. "Sentenced me to a purgatory without end?" Shaking her head, Consuela said, "Far better to know and find a way to come to peace with the blows life has laid in her path, than to not know the path. Or wonder at the destination. Give me this, cousin. Let me approach her. We can leave the decision to contact you up to her, but if you do not let me reach out, the answer will always be the same. Give her a chance to change your mind."

Consuela had more than redeemed herself, because today, Juanita's mother had called, and the two women had spent an hour on the phone crying and shouting and laughing. *Tomorrow*, Juanita thought. *I'll tell Watcher tomorrow.*

***

Watcher

"How you findin' Memphis, brother?" Watcher stared out the barn window towards the back of the house, smiling at an excited Bella draped over Spider's shoulder. The man was currently spinning in circles, and she was arched up, arms spread wide, as close to flying as she could get. Four more kids, three of Spider's and one of Watcher's, waited their turns nearby. "You've been there a few months. You get all settled in? That job work out for ya?" Watcher'd sent Andy to a friend of a friend, hoping to smooth the way. Bethy knew a guy who was looking for unobtrusive but efficient security, and as Spider had learned, Andy was far more powerful and skilled than he looked.

"Yeah." One word could carry a wealth of information, and with Andy's response, Watcher knew everything was not good. Shouted laughter pulled his eyes back to the window in time to see Spider fall to the ground, cradling Bella in his arms, Mela tackling them both.

"You ridin'?" Depending on what was eating Andy, blowing through a tank of fuel would likely set his head straight.

"Not as much. It's different here. I keep the bike locked up most of the time, catch rides or the bus to work." His voice held a note of melancholy. "Miss having folks around I can talk to. How's my Mela?"

Maybe we can lure him back here if he's missing riding with brothers, Watcher thought. Ignoring the question, he said, "Brother, you need to get your knees in the breeze."

"Yeah, just...there's been some shit going down up here. Got me thinking. A drug dealer named Ling killed a woman I knew. It seems he's notorious around here for that kind of shit. And Memphis, man, it's a hotbed of hard times. Everywhere you look, people struggling and then folks like this Ling making their lives harder. I had enough of that shit in my life with my mom, ya know? So it's all been weighing on my mind." And it would because Andy was like that, tender underneath his façade of impassivity.

"Maybe Memphis ain't the place for you. You thinkin' of movin' on?" Watcher paused, then threw a line in the water, fishing to see if there was a chance he could retrieve this man for the Soldiers. "Any chance you'll be rollin' back this way? Mela'd be excited to see you."

"Thinking north."

Fuck. Was worth a try. "Yeah? Got a destination in mind?"

"Chicago. Heard some good things about Chicago."

Spider was lying on his back between the kids, one arm pointed upwards at something. Bella had both arms up, gesturing with her hands as if she were shaping dough. Cloud watching, and she was explaining what she saw. *My girl's a dreamer*, he thought with a smile. Andy, however, needed to not have his head in the clouds because he was right; Memphis wasn't the safest of cities to be in. "Then you should go to Chicago. Or head home for a visit. Or come back out here. Get your head in the wind, brother. Roll those twos, man." Watcher shook his head. "I can hear it in your voice, you're a brother needin' a good ride." He paused. "Or a good brother to ride with." If Andy went to Chicago, Watcher knew he'd be able to hook his friend up with like-minded folks, help find him a permanent home. *Bones or Mason, either of them will welcome someone like Andy.*

"Riding doesn't solve everything, Watcher." From the humorous tone of Andy's voice, Watcher knew he threw it out as a joke, but Watcher wanted him to understand sometimes what we choose to do is a reflection of who we are.

"Brother, you know that ain't true. Motorcycles are like livin'. Either get the fuck on and ride or don't and sit the curb. Simple as that. Your life, your choice."

Silence for a moment, then Andy asked, "What about you?"

Juanita had walked out of the house and stood, smiling at the trio lying on the ground. "Me? Oh, hell yeah, I'm ridin'."

Never again

Watcher

"Jesus." Watcher twisted to look the other direction along the alley, hearing a grunt as Opie hit the wall beside him. "How many are there?"

"Got ten or twelve, but they're packing a serious arsenal." Another fusillade of shots came from the street running parallel to where they stood. Opie grunted again, tapped his earpiece and said, "On our way, brother." To Watcher, he said, "We gotta move. Spider's got two of them outside the safe room at the church."

"Outside?" Watcher didn't wait for a response. He jogged down the alley, knowing Opie and the other men would be directly behind him.

His own earpiece hit static for a moment, then, "Got forty rolling the bridge, Prez."

Fuck. He, Opie, and the other men here were in a better position to deflect the new wave of enemies. He tapped his earpiece, grunting, "Copy. Update with changes." Turning with one raised fist, halting their advance, he told the men at his back, "Bikes headed our way. We need to cut them off."

The Soldiers had been engaged in a running battle with the cartel for nearly three months. Each time Watcher thought they'd cut the head off the snake, it wiggled back to life. His Soldiers had worked hard to convince the coyotes it wasn't worth their lives to route through Soldier territory north of the bridge. Since the Soldiers claimed I-10 from Odessa, Texas, west through New Mexico to Lordsburg, and from El Paso up through Albuquerque, it didn't give Machos or the cartel much room to ease past them. But, carving out that section gave his men the bulk of the state as theirs, and outside of the Machos, it wasn't a claim to be questioned.

Colorado clubs stayed north of the Soldiers, and the western clubs weren't interested in anything other than Cali. Things should have been comfortable. Should have been, but the cartel also looked to be finding additional support in small upstart clubs, cycling cash and product through them in a way that ensured they grew out of control, imploding at the end. Even knowing it was coming, each bloody implosion still took energy to watch and contain. Mason, Bones, and Watcher had determined this was the cartel's intent. A tactic to keep enough shit stirred up to keep the clubs busy and on guard, giving the cartel time and room to seek out other avenues to peddle their product.

The way Watcher saw things, he could just about map how deep the Machos were in with the Columbians. He didn't expect they'd ever be able to claw their way clear of anything, and Raul reported the Mexican club had seen record defections. It looked like Machos had joined forces with the cartel to try and maneuver things so their men had no choice but to toe the line. This meant frequent forays into the US to bring back money to buy loyalty. Or, as they were today, they could try and flank the Soldiers and run a shipment through where they weren't supposed to be.

Tapping his earpiece, he barked a call number, then waited. A moment later Devil said, "Yeah, boss?"

"Routing to intercept." Their path was predetermined because he took this kind of shit into account when putting together a battle plan. "Cover base."

"Copy."

Base was his home, where his girls and Juanita were, and the Southern Soldiers' only clubhouse. Devil was either already onsite or headed that way because it was where their families had gathered. Today was supposed to have been a family party, interrupted by this bullshit business.

He used another call number, getting a response broken by gunfire in his ear. "Spider's got executive decision." Beside him, Opie laughed.

"Copy." The single word came through the earpiece, all sound crisper now the gunfire had ceased. "Spider's in control."

Cutting his gaze to Opie, Watcher muttered, "Gonna regret that, aren't I?"

"Oh, hell yeah, boss." Opie shrugged his rifle higher on his shoulder. "He'll lord it over everyone until we're sick of it, then you'll have to beat his ass." Laughing again, Opie said, "SNAFU. Dude should have it tattooed on his body, but he lives to deal with this kind of shit."

"True that," Watcher said, moving towards the mouth of the alley again. "Let's roll."

Five hours later, he and every Soldier member stood around the patio table beside the backyard pool and sang a very upbeat, if off-key happy birthday to both Carmela and Bella. The girls didn't share a birthday, but with only two weeks between, Juanita always thought it'd be more fun for both girls to celebrate them together.

Mela darted around the room, aiming her camera at the different groups, urging them to smile by angling her head around the device and grinning at them. Raul was nearby, not hovering, but close, the man quiet as laughter rang from the crowd of children gathered around the cake. This year should have been Carmela's *quinceanera*. Seeing the pain on Raul's face, Watcher firmed his resolve to do whatever it took to make it so no father ever had to look at their daughter with that expression again. *Never again. Not my girls.*

***

"'Nita, honey, stop crying." Watcher hated how his voice sounded, hearing the broken pieces of his heart exposed in the words. "Honey, please." Ass to the bathroom floor, he held her against his chest, one leg propped on either side of her shaking body. "Honey, stop. You're gonna make yourself sick." She yanked on his shirt, pulling hard, face buried against his chest. "Baby, stop crying. I love you."

She wailed, a brief tormented sound brutally cut off as she shook her head. "No." Even the one word was a struggle for her to get out, her voice catching and hiccupping. "Na...No, Watcher."

"You know I do, baby. I love you." Each time they went through this she questioned why he would stay with her. Over the years he'd run out of words, and instead tried every day to show her. She moved to push away, and he tightened his arms around her, holding her close. Watcher tipped his head, resting his cheek on her hair. "I love you, honey. Shhhh. You can't do this again, honey. You gotta stop this."

He'd woken as she crept out of their bed, carefully easing out from underneath the covers, trying not to disturb him. When she didn't return after a few minutes, he'd thrown back the sheet and seen the blood. She hadn't even told him she might be pregnant this time, which meant she'd endured the anguish of waiting alone.

"You and our Bella, our Mela? Right there, everything I need." He gave her a squeeze. "And I cain't lose you, baby. Cain't, not and stay sane. I'm gonna call the padre, get his wife to come wait with the girls while you and I hit the ER." She shook her head, and he gave her another squeeze. "Honey, don't even think you're gonna argue with me.

You should know by now, I always win when it comes to making sure you're okay." He moved, sliding out from behind her, frowning when he saw the growing stain on her nightgown. "Up you get. Wash your face, and we'll head into town." Phone in hand, calls made while he dressed, he grabbed her robe on his way back to the bathroom and came to an abrupt halt in the doorway. His heart squeezed in his chest, and fear paralyzed him for a moment, cold sweat breaking out all over his body. There was a large pool of red spreading out from where she lay silent and still on the floor.

"*Juanita!*" He stooped, one knee to the tile next to her, panicked when there was still no response. Gently he lifted her shoulders. As her head fell backwards, he caught it in one hand, cradling her. "*Jesus. Honey, come on.*" Nothing.

Careless of the blood, he gathered her into his arms and ran, racing through the house and barreling out the door and into the night. A car was pulling up as he closed the vehicle door on an awake but groggy Juanita, but he didn't stop to greet the woman behind the wheel. He was afraid he'd already wasted too much time.

Phone in hand, Watcher reversed down the driveway, the truck jerking and jumping when he spun the wheel, stopping with a jolt as the back bumper hit a fencepost, then he jammed the transmission into drive. Wheels spitting gravel behind him, he accelerated to the road, feeling the rear wheels jolting across the surface when he slid sideways, foot already buried to the floorboard.

Five minutes later he skidded the truck to a slanted halt in front of the ER doors, met by a corps of nurses and Juanita's doctor. Lifting her carefully from the seat, he laid her on the gurney, one hand on her leg as he raced up the hallway beside her, not caring he'd left the doors of the truck ajar.

Four hours later, seated in the surgical waiting area, Watcher was still waiting. Elbows to his knees, he was bent over, fingers of one hand rubbing across his forehead, back and forth. Staring at nothing, he ran the events through his head again and again. *Shoulda known.* The rasp of his callused fingertips rubbing across his skin was all he could hear. The hospital was quiet at this time of the morning. *I shoulda got up sooner.* He sighed, glancing at the clock and then back down to the floor. *Shoulda called an ambulance.* Footsteps in the hallway pulled him to his feet, and he was facing the doors when Opie walked in, followed closely by a half a dozen of his Soldiers.

"Hear anything?" That was Opie. He walked across the room, reaching out to grip Watcher's shoulder. Watcher shook his head. "Need coffee?" Fingers gripping tight, Opie held on as Watcher's mouth twisted sideways. Opie saw and swallowed hard, then asked again, "Need some coffee, brother?"

"No," Watcher got out, turning to look away. "Who called?"

"One-Shot's gal works ER," Opie twisted to gesture to one of the men now seated in the hard, plastic chairs beside the black TV. "She called him, he called me, I called them." He turned back to Watcher. "We'll talk later about why *you* didn't call." His grip tightened on Watcher's shoulder again. "For now, it's enough we're here." When Opie grinned at Watcher, it wasn't true, didn't hit his eyes, but he was trying. "I need coffee, and you're a bastard without yours, so I'll grab you a cup, too."

Two cardboard cups of stewed and burned coffee later Juanita's doctor walked to the doorway and paused, looking around at the men scattered around the room. "Mr. Otey," he called, and Watcher stood, not sure how to take the look on the man's face. "Come with me."

He didn't think he could walk across the room without falling to his knees, so shaking his head, Watcher planted his feet, waiting. "No." Somewhere he found enough strength to demand, "Tell me." The doc scanned the room again, his gaze coming back to Watcher. "They're my brothers, Doc. My family."

"Juanita's going to be okay. It was a...challenging surgery." They'd taken her away to stop the bleeding, the docs not sure what they'd have to do once they got started, but Watcher hadn't expected actual surgery. In the past, she'd had the procedures where they made sure she miscarried cleanly, but this sounded like so much more. Worse. "As you know, she'd lost a lot of blood. We had trouble keeping her stable during the surgery."

Watcher held tight to the doc's first words: *She's going to be okay.*

"Mr. Otey, we had to perform a partial hysterectomy." The doc paused like he expected Watcher to yell and scream, when all he felt was a profound relief. Never again would she have to go through this. *Never again.* "She's in recovery now, still under anesthesia, but once she's awake and alert, we'll move her to a room. Would you like to go back with me and see your wife?" Opie's hand pounded the center of Watcher's back, rocking him forwards as he nodded.

Watcher took a step, then turned back to Opie. *No more babies. Ever.* "Need you to bring Bella and Mela here, soon as you can." Opie nodded. "She'll need to see them. This is gonna kill her." Opie nodded again, lips twisting in sympathy. "Thanks, brothers." Watcher looked around the room, marking each face turned his way. "No words."

***

Watcher kept Mela visible from the corner of his eye, cataloging what was off with her. Bella had to be restrained from throwing herself at her mother, not worried about her so much as simply missing her. Even though she was older than Tabby had been when their mother died, Bella wasn't mature enough to understand mortality and what could have happened. And if Watcher had his way, he'd try to make sure she never experienced loss as he and his sister had.

Mela, on the other hand, older than her years, having seen so much of life, and not the good parts, seemed to know exactly how close they'd come to losing Juanita. Eyes to the toes of her shoes, she leaned against the wall on the other side of the room. As far from the door as she could be, but even though she kept her distance, she was still close enough to Juanita to reach out and touch if Mela wanted. Bella was hanging off the railing on the bed, talking a mile a minute to a smiling Juanita.

Juanita had taken the news better than Watcher expected. He'd led the conversation softly to where he needed it to be but hadn't held anything back. The bleeding was bad, the docs had tried to stop it, but couldn't. They also couldn't pour blood into her fast enough to compensate for what she was losing, so, midsurgery, a decision was made to save her life. Those were the terms the doc used, and that was what Watcher repeated. *So fuckin' close to losin' her.*

A touch on the back of his hand caused him to jerk and look down. Mela. She'd sidled in his direction while he'd been distracted, and now stood next to him. In a whisper, she asked, "She's gonna be okay, right?"

"Yeah, honey. She's gonna be fine."

Mela was silent for a beat, then with a small voice asked her question again, seeking a reassurance he didn't understand. "She really okay?"

"Yeah, baby girl, she really is," he responded, resting his hand on her shoulder. "She's okay, now and forever."

"Was it...?" Her voice trailed off, and she tucked her chin to her throat. Shoulders curling in, she stayed quiet until he prompted with a soft repeat of her words.

"Was it what, honey?"

"Was it because of what happened to her? Before?" Despite the quivering fear in her voice, she pushed onwards. "You know, before you saved her?"

Watcher stared at her, the anxiety bleeding from her at such levels he could feel it from where he stood. "No, Mela. This was something she needed to have done."

"But, how can you be sure?" He watched as she cut her eyes up at him, then back down, again studying the toes of her shoes. "Really, really sure?"

"Carmela." He called her name, wanting to put this fear to bed for her for good. "Juanita got sick once. Now, she doesn't make the right kind of stuff to help her stay pregnant. Isabella is a miracle, because when we had her, we didn't even know there was a problem. The surgery was because her body couldn't stand another pregnancy. Every time she got pregnant, the risks to her were worse, and I agree with the docs. I don't wanna lose her. It didn't have anything to do with what happened to her." He leaned in, needing to get it right. "Or you, honey. You gotta know this won't happen to you. What you went through doesn't mean you'll have the same problems. But"—lifting his hand, he stroked her hair, draping and smoothing it over her shoulder—"if this is something you're worried about, we can talk to someone, make sure you're good." She nodded, bottom lip trapped between her teeth, and he nodded in response. "I'll get it set up, honey." He pressed his hand to her back, gently urging her towards the bed. "Now go, say hello to Mama 'Nita. She wants to see you."

Mela looked up at him searchingly before she nodded. "I'd...thank you." He was surprised when she circled his hips with her arms, burying her face against his ribs. "I love you, Papa Watcher."

Cradling the back of her head, he bent deep, pressing his lips to the top of her head. "I love you, too, my Mela."

Enemies and friends

"Jesus fucking Christ," Spider muttered from behind where Watcher sat in a chair positioned along one long edge of a table. They were in the back room of a diner in Lordsburg, taking a meet with Shooter. Watcher hadn't expected this conversation to be contentious and, caught off guard, tried to school his face to an impassive expression. What Spider was reacting to was Shooter's demand of free passage across I-10. Not a request, but a demand. "Are you fucking high?"

Watcher held up one hand, silencing Spider. He stared at Shooter, taking in the man's relaxed pose. Casually leaning back from the table, ankle up on one knee, elbow propped on the back of the chair beside him. In any other setting, Shooter would be giving off the impression of a man who'd recently pushed back from a buffet table, filled and satiated. Comfortable, visiting with friends. At his back stood a small group of men, and one boy who wasn't trying to hide his dislike of every man in the room. Watcher lifted his chin, studying the boy. "Luke," he said, knowing this was Shooter's son.

Shooter brought the flat of his palm down on the table, slapping it sharply. "Talk to me, not my boy." Watcher didn't flinch. There was a slide of metal on leather from guns leaving holsters behind him, but he kept his gaze on the kid. The corners of Luke's mouth curled down, and his head moved side-to-side ever so slightly, disgusted in some way at his father's posturing. *Interesting.*

Shooter's father had gone down in Utah some time ago, about the same time Darrie had died, and since Justice Morgan's death, the Outriders had pulled back. It took a while, but Shooter had settled into the role he'd been training for since he was younger than Luke. This would be the Outriders' first attempt to venture into Soldiers' territory, and Watcher wondered if Shooter had chosen this direction because he thought Watcher still had some loyalty, or—and this thought pissed him off—if Shooter felt the Soldiers were weak in some way.

Outriders had never stopped doing any of the shit Watcher had noted and hated from his time in the club. If anything, the final few years Morgan had been over the club, things had ramped up on the drug and flesh trade. Their routes were up through Cali, though, not touching the Soldiers territory, and Watcher hadn't felt a need to deal with them. Now, though, with this ask which he was prepared to deny, Watcher knew there was about to be bad blood between the clubs.

"You got nothin' to say, Watcher? Got nothing to give me? Years under my patch, and you got nothing for me?" Shooter sighed theatrically, propping his head in his hand as if all this were too tiresome to bear. "Years as an Outrider, and you got nothing?"

"Oh, I got something, John." A strategy, to take back the man's road name, given to him by Mason. Take a moment to remind John he'd never called Watcher anything other than the name he'd earned in the service, but John Morgan had just been John when they first met. "You ain't gonna like it, and you're gonna have to suck that shit up, but I got something for ya." Leaning forwards, Watcher tapped the table with one fingertip, his controlled motion a menacing contrast to Shooter's wild slap moments before. "I got a big, fat hairy no for ya."

"'Bout right," Shooter drawled, tipping his head back. It wasn't a smart move because Watcher saw him swallow nervously and knew there was more riding on this meet than a simple route request. "Never did have any loyalty in your gut."

"And you never had any smarts in your head, considering it's been shoved up your ass for fuckin' years," Spider spit out, and Watcher had to fight a grin when Shooter's foot hit the floor with a thud. "Knew your daddy, see how you wanna be like him, but you don't got it in ya."

Watcher held up his hand again, once again having to fight a grin when Spider harrumphed.

"John," Watcher began, then stopped when Shooter's face flamed red. "Shooter," he corrected himself, aiming barely south of respectful. "You had to know the answer'd be no. Especially when you didn't come in here with a grateful heart I even bothered to fuckin' meet with you." Watcher shook his head, pushing his chair back from the table, catching the eye flare of half the men standing behind Shooter. Today's meeting was more important than Shooter let on. The Outriders needed this for some reason. "I took the meet for old times' sake. You"—he flicked a finger towards Shooter—"didn't make the right move. And now"—he pushed to his feet, seeing Luke's eyes narrow—"I'm done."

"You don't do this, then I got no choice in what I do next, Watcher." Shooter leaned one elbow on the tabletop. "I need a route. Not even asking for escort. Simply passage."

"You didn't *ask* for anything," Watcher reminded him. "Just came in actin' an ass."

"You weren't gonna give it anyway." Shooter stood, made a motion with one hand and turned to follow his men from the room. Luke stood still, eyes locked on Watcher until after his father cleared the room. Then he spun on his heel and stalked out.

"So…that went well," Spider quipped, and Watcher turned to look at him. "What?"

"Cracking wise ain't makin' me happy, Spider. You didn't help, brother." Watcher twisted to look at the door, swinging slowly back and forth in the wind, opening onto the darkness of the parking lot. "Make a couple of calls, get the brothers organized for a club-wide meeting tomorrow night. Everyone needs to know." He shook his head. "Shooter's a crazy motherfucker, and he's not above pulling family into shit. Gotta get ourselves ready."

***

Juanita

She leaned against the headboard of the bed with the welcome weight of Watcher's upper body across her legs. He'd come back tonight edgy and anxious, and together they'd worked the tension out of his muscles. *A workout for my muscles, too*, she thought. She grinned down at him, watching her fingers push through his thick hair, enjoying the feel of it against her skin. She loved the way he looked, hair scarcely beginning to go gray at the temples.

"What's the grin for, honey?" Pressing his head back, he lifted his chin in a demand she welcomed, rounding her spine so she could bend down to press her lips against his.

"Thinking that might be my favorite way to end the day." She pushed her fingers through his hair again, combing it back from his forehead. "And then I thought this might be better." She sighed, tipping her head backwards against the padded headboard. "I love spending time with you."

"Me, too." He twisted, turning to his side so his face rested on her thighs. "Like spending time with me, I mean."

She laughed and his voice joined hers, filling the room with joy. "Love you, Watcher."

"Love you, too, 'Nita." Rolling forwards, he pressed his lips to her belly, gracing her with a soft kiss. "Love you."

***

Watcher

Shaking his head, Watcher flipped his phone shut, disconnecting the call. He'd gotten off the phone with Mason, who had called him to check out the man Watcher'd sent to the Rebel Wayfarers bar. Andy had used Watcher's name, which led to the call. *Rebels would be a good fit for the kid*, Watcher mused, looking down at the paperwork on the desk in front of him. Southern Soldiers were in the process of buying a new pawn shop, and he'd been looking through the financials when Mason called.

Looks good on paper. He picked up the description of inventory, scanning down through the items listed, knowing fully a third of what was in the store wasn't actually on the spreadsheet. *Looks better in person*. Phone to his ear again, he waited for Opie's greeting. "Let's buy this one." Pulling another sheet towards him, he read off the name, "Locker Room. The pawn shop by the airbase in El Paso. We can have Devil on it, be good for him to get outta Cruces. Put Diamond on it with him."

Diamond needed something to do. Since getting winged in Mexico, he'd pulled back from the club, and Watcher worried about losing him. Putting him into play at a shop would give him a connection to the club, and him understanding how the shop's success helped every brother would settle him in other ways.

"Yeah, boss. I'll make the call." Opie agreed readily, and Watcher grinned. It had been Opie's eyes that found it, his leverage which located the vulnerable spot for the current owner, and his research had pulled together the info needed to make a decision. "Take a couple of weeks to finalize, but since we can pay cash, it'll go easier."

Watcher scoffed. "Easier once you show where the eighty-grand came from." One of the laws that came into play after 9/11 was accounting for large amounts of cash, which was why these kind of cash-heavy businesses were prevalent with clubs.

"You know I got it covered. Everything accounted for and logged, no worries, boss." Opie reassured him, and his voice trembled with the force of the grin he had to be wearing. "We'll be in possession before the end of the month, at least that's what I'll push for."

"Good deal." His phone beeped, and he pulled it away, looking down to see an unknown caller, but by the Chicago number, it was probably Andy. "I gotta go, got another call." He clicked over to accept the call, saying only, "Talk to me."

"My friend." Heavily accented English came through the phone and he unconsciously straightened in his chair. *Bones.* "How are you this pleasant day?"

"Good, Bones. How about you? You doin' okay?" *Speak of the devil.* He hadn't thought about the man in months and not fifteen minutes after Mason brought him up, Watcher got a call from him. Before Bones could respond, Watcher continued, "Heard you met my boy the other day. How'd you like him?"

"Your...boy?" There was an odd pause, then Bones asked, a thread of clear pleasure in his voice. "Of who do you speak? I was not aware you had a boy. When did your beautiful Juanita gift you with a son? And why did you not call me? I would rejoice with you at the news."

Watcher's stomach hollowed, lurching. Throat tight, he got out, "Andy." He coughed. "Andy Jones. Understand you ran into him on a run. Liked what you saw. Liked it enough you gave him a marker." The longer he talked, the farther he got away from the surprising pain, the stronger his voice became.

Not quickly enough to fool Bones, though. As ever, the astute man on the other end of the phone remained on target. "My friend." Bones' voice was low, and quiet, sharing his own discomfort through strained tones. "I did not mean to bring you pain. Your words took me off my guard. I apologize for the misstep."

"No apologies needed, Bones. Juanita..." He trailed off, not certain how to continue because he hadn't talked to anyone about this. It was private, but Bones knew so much about them. He was more like family. Swallowing around the lump in his throat, Watcher continued, stumbling as he tried to find the right words. "Juanita had to...there was another...but she couldn't. It busted, so they had to do surgery. She cain't...I mean, we can't have more." Sucking in a breath, he said, "We've got Isabella, and Carmela. All we need."

Silence for a long moment, then a ragged indrawn breath before Bones said, a curious intensity in his voice, "Of course they are. I am so sorry to learn of your Juanita's difficulties. So very sorry. I wish I could lift this from your path, my friend." Bones made a sound, clearing his throat. "Please tell her you are both in my thoughts. I will light a candle for her healing."

Watcher nodded, even knowing Bones couldn't see him. "She'd like that. I appreciate all you...your care for her."

"She is your queen. I can do no less." The statement was filled with meaning, and Watcher again swallowed hard, because every nuance was true. Juanita was his queen, his life, the breath in his body, and knowing his friend recognized the commitment and bond between them filled Watcher with a deep satisfaction.

"So Andy is yours? Why is he in Chicago?" Bones changed the subject, and from the surprise in his voice, Watcher knew this topic wasn't why he had called.

"Not *mine*, mine, but I sent him Mason's way. He was in Las Cruces a while. Worked at a bar we were buyin', got interested in the life. Hung with my Soldiers for a little bit, never got past the hangaround phase. He's a solid man, like so solid I was ready to patch him in. Woulda done it in a heartbeat. Had him ride into Mexico with me. Was there the day we brought back Mela." Watcher found himself recounting the story again. "She latched onto him, trusted him, even with blood runnin' down his leg. Dogs and kids, man, they tell the tale."

"I can see that about him. He was very collected when I ran upon him. We were mid, shall we say conversation? Yes, midconversation with the Dominos. He did not seem concerned about being caught up in our conversation, even as it raced down the street in front of him." Bones laughed, the sound rolling quietly through the speaker. "So he has landed at Jackson's and found a home in the Rebels. Why am I not surprised? Mason seems to be collecting quite the menagerie of people."

"What does that mean?" Even from Bones' own words, he had to know Andy wasn't odd. Andy was a solid guy, one of about a million simply looking for a place to call home. Not an oddity which would attract Bones' attention, except as someone he might like to recruit for his own club. This meant something else was going on. *Rumor and speculation, the bikers' gossip mill.*

"He has found a woman. She lives near to hand." *Interesting.* Mason wasn't known for taking tail home. "Mason has lost...focus."

"Lost focus in what way?" Unsettling news, because if the Rebel Wayfarers leadership wasn't stable, it could negatively impact dozens of smaller organizations in the Midwest. Mason had dedicated himself to cleaning up his old club, and once the members had settled onto their new path, he then devoted himself to expanding and growing the Rebels, but only in a sustainable way. Mason hadn't sounded unfocused when they were on the phone five minutes ago, but people could hide shit.

"I have known Mason almost as long as you." Bones was one of the few who knew about the childhood connection between Mason and Watcher, not a tie they tried to hide but didn't bring it out to chat about. Bones had met Mason back when he first came to Chicago, before he became the man he was. From Mason's stories, Watcher knew the history with Bones was forged in blood, Bones offering support in critical ways. "I have seen him in many situations."

Bones paused, and there was soft laughter in his voice when he continued. "*Many* situations. Stitched up his first encounter with a member of the nine tribe." Watcher grinned at the code for 9mm. "He has always held the club first. Even when the club itself did not deserve the loyalty, when it was under the reign of Deacon, a man who did not mind the streets running red, as long as it was not his blood painting them. Mason has loyalty and dedication bred deep in his bones. So you know I do not speak lightly when I say he has lost focus."

"A woman?" There'd been scuttlebutt about lots of things to do with the Rebels over the past several years, because Spider hadn't been the only one who believed Mason had acted a traitor to the idea of clubs. The Rebels had been cut out of several large sit-downs because of the way Mason took over, the bloody day when he killed patch brothers to save his club. Along with Bones, Watcher had worked behind the scenes to get Mason a seat at those tables again, even as Mason had done his own part to earn it, too. Remaining silent on the cause of his discontent was part of the reason the other dominant clubs let him back in, because other than strength, one of the things they most admired was the ability to keep a secret. "Where'd he meet her?"

"Interesting story there. She was Duck's obsession first." Duck was a Rebel member who came from West Texas. Someone who should have, by rights, been a Soldier, but he found himself in Chicago instead. "Then, she acquired housing next door to Mason. From day one he has been working to win her."

217

"No shit? She was Duck's and Mason stole her?" That wasn't right. Women weren't allowed to come between brothers, and certainly not between a member and his president. You didn't go there because it showed a lack of respect which could tear the fabric of a club wide open.

"It seems she was not Duck's in that way. An obsession, but not for himself. I am certain I do not have the full story yet, but you can be assured I am pushing aside the layers even as we speak." No doubt, because Bones would want to know as badly as Watcher did now.

"Tell me what you learn about the connection, yeah?" Still didn't say what Mason's deal was. "But what about Mason and the woman now? He's tied up in his neighbor?"

"He is tied in knots as I have never seen before, but the woman seems either immune to his charms, or ignorant of his interest." Bones' voice quietened, lowered when he continued, "He is distracted in dangerous ways, my friend. Many would use this opportunity to try and weaken the Rebels, and this I cannot allow. As things stand now, Mason and I have balanced the community in Chicago in ways which make us both strong. If he falls, there will be a void, and I am unsure of my Skeptics' ability to fully fill it, which would mean another player in town. I do not want that, Watcher. I have grown comfortable in my current role, and I'm happy here. My men live large in our world, ample supplies of everything they want or need. Mason's Rebels have their place, straddling the line as he has determined they will do. My Skeptics veer farther over into the darkness than the Rebels, and we are happy to because we reap many benefits from this *relacion cooperativa*. I called to speak to you because Mason is endangering my world, and he will not heed my words of caution. All I receive in return are reassurances of strength which exist only in his mind at the moment. I would like it if you could call him, talk to him, take his measure. See why he is wound about with the woman. Make him see sense and talk sense to him."

"I'll see what I can do—" Watcher hesitated, and then offered Bones something he'd been withholding for a long time. "—brother."

At the audible breath, Watcher knew it was the right thing to do. And then he knew what it meant because he got it back from Bones. "Thank you, brother."

***

Watcher bent over and pulled a bottle from the melting ice and cold water in the bottom of the cooler. He fished around for a moment, coming up with a second bottle before kicking the container, letting gravity slam the lid closed. Twisting the other direction, he held one of the bottles out, drops of water coating his fingers. "Here," he grunted, "last soldiers of the night."

"Thank you," Raul told him, reaching out to take the beer from his grip. "I needed...need to talk to you." Water dripped from the bottle, creating small darkened circles on his pants. Five hours in and Watcher still didn't know what had brought Raul north of the bridge. Carmela was at a sleepover with a friend, so he hadn't even gotten to see his daughter, even though Juanita offered to call her home. The way Raul demurred had caused shadows to gather in her eyes, and shortly afterwards Watcher brought the man to the bonfire area near the barn. He'd been waiting since, knowing sooner or later Raul would speak his mind. He hadn't expected it to take a half a case of beer to get him here.

"So talk." Watcher gestured with the bottle in his hand. "You got about ten minutes, then I'll have to get up and piss before I grab another six from the fridge." He settled back in the lawn chair, feet propped on a block of wood. "Talk. I'm listening, man."

"Carlos made many enemies." Carlos Estavez, the man Watcher most hated in this world. Before Watcher could respond, Raul continued, "Dangerous enemies. Men who I have cultivated over the past year and a half. Men who may not be my allies, but share my animosity for

Carlos. This gives us a common goal which I can leverage in my favor." Lifting his beer to his lips, Raul took a deep drink. "It's time to move towards this goal. I wanted to give you a heads up, because come tomorrow night, my hope and prayer is the fabric of my world in Mexico will look very different."

"You're making your move tomorrow, then?" Watcher's thoughts were hurtling a hundred miles an hour. If Raul took over the Machos, it would shift the entire dynamics in this region. *Who else knows?* "You bringing in other clubs on this, Raul?"

"No." Another lift of the bottle, another deep drink. "I will not be having conversations with anyone else on this. I know you understand why." Watcher nodded. He did, because Machos were large, international, and cartel supported. If Raul was successful, it was likely that particular affiliation would be severed, since they were the group who kidnapped Carmela. The cartel had their hooks in many places here in the southwest, including MCs like the Outriders.

"You need anything from me and mine?" The words were out of Watcher's mouth before he realized it, and only after they were spoken did he realize he'd put every Soldier on the line. *Fuck.* He didn't want Raul to fail, but a fight like this wouldn't be clean, and every man involved would be targeted for years.

"No, my friend. I would not ask that of you." Raul barked a laugh, then said, "But I thank you for the offer. The odds are...steep. Your response tells me you have at least a sliver of hope I will succeed. I will take the confidence with thanks." Minutes passed, and they sat in an uncomfortable silence, the fire's flames crackling and dancing in the pit in front of them. Raul shifted in his seat and broke the quiet with a heavy sigh. "My friend...Watcher. I would ask a favor of you. Can you promise me you will care for my Carmela, should anything untoward befall me? Can you promise me this?"

Without hesitation Watcher said, "Yes. Of course. As if she were my own."

Raul pushed for confirmation, the strain in his voice betraying deep fear. "Promise me, Watcher." The beer bottle reflected the flames, glinting as it was lifted again. "Promise me, please." Raul drank deeply, draining the bottle. He turned, and Watcher saw a determined look on his face. Raul's expression showing while he might know the odds were against him, he would not let the knowledge dissuade him from the course set in front of him.

"I promise you Carmela will be taken care of. Like my own family, she will be safe." Watcher swallowed, then fisted his right hand, pounding it against his chest. "My vow."

"Thank you, my friend." Raul paused, then Watcher saw the glint of his teeth reflecting the flames, giving him a sinister look. "Now, I would tell you my plans. Because you are one of the most intelligent men I know, and have a profound grasp of strategy. Carlos is on the move, but his destination is unknown, so I have plotted a course in his absence. You may, perhaps, see voids in my plans that, if filled, can make the difference in the outcome. May I share those plans with you?"

Raul knew if Watcher saw a chance to help, he wouldn't be able to stop himself, and this was one of those things he could do without endangering the lives and families of his men. "You got it. Lay it on me—" He paused, then gave Raul the same respect he'd given Bones two nights ago. "—brother."

Blowing shit up

"Jesus, Mason," Watcher blurted, interrupting his friend's recounting of a recent throw down with the Machos. Watcher hadn't heard from Raul in days, and from the sounds of what happened in Chicago yesterday, Raul's slim chances hadn't held. *Fuck*. He wouldn't say anything to Mela or Juanita, not yet. *Not until I'm sure*.

"Yeah. It was fucked up, man. Coulda been way worse, though." A harsh laugh escaped Watcher, and Mason reacted with his own gravel-filled chuckle. "Understatement of the fuckin' year, man. Walking into that club, not knowing for sure what'd gone down or who I'd find still standing." He paused, then hissed, "The stench." Watcher made a noise, because he knew exactly what Mason was talking about.

Firefights, especially when they happened inside a building, carried their own recognizable smells. Burnt gunpowder, the metallic tang of residue from so many guns, discharge gasses unable to disperse because these spaces weren't designed for ventilation like a range would be. Those were the first things someone noticed when they walked into a site like Mason had. Next would be the scorched scent of terror, smelling as rank as a hog trapped in hot sunlight. Bitter and cloying, it was a searing musk which would stick in the back of the throat, coating every breath with pheromones created in an intense fight-or-flight situation. Then, depending on the number of causalities, they would smell waste, the byproduct of terror and injury. Blood, feces, urine, vomit—any of these, and likely all of them—would be carried on the air, too. Perforating wounds, involuntary reactions to the gore left behind; unavoidable evidence of slack muscles of the dead. You never forgot the smells, or the sounds.

"You lose anyone?" If it were someone he knew, Watcher would have a trip to Chicago to plan.

"Prospect. Dirty Dan. Downed by the first shot, what started it all." Not a name he recognized, but Watcher questioned, wanting to be certain.

"Patched long?" Sometimes men jumped clubs, so even if he hadn't been in the Rebels long, Watcher might still know him from elsewhere. "From Chicago?"

"Yeah, a Chi-town native. He wasn't a patch, had barely rolled from hangaround to prospect. You don't know him, brother, no worries." Mason paused, and when he continued, there was a note of pride in his voice. "You remember Andy?" Watcher grunted in affirmation because of course, he remembered Andy. "He's a fuckin' keeper, man. What you said about Mexico, I got to see with my own eyes. Bones himself ran a recruitin' play right on the fucking spot. I literally gave Andy his vest an hour before this shit went down. Took me way too fuckin' long to talk him into it, but he finally took the leap. Then, the first thing that goes down is Machos getting up in my shit. The man took it in stride. Like a fuckin' rock. Slate. Only thing had him shittin' himself was worried he'd fucked up. Not the trash he took out, not the fact there was red runnin' through the room, only if he'd screwed up."

"Club. Family. Honor. Nice to know a man like him slipped through my fuckin' fingers." Watcher laughed. "Thanks for that, asshat."

"Thank you for letting him slip. I need men like him." Mason paused, then told Watcher the same thing he'd ended nearly every call with for the past eight years. "Need men like you, brother. When you gonna give up your hot-as-shit desert for a house by the big lake?"

"In your dreams, big boy." Watcher laughed, then sobered to say, "You sure it was Machos, brother?"

"Yeah, flyin' the green. No doubt about it." Cautious, Mason asked, "Why? What's got you tweaked?"

"Not tweaked, exactly. And I don't want to say anything until I know for sure, but you know who Machos' president is, know what the bastard is to my Juanita and Carmela." Watcher paused, unsure how much to say until he had a chance to check on things, and decided to err on the side of caution. "Hate to think he'd reach so far because of Andy."

"Slate." Mason corrected him idly, reminding Watcher of Andy's new road name, then tone sharp, questioned, "What do you mean, because of Slate? What's he got to do with Machos?"

"You know I got a beef with 'em. You know how deep it runs, how far the hate goes." These were statements, not questions, and Watcher didn't wait for a response. "You also know, because I told you and you don't forget a fuckin' thing, An—Slate went to Mexico with me and mine. I told you how Mela came to be mine and Juanita's, even before we knew she was a cousin. It is not a far stretch to believe Estavez could have tracked Slate. In fact, since this happened, I wonder about Memphis. How much has Slate told you about his time there?"

"Nada," Mason said quickly, anger tingeing his voice. "He ain't said shit."

"Ling." When Watcher called the drug king's name, Mason drew a breath. "Yeah, brother. Slate didn't get sideways of the man, but a woman he knew did, and I know Slate did some digging. Might have gotten himself on radar that way. Add that to the Machos having a hard-on for anyone who sides with me, knowing they back Ling and Ling sells all their product, including flesh? You can add it to him rollin' to you, and them knowing our history for as much as we've put out there, it ain't hard to tally up a pain column. Slate mighta brought this to your door, brother." Watcher shook his head, something wasn't right in the mix. "Feels like I'm missing something, though. It's not quite...right. Plus, if he did, I can guarantee you he did it unknowingly. Man didn't even know the difference between an MC and an RC until after he hit Chicago. Was a foreign language. Been educating him long distance, he's been a remote student for a while." This pulled a laugh from Mason, and Watcher smiled to hear it.

"I'll take over his schooling from here out, brother." Mason paused, and in the brief interval between words came the distinct sound of a match strike, then the harsh rush of air that signaled the first draw off a cigarette. "I know you're right. If he did bring the target, then he didn't even know he carried it. He's one of the most open and easy to read people I've met. Heart of gold, man. He feels shit deep. So fuckin' deep. Wants to be whatever is needed. Wants it in a way that can't be taught." Another rush of air. "Machos." A pause, then, "Shit, man, they been swirling around us for a long time. Wasn't him that told them my strip joint was neutral."

"No shit? You opened it up? I didn't know, brother. Thought Jackson's was your only neut. Good to know." This told him Mason was confident about his position in Chicago, something which gave Watcher relief after Bones' last conversation. Then his relief died when Mason laughed.

"Nope. I did not. Had a cut patch motherfucker passin' out bullshit. Well—" He paused, and Watcher listened carefully. "He wasn't a cut at the time. Is one now." The name seemed torn from Mason, and recognizing it, Watcher knew why. "Monster." An officer. *Fuck*.

"Shit." That was bad and pointed to a version of bad which seemed to echo what Bones had told him. Mason was losing focus, and if his members were revolting, then it would only escalate. "You cut him?"

"He took the path you'd expect, man. I allowed it and then encouraged his beat out. Earned a couple days in an assclown gown." This meant Monster had been allowed a choice. Drop his patches voluntarily and live. Was allowed to leave the club on his own two feet, but the fact he took a beating afterward said his chosen departure left him out bad. Monster wouldn't get another club to call home in the area, ever, and might not find another club ever ready to take a chance on him. "Officer, and he pulled this kinda shit. Fiends, I shoulda known." Rebel Fiends was the club Mason had killed, the first he'd joined and the precursor to the Rebel Wayfarers which he now ran. Monster had been a member of the previous club and had stuck with Mason through the coup which moved them to where they were now. Longevity as much as anything had gotten the man an officer patch, and now his true colors had been exposed. Assclown gown, that meant his beat down was enough to get him a hospital bed for a few days.

"Shit," Watcher repeated, the word not sufficient to the dread in his gut. "You holdin' your shit, brother?"

"Yeah, I'm holdin' it. I've got good men, patched in a dozen in the past year who are club to the core. The kind of members you know will carry the club on their backs until they bleed. Don't need fence-sitters or chair-fillers. Monster was both of those. Came to a decision vote. Monster'd fuckin' wait to see where the wind was blowing before he cast his lot." Like many clubs, Soldiers included, the Rebels used a system of markers to indicate a yes or no vote on any big topic. Black was no, white was yes, and the timing of when you laid your vote down told everyone at the table where you actually stood. Early voting was a passionate plea, even in a silent church when no argument was allowed. Men who didn't have a dog in the hunt waited to see which way the vote would sway, and then either cast their lot to cock-block if they didn't like the brother promoting the change, or throw it to ensure their favorite knew they had backing, regardless of the actual outcome of the vote. Chair-fillers were men who marked time in the club, looking for a better thing. They'd go from role to role in a club, trying to find something that fit, or, and this was arguably worse, they'd be all about the party, and roll from gig to gig there, too. "Him out, lets me nominate someone I want close. Open a spot at the table for heads who won't push as hard for the shit I'm still tryin' to stamp out."

Before Mason had taken over, the Fiends ran whores. Not slaves, but still owned girls. Women who didn't see any other way of living their life. Watcher had heard, but never asked, that the tipping point for Mason was when Deacon took payment for a shipment of product in girls. Bringing back a dozen undocumented women from Canada. As unwilling as it got, and sounding far too close to the kind of trafficking Juanita had endured.

"What's next for the Rebels, then? You got a line on the Machos? Gonna get your pound of flesh back?" Watcher knew he would be on the warpath if something like that went down for him.

"Holdin' my shit. Wanna see how this internal struggle in the Machos plays out. Bide my time and be smart, they might take care of my problem for me." Noise from outside and Watcher looked up to see Devil and Opie walk through the door into the barn. He acknowledged them with a chin lift as Mason kept talking, telling him more than he knew. "I've got my finger on the pulse of a half a dozen things right here in Chicago." One of those would be the pretty neighbor, no doubt. "Got enough of my own shit to deal with. Gonna let their shit run, see where it ends up. Bingo's in Indiana. We're expanding east for a change."

Watcher grunted, because it was news. "You sanction that shit?" Up to now, all the Rebel chapters were west of Chicago. South and west, but not too far west. Watcher didn't want to butt up against Mason in a struggle for territory and suspected Mason felt the same. East took the Rebels into potential conflict with a dozen other clubs, though.

"Yeah. I wanna keep the old bastard, and Bingo was struggling with a family issue meant he was needed in Fort Wayne. I'd already been talkin' to two small clubs there, trying to figure out if I wanted to start a support patch campaign. Now, at least one of them will be rolling into the new Rebel chapter." Mason laughed. "Give you one guess whose club it is."

DeeDee was Mason's cousin, from the same holler in Kentucky. Her old man was Winger, and he'd been the one to first introduce Mason to the life, way back when. They were in Fort Wayne, so the moment Mason spoke, Watcher knew who he had to be talking about. "No. You serious?" Tipping his chin down, Watcher grinned at the floor. "Lucky bastard. You always seem to have people right where you need them, when you need them." Opie grabbed the back of a chair and pulled it closer to the desk and then sat, Devil patiently leaning against a pillar next to him. "DeeDee know Winger's doin' that shit?" He laughed. "Full circle, brother. That's stellar."

"Yeah. Keepin' it all in the family, for sure."

Watcher's phone buzzed, and he narrowed his eyes as Opie and Devil reached into their pockets at the same time, pulling out their phones. A broadcast. *Shit.* "Well, you know what they say about incest." Opie's eyes lifted to his, and the expression on his face made Watcher's blood run cold. "Mason," he clipped into the phone. "Gotta go." Disconnecting, he pulled his phone away and looked at the screen, seeing three letters texted from an international number. *Fuck.* "Call the brothers." He stared at the screen for another moment, hearing Opie and Devil rushing to comply with his demand. *SOS.* "Call 'em all."

***

Hands loosely gripping the stick he had threaded through the center of the wire spools, Watcher shuffled backwards as quickly as he could without tripping and falling in the dark alley. He rounded a corner and dropped to one knee, feeling a presence at his back. Trusting his brothers, he didn't turn and look, simply pulled out his phone and dialed. "Team One in place."

"Five by five. Copy, One." They had abandoned their tech for this run, because the distance between teams and the construction of the surrounding buildings meant their communications might be spotty. He waited, several tense minutes passing before finally receiving the response for which he'd been waiting. "We're a go. Repeat, we are a go."

"Copy." While waiting, he'd not been idle, stripping the wires and connecting them to the small hand-held detonator he carried. Fingers working quickly, he connected the battery and slammed the cover into place. A moment later there was a rattling boom north of their position, and he spoke into the phone, "Team Two fired." He waited a beat, then said, "Fire in the hole." One finger on the toggle, he tugged it gently, feeling the click as it completed the circuit. Thunder rolled up the alley, pulsing past the niche where he and his team waited, dust following the noise. "Team One fired."

"Copy. Team Three fired." That was good news, because Opie's team was so far away he hadn't been able to hear their detonation. "Confirm all targets, boss. Repeat, all targets fired."

"Copy." A rattle of gunfire and Watcher held up a fist, silently telling his men to wait it out. The cartel's men would be expecting them to rush in following the blast. They were firing blindly into the dust raised by the explosion. When they failed to connect, he knew those men would begin making their way down the alley. Simple psychology to advance until they found resistance. No resistance, they'd make their way farther and farther from the base, opening the way for the Soldiers' final salvo which would completely destroy the target.

Once a sapper, always a sapper, he thought with a grin as he swapped the wires for the second pair. This was when he always felt the most in control. Where he was meant to be. Putting together the intel, laying out a strategy and watching as his men identified and understood what was needed. Looping the teams together, playing strength to strength in a way their everyday life didn't allow. And then executing the plan. Locating supplies, getting everything into place, and doing his damnedest to ensure everything came off the way it was supposed to.

The Soldiers had identified three cartel warehouses in Juarez, and their current operation was intended to destroy each base of operations for the cartel. The target wasn't simply the removal of hundreds of thousands of American dollars in product, but it was his intent to send a statement at the same time pushing back the cartel's hold. This would free the territory up for someone else to fill, and Watcher prayed the right ones would come out the winner. The first blasts were intended to breach the outer walls but without doing significant structural damage. The next ones would have a very different result.

The gunfire came closer, dust beginning to settle as the air cleared slightly. "Phase two," Watcher said over his shoulder, hearing the feet shuffling into position. "Team One is going again. Fire in the hole," he called into the phone at the same time he heard and felt the detonation. Much larger this time, a rolling vibration that transferred up through the soles of their boots. Bricks in the wall in front of him rattled and shook, releasing their own torrents of sand to join the maelstrom rolling up the alley. Cries of terror sounded, and the slapping of shoes on the hard dirt surface marked the advance of the cartel's men. The first runners flashed past the opening, and he counted only two seconds before there was a whump of air compressing, followed immediately by a flash of light. They'd triggered the closest trap. Shouts and screams still moving away, several seconds elapsed before the next explosion. "Blowin' shit up since 1986." Nervous snickers from behind him highlighted the tension everyone was working under right now.

From the phone came confirmation all three teams had executed their portion of the plan. *Time to get the hell out of Dodge, back across the bridge and into friendly territory.* Using the code preprogrammed into the traps, he remotely detonated those not already tripped, and led his team of soldiers turned bikers turned soldiers again out of the maze of streets.

***

Juanita

Juanita woke as Watcher settled on the bed behind her, pulling her across the mattress and into his body. Tense and tight, his muscles were stiff against her back. He'd been gone for three days with many of the club's members leaving their house, usually bustling with activity as men and their women moved in and out, quiet and eerie, only the two girls and herself to keep it full.

It was as if his thoughts tracked hers, even in the dark like this, when she was sure he couldn't see her face. "We need a dog," he muttered, lips to her neck. His beard was damp; he'd showered, but she could still smell smoke on his skin. Not cigarette smoke, but like he'd been near a big fire. "A big dog, like a mastiff. Horse-sized dog that'll scare off anyone. I'd feel better. Don't like leaving you here alone." His arms gave her a tight squeeze.

"I have my pistol," she reminded him, frowning when the bed shook with his laughter. "What? You showed me how to use it. Made me memorize your four rules, I remember them." Ticking them off on her fingers, she recited the words he'd drummed into her head. "All guns are loaded. Don't aim unless you are prepared to shoot. Finger off until you have it pointed at what you want to destroy." On the word "destroy," she knew she made a face and was glad he couldn't see it. "Once you pull the trigger, you can't take it back." Now she felt grumpy. "You even told me I was a good student."

"Yeah, I did, and you are, and you've got it right over there in the nightstand drawer. I know, baby. You showed me." He gave her another squeeze. "But you've also got a trigger lock on it and can't find the key." She stiffened, irritated that she gave that much away. "I wasn't supposed to find out, I know. Bella can't help herself sometimes." He nuzzled against her ear. "Don't be mad."

"I'm not mad." She could hear the crossness in her own voice and tried to tamp it down. "And the key isn't lost. It's just misplaced."

"Same as, baby." Teeth grazed her earlobe, and she shivered at the hot wash of breath across her skin. Desire curled in her belly, and she clenched her thighs together. Proving he was as in tune as she thought, he whispered, his voice gone ragged with need, "Wanna get busy with your husband?"

She arched her back, pressing her ass against his hips, shivering again when she felt the hardness there. *I'm his.* "Always."

"Mmmm." He nipped her ear again, skimming her nightshirt up with one hand to cup her breast, tugging on her peaked nipple. "Good answer."

***

Watcher

"Your actions ensured my victory," Raul Estavez said, giving Watcher a beer. This time, it was Watcher who'd come visiting, bringing three men with him deep into Chihuahua to Raul's current base of operations. "And without knowing you did so, you coordinated your efforts with those of the Malcontents out of California, who drew attention to themselves in Mexicali. With so many active engagements, the cartel pulled their support from the Machos, leaving them to me." Raul kicked the stump on which he'd been seated to one side, moving it farther from the fire. "And I was ready."

"And Carlos?" Watcher had heard the other Estavez brother had escaped north, making his way free of the skirmish lines.

"Does not have long left to him on this earth." Ass to the stump again, Raul stretched his legs out, soles of his boots to the fire. Watcher studied him, marking the differences in this man and the one he had first met. Leaner, which would come from the constant activity caused by the running battles. But he looked harder, too. More capable. Less the businessman he had been, and more like the outlaws he'd befriended. Where Raul's statement would have been laughable a year ago, dismissed as bluster from a man not capable of backing it up, now, it was a promise. "He had a small corps of loyalists with him, but we're tracking them. They are currently in the Denver area, and I will be headed there directly." Raul lifted his gaze, locking it on Watcher. "I will not fail in this. My Carmela will be safe."

"She already is," Watcher reminded him, because she was in a safe house with the rest of the women and children. Taking no chances, Watcher had ordered the move be made before he and his men stepped a foot across the border on this trip. "As safe as we can make her."

"No, Watcher. I mean she will be safe while living her life. Not locked behind walls, not looking over her shoulder. My friend, that is not a life. It is barely an existence. I want my daughter to *live*." Raul had leaned forward as he spoke, his passion ringing through his words.

"Brother," Watcher cautioned, "as long as we are the men we have to be, then our families will need protection." He shook his head. "We will always have enemies who want to take what is ours. Simply by defending what we have, we will gain more enemies. It's how people are, my friend. They want what they can't have, and hate those who have it." He sighed, leaning backwards and shifting away from the fire. "She's as safe as we can make it, and so is my Bella. Our kids are with people who love them and who would die to keep them from harm. All we can ask, brother."

"True. All we can ask of others. I can ask more of myself, so I will be leaving in the morning on my way to Colorado." Raul lifted his beer, but before he tipped it to drink, said, "Your old mentor is...has become an annoyance." He swallowed, then said, "Shooter overstepped. He has offered support to Carlos. The compound in Denver where my brother is producing and storing his heroin belongs to Outriders."

"I couldn't give two shits what Shooter's doing. He cut ties with me long ago, cemented the gap the last time I saw him." Watcher shook his head. "You do what you gotta do. No skin off my nose there." A pause, then he continued, "Except his kids. Don't bring his kids into it. Luke and Eddie. Let's leave them off the menu, like we want our girls left alone."

"Done." Raul immediately agreed. "Shooter, however, will be going down."

"Without a doubt. Lemme know if you need anything from my Soldiers on that front." Watcher stood, stretching his back, trusting the men he had on the perimeter to safeguard him, even silhouetted against the fire like this. "Rack time for me. Me and mine will be headed out early." Reaching out his hand, he gripped hard when Raul's palm met his. "Safe travels, brother."

"And to you."

Seven years

Watcher stood up off his bike and stretched, feeling his muscles complain at the movement after being locked into place for so long. Tense, he swept the parking lot with his gaze while Spider backed his bike in beside Watcher's, killing the engine. Spider swung his leg over and groaned. "Jesus, Watch, you are a machine on a cross-country run. I hadda piss like a hundert miles ago."

Rolling his eyes, Watcher walked towards the motel's office, calling over his shoulder, "Room should be ready. I reserved it while you were talking to the pretty thing at the last gas stop, which by the way was only fifty miles ago, so you havin' to piss ain't my fault."

"Whatever," Spider yelled back through his laughter. They'd ridden through the night, and Watcher was sure Spider was every bit as saddle-sore as he was. Five minutes later they had the bikes unpacked and were standing in the room, staring at the single king bed. Without a word, Watcher turned on his heel and stalked out, long strides carrying him back to the office. Ten minutes after that, they were in a different room, looking with some relief at two double beds.

"How long we got before we needa roll, brother?" Spider turned in place, dropped his bag to the floor and fell backwards, bouncing twice on the mattress. "I got time for a power nap?"

"A couple hours. It's only a five-minute ride to where we're going. I'm gonna want some grub before, though." Watcher set his bag on the built-in dresser, unfastening the buckles holding it closed. He pulled out a button-down shirt, frowning at the wrinkles in the fabric as he tossed it aside. Digging through the bag, he found a black tee and laid it across the bag. "Thought you had to piss?"

"Pissed outside." Spider toed off his boots, letting them fall with a thump to the thin carpet. "You go get food, come back, wake me up and we'll head over. I don't need to eat as much as I need sleep." He yawned, his mouth opening wide. "Fuck, man. I'm beat to hell and back." Lifting his head, he stared at Watcher. "We made it though. Sorry as fuck for the reason you had to come home."

"Ain't my home, not anymore," Watcher said, walking towards the bathroom. "I'll leave a key on the table, be back in time to get your ass up. Sleep, brother. Appreciate you making the run with me."

Two days ago he'd gotten a surprise call from Bethany, who'd heard from a friend that his Aunt Loretta had passed. No surprise his family hadn't contacted him, because other than his uncle, who Watcher wouldn't piss on if he were on fire in the street, he didn't have any. Some random cousins, but he hadn't seen any of them in so long, he probably wouldn't recognize them if he saw them. If it had been Ezra who'd died, he wouldn't have even called the florist, but because of what Loretta had been to Tabby, he'd made the trip to attend her funeral.

Seated in a booth at the front window of the diner, Watcher was fielding questions from the waitress, trying to remember her name without letting on he'd forgotten it, when the door opened and admitted two vest-wearing men. Watcher squinted at the one, thinking his face looked familiar when the other called his name.

"Fuck me, it's Watcher. Got a call about a pair of vests in town. Saw a bike out front, figured we'd find something in here. Didn't expect to see you. Hey man." Sticking out his hand for a shake, the taller of the two approached Watcher's table. Scanning the names on the front of the leather, he saw one he recognized.

"Patches, how you doin'?" *Jesus, he looks old.* The years rode heavy on the man, scars and sun-etched lines twisting across his face. Standing, Watcher waited with his own hand out, careful to avoid being pulled into a clinch.

"Good, man." Patches twisted and yelled towards the back of the diner, "Nancy, cuppa coffee for Beeman and me." He shoved at the other man, not introducing him and Watcher belatedly noticed the prospect patch above his nameplate. He'd already seen the Outrider emblem on Patches' back, which was no surprise. "What brings you back to Cynthiana? I didn't get the word you were headed our way; does Painter know you're in town?"

Watcher shook his head. "I've been on the road for two days trying to get here in time for Loretta's funeral." He lifted one hand, palm up. "I didn't make any calls."

"I got you, man. Get you covered," Patches said, pulling out his phone. He tapped for a moment, then laid it on the table between them where the screen would be clearly visible. "Hadn't heard she passed. Sorry, Watch."

"I have a man with me, too. Spider. You might remember him from Danger's services." Patches nodded, eyes on the phone. Watcher let the silence sit between them, waiting for whatever response they might receive. The waitress delivered the coffee to the table, topped off Watcher's cup, and quickly retreated behind the counter. She hadn't seemed nervous earlier, in fact, she'd joked with Watcher about him needing about fifty cups of coffee because he looked so tired. Now, she was making certain she had a solid barrier between her and these two.

The phone buzzed, rattling against the tabletop and Patches let out a huge sigh, exposing a lot with that one single action. He'd been worried about what the response would be. Watcher leaned in, reading the text upside down, **Prty 2nite. Bring him**. Patches typed in a single **Y** in response, then tucked his phone away, suddenly gregarious again.

When it was time to wake Spider, Patches and the prospect accompanied Watcher to the motel, waiting in the parking lot as he retrieved his sole backup. Watcher still wasn't entirely comfortable with their escort, but since he hadn't called ahead, he understood the need. Given their company, he abandoned the idea of the button-down shirt, pulling on the black tee instead, settling his cut over it as he patted down his weapons, ensuring they were all in place and secure.

After the funeral, during which his only emotion had been shock at the aged and infirm state of Ezra, Watcher verified the clubhouse location for the Outriders hadn't changed, and then led their small group directly there, regardless it was only three in the afternoon. His eyes narrowed when he saw the lot gate standing wide, no member on guard. The exterior of the building hinted at what they'd find inside, and the desolate feeling evoked by the exterior's peeling paint was reinforced by broken-down furniture and smoke-stained ceilings.

A few faces Watcher recognized turned their way when he walked in ahead of the Outrider members, shock registering first and then he was pleased to see smiles. He had left on good terms, Morgan not giving him guff about needing to support his blood brother, but while he'd seen some of the men at Darrie's service, this was the first time he'd entered Outrider property since dropping his patch. Pounding slaps on the shoulder, clasped wrists, and proffered fist bumps cemented the knowledge in him that these men held respect for him, which felt good.

By the time the party was in full swing, Watcher had slowed his alcohol consumption to a crawl, not wanting to make himself vulnerable. It wasn't that he didn't trust the men in the room, more a sense of self-preservation he'd learned long ago. A shout came from the door, and his caution proved prudent when he turned to see Shooter walking inside. Hands on his hips, Shooter stopped just inside the room, scanning faces until he found Watcher. *Fuck.* Their last communication hadn't been cordial, and he knew his refusal to allow passage through Soldiers' territory cost the Outriders in both face and money, since it meant they had to take a far northern route, negotiating with tribal clubs. So it shocked him when a wide grin split Shooter's face, and there was a shouted greeting of, "Mother*fucker.* Look who's in our house."

Watcher lifted the beer in his hand in a salute, feeling Spider sidle closer to his back as they both watched Shooter striding across the room towards them, hand already extended. Watcher allowed himself to be pulled into a clinch, surprised when Shooter's voice sounded from beside his head, regret in his tone, "Sorry for your loss, man." Stepping back, Shooter continued, "Got word you were in town, hopped the next flight out. I was sorry I missed the service."

Watcher felt his brow furrow when Shooter kept speaking, "Good to see you, Watcher. Miss the days we spent in this house, man." Nodding slowly, Watcher kept his gaze trained on Shooter. "We have some entertainment planned. You won't want to miss this." Shooter tipped his chin at Spider, who nodded his response. "Big show."

Whirling, Shooter shouted towards the bar, "Gimme three glasses, need some Jack, Jim, Johnny, and Jameson. Four horsemen are gonna ride." Turning back to Watcher, he ordered, "You'll drink with me." Plowing his way to the bar, Shooter left no doubt as to his expectations. The faces surrounding them were observing closely, and suddenly feeling as if he were behind enemy lines, Watcher followed slowly, feeling Spider crowding his back.

"Why didn't we fly, boss?" Spider's mutter made Watcher grin. "We'd be on our way home by now. Great excuse, brother. Just say, sorry, we can't stay for your bullshit party, we got a flight to catch." The thump against his back was Spider's fist, playfully pounding the center of his patch, physically reminding both of them they were in this together. "You suck, boss."

"I know," Watcher threw his agreement over his shoulder as he pulled to a halt behind Shooter. A glass slid down the bar towards him, and he reached out, managing to discretely spill half the contents onto the already swamped surface before lifting it to his mouth. Throwing a mouthful back, he swallowed hard, refusing to choke on the bite of the alcohol.

Shooter laughed, slapping his shoulder before shouting, "This party is about to get crazy." His eyes cut to something over Watcher's shoulder and even though his spine prickled, Watcher didn't turn to see what he was watching. "Oh, yeah," Shooter's voice had dropped to a mutter. "Gonna get fuckin' insane up in here." Gaze back to Watcher, he stared hard for a moment, then smiled, the expression on his face so far from humor Watcher felt Spider crowd him again.

"Got a private party. The two of you"—Shooter indicated Spider in the sweep of his arm—"are invited to do something only one of you has done before. Or—" He paused, tipping his head sideways to look at Watcher. "—I think you've done it before. Maybe not. You ever remember partying like an Outrider? No? We'll pop that fuckin' cherry tonight. Official invitation." Tipping his head back, he howled, this bizarre behavior echoed by several men around the room. "Shit's changed since you pussied out, Watch. We party like we fuckin' mean it now."

Shooter took a step closer. Close enough Watcher arched backwards, uncomfortable at the narrowed distance between them. Voice dropping to a hiss, Shooter said, "Come on, bro—" Making a show of interrupting himself, Shooter shook his head, eyes opened wide. Lifting one palm between them, he said, "Oh, fuck. Hold on. Gimme a minute. Jesus, I nearly fucked up." Shooter patted the air as with a theatrical sigh, he continued, "Lemme go again. I'll get it right eventually. Come on, *friend*, see what I've put together in your honor."

Behind him, Spider muttered, "On your six, boss," as they followed Shooter across the crowded room and through a door to what used to be an office. Pool table in the center of the room indicated the function had changed, and what was going on in the room was as far from business as anything Watcher could imagine.

A man, naked except for his vest which proclaimed him a prospect, was tied spread-eagled to the end of the table, ass up. Silent, his forehead pressed against the green felt, eyes squeezed tightly closed while behind him, a man in a full-patched Outriders' vest powered into his asshole. On the other end of the pool table, Watcher saw a woman was stretched out on top of a man. He couldn't tell from this angle for certain, but it looked like the man's cock was inside her. Her pose was similar to the trussed prospect, crotch to the edge of the table, forehead pressed deep into the muscled shoulder of the man on his back beneath her. Painter, who Watcher had lost track of once Shooter entered the building, stood behind her, pumping hard, his hand swinging and slapping her ass cheeks every time he withdrew.

Shooter stopped four feet into the room, and Watcher stifled a flinch when the door slammed closed behind them. "Party time," Shooter shouted, tipping his head back and howling again. The sound was only repeated by one man in the room, the cry muffled against the top of the pool table as the prospect uttered the first noises he'd made since Shooter had led Watcher and Spider into the room. "Fuck yeah," Shooter said, edging closer to the table as the man fucking the prospect pulled out, hand going to his cock and jerking, white spunk coating the asshole left gaping in his wake. "My turn," Shooter said, tossing a crazy grin over his shoulder to Watcher. "You don't get the pros. This is Outrider ass only." Jerking his chin toward the other end of the table, he laughed, the sound brittle. "Tail is for anyone." Hands fumbling at his belt, Shooter yanked his cock out of his pants and without pausing, slammed inside the prospect who took the assault without flinching.

At his words, the woman lifted her head, and Watcher stood in shock, recognizing the worn features of Carrie Sosa. *Jesus*. The expectation was clear, invitation more like a demand and turning down the club hospitality would be a mortal insult. Watcher was stuck, frozen between what he understood would get them out of this building alive, and what burned in his soul. Spider leaned forwards, his voice scarcely a whisper as he said, "You can't, boss." And Watcher wouldn't. For him, there had only been Juanita, and Spider had heard him vow to go to his grave with it only ever being her. Silent, he seemed to be waiting for Watcher's nod, because as soon as he gave it, Spider told him, "But I can."

Schooling his features to impassivity, Watcher stood, a silent observer as Painter finished in Sosa's ass, leaning far over and biting her back so viciously his lips were painted red when he stood. The man on his back under her had silenced her scream, clamping his hand over her mouth and nose with a grunted, "Shut the fuck up, bitch," removing it only after she'd collapsed back onto him, her spine leaving the agonized arch it had assumed in response to the pain.

The other men standing behind her gave way to Spider, moving out of line as he walked their direction. Fingers gliding across her side, his other hand went to his wallet, which he flipped open with a practiced motion. Condom in hand, he freed his already hard cock, rolling it down his length. Watcher's eyes were fixed on Sosa's face. Tears had left raccoon tracks around her eyes, crimson smeared along one cheek. She was thinner than he remembered, and looked used up, choices in her life having consequences written on her skin. The man under her grunted as she moved, sliding across his body an inch before he anchored her with an arm around her waist. "Fuckin' snug, dude. You the big dick in the house, no doubt." Watcher's gaze flicked to Spider who was now moving behind her, his head tipped back, eyes closed. *Not something either of us wanna remember*, Watcher thought, turning his gaze to Shooter who had stepped away and was tucking his dick back into his pants. They locked eyes as the noise level in the room gradually returned to what it was before, flesh slapping flesh as yet another Outriders member worked the prospect over.

Spider's groan echoed over the group, and knowing he wouldn't be in the room much longer, Watcher muttered, "Gotta piss." Turning to walk away, he was clumsy in his anxiety, struggling to keep his feet from tripping as he waited for someone to try and stop him. An intense itch started and grew in the center of his back, and Watcher knew the weight was Shooter's gaze on him. One foot in front of the other, Watcher moved to the door, trusting Spider to call a warning.

Watcher stepped through the door, reaching back to tug it shut as Sosa wailed again, a meaty smack sounding in the room. Movement at the base of the wall to his left drew Watcher's attention, and he looked down to see a boy sitting on the floor. Head bent deep, he seemed to be studying his crossed legs. Gaze up, Watcher scanned the room, seeing two men receiving blowjobs on the couch opposite, and a near-naked woman on the bar, her bellybutton serving as a shot glass. *Fuck.* "Kid." No reaction, the boy's dark hair had come untucked from behind his ears, falling forwards to curtain his face. "Hey, kid. Let's go outside." A flinch, subtly turning the boy's face away, adding avoidance to his posture. "Kid, you don't need to be watching this."

"Ain't lookin'." Muttered words, the tone snide as if he were educating an idiot.

"If you ain't watching what's going on right in front of you, then what are you doing sittin' here?" Watcher shook his head, squatting, one knee to the floor, trying to ignore the boy sliding another six inches away. "You shouldn't be in here, kid."

"I gotta wait." Petulant now, the boy clearly wasn't here of his own choice. "She'll be done soon."

Fuck. "She?" Which of the whores was this kid's mother?

The kid jerked his head to the wall behind him, his hair swinging with the motion. "Mom. She'll be done soon."

Watcher froze, taking in what he could see of the boy. Dark hair, a jaw that would one day be square and strong. The boy shifted, straightening and then refolded his legs. Watcher saw him dart a glance his direction, glint of eyes shining behind the fall of hair. "Your mom's in this room?" He reached out and touched the door behind him, wondering for a moment where Spider was, he'd expected his man would follow him out.

"Yeah. She'll be done, get her dough, and we'll get outta here." Fingers working at the folded seam of his jeans, the kid tucked and untucked the fabric bunched at his knee.

"How old are you, boy?" Silently he counted the years, measured the gulf between past and present.

"Twelve." Chin tucked to his throat, the boy stifled his own word until it was nearly unintelligible. "What's it to you?"

Fuckin' attitude on this one, Watcher thought. Then the boy tipped his head back, looking directly into Watcher's face and Watcher stopped thinking. Davis Mason's features stared back at him. Dark hair framing a face with high cheekbones, piercing grey eyes gazing at him. *Jesus.*

The door opened behind him, but he didn't look up, didn't move as he asked, "Got a name, boy?"

"Chase." The boy's gaze flicked over his shoulder, and he felt Spider's presence at his back. "Chase Sosa."

***

"Brother, I'm telling you, it's Mason's kid." Watcher paced the length of the motel room, passing between the foot of the beds and the TV for the fifth time. "Lemme tell you a story about the bitch you ass-fucked tonight."

Spider punched the pillow he had wedged behind his head, propping him against the headboard. Features on his face filled with unease, he looked up at Watcher and said, "And about that, boss. I want you to note I took one for the team tonight. Fucked that bitch in the ass, man's dick bumpin' against mine with every fuckin' stroke. Took one for the fuckin' team, and you needa remember this shit next time I fuck up." He waved his other hand, gripping the neck of the beer bottle. "Cut me a little slack next time you wanna whup me."

"Noted," Watcher grunted, then sighed. "Never seen an initiation of a prospect quite like that one."

"Jesus, boss. Did you see how many motherfuckers were lined up for a taste of the boy's ass?" Spider spread his arms wide in an imitation of the prospect's earlier position. "Him spread out and tied up like a fuckin' hog-tied calf bein' dragged shitter-first to slaughter. *Jesus*." Tipping his beer up, he took a long drink, then waved it again, "If we tried to pull that kind of shit, wouldn't nobody be patching in. No one we'd want, anyway. And they're working with some young clubs, too. Teachin' them that shit. *Jesus*."

"Hard to imagine he knew what was coming." Watcher shook his head.

"From what I gathered, every fuckin' prospect we saw in the main room will get the same treatment. At least one more of them is on the menu tonight because it's commencement night for the chapter. They have at least one party a month, two prospects earn their patch on their bellies. What happens in that room is a secret, and the wolf howl thing is a signal to the crowd saying the officers need to cut one of their prospects out of the herd. Get ready to take care of business. Howl at the moon like a crazy person, get your ass fucked until you fuckin' bleed. Fuck that shit." He took another drink, the expression on his face moving from disquiet to anger. "Fuck it hard."

Spider tipped his head up, looking straight at Watcher. "And you used to be one of them? *Jesus*, boss." His head shook back and forth, his features now strained. As much as he was trying to joke about tonight, what he'd seen and done had affected him as much as it had Watcher. "Glad as hell you got out when you did. Y'all some crazy motherfuckers in Kentucky. *Jesus*."

"You done?" Watcher leaned one hip against the table, fingers going to the curtains and twitching them back an inch to look at their bikes parked in the space in front of the room. "Because if you are, I have a story to tell you." He looked over his shoulder at a glaring Spider. "Don't wanna interrupt your recounting of the team support you provided tonight." He shifted, facing the room. "By all means, go on. I can wait."

"Fuck you, boss." Spider shot him an attempt at a grin, the humor not reaching his eyes. "Tell your tale."

Watcher took a breath. "You know Mason." Mouth twisting, Spider nodded. "You know he and I grew up together." Another nod. "You know I was president of Cynthiana chapter for the Outriders." Spider's eyes widened, and he shook his head. "Not surprised, they don't want shit getting out that their officer bailed. It's no secret I was a member, but I hadn't been patched a year when our prez died, and they installed me. Mostly because I didn't have a fuckin' clue what I was doin', which meant they didn't have anyone to argue the fine point of anything. Morgan assigned me a mentor." A noise outside drew his attention and he turned, twitching the curtain again in time to see a pickup drive out of the lot. "His son, John Morgan." Eyes back to Spider, there was an immediate look of recognition, so he snorted a laugh and comfirmed, "Shooter."

"Fuck." Spider drew the word out, scooting towards the head of the bed, sitting up straighter.

"Yup." Watcher grinned, knowing it probably looked as pained as it felt. "Thirteen years ago, I patched out of the Outriders, headed to Las

Cruces to work on building the Southern Soldiers with my brother. You were there. You remember." Watcher paused. "Darrie had started the club, but didn't have a clue how to deal with the politics needed to keep everyone safe and have the club be profitable. I did"—he snorted—"thanks in part to Shooter always fuckin' up. That man could fuck up an omelet if the only thing he had to do was throw away the eggshells." Watcher lifted a hand, scratched through his beard, then smoothed it back down.

"Thirteen years ago the reason I made my decision wasn't because I knew Darrie wasn't working things the way they should be. It was because Shooter made a play against Mason. Somehow, someway, he owned that woman from tonight. Her name's Carrie Sosa. Shooter had her dope Mason and get him to put his name on a piece of paper that made her Carrie Mason. Two full days Mason was so fucked up he didn't know his own name, and she did that. Two days before he finally sobered up enough to know something was going on. Brought her back to my clubhouse, and me thinking he'd already headed back to Chicago. He was still a Fiend then."

Cutting his gaze to Spider, he asked, "You know Shooter was a Fiend?" Head shaking slowly side-to-side, Spider kept his silence as Watcher snorted. "Course not, he doesn't like folks to know the number of patches he's dropped. But he was. This woulda been before Mason's takeover of the club. Shooter put Sosa's play together so he could fuck Mason. I had it out with her in that very fuckin' room, which was my office. Banned her for life, and we see how long it lasted." He snorted. "Got Mason free of her legally, and"—he leaned in an inch—"this is important, *she said under oath there was no child*. The boy you saw me talking to tonight?"

Spider nodded, eyes fixed on Watcher's face.

"Spittin' image of Mason. Looks just like the man when he was a kid."

Spider's eyes widened.

"Yeah, and he's twelve years old. And his name is Chase Sosa."

Shaking his head, Spider sat up, swinging his legs off the bed. He sat like that for a moment and Watcher let him gather his thoughts.

Finally, Spider led with a question. "You're telling me that kid heard me fuck his mom in the ass?" At Watcher's nod, Spider's head tipped back, and he stared at the ceiling. "With some other dude's dick in her pussy." Even though Spider couldn't see him, Watcher nodded again. "Kid heard everything." Bringing his chin down, Spider stared at Watcher again. "If the boy's twelve, what the fuck is his mama thinking?" He paused, then swore, voice hoarse in his fury. "*Fuck*, boss. Kid's probably more clued in on what's going down in that club than any of the prospects in the whole motherfuckin' room. *Fuck*. This leaves a bad taste in my mouth." The beer was discarded on the nightstand when he stood. "I need air."

"Don't go far," Watcher cautioned, moving to one side so Spider could get to the door.

"Won't." Spider paused. "What are you gonna tell Mason?"

"No fuckin' clue."

***

The voice on the phone was gruff, filled with a sandpaper rasp as if the man smoked two packs of cigarettes a day. "Heard good things about you."

Watcher rolled his eyes. He was parked at a gas station, waiting on Spider to come back out with whatever junk food had caught his eye this stop. Spider would eat it, then in an hour be looking for a shitter because it wrecked his belly. Made for a long run, if an amusing one, because after every assburning episode Spider would vow, "Never again." Then at the next gas stop, he'd do it again.

"Same," he told the voice on the phone. "Unsure of the context of this call, and I'm on the road. Means I don't got a lotta time, so if there's something I can do for you, we'll need to skip to the ask part of the conversation so I can tell you no."

Laughter rolled up the line and into his ear, and Watcher found himself grinning. At least the man didn't take offense at the up-front blow off.

"Don't hold back, man. Tell me how you really feel." The voice belonged to Blue Line, president of the Malcontents out of the San Diego area, a club Raul had worked with as he doggedly hunted Carlos, dismantling his brother's connections. "Not a LEO fan, I take it?"

"You know many MC who are?" Malcontents was a cop club, and as such, considered an enemy by nearly everyone in the life except other law enforcement clubs. Soldiers didn't go out of their way to avoid a cop club, but one would never be considered an ally, either.

"Fair, man. Fair." A pause, and Watcher looked up when the door to the convenience store opened, seeing Spider walk out holding two mustard-covered corn dogs in one hand and an enormous cup of something in his other, lips pursing and questing as the elusive end of the straw sticking up through the lid evaded him. Blue Line pulled his attention back to the call when he said, "No ask, man. Just reaching out because we have friends in common." Another pause and Watcher focused even more sharply when the man told him, "We have enemies in common, too."

"Who you got painted in your head as my enemy, Blue Line?" At the name, Spider's eyes widened, and he grinned around the end of one of the yellow smeared dogs. "I got one? A dozen? Go on, gimme what you got. Enlighten me."

"Outriders, from what I hear." Blue Line didn't beat around the bush, laying things right out in the open. "Man, there's a tape circulating. You seriously pissed off national by turning down hospitality."

"Fuck," Watcher muttered, remembering the gleeful look on Shooter's face when Watcher had turned to leave the room with Sosa still spread out underneath Spider. "Motherfucker."

"Yeah, he's all of that. Knows who his daddy was, still he's a bastard." Blue Line obviously knew who Watcher was talking about. "You need back-up, I wanted to tell you I got boys in Dallas, can run them up to cover you as you roll through Oklahoma."

This would be a give from the Malcontents without any promise of a marker, and this resulted in a very surprised Watcher. Malcontents were known for exacting payment for any assistance, bending the spirit of the law, even as they stayed within the letter of it. "Come again?"

"Fuck, man. Do you not know you're one of the good ones? One of the few I believe I could stomach dealin' with? Y'all's bullshit hatred of an LEMC? That shit goes both fuckin' ways, way some of these assholes act. Like Shooter. Assclown through and through, and, man, I find myself hatin' on him." Now Blue Line sounded frustrated, and Watcher tipped his chin down, focusing on what the man didn't say as much as what he did. "You, Raul, Mason, Bones? I might not want you in my family because you do shit—and I know you do shit—but I wouldn't balk at seating you at my table. Totally fucking rare in my world."

This was indeed rare, and something Watcher would need to mull over before he could decide what it meant. Something he could also take to Mason and Bones, get their take on it. He focused on the actionable piece of Blue Line's offer. "What do you propose I do in exchange?" It would be smart to have people riding alongside him, the more, the merrier, and with that in mind, Watcher had already made a call to his Midlands chapter. A half a dozen brothers were rolling east towards him right now. Still, wouldn't hurt to find out what else Blue Line had in his pocket.

"Keep breathin'," Blue Line suggested, and Watcher laughed.

***

Juanita

"Won't." The bed jerked underneath Juanita's body, and she rolled away from the source of the movement and towards the edge. Silence fell in the room again. She listened intently, not hearing anything untoward in the entire house. Settling back onto the mattress, she relaxed, feeling herself begin to slide the short distance back to sleep. Another jerk dragged her eyes open again. "Fuckin' won't."

Coming from the darkness behind her, Watcher's words were thick, slurred with sleep, and she knew he was exhausted from the hard run back from Kentucky. He and Spider had left Las Cruces only five days ago and gone to eastern Kentucky and back in that time, each leg of the trip taking about thirty hours riding time. He'd gotten home, kissed her and the girls, made two calls and crawled into bed. Even Bella's whisper-shout hadn't woken him for supper.

When Juanita undressed for bed, she'd picked up his clothing strewn on the floor, lifting his shirt to her nose to smell the unmistakable scent of the road. A mix of oil and sweat, it always reminded her of their first trip together on the bike, when she'd forced him to take her with him to Kentucky. She smiled as she dropped the shirt and jeans into the hamper. Now, lying beside him, she caught a whiff of a different smell she also recognized. *Fear.*

"*God.*" This pain-filled word came through clenched teeth, and when she rolled to face him, she could see the quivering strain in the muscles. His head arched backwards and he sucked in a deep breath, his body relaxing as he released it. Moving on from the dream it seemed, muscles all over his form growing lax again. His breathing deepened and slowed, and she hoped he was headed into a more refreshing sleep.

Suddenly he jerked, shoulders moving involuntarily as the dream reclaimed him.

He flinched, and his lips twitched. One hand lifted to fend something off in his sleep, then rubbed clumsily against his nose and cheek, as a child would. She was about to touch him, wake him, when he spoke again.

"Tabby, my baby girl." His voice was lighter, sweeter than she'd heard in a while, more like how he had spoken to Isabella when she was an infant. Near crooning, he whispered, his voice broken and halting, "My Tabby girl, so strong."

After several moments of stillness, he flinched again. More violently this time, so violently she wondered if he would awaken from the movement. "Preach told me. No accident." His voice was hoarse with pain, tears slipping from the corners of his closed eyes. "Wasn't no accident, honey. Why, Tabby?"

Juanita's breath froze in her lungs, eyes wide, she struggled to see Watcher's face, horrified. Tabitha had been his baby sister, and Juanita had seen the beautiful stone marking her grave in Kentucky, knew she'd died years before Darrie. But Watcher held his history close. *Or maybe you never asked?* Surely he would have told her if his little sister took her own life? He knew everything about Juanita, could pull stories out of her without even a question. For her to talk to him, it only took a look or the stroke of his fingers down her face. Would he keep a secret this painful?

"Why, honey?" His chest hitched, catching on a breath, tripping over the pain in his dream. *He would hate knowing I saw this.* Mind made up, Juanita reached out and laid her palm on his shoulder. He was a light sleeper, had been since she'd met him. The only time she'd been able to crawl out of bed without him waking was early in their relationship. Back when she couldn't believe he felt the way he did. When the only emotion she trusted was her fear, when most things looked hopeless, trying to escape without knowing where she would go. Where she *could* go. *Nowhere safer than here with me,* the memory of his voice echoed through her head. She found herself unsure and had to know he felt the same way.

"Watcher, you're dreaming." She gave him a light shake, and his body tensed, eyes flying open and she knew they unerringly found hers even in the dark. "*Papi*, you had a bad dream."

"I didn't hurt you, did I?" The question was immediate, and he knifed up, rolling to put an elbow on the mattress next to her head. This was followed by his hand smoothing up and down her side, across her chest, lifting to carefully cup her face. "Honey, I didn't hurt you?" He was close, so close air from each word rushed across her skin. His breath coming fast, ragged pants for air. She lifted her hand and placed it on his chest, feeling the pounding of his heart.

"No, *Papi*. You had a bad dream." At her words he fell back, lifting his hands to his face, scrubbing hard across his forehead, nails dragging down and through his beard. In recent years it had begun to turn silver, contrasting very well with his still dark hair, giving him a distinguished look. He'd been so handsome when she'd met him, the beauty of his face the first thing she'd seen in so many days, and now he was even more so.

"Thank God." His breathing slowed dramatically, and she knew it was because he was trying to get himself under control. "Thank God."

"Watcher, you were talking." He had been shifting, settling back into bed and at her words froze in place.

"What'd I say, honey?" Caution in his tone and she suddenly wished the lights were on so she could clearly see his face. Could see and read what he feared. "'Nita?"

"You...you were arguing with someone at first. Whoever you were talking to, you told them you wouldn't. I don't know what you were unwilling to do, but you repeated it, that you wouldn't." He blew out a breath and shifted, one knee lifting, tenting the sheet covering them.

"People always wantin' shit outta me. I tell a lot of folks no." One arm rose and crossed over her. Knowing what he wanted, she lifted her head, letting him wind his arm underneath, feeling his tug pull her across the sheet and close to his side. Her hand on his chest, she used the tips of her fingers to ruffle his hair there, rolling the pad of her thumb across one nipple. He hummed appreciatively, squeezing her and then relaxing again. "That it? Like you wantin' my sleep to be sweet, honey, but waking me up for that seems extreme."

"How did Tabby die?" She blurted the question, and the results of her prying were immediately evident as he turned to stone beneath her cheek and palm.

His breath was carefully even when he answered her question with one of his own. "What brought up Tabitha?" She realized she'd never before heard him call his sister Tabby. Always Tabitha, as if he needed to deny the affectionate name he'd said so lovingly in his sleep.

"You were talking to her in your sleep, too. It was sweet." She said this softly, quietly, not wanting to disturb the air. He was so tense and rigid it seemed the least provocation might force him to explode. She wasn't afraid of him, but rather for him, unwilling to trigger bad memories by blundering into a painful corner. *As if this whole thing won't already be painful for him.*

"Was a long time ago, 'Nita." He huffed out a hard breath. "Let's just go back to sleep."

She knew if she allowed his evasion, the topic would forever be buried. She also knew he was accustomed to her doing as he suggested. Following the safe path. Not that they didn't argue, but the kind of man he was, when he drew a line in the sand it was firm. Normally she respected this, respected those things he felt strongly about, and he gave the same back to her. Because she could hold firm, too. She lifted one hand to her neck and trailed fingertips across the ridges of the brand, edges still rough to the touch after all these years. Juanita hoped Watcher loved her enough to forgive her.

"Tell me about Tabby." She actually heard the muscles in his jaw creak, felt the shudder that rolled through him at her words. His arm became an iron band across her back, thick fingers digging cruelly into her hip in an unintentional, bruising grip. When he didn't reply, she repeated her request gently, "*Papi*, tell me about Tabby. Please."

"Fuck." He shifted irritably, head turning away so his next words were spoken to the wall, his tone blistering. "Cain't I get some fuckin' rest? I'm tired, Juanita." Rolling his neck, he kept his face turned from her, every muscle tense. "You get that I'm tired? Really fuckin' tired. Can you fuckin' drop it?"

She lay there, studying the parts of his face she could see. His jaw flexed, a ripple of clenched muscle running beneath his beard. Closed off, tighter than she'd ever seen, there would be no soul-baring conversation tonight. "Yes, *Papi*."

Her mistake clear, she rolled so her back was to his side, his arm crossing her breasts as she faced the edge of the bed. Silent, she lay unmoving, trying to relax, feeling his tension in the way he held her. It surprised her, how his rejection hurt, so much more than she'd expected. He wouldn't talk to her. *We're unevenly yoked after all this time.* She swallowed a sob. After a moment, he sighed and rolled with her, pulling her back against him.

"Honey," he said, lips to the skin behind her ear. "I just wanna sleep."

Juanita nodded, feeling his arm tighten around her, his lips drifting down her neck.

"Rode hard to get back to you. Wanted this."

She nodded again, unable to speak because her throat had closed around her words.

"Needed you, honey. Miss you when I'm not here. Was a shit run, for an even more shit reason. Stirred up things. I didn't mean to hurt you."

His hand moved, sliding up to rest at her waist, fingertips dragging as he drew loops and circles on her skin. His other hand cupped her jaw, tilting her face for a kiss she surrendered to, opening for him at his demand, sucking and tugging on his tongue. Giving him everything he wanted, everything she had. *He loves me.* She knew those words were true. Down to her soul, she knew he loved her. *I love him.*

The kiss slowed, and he finished it with a soft peck on the end of her nose, his whiskers tickling as they brushed softly. "Sleep, baby."

His head settled onto the pillow behind her, but his fingers remained in contact, slowly stroking across her lips, back and forth. She had not relaxed, still unnerved by the knowledge they'd been together for so many years, but he had never shared about his sister with her. Keeping pain-filled secrets, not trusting that she would twist herself into knots to help him make it better. Not trusting her with the core which was all of him.

His voice was hesitant, quiet, when he asked, "Why you wanna know about Tabitha...Tabby?"

Juanita drew a surprised breath, twisting in his arms. He lay there staring at her, and the moonlight coming through the windows exposed pain so raw on his face she wanted to weep for him. "She's your sister. You've never spoken of her, but you were dreaming about her." She paused, then pushed onwards, "It did not sound like a good dream, *Papi.*"

"Fuckin' wasn't, not what I remember of the dream, anyway. But Tabby...she passed a long time ago, honey. Not a lot to say. Taken too young." She pulled against his grip, and he relaxed his arms for a moment, letting her turn so they were pressed together, chest-to-chest in the bed. "Sucks when so much promise is ripped from the world. I wasn't even there for her. I was overseas, deployed and working my ass off to make the world safer for her. For you." His arm squeezed, and she melted into him. "She was back here, and then she was dead. Dead and gone, and nothing I did could bring her back. It's just...hard to talk about."

"She died in a car wreck, right?" She watched as the muscles in his jaw tensed, and his Adam's apple moved up and down as he let the silence build between them again for a moment. Then, licking his lips, he began.

"Yeah. She was not even seventeen. So fuckin' young. Like Mela, though, if you looked in her eyes, you'd think she was older. Born an old soul, that's what my Aunt Loretta said about her once. She was the only reason I had to keep goin' after Daddy and Momma passed. Daddy got caught in a collapse, Momma murdered a week later. It was just Tabby and me. Darrie enlisted, wasn't long before he was gone. So, for the longest fuckin' time, only me and her."

Now that the dam of his silence had been breached, Juanita lay and listened as he told her story after story about Tabby and Darrie, and growing up on the mountain. She learned of the dangers the miners faced, how his parents hadn't wanted that life for him. He told her what had happened to his mother, how his life had changed after that. About what happened to Tabby, and this portion of the story left the pillows supporting their heads soaked with tears.

He talked about being in the military, frightening her with stories of near-miss bombs and gunfire in the night. Watcher wove his way back and forth through the years, threading the stories together so they made sense, even if in one Tabby was six and the next fifteen.

Juanita lay and listened to the proof of something she'd already known in her heart: Watcher trusted and loved her. She wasn't something he would put aside when the novelty of her fears grew thin. Not a challenge of which he would grow tired. In giving her this piece of himself, something he'd had bottled up in his head for decades, he gave her so much more.

Soldiers and Rebels

Watcher

"No, my friend. There is nothing wrong. Just, I am worried about Mason. This woman, this Willa has him off his game." Bones had called hella early for a Monday and left a voice mail. Watcher had been up late the night before on a run, and still stretched out in bed when he'd returned the call. Juanita was up hours ago, headed into the church with food and clothing. They'd delivered a group of refugees to the rescue mission, and she worked hand-in-hand with the pastor's wife to manage the needs of the people they helped.

"How so?" Watcher yawned, rolling to his back and staring at the ceiling.

"Did you know she showed in Jackson's weeks ago?" Noise from deeper in the house distracted him, angry shouting coming from the kitchen. Watcher swung his legs from the bed, reaching for his jeans with one hand.

"So? It's the Rebels bar, man. She's hooking up with Mason, and he showed everybody at Slate's party that he was way into her. Why shouldn't she be there?" The shouting resolved into two female voices he knew well, Isabella and Carmela, and from the sound of it, Carmela was *pissed*.

"She did not know he was there, and he remained in the back. It was...odd." Bones tone sounded puzzled. "Then she showed up with him in Indiana. She is everywhere in his life." A pause, and Watcher used this time to stalk up the hallway towards the still shouting girls. "It is not at all like Mica."

Watcher had always questioned why Mason was so careful with Mica. Of course, he wondered silently because he would never voice his concerns to the big man who had been part of his entire life. He'd seen Mason frustrated, amused, enraged, and disappointed at Mica, but he'd never seen him be all of that at once, and then tender beyond belief. Not until this gal. When he was around Willa, the caring on Mason's face was clear for anyone to see.

According to the stories, since the day she had walked into a clubhouse party in Fort Wayne, Mason had protected her as if she was the most precious thing in the world. Watcher found it interesting to see him behave this way. It made him more approachable somehow, less jagged around the edges.

From what Watcher could figure out, talking to RWMC members, nobody had seen Mason so wrapped up in a woman, not for a long time, maybe not ever. Before Mica, Mason had held himself aloof from real relationships. He didn't abstain or deny himself; it was simply that he was very careful of his position as club president, not wanting to set precedence or grant power to the wrong woman. He'd fuck a club whore, hook up with a hangaround bitch, or find the occasional citizen who wanted a walk on the wild side, but they were all one-nighters. Or, if he did a repeat performance, he would make sure to be clear it was a convenience, not preference.

After Mica, Mason wasn't just aloof, he was fucking gone.

For as long as he'd known him, Mason had always been driven. Once he patched in, he was laser-focused entirely on the Fiends. Then, after birthing the Rebels, all activity was directed to claiming and keeping the club pointed on the path he'd mapped out. Everything he did was for the club. Businesses, citizen roles, bloody negotiations between other clubs. The club was his life, end of story.

Now that was no longer true. This woman was in his life, and Watcher was amused at how he'd changed.

"Should be glad it's not like Mica," he told Bones, rounding the final corner and coming to a halt several feet from the entrance of the kitchen. He could see both of the girls from here. Bella's stance was aggressive and angry, and she slammed a cabinet door shut with a loud slap.

"Stop it!" Mela screamed.

"I can't believe you!" Bella yelled back, not turning from the cabinet. With fingers gone white with strain, she gripped the edge of the countertop, chin tilting down. "You told him I liked him!"

"No, I told him I'd cut his balls off if he hurt you. I didn't say anything to him about you liking him." Mela shifted, one hand going to a hip as she swept her other hand out to the side. "He's a douche, Bella. Not what I want for you. Not what you should settle for."

Mela was always protective of her little sister, always looking out for her and it warmed his heart that Bella had this in her life. They might not be related by blood, but the bond his two girls shared ran just as deep.

"He's not a douche." Bella whirled, her blonde hair swinging wide. Dark-skinned, his daughter was a beauty, and her naturally light hair was a striking feature. "He loves me."

"It sounds as if you have your own drama, my friend." Bones' voice came through the phone and Watcher jerked, he'd forgotten he still held the device to his ear. "I'll let you go and deal with the crisis at hand. Do not be a stranger, Watcher. Give Juanita my love." Watcher grunted, disconnecting and shoving the phone into his pocket.

Mela tipped her head back, groaning, "God. He does not love you." She straightened and stared hard at Bella. "He wants to get into your pants. And he intends to get into your pants because no one's ever gotten in there before. And you're beautiful. And smart. You're fifteen, and so sweet Edwardo will never have a shot at anything like you again in his life because he's"—she leaned forward, her voice rising again to a shout—"a douche!"

"He's not a douche." Now Bella's voice was trembling, and Watcher was about to step out and sort the spat when Mela's next words pulled all the air from his lungs.

"He's a douche and too old for me, which means he's *way* too old for you. Edwardo defines douche, and the fact he's going after you makes it official. If you can't see that from where you stand, then here you go"— she held out her palm, pretending to offer something to Bella—"here's the stupid-as-fuck award of the year. Open your eyes, Bella. Please," she pleaded, her open palm fisting, thudding against her chest, "please open your fucking eyes and see what I see."

Before Watcher could say anything, the door leading to the carport opened and Spider walked in, sweeping the room with his gaze. "Fucking shit, girls. I could hear you shoutin' clear out to the barn. Your daddy's still in bed. Y'all are gonna wake him the fuck up, and he's gonna be a fuckin' bear."

"Too late," Watcher called, strolling into the kitchen. He pinned Bella with his eyes, watching as her face flashed red, then paled and she swallowed hard. "Daddy's up and wondering lots of things. Like who this

261

Edwardo is that's older, wants to get into my baby girl's pants, and is a douche."

***

"Jesus," Spider muttered, punching the back of the seat in front of him. "Get your ass back into your own fuckin' space." He punched again, harder, and the passenger in the row ahead of them quickly raised the seatback. Watcher saw her glare over her shoulder at the man seated beside him. "Boss, this is not how I like to roll."

"No shit, Sherlock," came from across the aisle and Watcher turned to see Opie grinning.

Spider shifted in the seat again, his leg stretched far out underneath the row in front of them. "Shut up." He twisted, staring at the wing, the only thing visible out the small porthole window. "Shut up until we get to Chicago. I'll kill you then. Fuckin' hate a cage. Hate a tin can worse."

Tipping his head back, Watcher silently agreed. Then he groaned when Opie poured gasoline onto the fire by saying, "You realize we don't deplane at O'Hare? We stay on this bird straight through to Fort Wayne." Even with his eyes closed, Watcher identified the periodic thudding sound as Spider beating his forehead against the plastic surface of the window.

Once on the ground in Fort Wayne, they were met at luggage claim by Hurley, one of the Rebel hangarounds. *If it were anyone but me, this'd be a hella insult*, Watcher thought, staring at the kid standing there, flipping a ring of keys around his finger. *Mason had to know I'd get it*. This must be a test for the kid, and Watcher readied himself to observe so he could report in later. Dressed in a tee and jeans, the only thing that could identify the boy as biker were the boots. *Or maybe it's about discretion*, Watcher thought, reconsidering, knowing that like everywhere these days, Fort Wayne cops had a hard-on for clubs. "Van's at the curb," the kid said, gesturing towards the doors behind him.

Watcher glanced the indicated direction and from the muffled laughter beside him, knew Spider saw the same thing he did.

"Van that cop is ticketing?" Hurley whirled and cursed. "Go see if you can talk him out of the ticket. We'll get our shit." Each of the men had checked a bag to bring their legal firearms. It wasn't so much they were expecting trouble, but a smart man was always prepared just in case.

"Boss?" Opie stood, duffle slung over his shoulder, staring out the doors and watching as the kid talked animatedly with the officer. "You gonna clue us in on what's goin' on?" Opie and Spider hadn't questioned when Watcher called and told them they were booked on a flight with him. They'd shown up at the barn, and Devil had driven them all to the airport, dropping them off in front of the terminal.

"Mason called." All he was willing to offer until after he talked to Mason face-to-face. "Soldiers stand with Rebels." The cop walked off, leaving an irate Hurley standing next to the van. Watcher gave it another minute, then led his band of men outside into the sunlight.

Watcher was surprised when Hurley pulled the van to a stop next to the Rebel clubhouse because there were zero bikes on the lot. Two cars parked at an angle next to the building, but other than the sign over the porch, nothing would indicate this was a motorcycle club's headquarters. Hurley didn't say anything, hadn't actually spoken except for his brief greeting at the airport, but given he wasn't even a prospect, it shouldn't really be surprising. He led them through the gate, waiting with his head up until it had locked into place behind them, manned by a member in a guard shack off to the side.

Walking into the building, Watcher came to a halt when he saw the crowd gathered inside the main room. A dozen patched members stood shoulder-to-shoulder in a line crossing the center of the room, positioned between a gaggle of women and children, and the outside door where Watcher stood. "What the fuck?" Spider's voice was pitched low, for their ears only, and Watcher felt unease bleeding off his two men.

"Thank fuck." The voice behind the heartfelt greeting sounded familiar, and then he saw an older, grizzled man push forward, arm out to clasp Watcher's. Bingo, the former Fort Wayne chapter president. "Watch, man, glad you could answer the call." He looked over Watcher's shoulder and introduced himself to Spider and Opie, "Bingo. How y'all doin'?" This encounter got more and more interesting. Bingo was a past president of this chapter, but Slate had replaced him more than a year ago. First a hangaround, now a greybeard with one foot out the club's door.

Watcher swept the room, taking in everyone this time. "Bingo, heard good things about you. Man, you sure you want company right now? Looks like y'all are on—"

Bingo heaved a sigh, interrupting him. "Lockdown, yeah. Mason wasn't able to get you on the horn before he had to leave. Y'all probably passed each other in the air somewhere." Turning, the old man walked away, giving Watcher and his men his back. "Come on back. I'll fill ya in."

The office behind the bar was stifling with hot, unmoving air, and the mood suffusing the crowded space was explosive even before Bingo made a motion to someone behind Watcher to close the door. With the skin on the back of his neck crawling, Watcher positioned himself in front of Spider, Opie to the side.

Without preamble, Bingo said, "Mason ain't here. You know that. Brother"—Watcher saw the already focused attention of the half a dozen Rebels in the room sharpen at the word, given freely, and not refuted—"you know the kind of shit Outriders are capable of. And this? *Jesus.* This might be the worst we've seen. Bar none."

Without saying anything, Watcher willed Bingo to keep going, because this, all of this, was not the beginning he would have wanted.

"You know Bear." Bingo waited for a nod from Watcher, indicating he knew the Rebel member. "You know his old lady." Watcher stiffened because Bear's old lady was Eddie, Shooter's daughter. He'd seen her and Luke, now called Judge, when Watcher had come to Fort Wayne for Slate's party. Outriders and Eddie in the same conversation didn't bode well. "Shooter wanted her back in Cali."

Watcher shook his head. That didn't make sense; Eddie loathed the club in Cali. For three years she and her mother had been on the run from Shooter, only coming back when her mother got cancer. Then, as soon as she could, she left again, landing here in northeast Indiana. "Eddie hasn't lived there for years. Years, Bingo. She's kept all ties to Shooter distant since high school. What would he need her in Cali for?"

"He found a use for her." Shuffling feet telegraphed the unease in the men around him. They didn't know where this was going any more than Watcher and his men did. "Auctioned her off. Needed her back so he could keep up his end of the bargain."

"No fuckin' way," Spider mumbled, and Watcher threw up a hand for silence.

"Auctioned her off?" Best to have clarity here, and so far, this was about as muddy as any creek back in Kentucky. "Auctioned her off to who?"

"President of some upstart club in San Diego." Bingo shook his head slowly. "Never woulda thought I'd see anything like this from the Morgans. Done gone past anything human, man. I've been in the life for a long time, rambled my way through a half a dozen clubs across the country, and been exposed to about any kind of man you can think of. This ain't right."

"Who? Who bought her?" Watcher thought of a better question. "What do you need from me?" *Fuck. I'm in Fort Wayne, I was closer in Las Cruces.* "Tell me what Mason needs."

"Blue Line."

It was Opie's turn to react, and his curse wasn't mumbled, but Watcher was already digging for his phone. Thirty seconds later, the call connected, and he received a brusque, "You got shit timing. Not a good time, Watcher."

"Oh yeah, it fuckin' is, asshole. This is me telling you to stand down." He waited for a beat, then when he got nothing in return, continued, "Stand the fuck down. Eddie Morgan is off fuckin' limits, Blue Line."

"*Jesus*." This was a breathy mutter from Bingo, then from the phone Watcher got, "A moment while I get private."

Like each man in the room, Watcher stood still, every muscle rigid, waiting, then Blue Line barked a question, "How in the fuck did you hear about this?"

"Don't matter how, only matters you hear me, motherfucker. I've been nice, been the good neighbor, eating your friend of my friend's bullshit, but you do this, and it's"—Watcher took a breath, then gritted out the word he knew every man in the room feared most—"war."

"It does matter how you heard because it could change the entire fucking play." An accent he hadn't noticed before threaded through Blue Line's words, either New Jersey or New York. Definitely not California, not the styled surfer persona presented in the past. "So you're gonna tell me right here and right now and be real careful to get it right. How the fuck did you hear about this?"

Eyes locked on Bingo, Watcher took a second to think about what he knew about the man on the phone. Loyal, faithful to his own agenda and beliefs, Blue Line had worked with Estavez but only where it didn't compromise his own principles. This man would no more buy a woman than Watcher would, and this was something Watcher knew down in his soul. So Watcher made a decision and went with it, ignoring the uproar all around him when he said, "Standing in the Rebel clubhouse in Fort

Wayne, called here by Mason, but he's on his way to you to stop this bullshit."

Shouts around him, but Watcher kept his eyes fixed on Bingo, staring at the old man over the front sight on the end of the barrel pointed his direction. He knew Spider had stepped to the side, and expected Opie had done the same. Knew it was three against seven, and he'd not be walking out of this room if he had chosen wrongly.

"Fuck," Blue Line ground the word out. There was a burst of noise on his end of the call, then a shouted, "Play's changed. We're going from a rescue mission to a fucking partnership on a fucking rescue mission. Someone get me word on a bird coming in, gonna be quiet and private, tell me where and when. Toto, get me a fix on Judge. That motherfucker does not slip this net." Louder, sounding closer to the phone, Blue Line's frustration was as clear as if he were still shouting. "Watcher, you didn't make this call. Never made it. Got that? You don't know anything, and if you're asked, you barely know me. Do not fuck me on this, or I swear to God you'll regret every breath you take from this moment forwards. You get those boys to agree. Do not fuck me on this."

"Fuck you how?" Watcher asked, shaking his head in disbelief and confusion. "What are you talkin' about?"

"I got a line on shutting Shooter down. I've been working it, and today I'm taking that line to the shore. I've been running with it, and I've got his ass, Watcher. Told you. Fuckin' told you. Taking his motherfucking son with him, because you've never seen wicked until you look Judge in the eyes. I don't have long, but I'll give you this and then I'm gone." Blue Line's voice changed, and from the intensity of his tone, Watcher braced. "This boy slips my net and gets in the wind, you watch your back. Watch your back, your front...fuck, man, watch your sides and over your goddamned head. I've never met a man with as much hate as he's got inside him. Now"—there was the noise of motorcycle exhausts and wind, and Watcher knew Blue Line had made his way out of whatever structure he'd been inside—"I got places to be, and people to fuck up. I'll update you as I can."

Dropping the phone to his side, Watcher saw the door had opened, admitting even more Rebels to the already tightly packed room, and even though the weapons had been lowered, every one of them had hostile eyes turned on him. Before anyone could ask, he volunteered what he knew.

"Blue Line is part of a cop club in SoCal. Through my Mexico dealings, I've had occasion to talk to him. According to him, he's not buying into the auction to get Eddie, except to get her away from her old man. Y'all know Shooter"—he scanned the room and saw heads nodding somberly—"and y'all know Judge. Blue Line's looking to take them both down. Which means"—Watcher focused on Bingo, who held the greatest sway in the Rebel club with Slate out of town on his honeymoon trip and now Mason out west—"he and Mason are working the same side of the fence. Blue Line's gonna update me when he can, but brother, you need to get a call to Mason, soon as you can. Would make life a fuckuva lot easier if he wasn't blindsided going into this mess."

***

"Slate's got a good woman." Watcher tipped the beer bottle in his hand up, listening to the music coming from the open back door of the clubhouse as he took a long drink.

A heavy sigh came from the chair beside him, then Mason agreed, "Yeah, he does."

"Like that chick for you. Willa. Don't think I got a chance to tell you last time. She seemed solid at the hospital yesterday." Watcher lifted his hand, pushing his hair back. *Need a haircut soon as I get home*, he thought, smiling at the idea of Juanita's hands in his hair, pushing and combing as she trimmed the ends.

"She's good to me," Mason said, and Watcher snorted laughter. "No, man, she is."

"She's good *for* you," Watcher corrected him, and Mason laughed.

268

"True story. I've never…" Mason took a breath, seeming to find his thoughts. "What you found for yourself in Juanita. That's what I've been wanting. What I've looked for. The best kind of give and take, where you don't have to be everything. You don't have to try to be what you're not, because what you can't be, she is right there and picking up the slack. I wanted that. Coulda had it, and looking back, I know I coulda, but fucking hell, man, I'm glad I didn't get my head out of the sand. I'd have missed what I needed, lost in what I might want."

"Juanita's all of that for me. Doesn't matter what kinda shit goes down, she's like a rock. With her background? You'd think she'd give the refugees a wide berth. You know the kind of conditions we pull people out of every day. Dig them out of holes in the ground, every single fucking day. Bring them over, give them a better life. A chance at what they need to make their family whole." Watcher drained the last inch of beer into his mouth then rested the still-cold bottle on his knee. "Juanita's there nearly every day. Giving. Giving of herself, organizing things, making sure Pastor has what he needs. Making sure the families coming through the mission get what they need. Giving herself to them. Every day." He drained the dregs of the foam out onto the dirt beside his boots, the drops quickly turning into dark spots which gradually lightened, fading away. "Every day, Juanita's that for me."

"I get it, brother." Mason leaned his head back and the two men sat in silence for a moment. "Bear's gonna be okay. You get a chance to say hey to Eddie?"

"Yeah, caught her in the hallway. Wasn't sure she'd remember me, but she did. She looks like hell." He shook his head. "Hard to believe John would do this kind of shit to his flesh and blood. I can't fathom the idea of a father caring so little for his baby girl. And Luke?" Goose bumps crawled up Watcher's arms. Dusting his palms against his jeans, he pushed to his feet, staring down at the shadows wreathing Mason. "Too fuckin' bad he wasn't there when Blue Line showed. I know you said Shooter saw him after Bear and Blue Line brought Eddie out, but that boy is dangerous. I hear word of him, I'll call." He paused a moment and saw Mason's head move in agreement. "You do the same, brother.

Fuckin' glad you got everybody back alive, Mason. Coulda been a serious shitstorm. Soldiers stand with Rebels."

"Rebels stand with Soldiers." Mason's response was immediate and gratifying. "Sleep, brother. Ruby'll have assigned you a room. You're stayin' here. All of y'all are stayin' here. Safety in numbers, yeah?"

Watcher stood and scanned the groups of men in the back lot of the clubhouse, saw lights on the first two floors of the building, and knew his men were mixed in amongst these. "Good to have your guys meet mine." Shaking off the chill which had settled on him when he'd talked about Shooter, he said, "Trust you with my life, brother. I'll sleep easy tonight."

With a lift of his chin, he left Mason staring into the night, and went in search of bed and quiet, so he could call Juanita and tell her he loved her.

***

"*Papi*," her voice reached towards the rafters, breathless cries saying he'd gotten it right, once again. Watcher held her hips in place with one arm, lapping at her. Varying the speed of each stroke of his tongue, he eased her down, down, down the mountain, letting her recover at her own pace. When she stopped undulating and began squirming, he licked once more, bottom to top, diddling her clit with the tip of his tongue for a triplet of strokes before he lifted on an arm, crawling up her body.

As he always did, he took a moment to look down at her, half-lidded eyes staring up at him, a smile curling the corners of her lips. Bending to brush his mouth across hers, he kissed his way to her ear so he could whisper, "Most beautiful woman I've ever seen." She giggled, bright and light as a girl, the sound making him smile. Teeth to the lobe of her ear, he told her, "Always wanna fuck you. Want my hands on you." Tipping his hips, he reached down to grip himself, angling his cock to her entrance. He waited for it, and she gave him what she always did.

"Love you, Watcher." Soft strokes up his biceps, she curled her fingers around his neck, palm to either side as she pulled him down, arching up into him, letting him seat himself root-deep in her. Legs curling around his ass, she used the leverage to meet him, thrust for thrust, working with him so he could make the same journey. Mouth to his ear, she told him everything he wanted to hear. "*Papi*, so good. You make it so good. My whole life. My wonderful man. I love you."

"God, 'Nita." He angled his head to the side, putting himself face-to-face with the only woman he'd ever loved. She leaned in, touching her lips to his, holding the contact so their breaths mingled. "My beauty. Love of my life."

His fingers stroked up the skin of her side, lifting and plumping her soft breast, dipping his chin to bring it to his mouth, drawing the puckered nipple deep like he knew she liked. "*Papi*." Fingers in his hair, she pulled his head up, anchoring herself with his mouth as she moved underneath him, driven by an urgency he recognized. That did it for him, and the coiling electricity spooling up his spine, muscles tightening as he lunged deep, deeper, holding still, feeling her clench and grip him, milking his cock. "*Papi*." Her cry lifted to the rafters again, and he silenced it with a kiss, letting her take his grunts down her throat.

"Jesus, baby," he muttered, wrapping one arm around her shoulders, shoving it between her back and the mattress so he could hold her close. Elbow to the mattress, he kept most of his weight off her, even knowing she could take it, wanted it sometimes, that closeness. "My hot mamacita." Brushing a kiss across her lips, he deepened it, stroking into her mouth with his tongue, taking everything he could from her.

Shifting to his side, he pulled her close, cradling her against his chest. "Love you, Watcher." Her breath drifted softly, scarcely disturbing the hair on his chest. Watcher bent his neck, pressing a kiss to the top of her head.

"Love you, too, Juanita."

Rise of the Diamante

"Whadda you mean, there's a new club in town?" Spider's words were pitched low and spoken slowly, lending a menace the man behind the bar could not mistake. "Ain't no new club, unless we say there's a new club."

"Man, I do not make up this shit to piss you off." Bernie, their guy behind the bar, threw up one hand in irritation. "I'm telling you these macho dudes were in here stomping around about an hour ago." He swept his hand out, indicating the destruction all around, smashed glasses and bottles of liquor, overturned tables. "Think I did this for fun? I do not make this shit up."

"And you didn't think to give us a call?" Watcher stuck the question in before Spider could open his mouth again. "Didn't think it worth your time, man? You work for me"—Watcher jerked a thumb towards his own chest—"and if you wanna continue working for me"—same thumb jerk—"then you"—a jab of a stiffened finger digging into Bernie's chest caused him to grunt—"needa make better choices."

"Jesus, Watch," Bernie said, moving back the two feet the space allowed. "Don't gotta get physical."

"Man," Spider muttered, "mind your mouth."

"I'm just sayin'—" Bernie began, and Watcher interrupted, cutting him off hard. This assclown didn't know what was happening up north, where Mason had recently absorbed two long-standing clubs, expanding his reach in a way that made other clubs nervous. Made other clubs look to his rivals to see who might fall next, and look to his allies, to see who else might be positioned for a move. Information like this had the potential to be nothing, or everything. He didn't need Bernie's attitude to color what he could tell them.

"Don't give a fuck. Learn or get your ass out. But you will tell me what you saw, who was here, what they said, who they talked to, and anything else you can think of, which will tell me who the fuck thinks they can come rollin' into my"—Watcher felt his control slip, voice lifting to a roar—"*motherfuckin' town.*"

Eyes wide, Bernie talked.

Standing in the alley behind the bar five minutes later, Watcher lifted his phone to his ear, waiting. He'd taken a long moment to think about who he would call, knowing the things swirling south of the border, and up in the northern states. Balancing friendship with need, Watcher knew whoever he called would be leaving themselves open if they provided assistance. Decision made, he'd shot a look at Opie and Spider, said one word, received a chin lift and nod in response. When the call connected, he didn't waste any time. "I got a problem. Need to call in that marker, brother."

Raul answered, as Watcher knew he would, "Anything you need, my friend."

***

"No. Got no idea." Fingers tight around the phone, Watcher's response to the question was clipped. He didn't have time for this shit.

"Think back, brother. Anyone you can think of who might own a strip club in Kentucky called Shinedown?" Gunny, one of Mason's officers in Fort Wayne, proved persistent in his questioning. He'd called ten minutes ago, had gotten right to the topic at hand, which Watcher appreciated, but wasn't taking no for an answer. Bella and Mela's voices came from outside by the pool, where Juanita sat on a lounger. Beer in hand, Watcher had been set to rejoin them when the phone had rung.

"Where in Kentucky?" If it wasn't his neck of the woods, he could put an end to this questioning. He understood why Gunny was all over this because he'd found the love of his life. Found her after she'd been beaten and violated by her ex-husband. From what Watcher had seen and heard, Gunny felt protective of her. Extremely protective. Like Watcher was with Juanita, making sure nothing like she'd lived through could touch her again. Because of that, he'd give Gunny another minute to route him to a more productive avenue for his search.

"Cynthiana, or right outside it." Gunny pulled in a breath. "Said the owner's name was John, and he was a good guy, but they had rough clientele. Rough enough to make her abandon all her shit, brother. Just pick up stakes and walk away. I'm looking for whatever I can find for her, man. You're a lead for me because you and Mason grew up there. Help me find something."

"Why do you think I'd know anything? I haven't lived there for decades. Turned my back on that town and still say good riddance." Thinking furiously, Watcher was running all the bars and strip clubs he knew of in the area through his head, trying to find one which could match the description.

"That rough clientele? Sharon said they were bikers. But she didn't say bikers like she was talking about the Rebels. She said it like what she really meant was a gang." Gunny paused a second, then said, "Know you were an Outrider, man. Mason's not made any bones about some of the shit he dealt with back in the day. We've barely come off a fucking hellhole run you saw the tail end of, and I gotta say, all of that hellhole was Outrider. You think they own this club? Think they were the motherfuckers she was talkin' about?"

"No idea." Gunny made a frustrated sound at that, so Watcher gave a little. "I'll check around."

"Quiet like," Gunny shot back, not wasting any time in taking what was offered, and his speed in doing so told Watcher this was more important than the man had let on so far.

"Quiet like," Watcher agreed.

"You get something...anything, you call me direct. Don't worry about protocol. I'm Mason's voice on this." Gunny didn't wait for him to respond, simply disconnected the call.

"Jesus," Watcher muttered, lowering the phone as he stared out the window but he did this not seeing his woman and kids poolside. Instead, he remembered the scene in his old office at the Outriders' clubhouse. "Rough clientele. Fuck yeah, I'd say so."

Coulda mighta

In an aggrieved tone, Bones complained, "Why is it there always seems to be another viper striking at our heels?" Watcher laughed aloud at this, leaning back on his bike, listening to Bones on a tear about some upstart club. "Do not laugh, Watcher. You have the same problems there with the Diamante."

"It's true they're here and in the way," Watcher agreed. "But I'd classify them as more of an annoyance than anything else. A gnat as opposed to a viper."

"Then count yourself lucky, and tell me how you will be helping me." At this, Watcher froze in place for a moment. Bones never asked for anything, and for him to do so now was telling.

"What kind of help do you need, man?" Not quite an offer of assistance, Watcher was more testing the waters to see what was eating at the man he'd come to know so well. "Talk to me."

"Every time I roll past my own borders, I find they have fallen in behind me, pushing the boundaries as they can. Mayhem, mostly, but an annoyance which has quickly grown into something that is dangerous for their continued good health. I push back, of course, but we are in a vicious cycle of take and take back, and it cannot stand. This running battle has come to the point where I cannot assist Mason in even the smallest request." Bones took a deep breath, this alone signaling the man's rage. Normally he was so closed off and controlled, to hear him rattled was disturbing.

"What do you need from me?" A tractor-trailer passed by where Watcher was parked on the shoulder of the road. Winds caused by the vehicle whipped around him and carried sand and grit in an abrasive wave that coated Watcher and the bike. "Talk to me."

"I do not expect anything from you, my friend. You have enough on your plate without accepting a serving from mine. This was a call to commiserate, more than anything. I find myself frustrated with Mason, and what he is doing, or more to the point, not doing, and that, I suspect, is something I should immediately take up with him." Another truck rolled past, closer, and in the noise of its passage Watcher lost the next thing Bones said, "...pted things in my neighborhood." A horn sounded and distracted again, Watcher jerked his gaze up to see a pickup stopped in the road on the other side of the median. Halted on the inside shoulder going the other direction, the driver stared at him. Watcher gave the man a thumbs-up, receiving a wave in return as the vehicle drove away. "...splaced something important to me."

"Jesus Christ," Watcher muttered when another vehicle slowed, and he was about to give the same thumbs-up to indicate he wasn't broken down when he saw the barrel of a gun extending from the barely opened window. With a shout he threw himself from the bike, scarcely getting out of the way as it lurched and died, toppling sideways towards him. Metal striking metal reverberated as the bike shuddered, and he saw a spark as a bullet ricocheted off the motorcycle's frame.

Gun in his palm, he rolled, putting the handlebars between his head and the now speeding away pickup. Elbows to the sand, he propped his gun hand in his other palm and squeezed off three shots before an oncoming vehicle cut through his line of sight. "Fucking shit." He lay there a moment, then blinked, his left eye stinging. The car sped past, carrying another wave of sand to lash at his exposed skin. Lifting a sand-covered palm to sweep the sweat from his eye, Watcher was startled when it came away covered in red. Sand and blood.

Fingers to his head, he found a furrow in his scalp. The wound was bleeding profusely, and from the corner of his eye he saw the shoulder of his shirt was already saturated. On the air, he smelled blood mixed with gasoline as fuel leaked from the bike lying on its side. Scanning for any additional threats, he didn't see anything, not even any more traffic. The lone vehicle which passed during the skirmish hadn't stopped. He was alone. "Fucking shit."

Scooping up his phone, he held it in one hand as he stooped to grip the handlebars and frame. Scanning again, still not seeing anything, he pulled, grunting as he heaved the bike upright, lifted it from the ground and shoved the kickstand down with the heel of one boot. Looking at the phone's display, he found the call to Bones had disconnected. "Shit." Shaking his head in an attempt to clear the ringing, he saw splatters of blood land on the bike, the random pattern taking all his attention for a moment. "Shit."

Vibrating on the seat where he'd laid it, the phone indicated an incoming call from Opie. "Good tim—"

"*Where the fuck are you?*" Opie's roar cut off what Watcher had been about to say. Breathing heavily, his words came out with stuttering pauses between. "Boss, where...the fuck...are you?"

"Out on Highway 70, out by the Rio. Opie, I need—"

Opie cut him off again. "On our way. We're only two from you. Hold, boss. Fuckin' *hold*." The call disconnected and Watcher stared down at the phone, engrossed at the sight of a smear of blood across the screen. In the distance came a deep rumble of bikes, and he recognized from the sound and reverberation through the air that it was a lot of them. He went to recent calls and was perplexed to see it had been nearly thirty minutes since he was on the phone with Bones, with no traffic coming past for almost as long.

In the distance, beyond an overpass that looked to be about two miles away, there was a pillar of smoke. Black and rolling, it lifted to the sky, winds at altitude tearing it apart, dispersing it across the heavens. "Hey, mister?" Watcher heard the shouted question and jerked, looking across the divided road, seeing a pickup pulling a camper stopped on the shoulder, "Are you okay?" Lifting one hand, he gave the family in the truck a thumbs-up, hearing the wife warn her good Samaritan husband, "Honey, he's in a gang." The window closed, and the truck pulled away as dozens of bikes swept into view. The double line of his men crossed at a dirt-covered culvert about a half a mile up the road, coming into the lanes nearest him going the wrong way against nothing.

He stood straight, boots planted wide to hold on the shifting sands underfoot. Watcher was thankful he was no longer reeling from what he knew had to be a ricochet he'd taken to the skull. Counting thirty bikes, he jerked his chin at Opie and Devil as they rolled to a halt in front of his motorcycle. Opie's eyes had narrowed, and he was shaking his head back and forth. Without a word, Watcher pointed to his bike, lifting a drop of gasoline from the bottom curve of the tank with one finger. He shook it off, and then told them, "Sprung a leak."

Devil laughed openly as he got off his bike, bending to the tool roll on his front forks. A moment later he held up a tube and a roll of tape. "Got a fix."

"Good deal," Watcher said, letting his gaze roam up the line of men now milling on the side of the road, walking out into the lanes and looking towards the smoke, eyes shaded with palms. "Opie, wanna send a couple guys to check that out? I mighta clipped the bastards who put a dent in Bertha." He patted the tank, still not smiling when he said, "I'm partial to all the fluids being inside, where God intended."

"On it, boss," Opie said. His mouth twisted and he obviously wanted to ask questions, but followed Watcher's lead, turning to direct a half dozen of the men to go check out the smoke. "Meet y'all back at the clubhouse." His closing instructions gave them permission to follow whatever they needed without having to worry about hooking back up with the main column.

Turning back to Watcher, Opie got close, looking to see what Devil was doing to the leaking hole on Watcher's tank. "Epoxy won't stick to that paint," he warned, "needa use the tape as a short term. We'll get it taken care of when we get back to the barn." Not looking at Watcher, he muttered, "Fucking hell, boss. Bones called. Said you were on the phone and then you weren't, but there was gunfire. He couldn't raise you so he called me." Devil glanced up, but Opie beat him to the question. "You okay? Fuckin' covered in blood."

"Head hurts. Got my bell rung, but I'm okay. Wanna get off the side of the road." Watcher lifted his gaze, seeing a line of bikes and men between the three of them and the highway. Human shield, in case the shooters returned. Each man either had a gun in hand or had their vest moved so they could easily get to their pieces. Club. Honor. "And before you ask, I got no fuckin' idea. Was a pickup truck. Coulda been any farm truck. White stepside, about an '05. Coulda been anybody, Opie. If I'd been a second later seein' the barrel, they'd 'a had me."

"But you did. Can't play the coulda mighta game, boss." Opie shook his head. "Want me to look at your head here?"

"No. Let's get off the road. Time enough to deal with this at the barn."

"Wanna wash—" Devil started to say something, but Watcher cut him off.

"No, if you're done, let's roll."

***

Juanita

She lay in bed in front of Watcher, fingers curled around his thick wrist, holding his arm in place. She didn't want an inch of space coming between them. When the men had ridden into the area beside the barn, Juanita had gone outside to greet them. The first thing she saw was Watcher, covered in blood from the top of his head to his hip, where it had soaked into his jeans, coating the leather of his belt. He hadn't been prepared for her reaction, had held her while her terror leaked out as tears, silently weeping against his shoulder. Even knowing he'd ridden his bike home, gotten here under his own power, she was petrified. She'd allowed herself only seconds, and when she'd pulled back, he had frowned, lifted a finger to her cheek and trailed it through the wet there, coming away covered in his own blood.

After that he hadn't argued, allowing her to retrieve the huge box used for first aid supplies. Heading towards the back room where it was stored, voices rose in a blur of murmurs and shouts behind her, individual words unintelligible. As she'd returned to the main area of the barn, the men quieted, and she knew they had been discussing whatever had happened, the business they felt she had no right knowing. Inwardly fuming, because this was her husband who'd been shot, bled, and come home wounded, she had held her peace. It was the way of the club life.

Once convinced he was okay, she'd stitched the gash in his scalp, his fingers gripping bruisingly hard on her hips as she tugged the curved needle through his flesh. Something she'd had plenty of experience in over the years. She'd then retreated to the house and waited, knowing he would come to her when he was ready. Her part was hard, the waiting and not knowing, the knowledge that threats circled her man of which she would never know. But the rewards were so worth it, she thought now, stretching and feeling the pleasant soreness between her legs.

He had been nearly frantic in his lovemaking. Had burrowed his face between her thighs, insistently plying her with intimate kisses and caresses, pushing her to fly again and again. Flipping her to her stomach, pulling her ass to meet his hips as he drove himself home inside her. Pounding into her, his grunted oaths filled the air. "Love you, Juanita. I love you. Love you all my life. Love you long as I'm breathing. Never doubt. Always love you."

Staying connected, he had eased them into the mattress when he was done, nestling behind her as tight as he could manage. One hand cupping her sex, the other captured her shoulder. Only then did he tell her what happened. Even then, she knew it was a sanitized version. Every word spoken sounded deliberately detached, carefully chosen so as to not expose any fear. Not letting on he'd been worried in the least. Just another day.

Gradually, his words had slowed, and when he shifted, pulling her more underneath him, she went with it. Happy to take his weight, allow him to pin her to the mattress because each breath was a miracle tonight. Finally asleep, his hands relaxed, and she'd captured his wrist, wanting to hold onto the safe feeling as long as she could. Keep him in place behind her, around her, and in her heart.

***

Watcher

"Are you certain this is what you want to do?" Raul's voice sounded scratchy on the secure line Opie had set up for them. Scratchy, and tired. Because of it, Watcher tried not to read anything into the question. Tried not to have any second thoughts.

"Yeah, Diamante need to go the fuck away." Watcher forced confidence into his tone, tried to make the steel in his spine sound through his words. "Nip it in the bud out here."

Bernie hadn't been wrong when he'd talked about the macho wannabes who had smashed up the Southern Soldiers' bar. Those men had been Diamante, patched into the newest chapter right in his backyard.

In a roundabout way, it sounded like Diamante had also been behind the incident out on the highway. A chance encounter, one of their hangarounds had seen him parked on the side of the road. Turning around at his first opportunity, the man was hoping to make a name for himself by offing a national of the Soldiers. Watcher's return fire had clipped the guy, and he'd eventually wrecked, but ghosted from the accident scene. The truck had been stolen, so the only thing they had was a whole list of dead ends. All of this told as a story at a bike rally in Florida, traveling word of mouth back to him, making his stomach roll at the idea of the sheer randomness of it all.

The Diamante chapters were a young club, in every sense of the word. A mixed bag of American and rice burner bikes allowed, observers were as likely to see patched members riding crotch rockets as more traditional cruisers or bobbers. Kids, punks mostly, who didn't have any sense of what the life was about. Hadn't seen the inside of a real clubhouse, so they made up their own, taking over rundown buildings, spraying graffiti on the outside, making themselves feel like the big man in town. Set up like a Ponzi scheme, they were drawing a huge amount of government interest. By charging support clubs monthly rent on patches, the more patches a chapter rented, the higher they were on the list for nationals. RICO was a frequent visitor wherever they copped a squat, with seizures and indictments coming left and right. All the kinds of shit Watcher had been diligent in avoiding over the years, focused as he was on his mission. And now, one of their chapters had set up camp in Watcher's town.

He'd watched them for weeks, gathering intel, trying to lay a plan together. They were all over the map, however, making it hard to narrow down his targets. The club moved members and officers in and out like they were changing linens at a rent by the hour motel, and the here-today, gone-tomorrow aspect was daunting. Through it all, however, there seemed to be two members who returned time and again, and he'd focused his attention on them. Lalo and Chismoso. Cousins from Mexico, born in a village not far from where Juanita had grown up.

A village directly in the middle of Raul's territory.

"You hear the shit they pulled in Florida last month?" Watcher had, and he was certain Raul had, as well. Diamante had roped a prospect from another club, the dominant in the area, and had dragged him to death behind a bike. The authorities had picked the guy up in pieces, using twenty-three different body bags. Pictures of the destruction left behind every incident with Diamante had circulated through all the clubs, but everyone was tiptoeing around what needed to be done. No one wanted an event that would bring even more government scrutiny to bear on the community as a whole. No one was willing to step up and do what they all knew needed to be done. Silence from the phone, so Watcher asked a different question. "You think they'll stay north of the border, amigo? Think again. These assholes don't discriminate who they fuck over. You hear what happened to Skeptics in Chicago?"

"I did. Bones has lost control of a very lucrative warehouse." Raul now sounded resigned, and Watcher would take it as long as it meant he got what he needed, but he wanted to set things straight first.

"Two warehouses. They've locked him out of half his territory, even if he can't admit it aloud. He's hurtin', man. I suspect he's on the phone with Mason right now." *Fuck, hadn't meant for that to slip out*, he thought, and Raul jumped on it, like Watcher knew would happen.

"Which is why you are on the phone with me." At least he could hear the humor in Raul's voice, which would mean the man wasn't too pissed. "Tell me what is planned. I will see if I can assist. I already told you I would, Watcher. I am only...what do you say? Busting your balls."

"Fuck you." Watcher's shoulders dropped two inches, and only then did he become aware of how tense he had been. "But you're right, there's a campaign planned in Chicago, and we'll want to coordinate with Mason and Bones so we all keep our targets suitably distracted. So—" He pulled in a breath, propping one hip against the desk, looking over to where his officers stood, listening. "—here's how it's going to go down."

Club. Family. Honor.

Watcher leaned back into the sectional couch, draping one arm across the back and the other propped on the arm, hand holding a coffee cup. He stared across the room at the extremely nervous boy sitting in the armchair nearest the door. When Mela had let the kid in, that was as far as he made it, looking like his legs would collapse if he had to take another step forwards under Watcher's scrutiny. *Jesus*, he thought. *My Bella can really pick 'em.*

Instead of doing what he wanted to do, which was lean his head back and sigh, or the other alternative, get the fuck out of the room, or the best alternative, pick the punk up and throw his ass out the door, Watcher instead tried to be civil. "So, you go to LC high?"

The kid quivered in place, head shaking back and forth so fast Watcher thought his features blurred for a moment. *Jesus.* "No, sir, Mr. Otey, sir. I go to Arrowhead."

Slightly impressed, because Arrowhead Park Early College was a tough program to get into, Watcher said, "Nice. What college are you aiming towards?"

"Well, I hope Harvard." The kid's head did that shake thing again, and Watcher had to stifle a laugh. "I'm on the medical side of Arrowhead."

"*Jesus.*" This one slipped, and Watcher saw the kid's eyes widen, and his hands twitch like he wanted to cross himself. "Good on ya, kid." Mela had chosen to not do college until this fall. She'd instead spent her years after graduating bouncing between her father's house in Chihuahua and the one here. She also hadn't ever brought a date home, nor had one pick her up. When it came prom time, she'd opted out of the experience entirely, staring him into silence when he tentatively tried to suggest he could get a prospect to take her. So Bella and Mela would be hitting the local campus at the same time, his two girls in lockstep like they'd been nearly since he'd brought Mela home, the six-year difference in age didn't matter to either of them.

"So moving out east?" The quiet in the room was oppressive. He glanced towards the kitchen, then the hallway leading to the bedrooms, mentally pleading with any of his girls to come save him.

"Yes, sir, Mr. Otey, sir." The kid could nod nearly as fast as his shake, and Watcher focused on his hair for a moment. It didn't move. Not an inch. The kid's head was flopping around on the end of his neck like a fish on a dock, and his hair wasn't moving. *That's not natural*, Watcher thought.

Elbows to his knees, the kid leaned forwards, making Watcher jut his chin out, getting an inch closer so he could hear whatever it was the kid was about to say. "Mr. Otey, I want you to know I respect Isabella."

"Yeah, you fuckin' better," Spider's voice came through the window right before he flung the door open. "She's got a hundert brothers who'll have your ass you disrespect her."

The kid looked between them, and Watcher saw his Adam's apple bob up and down as he swallowed. In a tentative voice, he questioned, "Mr. Otey?"

His attention flashed between the two men when Spider grunted in amusement at the same time Watcher muttered, *"Jesus."*

This time the kid did cross himself.

"Yeah. That's me." Watcher took pity on the boy and leaned forwards, putting down his coffee cup and adopting the same pose, trying like hell to pull out whatever it was the kid needed to say. "What's your name, kid?" Surely this wasn't the Edwardo Bella had been sweet on. *Please God, say it's not.*

"Walt," the boy said, and Spider choked, the sound of his laughter coming out strangled.

"Okay, Walt." Watcher let a beat of silence fall, then deliberately lowered his voice to rumble the question, "What did you want to say about respecting my baby girl?"

"Um." Walt's eyes sliced to Spider, then back to Watcher. His words came fast, nearly tripping over themselves on their way out of his mouth. "Just that I respect her. She said her curfew is midnight, and I'll be sure to have her home by then, sir. Safe and sound."

"That it?" Watcher jutted his chin a bit more, making sure the kid was done speaking. When Walt nodded, he sighed. "That's good, Walt. Good plan. Because her Uncle Spider there behind you isn't kidding. You know who I am?" Walt nodded, again going so fast his features blurred. "Then you know she's got a hundred men who would hunt your ass down and cut off—"

"Daddy," Bella scolded from down the hallway, and with that, he knew this was a set-up so the kid could reassure him.

With a grin, he continued, "—your access to the Internet, and then how would your homework get done? You'd have to kiss Harvard good-bye."

Spider's voice was awestruck when he said, "Holy shit, Bella. Hey, Watch, lookie at our girl."

Twisting off the couch, Watcher stood, and as he did so he registered that Walt had also risen to his feet to watch Bella enter into the living room. Blonde hair pulled back into a bun low on her neck, it contrasted beautifully with the dark skin courtesy of her mother. Bella had on a shimmery gold dress which barely reached her knees, long legs ending in…

Watcher frowned. "You ain't wearin' those shoes." He paused. "Or that dress." Spider laughed, not bothering to swallow his humor this time. "It didn't look so short in the pictures you sent me, Bella. Did you take shears to that skirt?"

Juanita walked out behind their daughter, followed by a laughing Mela. Both of them came immediately to him, one to either side, arms around his waist. "Have a very good time with Walt, bebe," Juanita told Bella, getting a grin out of her.

Watcher muttered, "Not too good. Think about Harvard, Walt." Spider laughed again.

Mela gave Watcher a squeeze, then reached to hand her sister a flower box. "Boutonniere, Bella." Wrinkling her nose at her father, Bella took the box and fumbled it open, managing to only stick herself once as she pinned it to the boy's shirt. Watcher saw with relief that what the boy held was a wrist corsage, so he wouldn't be going anywhere near anything that would require Watcher beating Walt's head in right here on the spot.

Pictures and more pictures, Mela happiest when she was hiding behind the camera as usual. Spider getting in on the action by sneaking into a couple of the shots, and then it was Watcher standing with his arm around his baby girl, staring at the camera held in Mela's hands. *Blessed the day she came to us*, he thought. Watcher looked down at Bella, remembering again how it felt to hold her slippery body, all the emotions swelling in him at the moment she came out of Juanita and into the world. "My miracle," he murmured, bending to brush a kiss against the top of her head. "When did you grow up, baby girl?"

"Daddy," she said softly, giving the same tight squeeze Mela had moments before. "I'll never grow up."

"You see to that immediately," he ordered, and she laughed.

***

"God, I love her," Mela breathed as the door closed behind Bella and her date.

Watcher smiled at his oldest child, the daughter of his heart who had come to him second, after his daughter of the body had been born. A girl who had grown into a beautiful woman, one he hoped would never doubt her place in his life. "She loves you, too, honey."

He and Raul had decided way back on the first visit Mela's parents had paid to them, that with what had happened to her, Mela would have a definite say in where she lived. After Raul had solidified his position, when given the choice, she opted to stay in the States with Watcher and the people who had become her second family.

"I'm so glad she's over her bad boy phase," Mela muttered, cradling a coffee mug to her chest, picking up the remote to turn on the TV.

"She had a bad boy phase?" He threw himself into the chair the kid had used, reaching with the toes of one foot to hook a leg of the ottoman and drag it closer so he could prop his feet up. "When was that?"

"You remember, Papa." He did, but he hadn't ever gotten a complete story out of either girl about their massive fight. A fight which ended in Bella holding a grudge for an unheard of two weeks. Normally his Bella was as sweet as they come, slights real or imagined gone in minutes, but she'd held onto her anger from the fight for a long time. "The douche."

"Which one was that?" He stared at the guide she had on the screen, watching as the selector flew down and down, pausing at the sports channels for a moment, then settling on one of the dramatized bike shop shows. His girl knew him well. "I can't remember."

"Edwardo Suches, the wannabe." She shifted forwards to toss the remote to the coffee table, settling back by tucking her feet underneath her on the couch. Juanita fussed in the kitchen, probably getting ready to plate his supper. He'd made it home after everyone else had eaten, but in time to suffer through Walt's unimpressive entrance. Mela rested her head against the back of the couch. "The one who wouldn't come to the house. She always had to meet him somewhere. He'd call, and she'd pick up and be gone in a flash. He didn't treat her like she mattered. I'm glad she finally had enough."

"What happened, do you know?" His Bella had cried for two weeks, and he'd listened to Juanita comforting her quietly one night, murmuring about Edwardo, so he assumed the kid had broken it off with her.

"I don't know. Edwardo was gone for a while, and when he came back to Las Cruces, he was different. Even more of a douche. Had changed from being a rocket jockey to riding a panhead. Got himself new ink and a new vest, but had the same old douche attitude." Watcher's ears perked up at vest, because he hadn't been aware Bella was interested in a rider. She'd ridden on the back of his bike since she was big enough to hold on, and even before that cradled in front of him, her little legs straddling the tank. She'd even ridden with some of his older members, but shied away from any of the men closer to her age. Mela continued, "She didn't expect him to drop her like he did, but that wasn't the worst. *Pinche cabron* hurt her, Papa."

Watcher froze, holding himself in check, forcing his stare to stay on the screen, not seeing anything, only red. "Whadda mean, he hurt her?"

His tone must have given away his rage, because she sounded way more careful when she answered, "Long in the past, Papa." In a clear distraction tactic, she asked, "What are they doing with that exhaust system?"

"Mela." He swung his head to look at her, watching her lips press tightly together. "This Suches, he hurt her?"

"I took care of it." She blurted the words and clapped a hand over her mouth. "Bella never knew."

"How'd he hurt her, Mela? What did you take care of?" Everything around him stilled until the pounding of his blood was all he could hear, all he could feel, smashing through his heart, keeping pace with his rage. "What. Did you. Take care of?"

"He pushed her down. Grabbed her arm and pushed her down. I saw it. I was on my bike at this taco place. She was meeting him there. She didn't know I knew. She didn't know I saw. She wasn't hurt, not really. She got up and ran to her car, tore out of there and came home." Mela leaned forwards. "But he put his hands on her in a way I didn't like, Papa." She leaned back and took in a deep breath, blowing it out through her nose.

"I took care of it. He didn't call her again. Nothing left to teach him because he learned his mistake. Right in front of his boys, learned he made the wrong move, Papa. Don't mess with the Oteys, we mess back." She stared at him, then tipped her chin. "I remember what you've taught us, Papa Watcher. *Club. Family. Honor.*" The emphasis she put on the words made them sound as if they'd come from his mouth. She had learned his motto early on, adopting it as her own.

"When was this, baby?" Struggling to stay seated when every cell of his body demanded he go find the motherfucker and kill him, Watcher tried to correlate the timing with anything to figure out where he'd been, why he didn't know his girls needed him. "Where was I?"

"You were with my *papá*." She smiled, one corner of her mouth lifting her lips into a crooked grin. "Hangin' out down in old *México*. Downing his special reserve cactus juice."

"You'll tell me if anything like that happens again, right?" He kept his gaze trained on her, seeing her mouth quirk sideways, knowing she was about to lie. Her tell, and pray Jesus she never figured it out. Teasing, her crooked smile. Lying, that cheek-chewing quirk.

"Sure. Absolutely, Papa. I will." Tipping his chin down, he glared, and she blinked, recognizing how serious he was about this, and her expression changed, accepting her role. "Of course, Papa Watcher. I would tell you."

"Good girl." Gaze to the TV, he told her, "Turn it up, I can't hear this fucking idiot."

***

Watcher was scrubbing at the chain grease under his nails, knowing from experience it would take time and patience to get it all and for a moment he was struck by a memory. His mind cast back to when Mela first came to live with them. They'd been sitting in the yard out by the bikes when she'd asked if she could stay forever. *Make you clean again*, he remembered telling her, wiping his hands with a greasy rag. *Mama'd like her*, he thought, smiling down at his hands as he scrubbed them together under the running water.

Would Ma be proud of me?

The thought came out of left field, and he glanced up, catching his own startled gaze over the half-glasses he wore to read the Sunday paper. *Would she be proud of the man I've become?* He took a breath.

Would Darrie? Tabby? Would Pa? Would he understand how I got to where I am?

Looking down, he finished washing his hands and picked up the cotton towel laid on the edge of the sink, slowly drying them. No longer thinking of the bikes or the grease or even Mela, he was stuck on the ideals his father had left with him. The lasting legacy of a man he revered more than anyone else on this planet. *Family and honor.* Something Watcher had stretched to also cover his claimed family, the brotherhood on which his life was built. *Club.*

Watcher idly finished wiping the last droplets of water from his hands and leaned back, shoulders to the wall behind him. Staring into the mirror, he crossed his arms over his chest. The stark white of the towel loosely gripped in his hand contrasted strongly with the dark tan of his arms. *The things I've done, I've done for the right reasons.* His mother, always pushing him to be more, to do more, to strive for something higher.

He remembered the framed diploma over her desk, wondering not for the first time where the desk had gone once he had to leave for the military. Aunt Loretta made sure Tabby had everything from her room, and saved some of the pictures which had survived the destruction of their home, but he didn't know about things like his mother's desk or rocker. Still, he had the memories of her sitting in the rocker, laughing out loud as she read letters from home. Memories of her seated at the desk, looking out the window at Tabby playing in the yard, smiling as she composed her own letters he hoped had been filled with contentment.

I did my best, he thought, shifting uncomfortably. *For Tabby.* Did everything he knew how to do to keep her safe. *Might not be an accident*, Preacher's voice ran through his thoughts, and he shook his head, dislodging the idea. *Done right by Juanita.* Chin lifting, he stared at the reflection of his eyes. *And by Mela. My Bella.* The near-on thousand women and countless children rescued on his orders. *Family. An honorable legacy.*

Pa would understand about the club, too. Watcher sighed. Pa had made his own hard decisions back in the day, and Watcher remembered more than one moonlit trip through the hollers with him. Sitting in the back of the truck, Mikey would hold the clear bottles upright. Stopping at bridges and mailboxes, shadowy figures coming into view. Pa would swing out of the truck, leaning over the side rail and passing along the order for one or two bottles, straight shine or apple pie. Exchanging mountain liquor for hard cash which could be spent in places the bank's checks weren't welcome. Paying for Tabby's midwife with hours of patient tending over a still. *Cash crops, wherever we could find 'em.* Tobacco. Morels. Shine.

Leaning forwards, Watcher untucked his arms, hands to the sink, staring into the mirror. Craggy features he would never label as anything except hard. Scars trailing through his beard, now more gray than ever, the dark it had once been giving way to the advancement of age. Each mark a reminder of a mistake or misjudgment, each a reminder he was still alive to talk about it, which meant it was a story from the past. *Got the Otey hairline*, he thought, lifting one hand to ruffle his still-full head of hair. Also graying, but there. *Lucky as hell Juanita wanted me.* He tossed the hand towel to the back of the sink, turning as footsteps came running up the hallway past the door.

Mela's voice lifted, sweetly shouting, "I'm out, Papa. See me latah!"

He grinned, pausing to see the reflected expression of joy on his face. Shaking his head, he grabbed the handle and yanked the door open, yelling, "Put your helmet on, Mela. Love you, honey."

He got back the one thing he never took for granted, the one thing that kept him going. Didn't matter which of his girls said it, it always hit him the same way. "Love you, too, Papa."

If it were me

Watcher separated himself from the group of men standing outside a military bunker in the mountains of Utah. "Need a minute," he muttered, hearing Bones' grunted response. So much had happened in only a few weeks, and then today had been chaos from beginning to the end he'd witnessed only minutes before. A noise he recognized came through the open doorway behind them, that of a heavy load being dragged across cement, the scrubbing sound of fabric marking the movement of a body.

He'd been present when family turned on family before. Stood there when Raul finally cornered Carlos. Did not judge the man for taking it slow, taking his time. Knowing what Watcher knew about the betrayal Carlos had done to Carmela, he would have been disappointed if Raul hadn't spent the hours he did gutting and killing the man. Given the chance to get retribution for the hell Juanita survived, he would have dealt the man the same.

He'd seen patch brothers turn on each other, too. Remembered the scene not four years ago in Kentucky, when he'd known without a doubt in his soul he'd made the right decision to leave the Outriders so many years ago. The bullshit they were doing with the prospects wasn't about building a club, wasn't about making men into strong brothers. It was as horrendous a betrayal as anything he'd ever witnessed, turning the man into an accomplice in his own debasement.

Honestly, he didn't know if he could have held himself together like Mason did, taking care of needed business with no more than a single bullet. He knew it was only because Mason hadn't seen the video, believed that was probably Judge's salvation. Watcher shuddered, his mind unable to release the idea of Juanita and Carmela suffering the kind of torture Shooter's son had put Mason's woman through. Willa was strong. Watching the video where she faced down her rapist and shot him, then shot him again, proved her strength beyond a shadow of a doubt.

It was hard to reconcile the kid he'd met in the back room of a business in New Mexico with the hard-faced man from today. Harder still to reconcile the stories that Morgan had told all those years ago about his grandson, a sweet boy from the tales, and one that Morgan had doted on. What he did to Willa...hell on earth. Willa was lucky Judge didn't understand her strength.

Her fate would have been certain. Every man present knew it, based on what they'd found in one of the other cells. Carrie Sosa. Dead. Not even at rest, but stinking and dismembered, dead for days and thrown into a heap on a bed, the mattress sodden with decomposing fluids. No one deserved that. Watcher realized his head was shaking back and forth, the movement involuntary. *Not even Sosa.*

Two more cells empty. Inhabitants unknown, because the camera had been trained solely on Willa's prison. Judge had stacks of tapes from the days he'd held her prisoner. Sosa, who the hell knew when he'd taken her. Willa had been missing, but not really on the radar as taken. Mason had called a dozen times over the past week and a half, searching for any news of her. It had taken Mica's abduction to stir Mason's ass from Fort Wayne, he'd been so certain Willa was running

297

from what he wanted to build with her. *Man picks some fucked-up broads*, Watcher thought, remembering Mason's voice telling him Juanita was damaged.

Watcher had been staring at the wall of trees for a while when he heard Bones behind him. "This, my friend, is not something any of us will easily forget." Watcher shook his head, agreeing with the words. "They are preparing the building for disposal." Fire, a way to sweep things away cleanly. "I think Mason will want the tape."

"Jesus." Watcher twisted to look down at Bones, surprised as he always was that this man who was a force to be reckoned with lacked the stature his presence demanded. "Even if he wants it, if that shit's ash, he can't fight it. Burn it, Bones. Don't let him see."

"If it were me, I would want to know," Bones counseled quietly, stepping in front of Watcher and turning so they were face-to-face.

"It's been me, and I'm here telling you I do not want that kind of shit in my head. And I don't want it for Mason, either. Gonna eat at him if he knows what Judge did. He hears her voice crying out as we heard? Gonna eat him up inside, because he'll *know*"—Watcher leaned an inch closer—"he should have taken his time killing the motherfucker. Taken a fingers width of skin for every second she suffered." Watcher straightened. "If I could do that to the men who hurt my Juanita, I would. And that's with only her stories as fuel to the flame. If I'd seen it? Heard that? Wouldn't be any stopping me. And if I couldn't deal out my anger on their asses? Would eat at me. Eat and eat and eat." He took a deep breath. "Burn it."

"I think he should have the choice." Bones tipped his head to one side. "He carries a lot. So much. I do not think he would want us taking this from him without his voice."

"Well, you do whatever the fuck it is you have in your mind to do, then. Because you clearly got an agenda here, friend." Watcher turned, looking away, seeing movement in the trees at the same time Duck called softly, relief clear in his tone, "Hoss found them."

"Thank fuck," Watcher muttered, turning his gaze to Mason, seeing the man's singular focus as the little group came out of the woods and into the sunlight. If a person didn't know him, they might think him impassive, uncaring, but the tension in his stance sang through every muscle of his body. It was torture for him to stand in place, but Watcher understood the need. Willa had to want to come to him. Had to want to be comforted. Mason was strong enough to let her set the pace, understanding in this space of time it wasn't about what he needed. Without looking, Watcher told Bones. "You're right. Bring the tape."

No response, just the sound of retreating footsteps marking his friend's movement.

Watcher looked back at the women, seeing first Willa, and then Mica. They knew Willa's identity from the evidence in the building. Mica they'd anticipated, because of how she went missing. But the third woman was a blow Watcher hadn't been expecting. Worse, somehow, than Carrie Sosa, was recognizing Bethany walking behind the other two women, head held low, hair in her face, a defeat he'd never seen in her posture. Not even when she'd stood in front of Zonder, confessing the things she'd suffered with the complicit approval of her father. "Jesus."

All these women intimately connected to Mason through blood or love. He glanced at Mason and saw the same knowledge had settled on his shoulders. Looking back to the women sandwiched between men loyal to Mason, Watcher knew this alone would eat at Mason. His nephew, dead at his hand. His woman, his boy's mother, his sister, and a woman he had vowed long ago to protect, all damaged through their association with him. *That's how Mason will see it*, he thought. *How I'd see it. Gonna have to steer him differently, make him see he can keep what he's got in Willa. Otherwise, he'll turn her away, afraid of all the what might have beens.*

A month ago Watcher had called, talked around the edges of what he wanted to say, knowing Mason would see through to the heart of it, and his friend had. Had told Watcher exactly what he needed to hear, and listening to his idea put to words cemented it in his head how this was the right thing to do, eventually. Not right then, and hell, not now, but at some point in the near future he would hand over the charter papers he and Darrie had worked on side-by-side, bent over a piece of plywood laid on top of sawhorses in the barn. Mason had spun up a Rebel Wayfarers chapter in Oklahoma a few months ago, and Watcher saw the benefits of their close association immediately. It would only be a matter of time before the patch on his back changed, and the Southern Soldiers were no more.

That wasn't today, though. Today was for celebrating the win they were taking home. Three healthy women, one solemnly carried bundle, and near a dozen men who claimed the tightest bonds of brotherhood which existed on the planet. Today was also for what they left behind, a black plume of smoke rising into the sky, marking the end of a dynasty.

On the plane headed to Fort Wayne, Watcher was pleased and surprised to see Bethany already bouncing back. After settling her in Nashville, he had been determined to keep ugly at bay for her. *At least I helped give her a firm foundation, so when things got rocky, she was still standing at the end of the day.* He could tell from the set expression on her face she was determined to beat it back. "You keep doin' that," he whispered to her, knowing she couldn't hear him. With a thankful heart, he took in the loving interaction between brother and sister, grinning when she broke into laughter. "Beat it back."

Only for you

Opie walked into the barn and stood in front of the desk, staring at Watcher, not moving for a minute. "What?" Watcher asked, bending back to the laptop in front of him. Opie didn't respond so Watcher lifted his eyes to his brother's face again, seeing a peculiar expression lay uneasily on his features.

"I wanna look at your sump pump set-up." Opie nodded like he was trying to convince himself. "Monsoon weather is coming." Watcher tilted his head, staring in confusion. It was months to monsoon season. "You've never had problems with yours. Do me a favor, come show me the sump pump, Watch?"

"Right now?" Watcher asked, incredulous. He glanced back at the laptop in time to see it closing, moving his fingers before they were pinched by the clamshell as it clicked into place. Opie nodded without responding, so, shaking his head, Watcher stood and walked around the desk. Once outside, he turned and opened his mouth to ask what was up, but Opie shook his head, eyes darting to the eaves of the roof before he walked across the yard.

The building that housed the pool equipment as well as the sump pump was on the other side of the property. An area Watcher didn't frequent except to mow as needed. Once they rounded the corner of the house, Opie reached out, plucking Watcher's phone from his vest pocket, finger to his lips as he bent and laid the device alongside his on the ground. Then across the remaining distance quickly, through the door of the equipment shed where Opie tugged at the string to turn on the overhead light.

"Cameras," Opie said before Watcher could ask anything. "I found five of 'em, boss. Not ours. They're piggybacking off our signal, but I got Mason's guy to run a check, and they are feeding back to an outside source. Myron's still digging, but I had him go gentle. Whoever it is, we don't want them to know we have a fuckin' clue they're watching us."

"Fucking hell. Where?" Watcher didn't bother questioning if Opie was sure because if he weren't sure, he wouldn't have said anything.

"In the office, outside the barn, near the pool"—Opie hesitated, then continued—"and two in the house, boss."

That hesitation told the tale, and Watcher was sure he wasn't going to like this. "Where?" This time, the one-word question was husky. Watcher felt his throat quivering with rage. *Eyes in my house?* Opie hesitated again, which told Watcher exactly how much he wasn't going to like this answer. "Where in my house, Opie?"

"Girls' rooms." Quick to react, Opie reached out, slapping the already opening door out of Watcher's hand, using all his weight to shove him against the wall and holding him there. "Boss, you can't. Not until we know who it is."

"*My girls have eyes on them?*" Watcher breathed like the oxygen in the room was gone, sucking at nothing. Desperately trying to keep his cool, pressure pounded in on him like a diver's bell, feeling his ribs crack under the strain. "Fuckin' *cameras* in their motherfuckin' *rooms?* And you expect me to not *do* anything?"

"Yet." Opie breathed the word. "You know, we need intel. Cannot plan an op without knowing what we're up against. So you're gonna do exactly what you gotta do. *Hold*, brother. Don't do anything yet. We have to know more before we cut the lines. Get the girls out of the house, get Juanita out of the house, but hold."

Rigid with anger Watcher sucked in a lungful of air, then another. Pausing on the exhale until he was sure he could speak without raging at a man who had no wrong in this, Watcher finally released the breath and asked the only thing that would let him walk out of this meeting without losing his mind. "How long before we know?"

"Fast as I can make it happen. My patch, brother. As fast as I can make it happen."

He had to come up with a reason to get them out of the house tonight. *What would be believable to Juanita?* Trust came hard, and with what he'd come back from in Utah, Watcher couldn't see sending them north. *Where's the last place anyone would look for my family?*

"College starts in a month. Juanita and I were talking last week, our girls need a vacation. I might be crazy, Opie, but San Diego seems right." Watcher nodded slowly, growing convinced with each thought flickering through his head. "Sun and surf, beaches and boys. Girls will love it. Juanita will enjoy the time away, too. Leave me here at the house. Won't seem like it's odd, either, with the semester starting so soon. San Diego."

Opie shook his head, "Not followin', boss."

"Cain't send 'em to Mexico. Raul's got his hands busy right now. Columbians are itchy for more, and he's dealing with them routing through his territory whether he gives way or not. Means Mexico's out." He pointed to a square patch high on Opie's shoulder, the RW in stark white stitched on black. "We support the Rebels. Made it official a while back when we took on their support patch. Don't mean they're our only ally. Much as I love Mason like a brother, the man's shit is thick up north. He can't turn one way or another without running into enemies. Look at what happened in Memphis. Jesus, man, they fuckin' dismantled the town, tore it wide open and had to pour blood and men into the breach so it didn't fuckin' spread."

The Rebels had, too. They'd taken on Columbia cartel in a big way. So much death, the rumor was every highway construction site had unexpected filler added to the deep base of bridges and roads. Killed the drug dealer Ling, ran the Diamante chapter out of town, then pulled in a dozen clubs to talk about what would happen in Memphis in the long term. Solidified their position as dominant in the area by taking over and holding tight, forcing everyone to their path. "Rumor and speculation, but I trust there's more than a grain of truth."

He waited for Opie to argue, and when he didn't, Watcher continued, more convinced than ever he was right. "Then right there in Chicago, we got Bones. That man is on the cusp of rolling Skeptics into the Rebels, and I can't blame him. Strengthens both of them in a way which makes the world take notice. It's gonna back some of the shit off their doorstep, but until it happens and is recognized, north can't be an option." Watcher shook his head. "Florida, I ain't got but a couple of names. I got folks in my pocket in Alabama, but not sure I wanna stir that pot. Retro got sucked into some shit with the Rebels, he's been on federal radar ever since. Sending my girls to him isn't a good option."

"So what's in San Diego?" Opie looked puzzled, and he should be. This wouldn't be anything any outlaw club member would expect.

"Blue Line and the Malcontents."

"Fuckin' LE? Are you kidding me?" Opie's response was immediate and exactly what Watcher expected, and he smiled humorlessly.

"Not kidding, brother. Give it a minute, and you'll see the reasoning. LE isn't just off radar for most clubs, they are off the planet. No one scopes and watches what they're doing or who is coming and going." He shook his head. "Unless they're pulling dumb fuck shit like a couple of the cop clubs. Blue Line, though, he's different." The fact he was Bear's brother-in-law was a secret for now, but it was another of the reasons Watcher felt the man might be trusted with his girls.

"Malcontents stick to their own shit. They don't fuck with other clubs. They even manage somehow to stay out of the way of the dominant on the west coast, and you and I both know how fuckin' hard it is to run under radar side-by-side with a club that big. Malcontents can keep them safe. Juanita would—" He swallowed, hating to expose her fears, even to someone who loved her without reserve, like Opie did. "Juanita wouldn't be comfortable going anywhere without me unless I can tell her she'll be safe. I think I can make that promise in good faith if they go to Diego."

"Then San Diego it is. We'll sort through this fast, boss. Myron's on it, and he's good." Opie reached behind him, pulling the door open and letting the heat of the day roll through the tiny building. "We'll have the girls home before you know it."

"And we'll deal with the motherfuckers who put eyes in our clubhouse, on my property, in my little girls' rooms. Do a little forty-five persuading." Watcher reached up, tugging the string, plunging the corners of the building into darkness. "Take care of family."

***

Staggered from what he had just learned, Watcher stood, rubbing the top of his head. He saw the man who had just released him from a headlock familiarly greet Duck.

Gabe Ledbetter, his cousin. The last time Watcher had laid eyes on him was Tabby's funeral. *Son of a bitch.*

They were standing in the back of a bar the Soldiers had purchased a year ago in Lamesa, Texas. Watcher had approved a charter here before that, letting the half a dozen men run the club out of a garage until they had an official building in town. Now the clubhouse was housed in the backroom of the bar, extended downward recently as they hand dug a basement room. Soundproofed and well-stocked, it had many uses. Right this minute it held a dozen women and children they'd rescued from a slave farm five nights ago, the activity which had brought him to town in order to organize their escorts to host families.

Duck pulled Gabe close, muttering softly into his ear and Gabe turned amused eyes Watcher's direction. "Watch...Michael," Gabe yelled through his laughter. "You keepin' secrets, cuz?"

Watcher expected to see Gabe at Aunt Loretta's services, but the man had been a no-show, pissing Ezra off. He'd heard through the grapevine Gabe had joined a club, but that was years ago, somewhere down in the Carolinas. His redheaded cousin had fallen off the grid for him, especially when Watcher followed Darrie's move to New Mexico and his focus turned out here.

In the club world, there'd been talk of a man named Fury for months, popping up in conversations with a dozen different clubs, but most persistently when Watcher spoke to Mason. The man had played a part in Memphis, as well as played a role in the club absorption process in Chicago. Played a part of what Gunny and Duck had found in Cynthiana with the Outriders, taking over the territory fistful-by-fistful until Shooter had to pull back. That happening even before Shooter wound up in prison for his part in kidnapping his own daughter. Fuck, Fury even played a role in his own dismantling of the rival club here. But that Fury? He had been a Diamante, one of the enemy until he'd proven himself, moving his chapter to Fort Wayne and then burning his charter, rolling every one of his men into the Rebel Wayfarers chapter there.

Unreal that Fury was his cousin. Gabriel, one of Loretta and Ezra's boys. Watcher had memories of the redheaded kid he'd fished with, stories told by Tabby of how Gabe had stuck up for her against shitheels at school. Gabe had been born in Louisiana where their mothers were from, raised in Kentucky. Stick thin, hair in a short buzz cut leaving the barest crimson halo around his skull as they waded up the creek, turning over logs and rocks to find mudbugs. That was the Gabe Watcher remembered. Not this muscled, bearded man wearing a Rebel Wayfarers patch on his vest.

Duck was here in Lamesa because he'd been born here, and still owned land and a business in the area. Watcher had run into him four days ago, shocked to see the man. Not in the territory, because that had been asked and answered via a phone call from Mason before Duck left Chicago months ago. No, Watcher had been shocked to see Duck without a vest on. It had felt like a hard kick to the chest. To Watcher, it seemed to telegraph that the Rebels didn't trust him, or his men. Duck running anonymous in his own hometown because he didn't believe the word of the Southern Soldiers' president that he'd be safe.

Pissed as hell, Watcher had called Mason, ready to rip the support patch off his own shoulder. With everything going on, Juanita and the girls finally getting home after three weeks in California, Watcher then having to be away from his family and home on move-in day at the dorms, he'd been pissed as a wet hen, and scarcely a breath away from calling war. *Too much shit*, he thought now, gesturing to the bar for beers. Mason had put the kibosh on his anger, calling him out on his mistakes, reminding him neither of them were mind readers.

Settling into a seat, he listened as Fury and Duck brought him up to speed on everything that had been going on in the Rebel world. Sitting quietly, keeping his own counsel, he let them talk on, switching the narration back and forth between them until they'd run out of stories and news. After a few moments of silence, Watcher was somehow not surprised when Fury tipped his head to the side and said, "Heard Myron helped out with some info a few weeks ago. Everything shake out okay from that?"

Watcher sat for a moment, because it had, but it hadn't. "Had someone put up cameras at my place." Duck's eyes sharpened, and Watcher was reminded of his intelligence. This man, nearly as well as Slate, could look at a problem and see fifteen ways to solve it. *Mason's got a stable of keepers*, he thought. Spider. Devil. Opie. Diamond. *So do I.*

"FBI?" Fury asked the question, and Watcher shook his head.

"Not fed. They were my first thought, too. Then, we traced the signal back to a truck parked about three miles away. Had some equipment in the bed, about half of it tarped, half open in the elements. When we found it, based on what we saw it seemed a remote set-up. Isolated from everything. It looked like there were about two weeks of data stored, so Myron figured whoever had put it into play only came in every so often to gather what had been captured on the cams. He didn't see any way to remote into the system. Meant they'd be back, so we staked it out. No one approached. But"—he shook his head, because this was maddening in so many ways—"about two weeks into our stakeout, it took a burst of power from something. Zapped the entire rig. Fried everything." Lifting his beer, he took a long drink, his throat tight with remembered anger.

"When we realized it was useless, we went to move it." The hospital visit slid through his mind, men covered in blood and sand, looking exactly like he never wanted to see his brothers. "Fuckin' IED under the wheel. Blew a crater and sprayed my guys with shrapnel. Afterwards, we found a battery under there with a sensor. That's what had fried the rig, it was hooked to the frame. Whoever did it was able to kill the system remotely by opening a connection. Set a trap." He took another drink, scanning the room with his gaze.

"Found a room...a cell buried under the truck. Two women. Devil figured they'd been dead about four days." Eyes back to Fury and Duck, he scoured them looking for any sign of contempt. "We sat on our asses for two weeks while they starved to death. Sat there eating chips and drinking beer, watching a fucking truck in the middle of the desert while two women starved to death in a metal fucking box under the truck. A truck filled with videos of my house, and my wife and daughters."

Watcher pushed his chair back and stood, "So no, I don't consider that shaking out okay." Two steps away, he paused. Without turning around, he huffed out a breath and said, "Back in a minute, just need...some air." As he walked out the door, stiff-arming it open, a buzzing swell of animated conversation came from behind him. Fury and Duck dissecting his tale, trying to figure a way to help him.

Brothers. Family. Standing in the heat outside, he leaned his shoulders against the wall. Two men had been injured when the can of bolts exploded, one blinded, forever losing sight in an eye, something no amount of money could make better. *Because I was so focused on finding out who was watching my girls, I forgot to pay attention to anything else. On me. That's on me.* Club. Honor.

A few minutes later the door opened, and Fury stepped out, moving to stand beside Watcher. "Had no idea, Mike." Watcher grunted in response. "We got some thoughts on it but have questions first. You up to comin' back inside?" In answer, Watcher pushed away from the side of the building. Fury turned and opened the door, holding it so Watcher could enter first. As he walked past, Fury lifted a hand to grip the side of his neck, squeezing tight for a moment, muttering a word that shocked Watcher. "Prez."

***

Leaning against the motel headboard, Watcher grinned as he listened to Juanita verbally reenacting the day. She and the girls had moved Bella into her apartment with the help of Spider's two sons. Not a dorm as he'd thought, but a suite of rooms where she'd have more space. "And then the boys dropped her suitcase. Watcher"—Juanita was laughing so hard he could barely make out the words—"it busted open, and they were working to scoop up the clothes. Then"—laughing harder, she was taking in great whooping breaths between each word—"they realized they were holding her panties." Now he was laughing alongside them, this picture in his head in a way he both liked and didn't like because he didn't want to think about Spider's boys with their hands on his Bella's panties.

Mela was in the background, howling with laughter as she shouted, "Hot potato, Papa. They were throwing her thongs"—*I did not need to know that*—"back and forth, like a game of hot potato. Throwing them towards the suitcase, missing, having to pick them up again. Then Bella came out of her room—" At this point Mela lost it completely, laughing so hard she couldn't continue.

Juanita picked the story back up, "—and screeched, 'Put down my underwear!' It was hilarious, *Papi*."

"Wish I'd been there to see it," he told them, and Mela laughed even harder.

"Oh, no. No, Papa. No, you don't. You'd have shot them." Mela's voice was muted like she was moving away from the phone and he recognized the ending tones of the doorbell in the background.

Juanita, still giggling, her voice soft but threaded through with her love for him, said, "Wish you were here, too, *Papi*."

He thought about the women moved from the bar's basement room today, put on transports taking them to host families. Some of them had babes at the breast, two of them with older children, and Watcher said another prayer that God would watch over those babies, keeping them safe and blanking their minds of what they had seen. *Like you helped with my Juanita and Mela, God.*

"Box for you, Papa," Mela called, and he smiled to hear how light her voice sounded. She would start classes the same day as Bella, but had opted to continue living at home. Her safe place in the world. *Let those children find a safe harbor too, God*, he finished. *Amen.*

"Put it out by the barn door, one of the boys will take it in for me." Noise in the background and he waited a moment, knowing it was her leaving the room. "Juanita?"

"Yes, *Papi*?" *I never get tired of her voice.* The sound quality changed and her voice could have come from right beside him when she murmured, "What is it?" *Took me off speaker, wants a different kind of fun now.*

"Love you, mamacita." He smiled and then reached down, adjusting his jeans around his thickening cock. Simply the sound of her voice could do that to him. "I'll be home tomorrow. Be good."

"And if I'm bad?" *Jesus. Killin' me.*

"Then you'll earn what you get when I get home, won't you?" She giggled again, sounding nearly as young as their girls when she was playful. "My Mama gonna be bad?"

"Only for you, *Papi*." Fingers to the waistband of his jeans, he opened and pushed them down, taking his cock in hand. When he groaned, she asked, her voice breathy, "What are you doing, *Papi*? Do you need me to go?"

"What do you think, honey? You gonna talk to me like that and I'm this far away? Oh no, not a chance in hell you're leaving me high and dry, honey. Thinkin' of makin' me hafta take care of business by myself?" The sound of her breathing sped up, and she whimpered. "Leave me with only dreams of you, baby? Burying myself in you? Oh, no, Mama. Least you can do is listen."

Their call didn't end for another thirty minutes, during which he directed his wife go to their bedroom and lock the door. Then he talked to her, listening as she took herself over the edge of a much smaller mountain than they found when together.

***

"How'd you...?" Watcher paused, because this wasn't a question he'd ask anyone else, but this was Gabe, so he forged ahead. Even as he did so, he was careful to set the stage as to where the inquiry was coming from. "How'd you wind up where you are, man?"

"Might as well ask how the grass grows, brother." Fury lifted his coffee cup and blew across the steaming liquid, then sipped.

Watcher and Fury were seated along the short edge of the bar, the cleaning crew moving around them to finish their job. Watcher was hoping to be on the road by noon, make it home by dinnertime so he could take Juanita and his girls and Bella's apartment-mate out for a meal. Make up a little bit for missing move-in day, even if it had sounded like they'd managed fine without him. With that in mind, he'd asked Fury to meet him early, knowing they'd have some privacy. The Soldiers members in Lamesa were all staying at a local motel until he could find a decent house to buy. The motel was cheap digs for now, and cheaper yet because his men had run the meth heads out for the owner, so she was cutting him a deal on their rent.

"Gotta be a story in there." Leaning his elbows against the curve of the bar, Watcher dangled his hot mug from the fingertips of one hand, reaching for a stirring straw with the other. Twisting his neck, he called, "Crema, Lizetta. *Leche para mi café, por favor.*"

One of the women sweeping paused to flash him a quick glance, anxiety flooding her features. She ducked her head and mumbled, "*Si, señor.*"

"Lizetta," his tone was scolding, but he pursed his lips in a tease, smiling at her.

"*Si,* Watcher."

"*Gracias, señorita.*"

"Why's that shit matter to you? Caught it the other day, too, you making them call you by name. What's the deal?" Fury waited to ask until after the girl had walked away, headed into the back where supplies were kept.

"She's one of the girls we've rescued. Got her free about a year ago. It took her three months to speak." Watcher glanced around the room. "These women? They're all rescued slaves."

"Jesus," Fury muttered, his eyes following the same path. "How many have you freed?"

"Nearly a thousand." Watcher took the creamer containers from the young girl, careful not to touch her. "*Gracias.*" She nodded and went back to sweeping. "Since we started keeping count." He dumped in several tiny buckets of white liquid, stirring slowly, watching the color seep into the darkness inside the mug. "And it matters because they had to call their customers by title. I don't want to be on the same level with those animals, ever. In any way. So I insist they call me by name."

"No doubt," Fury muttered, sipping his coffee again before returning to their previous topic. "Did a stint in the navy, didn't like it. Bullshit everywhere I looked. Guys with family got the cush, guys like me got the short end. Did my two, didn't re-up. Drifted a while. Found a bar, worked there. Liked it. Liked not seein' the same people every day, but seein' some people enough so you got to know 'em. Regulars. One of those regulars was in a club. Talked a game." Fury laughed, his teeth glinting white in his red beard. "Big game. Good game. Totally a game. Turned out to be a pansy ass RC more than anything. Fuckers would meet at the local burger joint to ride. Hang out on the corner like punks for hours waitin' on a brother to decide to roll. I didn't know any better, so I took it as gospel. Put that shit on a vest, got my ass on a bike. Lucky for me the one I liked was American iron, yeah?"

Watcher prompted him to continue, knowing there had to be more to the story. "Don't sound like the worst thing. Working and riding."

"One of the boys got crossways with a half-assed real club in the area." Fury shook his head, beard brushing his chest as he looked down for a moment. "Started wreckin' us up. We had four guys get put in ICU. One after the other. Bam. Bam. Bam. Writing on the wall. My options were to take it"—he cut his gaze to Watcher—"or take 'em down."

"Door number two?" Watcher guessed, and Fury nodded.

Then he laughed and shook his head. "Actually, I picked curtain number three." Shaking his head, Watcher opened his mouth to ask what it meant, but Fury talked over him. "Took a meet. I'd spent two months working up the ranks. Didn't take long, these guys were serious pussies. Threaten real pain and they'd offer up their officer patch. So I climbed way up the fuckin' pole wearin' the president patch and set a meet. Took that meet. Walked in outnumbered in a way you wouldn't expect I'd be comin' back out." Fury paused, pulling in a breath. "You'd be wrong. Walked out, but without a patch on my back. All the men who walked out, did the same, both sides." He laughed. "I had a plan."

"I bet you did," Watcher muttered, staring at Fury. The story was fascinating because here sat a man like him. Family. One who had come from the same background, joined the military but had a different experience. Got into club life, but also had a very different experience. Yet they found themselves at the same crossroads, Fury having gotten there slightly sooner than Watcher's decision. Rebel Wayfarers MC.

"Plan was to take the elimination of two rivals to Diamante, secure a place deep inside. I wanted inner circle, not biding my time and building support. I wanted it all." Fury shook his head, laughing. "Stupid punk."

"What happened?" Watcher lifted his mug and drank, making a face. His coffee was nearly cold, forgotten as he'd gotten caught up in the story.

"Diamante schooled my ass. They weren't opposed to having less competition, but they were not excited about having an unpatched rag of a baby rider comin' in thinkin' he was gonna be throwing his weight around." Fury set his empty mug down, waving off one of the girls who moved their way, likely to refill it. "Schooled my ass good. Took me a month to walk without limpin'." He tipped his head, hair falling over his face, blue eyes pinning Watcher to the stool. "Took me two days to deal my own version of shit back to them."

"Jesus."

"Yeah, was some callin' to the Lord that day. Not from me, though. End of the day, I was king of the rock. Kept the position by force, making sure to move as often as I needed to keep my footing secure. Wound up back home, Cynthiana." His gaze dropped to the bar as he poked the coffee cup with one finger, turning it to and fro. "Mom and Dad weren't pleased to see me. Can't say I blame 'em." He cut his eyes back to Watcher, then back to the bar. "Heard you went back for Mom's funeral."

"I did." Watcher waited, sensing Fury wanted to ask a question, but instead he changed topics.

"You know Duck's woman is from Cunthiana?" As he used the mockery of the town's name that some locals used, Fury snorted. "Talked to her last night, was all I could do to keep that word off my lips." He reached out, picked his mug up and set it on the inner rail of the bar, seeming to want to keep his hands busy. "You remember how Tabby died?"

That was straight out of left field, and Watcher lurched, unable to hide his physical response to the question. *"What the fuck?"*

"Sorry, man. I got blurtitis today. I mean you remember there were questions about the accident? I know you thought she might have...you know." Fury seemed uncomfortable with this line of conversation, and Watcher didn't blame him. In only a few breaths his cousin had stripped away years of veneer from Watcher's grief, leaving him raw.

"Killed herself? Yeah, I know all about that." Watcher didn't try to hide his anger, not until he saw several of the girls look up with fear on their faces. *Fuck.* He moderated his tone to continue. "Of course I know; she was my baby sister."

"What if she didn't?" Fury whispered this, and Watcher leaned back, reeling from another blow because this was what he'd wanted for the longest time. *She'd beat it back.* Bethy's voice was a ghost in his head, making him glance around because for a moment it sounded as if she were in the room. She was supposed to be here in town, that he knew, part of some show at the rodeo grounds involving Mason's boy, Chase. *Beat it back.*

"What if she didn't, Watch? Brenda's folks were killed in an accident a few years before Tabby. She talked about it last night, so I looked it up. Didn't like what I found, so I dug a little deeper. Didn't like the next layer, so I put Myron on it, because Mason's hot to know all about Duck's woman anyway." With one look at Watcher's face, he shook his head. "Didn't say squat about you. Not a word, brother. Not you, and not Tabby. That's yours, not theirs."

Fury continued, his gaze intense. "What Myron found? Sixteen *accidents.* Exactly the same MO. Exactly. Sheriffs didn't put it together because those two wrecks happened on both sides of the county line. So we had one group looking at Tabby's and another lookin' at Brenda's. Man rescued Brenda, brother. Walked down the mountainside and dragged a cryin' six-year-old out of the car. Rescued her and took her to the hospital. Took his time to write down her shit and pin it to her fuckin' coat." Fury tapped one fingertip against the wood of the bar. "It's too big a coincidence, brother. So I had Myron look deeper. Sixteen wrecks, all the same way. All within ten miles of each other. There's a place on the shoulder of the mountain where three counties come together. That's some sick motherfucker's playground. I'd bet my life on it."

"I grew up with Tabby. She was closer to me than my own kin, Mikey. No way she'd have done that to you, to Darrie." Face resolutely tipped down, gaze on his finger still tapping on the bar, Fury muttered his next words, and Watcher wondered at the anguish hidden behind them. "Wouldn't a done it to me, man." They were quiet a moment, then Fury said, "Tore a hole in my chest the day we put her in the ground. Then to find out about what old man Mason did to Bethy. I...that shit...I can't even imagine someone doing that to a woman, let alone a little girl. And Tabby had come back from it, Mikey. She had. Loved that fuckin' truck. Loved you, and Darrie, the girl couldn't wait to see you your next leave. She'd talk about it all the time."

The corners of his eyes crinkled, and Watcher knew he was smiling, staring down, seeing something far different from the scarred surface in front of him. "She made me promise I'd call every Sunday. Just in case you boys had written. So every Sunday she'd wait, and then read me every word y'all wrote. Tell me all the stories. She loved you, man. Tabby wouldn't a done that to you."

Lifting his head, Fury stared at Watcher. "I never believed. Couldn't." It scored deep, and Watcher didn't try to hide the pain. "Nothing against you, brother. You didn't have a chance to really learn the woman she was becoming. Shit forced you down the road you had to take. Shit that brought you two closer in ways no one could predict. But it also forced you apart. You never got...she was your Tabby, and that's what you saw. No wrongness there. But she was growing up. So smart, she coulda done anything, Mikey. But I knew she'd a never done that. So I never stopped looking. Even from where I found myself, I looked as I could. Couldn't go back home, not with how things were between my old man and old man Mason. I never wanted to know if he'd been part of anything up the mountain, but I have my suspicions. Oh yeah, I got those. Spent my life trying to put those in my rearview. Jumpin' jobs and clubs. Takin' what I needed. Didn't much give a shit about anything, being as I couldn't turn back time and change what mattered." Fury shrugged. "So I kept hoppin'."

Watcher carefully settled the mug holding his cold coffee on the bar's surface, trying to still the trembling in his hands. All this was too much, too fast. Impossible to process, and dragging up emotions and anger he'd thought long buried. "So why'd you pull up stakes this last time? Why Rebels?"

"You met Mason?" Fury snorted. "Man's a force. Climb on his barge in the middle of the river, or drown in his wake. I like breathin', brother. He's about to decimate Diamante, and they know it, running scared. But in their blind running, they're tearing shit up you would not believe. Running Russian and Chinese gals out of Kentucky. Trying to force me into their business and I wasn't having anything to do with it. Shooter gobbled that cock right up, through." He cut his eyes to Watcher. "Heard about Utah." Watcher jerked his chin up. "No, brother. I *heard* about Utah."

Watcher pulled in a slow breath because it sounded as if Fury had critical information he'd withheld. Information that wound up with Bethy put in harm's way. "You wanna be careful what you say next, brother."

"You honestly think I'd have let Bethy walk into that shit? No fuckin' way. No way. Man, I didn't hear who, didn't even hear Mason's name mentioned, but Shooter wasn't quiet about what kind of holding facility someone was putting together up there. What he *was* quiet about was who it was and, brother, that bothered me." Shaking his head, he looked up the bar. "Too early for a shot?"

Wordlessly, Watcher slid off his stool and walked behind the bar. He turned to face Fury, holding his hand out over the liquor bottles, and taking one small, slow step at a time, walked backwards until Fury nodded. Watcher settled his hand on a bottle and looked to see a cheap whiskey in his grip. Shifting up a shelf from rotgut, he pulled a different brand, catching Fury's humorless grin. Grabbing a highball glass from the shelf, he queried, "Ice?" With Fury's headshake in response, Watcher tipped the bottle over the glass, counting out about six shots.

He moved back towards Fury to exchange the brimming glass for the empty coffee mug. He studied the man as he picked it up, hands steady as a rock, throat moving as he gulped at the contents.

"He was quiet about it, and I looked into it. Didn't like what I found. You knew Judge." This wasn't a question, but Watcher nodded anyway because Fury seemed to be waiting for something. "Got Judge good and drunk one night. The boy couldn't keep his mouth from running at that point. His granddad ain't dead. Justice Morgan joined forces with Deacon, both of them hating Mason, but I didn't know that then. Didn't have any inklin' they'd scoop up Bethany. I think Judge got lucky with surveillance because Mason had gone down to visit and someone saw. You know who Deacon is." He paused, and Watcher nodded because he'd known that man a long time.

Watcher interjected, "Told Mason more than once it was a mistake to leave him breathin'." He leaned a hip against the cooler under the bar, hearing the muffled clink of his gun against the metal, adjusting automatically so it didn't dig into the small of his back. "He never shoulda let that man walk outta his clubhouse."

"Agreed." Fury nodded. "But he did, and now he's got this shit to deal with. Deacon hates him worse than anything I've ever seen. All this, because Mason bested him and tore the club outta his hands. But more because Mason's made a success of it. He didn't falter and fall, didn't disappear into the woodwork. Not Mason. He's made quite the splash, sitting at tables with worldwide clubs who come to him. That's something Deacon wanted and never managed."

"Couldn't keep his nose off the line," Watcher muttered, and Fury nodded again.

"Still can't. He's coked up most of the time. The new normal. Makes him unpredictable, though." Fury lifted the glass and slugged back another mouthful of liquor. "Mix him with Morgan, and it's a volatile concoction. Not something I'd want close to me or mine. But sometimes it's better to be close to the target so you can at least see the hit comin'."

He lifted the glass, draining the last of the whiskey. "And that brings us to today. I saw a club I wanted to be part of, worked my way into a position where I could bring value with me, and then made it happen." He slid the bottom of the glass against the bar top. "Simple as that."

"Ain't nothing simple anymore, brother," Watcher muttered, reaching to gather his mug and the empty glass, setting them in the sink under the countertop.

"Agreed." Fury stood, stretching. "Storytime's over, old man." He reached out, gripping Watcher's shoulder. "And I have a protection detail to get on with."

"That why you're here?" Watcher had wondered and thought it likely the reason, but hadn't asked yesterday.

"Yeah. Prince is coming in." Watcher tilted his head in a silent question, and Fury burst out laughing. "Sorry. Talkin' about Mason's boy, Chase. Chase is flying in today. Mica's gonna be here. Her sister's already here. She's like extended family. Mason is coming down without Willa, but Bethany is supposed to be here, too. Prince, princess, king, and whatever the fuck you wanna call Bethy. All of that and a piss poor detail of Duck and me."

"Explains the call I got from Slate last night," Watcher said with a grin. "I've got a dozen of my guys headed to the rodeo grounds right now, looking for Duck's woman to get instructions on what's needed. I'm thinkin' you'd have better info than Brenda would."

"Agreed." It was Fury's turn to grin. "Send 'em my way. You got my cell, go ahead and pass that shit out, brother."

Watcher's head was bent to his phone when Fury spoke next, and Watcher didn't look up, not wanting to see the emotion on his cousin's face. "Sorry as fuck about Darrie, Mikey. I wasn't in a position to offer condolences at the time, but I heard about the run you made and what happened. You lost him to a good cause. Glad as hell you found Juanita." Unable to speak, Watcher nodded, eyes fixed on the screen of his phone. The door leading outside opened, light flooded the room and then disappeared, taking Fury with it.

Escalation

Heart racing, Watcher leaned the bike into the corner, knee out, balancing the machine even as it fishtailed on gravel near the edge of the road. His destination was around the next curve, and he wasn't slowing down until he saw his girl was okay. Sitting up, he punched down through two gears and sped into the gas station parking lot, eyes fixed on the grouping of bikes and men on the far side of the building. Braking hard, he skidded to a stop, had the kickstand down and was off the motorcycle before the growl of his engine left the air.

"Where is she?" He couldn't help barking the question at the men. Spider tipped his head, indicating the bathroom door at the back corner of the building. Five running steps and he was there, closed fist pounding on the metal, hearing the racket echoing off the warehouse next door. They were on the edge of an industrial complex and for the next few miles, the road boasted huge building after building, half of them empty as jobs moved overseas.

"Mela, open the fuck up. It's Papa." *Like she wouldn't know who it is*. But she hadn't called him. She'd called Juanita and asked for a ride. Tried to lie about what happened, and no way was he going to let her do that. *Not my Mela*. His brave girl, always pushing the envelope. *Strong, so fucking strong*. "Mela—"

That was all he got out before the door lurched open, pushing against his hand still hammering and then Mela was in his arms, burrowing into his chest, her arms wrapped around his waist and she was shaking. Shaking so hard her hair was moving. "Shhhhh. Honey. I got you." The door slammed into the frame, causing her to jerk and pull away, her head lifting in fright. *Jesus, she's so scared*. "Got you, baby girl. Got you."

Boot leather scuffed on gravel, and a moment later Spider said, voice low and soft, "Watch, she's gotta tell us what happened."

"Give her a fuckin' minute." His snarled reply was followed by the sound of leather on gravel again and from the corner of his eye, he saw Spider hadn't moved away, was just shifting from foot to foot. *Fuck*.

Mela had phoned Juanita with a story about being stranded, and even without him being there, Juanita, knowing how Watcher would want it handled, had immediately run to the barn, calling for help. Spider had mobilized the men, getting a location from Juanita and then heading out. Not urgently, because Mela hadn't been up front with everything. By the time Spider got to the station, she'd opened up to Juanita, which meant Watcher had gotten two calls: one frightened out of her mind mama bear, and one slightly confused member who couldn't locate his target. That slightly confused didn't last long, because Spider already had a bad feeling, and finding out Mela was hiding tipped him straight to pissed.

Watcher stood tall, eyes pressed closed, memorizing the way his child of the heart fit in his arms. *My baby girl, don't matter she ain't mine*. His words echoed his thoughts. "My baby girl. Strong as you need to be. Pull it together, honey." And for him, she did, sucking in a hard breath that stuttered in a dozen places, then was pushed out in a trembling stream. Her arms tightened around him, and he cradled the back of her head, pressing her cheek to his chest. "Don't gotta move, honey. Just tell me what happened."

All she'd told Juanita was her bike had been stolen, and she'd confronted the man doing it. She'd run when he'd pulled a weapon and hid in the bathroom. But it didn't explain her extreme terror. And it didn't explain her not coming out of the bathroom when Spider and the boys got on the lot. If anything, she should have run to them, knowing they spelled safety no matter where or what was going on. The fact she hadn't made Watcher's gut twist, and he was dead certain something more had happened.

Mela trembled violently as she breathed his name, "Papa." Every other noise ceased for Watcher, until all he could hear were her indrawn breaths as she struggled for control. He'd never seen her like this. Not even right after her rescue, when she had been wary but not scared out of her mind. *Slate. Ruby.* He ran people through his mind who she might talk to, but kept coming back to her being his girl. *Gotta be me.*

Lips pressed to the top of her head, he whispered, "Ain't nobody hurtin' you, Mela. Spider and the boys got us, honey." Maybe acknowledging his own dependence on the men would reinforce her belief they were absolutely as trustworthy as she already knew. Had always known. "They got us, so you can give me whatever is tearin' at you, honey."

"Edwardo." She flinched as she said the name and Watcher realized it was because his arms had tightened around her reflexively. He hadn't forgotten her story about facing the man down who had put hands on her sister. Hard to ignore something which invoked two very different but profound emotions like puffed up pride and a dangerous rage.

"Edwardo stole your bike?" She nodded. "He touch you, honey?" Watcher marked that every muscle in her body, already tight, tensed even more. Her cheek scrubbed against his tee, a slow up-and-down she had no way of knowing held the exact same result as an emperor's downturned thumb. "He hurt you, my Mela?" Her quick headshake freed the breath stuck in his lungs.

"Edwardo?" Spider's voice was hard, and Watcher looked up to see Spider making a face like he'd tasted something bad. "Edwardo Suches?"

Mela pushed against Watcher's hand, pulling away only as far as it took to angle her eyes to where Spider stood, two feet away. Watcher felt rage rolling off the man and wondered what she'd confessed to Spider in the months since Bella's senior prom. "*Si*," she whispered, "*su nombre es* Edwardo Suches." At her reverting to Spanish in this setting, Watcher tightened again, because it was another thing that spoke to her level of fear.

"Boss." Spider seemed to rip his gaze from Mela's face up to Watcher's with effort. With a jerk of his head, he indicated the back corner of the lot. "Talk." When Watcher shifted Mela to his side, intending to bring her with him, Spider stopped him with a quick, vicious shake of his head. "No."

Staring at his brother for a long moment, Watcher nodded and bent his knees, putting his face near Mela's. He wanted to be all she could see, wanted her to understand how treasured she was, that she was safe. "Gotta talk to Spider, but I'll be right back, honey." Her fingers twisted tighter in the fabric of his shirt for a second, and he watched her gather herself. Eyes slipping closed in a slow blink, a shallow breath followed by a deeper one, and then she stared at him as she released him, empty hands falling to her sides as they closed into fists. He watched as the men shuffled in, protectively surrounding her, and he nodded as he swept the group with a glare he hoped each knew was a sign of trust. Turning, he followed Spider, letting him decide where to stop and turn so they could get on with whatever it was he needed to say.

"Suches is Lalo." Those words hit Watcher like a punch in the stomach, and he struggled for a moment to remain upright. Lalo was the rabid bastard Watcher had run out of his territory more than once, had been president of the Las Cruces Diamante charter until Watcher laid that chapter to waste. Diamante, the bastard club that left destruction and death everywhere they landed. Lalo had been after his little girl, and he hadn't known. *Fuck.* "Lalo had his hands on our girl." Spider kept talking, shaking his head. "Forget the fuckin' bike, he had his hands on our girl. What the hell was she doin' out here, boss? We gotta know."

Teeth clenched together, Watcher ground out the admission, "Hands on both our girls." The jerk of Spider's head told him Mela hadn't shared about Bella's experience with Suches. "Mela told me months ago, but she said he'd cleared the county, moved out east." Watcher ran his fingers through his hair, brutally gripping and tugging hard. "*Fuck.* She was pumped because she'd taken care of him. Taken care of business. She said the way she put him down in front of his boys, no way he'd come back. And a *boy*," he bit out the word harshly, "wouldn't come back. Lalo, however—" Watcher shook his head. "—he's one sick motherfucker."

"We gotta know more, boss. She's gotta give us everything."

"How the fuck did I not know his name?" Spider didn't answer. Watcher turned to look at Mela where she stood. Frozen in place like a pillar, she wasn't moving, even as his men milled around her. "I need to get her home. Get her safe. I won't do it here."

Mela dropped her head, eyes to the ground in front of her and he could almost see her trembling where she stood. *Gotta get my girl home.* "Let's roll out. She'll settle by the time we get home." Spider's hand fell on Watcher's shoulder and he gripped hard, pulling Watcher's attention away from Mela for a moment. Distracted, still focused on what he'd just learned, Watcher muttered, "I'm gonna call Juanita, let her know Mela's safe. Let's get our girl loaded up with some sugar. Hit the store for me, yeah?" Spider nodded, and walked away, headed to the convenience store portion of the station.

Five minutes later they were on the road, and an hour after that, Juanita was curled up in their bed, curved around a cried-out and sleeping Mela as Watcher again hit the road, his destination and plans driven by rage.

***

On a dirt road just outside Tulsa, Watcher stood staring as flames licked up the sides of a building. Smoke billowed from the peak of the roof. He glared, waiting, making a satisfied sound when the fire blistered the paint off the wall, the word "Diamante" disappearing. *Wish those fuckers would do the same*, he thought, finally turning away. Sixteen men stood behind him, two additional ones on their knees.

"Where is he? You know who I'm after. Everybody fuckin' knows I want Lalo." Not trusting himself to get closer, Watcher stood, fists to his hips, looking at the men on the ground. He gave them an offer he hoped they'd accept. "Alter your fate, you talk to me. One chance." He swept one hand out, indicating the fire behind him, watching the men's faces turn to look, then swing back to him. "Need to take it. Fuckin' club's ash. City by city, we'll scour it from the fucking earth. Give me Lalo, even a scent of his trail, and you can walk away."

The two men, arms bound behind them, glanced at each other. One shook his head as the other one nodded. Without looking at Watcher, the one on the left asked, "Safe harbor?"

Was it worth taking them in and protecting them against any blowback from their club. *Fuck yeah.* "Yes." A creak came from the building, then a window exploded and with fresh oxygen to fuel it, the fire roared, heat pounding at Watcher's back.

Illuminated in the leaping flames, he saw fear on the faces of the two men, resolve on the sixteen.

"Adken, Florida. Just outside Tallahassee. He's in Adken. That's where the officers all go."

***

"Nothing." A report he did not want to hear came through the speaker and Watcher skimmed the group in the room with his gaze. "If it was Lalo, he's gone to ground, brother." Mason sighed, the sound audible over the phone. "You get anything from Estavez on Lalo's family down there?"

"Same from his side of the bridge." Watcher stared at the wood of the table that lay beneath his hands. "Lured her out there with the promise of a job." He squinted his eyes, trying to control a tic in one lid. "Answered a fucking personal ad she'd posted, wanting work as a motherfuckin' photographer." He reached up, rubbing at the jumping muscle. "She got to the place and saw it was a shutdown plant. Put it down as a scam, started to roll home. Stopped at the gas station for a drink. He jumped her before she got off the bike. She got one in on him, clocked him upside the head. He'd have had her, though. He'd've had her, Mason." The thought made him sick. *Didn't happen, hold to that*, he told himself. "But the dude with him pulled Lalo off. I'm thinkin' Chismoso, but don't know if I'm right. She scrambled into the bathroom and locked the door. Keys were in her bike, so he just got on and rode away. Didn't even need a fuckin' trailer. There was nothing but her in a four-by-four room to show anything happened."

"I'm surprised there's no security at the station. Bet there's something." Mason sounded thoughtful. "Gotta be. Want me to get Myron to take a look at the area, see if there's anything techy he can find?"

"Be appreciated, brother," Watcher muttered, raking fingers through his hair, picking up the phone and taking the call off the speaker. "Thanks for takin' my call."

"Watcher." Mason hesitated, which got Watcher's attention in a way that caused the hair on his arms to stand on end. "You know Rebels stand with Soldiers, yeah?" Watcher made a gesture, watching as the room cleared, the door closing on a questioning look from Opie he ignored.

"Yes." Watcher kept his response to a single word but made a firm statement. Still as much a commitment as anything he'd ever said to this man.

"You wearin' my support patch, brother." This wasn't a question, but Watcher treated it as such, giving another affirmative. Mason continued, "You know I'm open to other options. Not something we've discussed directly, but I wanted you to know if it's on your mind, you can talk it through with me, brother."

"You're talking about me dropping my center and charter, picking up the Rebel colors." He knew his tone was sour, because his mouth filled with saliva merely considering closing the doors on the Southern Soldiers.

Mason took a breath, and his voice was rough when he continued. "Watcher. Brother. Way the world is these days? There is definite strength in numbers. I never would have believed it ten years ago, but here I am, having sat at the table with five club presidents, watching as they ashed their charters. It's not been without bumps, but the benefits outweigh. Scales definitely tip in favor of both groups each time. Chapters retain their own personality but adopt the larger culture. Which you and I know won't even be a blip if we get to that point between us. We *want* the same things, Watch." His voice was strained, and Watcher listened with growing intensity. "We *believe* in the same things. Club." Mason paused, and Watcher finished for him.

"Family. Honor. I know. I get it, Mason. I just can't see it happening right now. I got too many irons in the fire—"

Mason interrupted, "Exactly why this is when we need to discuss it, brother. Because Soldiers do not have to stand alone. Let me in, *let me help*. Let me give you what you need, and we both become stronger."

"I'll think about it, Mason. Best I can do." Watcher reached up and pressed a fingertip against the twitching muscle. "Best I can do."

"All I can ask, brother. I'll drop a note to Myron now, get him dialed in on where the shit went down with your girl." A pause, then Mason said, "If I've learned anything over the past few months, I learned when I feel it, I need to say it. Love ya, brother."

"Pussy." Watcher laughed, leaning back in his chair. "How's your boy?"

"He's good, asshole. Chase is doin' good. Talk soon, yeah?"

"You got it, Mason. Talk soon."

After the call disconnected, Watcher sat for a long moment, staring at dust motes swirling through streams of sunlight coming in the window. Mason was right, and wrong, in the same breath. Combining the two clubs would give them both a wider base of resources, which in a numbers game was critical. But killing Darrie's dream? "Not happenin'," Watcher muttered, hearing his phone buzz. Looking down, he saw a text from Myron asking for location specifics on the area which needed scrutiny. "Not happenin' *today*."

***

Juanita

Juanita picked up her phone as it vibrated again with an incoming call. Watcher was sitting in the living room, muttering to himself, and she smiled at his loving and irritated tone. That smile fell away when she saw an international number on the display, and knew there was grave caution in her own voice when she uttered a single word in greeting. *"Hola?"*

An unrecognized male voice responded, his tone brusque when he demanded, "Watcher."

"*Que?*" She was ready to throw the phone, slippery in her suddenly sweaty grip, fear grasping at her belly.

"Watcher," a pause, then, "*por favor, señora*. Watcher."

She moved to the doorway and the moment Watcher caught sight of her face the expression on his changed, hard lines creasing his forehead, jaw suddenly tight. "Is that her?"

Who he was talking about, she didn't know, but the voice definitely wasn't female so she wordlessly shook her head, holding out the device. He took it from her and barked a questioning, "Yeah?" A pause, then, "Lemme speak to him then. What the fuck is up? I'm waiting for a call here." Another pause and Juanita sagged against the countertop with his next words. "Estavez, what do you need?" Watcher's face paled and his gaze cut across her, unseeing, focused on whatever Raul was saying. "Yeah? What about Lalo?" That wasn't a name she knew, so this had to be club business. *But why would Raul call on my phone?* Still, it couldn't be about anything else so she began turning away, prepared to return to the sink when Watcher made a sound far down in his chest. Dragged out of him, it was pain filled and raw, and she whirled back in time to hear him push out a single, fierce word through tightly clenched teeth. "Where?"

The next moments were frustrating because he didn't take a moment, only ended the call, threw her phone toward her, uncaring of her fumbling attempts to catch it and was gone from the doorway. Phone clutched to her chest, she followed him, seeing all the things he kept inside him exposed. He was furious and frightened. *Dios.* Anger. Fear. *So much fear.* Phone to his ear, he waited but a moment, then in a voice vibrating dangerously on the edge of control, said, "Mason, Lalo's got my daughter."

Pressing her fingertips to her lips, she held herself rigidly. *Our Bella.* Juanita flinched as rage slapped through the air in the room, Watcher's fury was palpable as he gritted words out between clenched teeth. "Estavez got a call. They've had her four days, Mason." He scrubbed at his face with a palm, hair on his head already standing up from fingers raking through it. "Four damned days." His voice dropped to a whisper. "My baby." Corded muscles stood out in his shaking arms, tension evident across his entire body. "Mason, after Utah..."

Watcher was silent a moment and seemed to be listening to Mason. His phone dinged, and he pulled it away from his face, tapped a button and suddenly voices filled the air. "—address, phone, a list of friends, car license and registration—" ... "—wouldn't dare do anything to her, Watch. No—" ... "Jesus, fuck me. Where's Mela—" ... "to focus on where—" The words and questions overlapping so she couldn't follow a single thought to a conclusion, but Watcher seemed to be able to decipher the need because he began firing back rapid answers.

"Myron, texting Spider, he'll get you what you need. Her apartment is on-campus—" Juanita made a noise and Watcher lifted his head, looking at her. He barked, "What Juanita?"

"Off." She shook her head, taking two steps closer so the men on the phone could better hear her words. "Her apartment is off-campus. It's in a small building on Wyoming." She gave the address and followed with Bella's phone number, then without being asked gave her birthday. Keeping her eyes locked on Watcher's face, she knew her lips were trembling when she gave a physical description of their daughter.

The man's voice on the phone was soft, encouraging when he said, "That's good, Juanita. Really good. If I give you my phone number, can you text me info on her friends and their numbers?" She nodded, and Watcher answered for her.

"She can. She will." Snapping each digit, Watcher gave the man her number, and only a moment afterwards, there was a vibration at her chest where her hand still clutched her phone. She didn't look, didn't move. Couldn't, watching as she was to take her cues from her husband. Her precious daughter's father.

"Mason, I got to get my boys rolling. Need to secure Juanita and Mela, in case this is a strike. Fucking Columbians have been circling, and they—" Watcher swallowed hard. "They don't care who they scoop up. We've seen it before. I know Estavez said Lalo, but we both know that motherfucker has as many connections south of the border as Estavez." Juanita stepped closer and reached out, resting one hand against his chest, breathing deep when Watcher lifted his hand and covered hers, pressing their threaded fingers deep into his flesh. "Help me find my girl."

"Duck and Fury are in Lamesa, already got Duck headed your way. Myron's gonna work the info side of things. I'll get a flight booked brother, be there before you know it. She's gonna be okay, man." From Watcher's flinch, she knew it was an empty promise and leaned her head against his shoulder, resting her weight on him. He took it, supporting her as she knew he would.

The back door burst open, and voices filled the living room as eight Soldiers flooded in, demanding to know what was going on. Watcher terminated the call, bent to put his face close to hers and reminded her, "You got a job, honey." She nodded, blinking fast, feeling her lips tremble again when his big hand cupped her cheek. "Get to it, yeah?"

Retreating to the kitchen, Juanita saw this faceless Myron had asked simple questions, numbering each so she could keep track of what she'd completed. In minutes she'd sent him everything in the first requests, and then spent time filling in some follow-up info he wanted. Waiting for the next round of questions, she was staring down at her phone and jumped when Watcher's form fitted to her back, his arms crossing as they rounded her belly. He held her for a moment, and she took strength from him as he knew she would. "Gonna go find our girl. Carmela's on her way here. Neither of you leaves this house, Juanita. I need to focus on Isabella." The unspoken part of his demand was the shared knowledge that containing Mela would be hard, and he knew what he was asking by laying it on her shoulders.

"Find our baby, Michael." Twisting her neck, she looked up at him. "Please."

He lowered his head and kissed her, deep and brutal, leaving her lips bruised when he retreated an inch to whisper. "Promise."

Miracle twice over

Watcher

The words rolled through his head, again and again, no shutting off the rewind, not knowing what he knew now. *Tellin' you, Watch. I don't think you're makin' the right play.* Watcher shook his head to clear it of Mason's voice as he leaned closer to the tank of his bike and twisted the throttle harder, hand slipping on the sweaty grip because it was already pegged. *Fast as I can, baby. I'm on my way.*

He and his men had been south of the Rio when he got the call. He kept his earpiece in place because even in the wind Watcher demanded he receive updates every fifteen minutes, good or bad. Three hours earlier, he'd gotten news. Duck had found Isabella. In Las Cruces. The place where he'd pulled every damned resource from to throw into the fray in Mexico. *Wrong, I got it wrong. So fucking wrong.* That was the pulse of his guilt as his bike tore through the night.

Skidding sideways in the street, he barely kept the bike under control as he whipped it around the truck parked there. Sliding to a halt near a building which was only two blocks from where Mela had nearly been

335

abducted, he was off the bike and through the door before any of his men made it onto the lot. He shouted into the phone, "Where?"

"Left, then right." Myron's steady voice fed into his ear as it had for three hours, and he was already running, rushing past empty doorways, the light ahead drawing him forwards, pushed by the sound of pounding footsteps behind him.

The room where the hallway terminated was empty but for a couple pieces of furniture and stacks of refuse along every wall except one. *Fuck. Jesus. Fuck.* Watcher screamed, "Duck, where the fuck are you?"

An immediate response, muffled and distant, of, "Here. I'm here," had Watcher looking around frantically, trying to determine where the voice had come from. Pops and Spider surged around him, hands scrabbling along the wall to pull open a low door Watcher hadn't seen. He launched himself at the yawning opening, hearing Duck again call, "Here! Need a rope."

Jesus. Fuck.

The limited light showed dirt. An expanse of dirt with small piles here and there, and a much larger heap out near the middle, but no Bella. No Duck.

Duck's voice again, coming from everywhere in the room. "I got her, but can't get her out."

Toes and hands digging for traction, Watcher threw himself across the dirt towards what had to be a hole. *She hasn't said anything. Why isn't she talking?* The only sounds were a man's heavy rasps of breath accompanied by the slippery sound of dirt sliding, punctuated with a periodic faraway ping of small stones hitting something metal. The scent of sweat and pesticide filled the air, the close atmosphere of the room suffocating him because his Bella wasn't talking, wasn't calling out to him. He couldn't even hear her breathing. "Bella. My Bella. Duck. Is she...my *Bella*."

Stretched out on his belly, Watcher shoved his shoulders over the lip of the excavated area, seeing Duck halfway up a steep slope, his head only inches below the opening. Legs spread wide so his feet could dig into the sides of the narrow hole, Duck had his arms wrapped around Bella. Back to his front, Bella hung lax in his grip. Unmoving. Neck drooping to the side, her hair, usually glossy and beautiful now hung greasy and dirty, red-stained strands of it stuck to her cheek, a sheet of it obscuring her face. Her arms were draped over Duck's, elbows akimbo, hands and fingers slack. Duck was filthy, covered to his elbows in caked on mud and dirt mixed liberally with blood. *Jesus. Fuck.*

Frantic, Watcher flung himself over the edge, dropping feet first down the hole, sliding to where they were wedged into the loose soil. Duck's voice droned on, his words unimportant, nothing factored any longer. Not once Watcher lifted her chin and saw bruises like a necklace on his baby girl's throat. Huge welts and smears of blood obscured her beautiful features. Her skin was cold, so cold it chilled him to the bone to touch her.

His heart stuttered and stopped in his chest, arrested until there was a gentle puff of her breath across his skin, until he felt the beating of her heart against his palm. Focused on getting to her, he plucked at Duck's hands, insistently moving them, carefully gathering Bella to his body, feeling her head swing and wobble like a newborn against his shoulder. His world narrowed to her face, willing her eyes to open. *Please, God.* No matter how hard he prayed, nothing happened. No movement that didn't come from their handling of her, nothing that wasn't directed by him or Duck. *Jesus, please.* She showed no awareness of anything. Lips blue, tinging to purple, colors which would forever symbolize terror for him. Her mouth dropped open, and he saw her teeth, stained black with dirt and blood.

Lalo.

A force pulled her up and to keep his hold, he had to scramble, kicking footholds into the dirt, crawling and pushing with his heels, keeping her body tight to his. Over the lip of the hole and onto the flat dirt and then hands tried to take her from him. With a growl vibrating painfully through his throat, he beat them away, cradling her to his chest, stripping a rope away which had appeared out of nowhere, in his way. He fought it for a moment, finally freeing her.

Struggling with her dead weight—and oh, how his mind shied away from that word—Watcher pushed to his feet only to be confronted by a waist-high door. He felt a movement and stared down, seeing her hands captured between their chests jerk and twitch. Only barely, but enough that he knew he needed to get her out of this place. *First, the door.* Falling to his knees, he crawled through, bending and twisting to fit, curving around his daughter. The top of the opening scraped across his back, and he pushed harder, forcing his way through, not caring if it tore caverns in his skin. *Couch*, he thought, knee-walking there and leaning over, gently resting Bella's back against the cushions.

Pale, so pale, but her lips were pink now. Nostrils quivering with each draw of air. She would hate having people see her like this. *My Bella.* Scabs dotted her temple, drawing a line to a deeper gouge above her ear. Someone did this to her. Someone touched her, hurt her. *Made her dirty.* His mind shied away from that word, too. *She'd want to be clean.*

Snapping his fingers in a silent demand, a bottle was pressed into his hand, and he spun the lid off with his teeth. Pouring a little water into his palm, he wet his fingertips and started cleaning the blood away, each swipe revealing more bruising. The membranes inside Bella's mouth were dry, so he tipped water between her lips, a drop at a time, not wanting to risk choking her as she lay unconscious. Bodies crowded around, words and instructions shouted, but his gaze didn't waver. *Bella. I went to Mexico and wasn't even here. I got it wrong. Wasn't me who found her. Duck saved her.*

Bella's breathing turned ragged for a moment, became terrifyingly uneven, and Watcher felt his own lungs struggling for breath along with hers. Her chest rose and fell in lurching movements, and Watcher wondered for a moment if he'd imagined a barely-there whisper, "Papa." That single sound repeating broke the vacuum around him, a cacophony of voices crashing down on him. "She's alive," Watcher heard Pops say at the same time her lashes fluttered on her cheeks for the first time.

Then it was quiet, and there was only one voice, strong and steady, confident as it said, "I got her." *Duck.*

He twisted to look, seeing the room filled with his Soldiers. So many men, so much on which to focus. Devil had started an IV, Watcher not even knowing when he'd stuck the needle in the back of Bella's hand, and there were three men reverently washing the dirt from her skin. Duck sat propped against a wall, exhaustion evident in the mask of weariness on his face. Just as he became aware of the stinging on his own skin, he recognized the marks of chemical burns on Duck's face and hands. Looking more closely, he took in more damning evidence of Duck's single-handed struggle to save Bella. Bent and broken fingers, deep cuts on his hands, still weeping blood, runnels of it traveling down his fingers to plop in fat droplets to the floor.

The murmur of voices in the room died away as Duck told the tale. Explaining what he'd found, what he'd seen, and what he'd done. A miracle he'd located this place and an even bigger one that he'd managed to save Bella. Odds stacked against her so high, nearly obliterating survival, all of it evened by the actions of this man. The hole in the ground leading to her cell, dug by his bare hands. Watcher sat mute, aware if it had been up to him, Bella would have died today.

It didn't take a genius to draw correlations between Bella's prison and the one his men had watched for two weeks, unknowing as two women died. *Coulda been Bella. Woulda been. I was wrong. Decamped and lit out. Took my ass to fuckin' Mexico.*

Then Duck said a name that made Watcher's back snap straight, because he'd heard it recently from Fury: Deacon. *If I'd been paying attention, I would have called Blue Line, or Bones. Fuck, all I did was reach out to Mason. Then I ignored his advice and trucked off on my own anyway. She'd be dead if it weren't for Mason. I was in* Mexico *and didn't even call Raul.*

Watcher tried to take a breath, but the weight of his knowledge settled onto him, choking and strangling everything inside him. *Killin' me. Nearly killed her.* Neck bowed, he thanked God for the help He'd sent. Because, in the end, all that mattered was Bella was safe. The only thing. *I've already fucked up today.* He had to stay focused and make sure he didn't miss anything else. *I can flog myself later.* Right now, there was a score to settle, and Watcher knew where his attention would be directed. *Diamante.*

Duck stared at him, looked at Bella, and then back at Watcher. "I got her." Watcher's eyes slipped closed, weighted down by the knowledge of how close it had been. From Duck's recounting, Bella should be dead. But she wasn't. "Deacon didn't win, brother. I got her." Watcher nodded. The only thing that mattered. *Amen.*

***

"She cain't stay here, Juanita." Watcher sighed, explaining the reasoning for what seemed like the hundredth time today. First to Mason, because it was a huge ask. Then to Spider, feeling the look of betrayal the man sent him like a knife in his back. Deserved, because by sending her away, he was telling each of his men he didn't believe they could keep their princess safe. Not the message he wanted to send, but it was unavoidable. None of this their fault, all blame could be laid directly at his feet. Still, they took it on. Spider most of all.

"I know, Michael," she whispered, not lifting her eyes from Bella's face.

Bella had fallen into a blind panic when Watcher and Spider gently tried to question her. Panicked and was striking out, not seeing anything around her, she'd been trapped in the prison of her own mind. Devil had pushed a cocktail through her IV to knock her out, and the minute Bella collapsed, Watcher had gathered up his girl, cradling her close to his chest and carried her to her room. Juanita had dragged a chair in here, angled it near the head of the bed and planted herself there. She'd held vigil since, remaining only inches from their daughter, wanting to be available the moment Bella woke.

Juanita had been quiet as Watcher lifted Bella out of the truck and carried her through the door. Pops had called from the warehouse, so Juanita hadn't been left wondering, but something wasn't right with her reaction. Watcher read censure in her tone if not her words, and she wouldn't look at him. Hadn't looked at him since he arrived.

"Honey, we found her." He took a step into the room, stopping when Juanita stiffened. "But she's not safe."

"I know, Michael." Even if her repeated words were soft, they still lashed him, leaving pain in their wake.

"Baby, I didn't know this was on radar, or I'd have had guys on her." Juanita had to understand he'd do anything for her or the girls. "And now we do, we need to make sure she's safe. Mela's headed to Estavez and Bella will be in Chicago, as far away as we can get her. You're going to the church with the other women. Only until we get this sorted out, honey."

"Will you?" Still soft, but her voice was trending upwards with the question. "Will you sort it out?" Juanita turned in the chair, half facing him. Gaze not rising to his face, she stared at his chest. Strong chemicals laced through the dirt had burned him. Not as bad as Duck, because that man had taken the brunt of it with the length of time he'd been in contact. Between Watcher and his men, they had washed Bella free of the stinging coating, but since Watcher had insisted she be assisted before he was, he'd gained some burns. The worse ones were at the top of his chest, right at his throat, where Bella's head had rested. Juanita stared at those wounds, blinking back tears. "Will it ever be sorted out?"

"Juanita, I'll—"

She shook her head and called, "*Papi.*"

When she gave him that word Watcher's knees gave way, and he was falling because she'd been holding it back, hadn't given him any sweet since the call came in and he had to leave her, and then he made the wrong call, and she couldn't forgive him, and he was lost. "*Papi,*" Juanita's arms were around him, her steady hand cradling the back of his head, pressing his face into her neck. "You weren't lost. You were doing the best you knew how to find our girl." She squeezed him, rib-cracking strength in his wife's arms. "You've always told the girls if they did the best they could, then you couldn't ask for anything more. *Papi,*"—heat hit the side of his face, kisses dropping like tears—"I don't...can't blame. There's no blame in this house. That belongs out there,"—pressure released and then returned, her arm flung wide for a moment, coming back to anchor him—"and never, ever in here. But I'm afraid. I'm so afraid. If she...*Papi.*" Her voice broke, and she buried her face in his shoulder.

Watcher knelt on the floor of Bella's bedroom and the strength from his wife, his Juanita, seeped slowly into him. Gradually their positions changed, easing them back into the well-worn roles they held between them, where he was the strong one, and she allowed him the belief because he had to know she could count on him.

"She'll be safe in Chicago," Watcher promised, holding those words as truth in his heart. "My cousin will take her up." Watcher would rather fly her, but the stark fear on Bella's face when he'd mentioned it had set those ideas aside. "When she wakes up, I'll have Devil here. He'll give her some meds, honey. We'll get her comfortable and then she has to tell us everything. I can't imagine making her relive it, so he'll get it so the memories aren't fresh. She'll talk through it, but he's gonna make it like it happened weeks ago. A little help for her head. Then I take her to Lamesa." He paused, and said again with emphasis, "*I* take her. And then"—Juanita's arms tightened around him—"I hunt."

*** *** ***

"Congratulations, brother. Another boy. What'd you name him?" Watcher was lying on his back next to Juanita, arm curved around her shoulders. Knowing it would be hours yet before Bella woke, he'd finally talked her into laying down, leaving Spider to watch over their girl. Juanita's sleep had been uneasy, so Watcher had crawled into bed beside her, holding her close.

He hadn't slept. Felt as if he might never sleep again with how his brain was racing. So at least Mason hadn't woken him with this phone call. So much had happened so quickly, Watcher hadn't been aware Mason was stuck in Fort Wayne. For the best of reasons, but still stuck.

"Garrett Davis Mason." Spoken with ringing pride in his voice, Mason didn't hesitate to push past this good news and into the bad. "Watcher, I got ears in a lot of places. I hear chatter, wanted to run it past you."

"A minute, brother," Watcher muttered. He carefully extricated himself from Juanita's grip, flicking open a light blanket and tucking it in around her. At the door, he turned and looked at her a moment. Gorgeous dark hair with only a few strands of silver, her skin was as flawless as a child's, and her beauty had not faded. Stunning. From here he could barely see the faded brand on her neck, which to him had become so much a part of her he nearly couldn't imagine her without it. *My queen.*

He quietly pulled the door closed, walking up the hallway to glance into Bella's room, seeing Spider seated in the chair, head up, alert. Watcher gave him a wave, which went unreturned, and moved past the doorway and into the kitchen. "Okay, Mason. What's up?"

343

"Lalo's finally in Florida, best as we can tell." Every muscle in Watcher's body locked up at the unexpected words.

"A gift, brother. Send me a damned address so I can collect." Watcher wasn't sure where he got the air to push out those words. Death birthed in a whisper. Guaranteed.

"Cannot do that. I want to, but cannot." Before Watcher could make any demands, Mason continued. "DEA picked him up. Got him tied up tighter than a cop's ass in lockup. He doesn't make a move without a dozen agents on him." Mason paused, but Watcher couldn't speak. To know where this motherfucker was and not be able to reach him was torture. "Good news outta this, brother. Means your family is safer than we thought."

"Mela's in Chihuahua. Juanita goes to a safehouse as soon as I roll to Lamesa with Bella, and Bella's still coming to you." Watcher's response was immediate and sounded as determined as he felt.

"I think it's the right course, too, brother. Wanted you to be able to breathe easier for a few." Silence settled between them, comfortable, reminding Watcher of how well he knew this man. *Club. Family. Honor.*

"Brother." Watcher's throat tightened, paralyzing emotion choking off his words, but they weren't needed. Mason knew everything he was feeling right now.

"I always got your six, brother. Always. Ain't ever changing, no matter what." Mason's words vibrated with emotion, Watcher's heart pounding in time.

"Tell me about your boy." Watcher could get those words out, could extend their time together a while, filling in the moments until Bella woke and he had to submerge himself in the horror of what happened to her. *If I think I can't sleep now, imagine what I'll be like with that in my head.*

"Willa did amazing, brother. I got there in plenty of time, wasn't sure I'd make it, but damned if I didn't. He's good, back and forth between sleeping and suckin' on the nip like she wants him to." Mason paused, and Watcher heard him sigh deeply, his tone rough when he said, "She keeps asking if I think he looks like me. Slippin' it in like I won't notice. And the look on her face, brother. Kills. Doesn't matter how much I tell her, she keeps askin'."

"*Jesus.*" That slipped out before he could stop himself. Utah seemed fresh still, like it had been only days ago but the truth was nine months had elapsed. Mason hadn't said a thing, but anyone could do the math. Hard shit, held close between friends. Since he'd brought it up now, this meant there was a need to talk about it, and that knowledge gave Watcher courage to ask what he did next. "Does it matter, brother?"

"Not a fuckin' bit. Boy's mine." Mason's words were firm, not leaving any room for doubt. Still, raising a cuckoo's child would be painful, if it were true. Anxious for something to keep him busy, Watcher grabbed the carafe and shoved it into the sink. A twist of the faucet had water running as he opened a cabinet to pull down the coffee. Listening. All he could do, but he'd do it. "He's mine, and she's mine. Ain't nobody gonna fuck with that, especially not a dead man."

Measuring his usual spoonful or three of grounds into the basket, Watcher asked, "How you gonna convince her of that?" He shoved the basket into the coffee maker, grabbing the now-full carafe and pouring it into the reservoir.

"One breath at a time." Mason snorted a laugh. "You makin' coffee, motherfucker?"

"Yeah. Gonna be a long day." Gut-wrenching sounds came from up the hallway. Frantic, Bella's high-pitched voice was countered by Spider's deeper one. A quick pattern of words followed by silence. "A long fucking day."

"Hear that. I'll let you go. Just—" Mason paused a second. "—needed to know you're good."

"I'm good. She's alive." Watcher stopped moving, focusing on what he wanted Mason to know. "She's alive. Miracle twice over. Your man got to her and saved her. I'm in his pocket for life, and I told him he owns a Soldiers' marker, but he was so fixed on gettin' home to his woman I doubt he heard me. Remind him, yeah?" Watcher brought three mugs down from the cabinet. "I'll see Fury in a few hours. I'll text him before I roll so he's expecting us. I appreciate you being willing to let him bring her, brother."

"Anything you need."

"Back atcha." Watcher disconnected as he poured himself what would be the first of many cups of coffee that day.

I'll give you everything

Isabella

"Please no. Please. No, please." Isabella chanted the words to the man who had been assigned to her. In the time since her just-met cousin had dropped her off here in Chicago, she hadn't been offered many decisions. Where to sleep, how to spend her time, even what to eat was all dictated by this man, Tater.

Growing up around her father's club, she had long been accustomed to the behaviors and attitudes of this kind of man. Growly and gruff, taciturn by nature, they were what her mother called salt of the earth. Resolutely no nonsense and Bella had long ago given up arguing with any of them. Her sister Carmela never stopped and Bella had often sat back and watched, confused because the men seemed to approve of Mela's rough behavior more often than not. That was at least until she'd matured. Since then they'd been less forgiving, turning her away when she would act out.

Tater hadn't given anything away. No emotions, no condemnation, but also no indication he understood her fears. He'd escorted her in and out of buildings, staying close, hand tight on her elbow. Palm pushing to tilt her head as he helped her into and out of cars and trucks. Not on the back of a bike. Never near a motorcycle. Even if she missed the thrill of riding behind someone, Bella tried to tell herself staying away from bikes was okay with her because the ride up with Fury had been terrifying. He had given her scarcely any time to rest, and hardly any time alone. The level of tension he'd carried had transmitted to her, building what she was already dealing with up to unbearable levels. She hadn't been ready for the trip, not for the way the open spaces made her feel, and not for the chill she couldn't seem to shake.

Her thoughts drifted from Fury and the chill in her bones to what had come before. Nothing had prepared her for the memories that wouldn't go away. Wouldn't leave her alone, invading her mind whether she was asleep or awake. Memories of being forced onto Edwardo's motorcycle. Bound wrists secured to the frame, her body bent backwards over the tank as slim hips shoved between her legs, clothing seeming a too-thin barrier. The ride had lasted a lifetime as with every chance his hand explored her body in ways she'd never given permission for. Never would have, if she'd been given the choice. He'd enjoyed humiliating her, pinching and twisting at her flesh, fingers digging into her throat.

Edwardo had hurt her. More than she'd told Daddy. She couldn't imagine telling anyone the things he'd done. Things he'd made her watch. She had been so frightened when he was yelling at her. Then terrified when he'd yelled at people who weren't there. Talking to the air most of the time, one hand twisted in her hair, the other swinging back and forth, slapping her ruthlessly, and shouting about enemies who seemed to exist only in his mind.

Bella snapped out of her memories when something moved right in front of her. She recoiled, knew the movement meant she had cowered back into the couch, but couldn't stop the instinctive retreat. Everything seemed like a threat now, and she kept getting lost in her own head. Looking up, she recognized Tater. He repeated his words from earlier, the ones she had refused. A demand that shouldn't carry terror, but was filled with the emotion. "Come on, Bella. Time for lunch."

Shaking her head, she pushed deeper into the cushions, hoping he would give up. And, as ever, he refused to change plans, bending close and gripping her wrist. He was patient but firm, and Bella didn't know why she fought him. *I won't win.*

"Honey." The moment Tater said that word with the pressure of his fingers circling her arm…she was gone. Back in the cell, Edwardo's face pushed right up into hers, his shrieking voice echoing in her head and the enclosed space. Pulling, struggling, she struck out, connecting once, twice, screaming and shoving to get away before he hurt her again. Arms wrapped around her, pinning her hands against her chest so she couldn't move. "Not gonna let you go, Bella."

"Let me go. Please. *God*, please. I don't know what you want. I won't tell anyone. I won't. I won't. Not anyone. You can go. Go. Just go." Words fell from her lips in overlapping sounds, and she struggled still, twisting and shoving with all her strength. It wouldn't matter. It never did. "Let me go, Edwardo. I won't tell." *He always wins.*

"Bella, not letting you go. You're with me. Tater. In Chicago. Bella, you're with Tater. You're safe." Gradually she heard the words. Recognized the voice and knew it wasn't Edwardo. It was steady and safe and calm. So very calm. The very steadiness gave her strength, and with that small bit of composure, she rested her head against the wall of muscle in front of her, feeling the rumble of his words, "You're safe with me."

"Never be safe again," she whispered, each sound falling like a brick building a jail cell, locking her into her head. "Never again. Never safe."

"Yeah you are, honey. Safe with me." Warmth suffused her chest, and she tasted salt in her throat. "Safe, Bella."

Lifting her head, she closed her eyes, the tips of her whipping hair stinging her cheeks. "No. No. *No.* Not safe. Never again. Never safe."

"Safe." He reassured her, and hands were cradling her face. Firm. Hard, but gentle, not frightening. "Safe, honey." A tingle in her arm preceded the darkness swallowing her, but the last thing she heard was that same voice. "Safe."

It seemed hours later when she woke up in a bed. Curled on her side, she faced a blank wall, the grooves in the stained paneling giving her something to focus on as she blinked the sleep from her eyes. Dim light illuminated the room, and when she lifted her head to look over her shoulder, she saw Tater sitting in an armchair near the door. Not sleeping, he was watching her. Impassive as it always was, his face didn't give her any indication of what he was thinking.

Bella remembered her meltdown and let her head drop, curling her legs to her chest, pulling into as tight a ball on the mattress as she could manage. *Maybe I can disappear*, she thought, curling her toes as hard as she could, trying to make even her feet smaller. Gradually she became aware of the sounds of his breath, deep and slow and calm. Unceasing, in and out, and even more slowly she relaxed, unaware her breathing had progressively matched the same cadence.

"Bella." She liked the sound of Tater's voice. It was deep, melodic, and sturdy sounding. *He's a sturdy man.* "You can't go on like this." She swallowed, aware her throat was dry, clicking loudly through her ears to echo in her head, nearly drowning out her thoughts. *I can't go on.* "You need something."

She twisted, looking at him again to see he'd bent forwards and now sat with his elbows on his knees. Staring at her. He didn't smile, didn't grin, didn't offer anything other than his words. "You let me in, I can give you what you need." *I don't know what I need.* "You need me." *He took everything.* "You need what I can give you. Let me into your head, Bella. Talk to me, let me in."

"He took everything." Turning her back on Tater, she curled up on the mattress again. *Small, smaller, smallest*, she thought, curving her back and bringing her arms into her chest. "Everything, everything."

"No, he didn't. And I can give you back what you think he took." She shook her head, pressing her forehead into the pillow. "Bella, I can give you what you need. But you gotta let me in." Her hair rustled on the pillow again, moving with each sharp shake. "Gotta let me in, honey."

"He took that. Called me that. Took it. Took it. Took it. Took it." Thumb and finger met with a fold of skin between and she pinched, twisting viciously, the pain pulling her back from the edge. "Don't call me that."

"Bella." He pushed a heavy breath out and in that sound, she imagined echoes of Edwardo's breathing. *Gusting and hot past her ear as he rubbed his crotch, his other hand tight around her neck. Words filled with so much hate, she could feel it on her skin. Puta. Worthless puta. Chinga tu madre.*

Sharp as the blade of a knife, her name rang through the room, cutting a swath through the fog in her head. "Bella."

"Yes?" *What does he want? Why doesn't he leave me alone?*

"Look at me." She rolled onto her back, keeping the tight pinching pressure on the inside of her bicep. "I can give you back what he took." His hand covered hers, hot and scorching as he pried her fingers apart, the blood rushing back into the muscle and burning when it flooded the bruise. Tater kept her hand in his, not crushing as Edwardo had, only holding her loosely, cradling her fingers. "Give you everything back." Tater stared at her, and she heard him, the sounds echoing throughout her body, diving deep into her chest, setting up a resonance that made her believe. "Everything."

Uncommon name
Watcher

Jesus, keep her in the palm of Your hand, Watcher thought, staring out the window in the barn. "That fast?" Filled with memories of a silent Juanita surrounded by blood, it was the only thing he could think of to ask, hoping to hear that when Hoss' woman died, she at least did it quickly. Painlessly.

"Yeah." Mason's words were soft, reverent, and full of pain. "Docs said she was gone before he hit the floor beside her. Nothing Hoss coulda done. Nothing anyone could do." Silence on the line for minutes, and he knew they were both thinking the same thing. *There but for the grace of God.*

"Services?" Watcher began putting a list of members together in his head, an honor escort to go to Fort Wayne for her funeral. He liked Hoss. Knew him to be a solid club member and friend, and liked him even more after hearing stories from Fury about how Hoss had taken in the woman and her boy, making himself a family in the process. *Fuck, I just saw the man.* Watcher had been in Fort Wayne last week, and Hoss had provided more detail as to what had gone down in Memphis then tore out of the clubhouse to get home to his woman.

"Seems the only reason I get up north is to visit the boneyard." It had been only a few months since Bingo had died from cancer, and Watcher had ignored the dangers dancing around Las Cruces at the time to take half his club up out of respect for one of the long-time Rebel members. Old school biker, one of very few people who had remembered the heady days when clubs first sprang up across the country. Bingo could tell stories for days, and the man had captured a bunch of those memories in poetry.

"Yeah, we're waiting on word, but Hoss should be able to bring Faith home from the hospital in a couple of days, so probably the day after that happens."

Faith Inez, Hoss' baby daughter. He'd gotten the text and the picture of a proud momma and daddy cuddled close to a tiny pink bundle. A moment that should have been filled with nothing but joy, had turned to ruin and devastation.

"Jesus." Silence again. Watcher saw the backdoor of his house open, and Juanita stepped onto the patio and walked to the pool. She dropped the towel, and he was lost for a moment in the vision of her in a skintight bathing suit, dipping the toes of one foot into the water before bending at the waist and cleanly parting the water with a dive.

Mason broke his reverie with a question. "Why ya askin'?"

"Coming up, brother." Pulled back to the conversation, Watcher answered quickly. "I'll sort guys and we'll head out today. Make it there in plenty of time. Pay my respects."

"You coming, Watch?" The skepticism in Mason's voice wasn't expected so Watcher stiffened, his angry rigidity not going away at Mason's next question. "You sure that's a good idea?"

"Why the hell wouldn't it be? You don't want Soldiers there, man?" His pride stung at the slight, Watcher waited impatiently for Mason's response.

It started with a heavy sigh.

"Fuck, Watch. I'd be obliged if you didn't take everything so fuckin' personal, brother. I'm thinking of all the shit you got going on. You've been running every lead to the ground, rolling twos nonstop. Juanita's back home, and Mela's still in Mexico, but Bella's up here in Chicago which is close to fuckin' Fort Wayne, and before you get your ass in a twist about that, she's welcome to stay here for as long as it takes. You know this, brother. But you on the road makes you vulnerable, and you fuckin' know that, too." Mason sighed again, the frustration evident in his tone. "You are the closest thing to a brother I have, man. You know it. Know all my family's secrets, and still you're there for me anytime I call. I'm fuckin' honored every time you pick up, knowing I'm gonna have an ask. I wanna keep you on this side of the sod, brother. You mean a lot to me. Kinda used to the idea of you breathin'."

Jesus. Watcher absorbed what Mason had said for a moment, then in a voice he knew was thick with emotion, he told his best friend, "Love you, brother. You'll never know, man. You being there for me when Darrie died. And then, *fuck—*" Watcher broke off for a moment, unable to continue, struggling to keep the tears flowing down his face from sounding in his voice. "When my Bella...when it happened, you rolled everything you could. Balancing your own needs, you still saw to me and mine. Fuckin' love you, man."

"Returned. Straight up, brother. Returned."

***

Watcher

Watcher stared across the funeral home parking lot at a patch from a Utah club, not trusting his eyes for a moment. He moved towards the group who had been speaking to the biker now rapidly walking away. "Hey," he called, trying to place the face of the man in the group. He looked a lot like Grant...Deke, from the army, but it couldn't be. By the time Watcher had gotten out, Deke was long in the wind, and they'd never reconnected. Watcher called again, trying to remember if he knew this guy's name. One of Mason's from the patch, and Watcher needed to know who he'd been talking to a moment ago. Because that was another face which looked all too familiar. "Hey."

Still about twenty feet away, the guy was walking with his arm around a weeping woman, and walking beside both of them was Willa, Mason's wife, carrying her baby. "Hey," Watcher called again, but they didn't pause. Angling across the lot, he squeezed between groups of men and women, keeping his eye on Willa. "Hey." At last, the guy's head came up, and he looked at Watcher, eyebrows lifting in a question and recognition hit Watcher in the chest. *Jesus, it is Grant.*

"Watcher." Deke got out a greeting, stopping to shove out a hand, but not taking his other arm from around the woman. "Good to see you, man. Been too long."

"Deke." *How did I not know Deke was one of Mason's?* Watcher marveled for a moment as he accepted the tight grip, letting Deke pull him in to bump shoulders. "Jesus, brother, good to see you, too." *Every time I start to waver about rolling into the Rebels, I find another reason to stay the course and make the change.* Movement from across the lot caught his attention again, and he remembered his original intent with talking to the trio. "Who was that guy back there?" Watcher asked, gesturing to where they'd walked from. Deke twisted to look behind him, then back to Watcher, the expression on his face clearly puzzled. Watcher repeated his question, tamping down an urgent panic threatening to overwhelm him. "Who was that guy?"

Willa shifted baby Garrett to her other shoulder, palm smoothing down his back when he fussed for a moment before settling down. "Are you asking about Ripper?" She glanced over her shoulder, and they all heard Mason's voice calling her name. "We have to go in," she told Watcher apologetically, as Deke tightened his arm around the woman who had burst into renewed tears. "Mercy is Hope's sister. They need us in there, Watcher."

"Yeah, sorry," Watcher muttered, stepping back and out of the way. "Deke, we'll catch up later."

Ripper wasn't a common road name. You might hear of a dozen guys called Gypsy, a hundred with a variation of Drivetrain or Overdrive or Harddrive. He knew of one club in the Maryland area that had four officers in different chapters who all answered to Hawk. Watcher had only ever heard of one Ripper, though. Not someone he'd ever met, but it was a man long dead. A man dead because of Shooter, back before Mason took over the Rebels.

Watcher turned and stared across the lot, seeing a lone bike pull out of formation and idle to the street. It turned to the right, which meant following the drive around a sweeping curve that would bring it closer before it reached the highway. Without thinking about what he was doing, Watcher took off at a run to the end of the building nearest to where the curve was. He got there just as the bike flashed past, already in third gear and accelerating. That didn't stop him from recognizing the man, someone he had met, but who had been out of the club life for a long, long time. Someone who hated Mason more than anything. Someone who, if he'd read the body posture right, had nearly gotten his hands on Mason's boy.

Deacon.

Everything changes

"Tell me again." Watcher stood, back to the kitchen counter, eyes on the redheaded man who had just walked through the door.

"Hello to you, too, cuz. Jesus," Fury clipped, reaching back and slamming the door closed. "Can a man have a sip of water to wash the desert away before you start grillin' him?"

"Bottle. Fridge." Waiting for a beat, he let Fury swig twice before he repeated his question, elaborating this time so Fury understood the need. "Tell me again about Deacon and Morgan, how they've hooked up. Tell me what you think Shooter's doin' from his jail cell. Tell me again what kind of vengeance the Morgans are going to be looking for with Judge's death." He folded his arms across his chest, leaning backwards. "Tell me why I saw Deacon at Hope's funeral."

This last earned a reaction he hadn't expected, and both he and Fury looked down at the water spreading out across the floor, ejected in an eruption from the bottle crushed in Fury's fist. Watcher kept his tone carefully neutral when he offered his observation. "I think there's something here you haven't told me, brother."

"No." Fury shook his head. "Told you how me and Hoss saw the woman the same time. Told you we both recognized what she could be." Fury tipped his chin down, fingers going to strip the tangles from his beard. "Told you she wasn't an option for me."

"Seems a little raw to be sniffing around Bethy as you are." Watcher shook his head. "Don't make her be a consolation prize, man. She deserves more."

"Fuck yeah, she deserves more." Fury's tone was thick with anger. "Bethy ain't a consolation prize, man. Not at all. She's…different. Hope was the first clean breath of air I'd had in years. Never a possibility for me, not even if circumstances were different. But the *idea*? That ideal? The idea of her was real and something I used to get through the waking hours, those last weeks in Diamante." He shook his head, glancing up at Watcher, pain gathering on his features.

"World doesn't need to lose people like her. No one deserves to lose the ones they love, not ever. And to lose her like he did? I cannot imagine how Hoss is feelin'. Weight of the world on his shoulders." Gaze still fixed in place, but Watcher could tell Fury wasn't seeing him or the inside of the kitchen right now. "That baby girl? Her little boy? Knowing you have to be everything for them, stay strong for them, even when you wanna break." His eyes focused, and Watcher flinched from the pain. "Hope was an ideal for me, nothing more. An ideal that led me to believe I could have everything I wanted. I didn't know what I wanted until I saw Bethany again." He shook his head again. "She ain't no consolation prize. She *is* the prize."

"You're damned right she is," Watcher growled, still as protective of Bethy as he was of his own two girls.

Fury flashed a grin at him, then the expression on his face sobered, and he said, "You saw Deacon at Hope's funeral?" Watcher nodded. "At the service?"

"Outside, just before. He was talking to Mason's woman. Right outside the funeral home. I wasn't sure it was him at first, it's been years." Watcher hesitated, then asked, "You know anything about Mason's time with the Fiends?"

"A little. Mostly rumor. Not something the big man talks about. You hear about Lalo turning up at Duck's place in Lamesa?" A sound from the hallway pulled both their gazes that direction and Watcher saw Juanita come out of Bella's bedroom, wiping at her cheeks with both hands. Without looking their way, she turned and walked towards the back of the house. "Wanna take this outside, brother?" Fury's question was quiet and filled with understanding. Watcher and Juanita were sudden empty nesters, and neither of them was dealing with it as well as they'd like.

Watcher nodded, tossing a pile of napkins to the floor, swiping them across the tile with the toe of his boot before scooping the wet paper up and throwing them away. *If only everything could be cleaned up as easily*, he thought, following Fury outside and across the yard to the barn.

***

Isabella

Bella sat on a stool, uncomfortable for more reasons than the lack of cushioning, squashed flat by countless other bottoms. Wedged into the corner of the room, protected at her back and sides by walls, protected above by the ceiling and below by the floor, she still felt exposed and vulnerable. Tater stood across the room, leaning against a column near one of the pool tables, nonchalant and comfortable. A beer dangled from his fingers, and he smiled, listening as one of the men near him told a story. When the other people in their group laughed, he did too, but his head tipped back as he gave open-mouthed approval to whatever had been said. His just-shaved chin lifted, exposing the cords and muscles in his throat and even from where he stood across the room, the timbre of his laughter wrapped around her.

She'd been in Chicago for five weeks. And he had done as he promised. He had helped her move past the paralyzing fear that had coated every one of her emotions, her mind, stripping her of the ability to do anything other than breathe. He had helped. *He fixed me.* One of the waitresses angled her direction, and before Bella could even tense up, he had redirected the woman, keeping the space around Bella clear of anyone. *Gives me what I need.*

She sat and watched him, not noticing when other men came and went from the group, focused solely on Tater. What he did, how he moved, his reactions to the room and the men and women. The women. He had a type, she saw this. His type walked on the slatternly side of sizzle. Tall shoes, short skirts, tight tops. Bella glanced down at her sneakers propped on the rungs of the stool. Her fabric-clad legs extending down from where her white tee was tucked inside the waistband of those plain blue jeans.

The women he looked at had teased hair and bedroom eyes crafted with an expert application of makeup. Bella's fingertips trailed across the smooth skin of her cheek. A strand of her hair had come loose from the simple ponytail, and she fingered it for a moment before tucking it behind her ear.

He looked up at Bella and noted her study, angling his head to the side. She lost his eyes when a woman near the pool table pretended to stumble. She tottered skillfully backwards and he had to catch her arm, preventing a fall. Tater bent his neck, mouth near the woman's ear and Bella could make out the movements of his lips. The woman pulled back, sour twisting her lips and she shot a daggered look Bella's direction before flouncing away. Bella looked down, staring at the toes of her shoes, watching the fabric flex as she scrunched and unscrunched her toes.

An hour later she was still lost in thought when Tater's boots strode into view. There was a deep scuff on one side, and the top of his left boot had a permanent dent in it from shifting his motorcycle. She knew this because her father's boots bore the same mark. "Ready to go?" His deep voice rumbled through the noise in the clubhouse, a rumble which had been audible from across the room, and now vibrated in her belly from this close. She nodded. She'd been ready to leave before they got here. His hand rose, and she shivered in anticipation, knowing when his fingers tugged at hers, they would be chilled from the beer bottle. "Come on, then."

She was surprised when he walked her to the door that led outside, because most nights she slept in a bedroom on the second floor of the clubhouse. One weekend he had moved her to the club's compound in Wisconsin, but they'd returned to Chicago by Tuesday of the next week. Back at the clubhouse, back into the routine of sleeping with him in the room, showering with him seated outside the only door, eating with him standing at her back. So after weeks of the same, weeks of settling into this normal, Tater leading her outside wasn't routine. Wasn't normal.

Bella's muscles tensed, and she knew her sudden fear had transferred to her grip on his fingers when he stopped and spoke to the top of her head. Tater had ceased trying to make her look at him weeks ago when he'd realized she was still listening with her entire being no matter where her gaze rested. "Mason's house is empty. Got good security. We'll be staying there for the foreseeable."

Bella nodded and followed the tug on her hand when he started them moving forwards again.

Their forward momentum came to a screeching halt when he tried to lead her towards a bike. *No. No. No.* Tater crowded close, dwarfing her with his size, his muscles, his strength. "I won't let anything happen to you, Bella." He never called her honey again. Not after she told him about Edwardo. Never called her anything other than her name. She missed the sweet and silly words her father made up, missed being anything other than what she was. Isabella. In her mind, she'd given herself a title: *Isabella, the damaged*.

"Ride with me." Bella realized she was leaning towards him, her shoulder bumping against his arm, needing to borrow a little more strength from him. Tater took her silence for consent, moving them towards the bike. Keeping hold of her hand while he mounted it, he guided her onto the seat behind him. *Behind him*. His grip brought her fingers to his side and wrapped them around his belt loops. She waited for him to start the engine, then leaned forwards, rested her cheek against his spine and held tightly to his belt with both hands.

Then they were moving, rolling, gaining speed only to lose it as lights changed ahead of them, cars on either side, cars behind, people everywhere. Bella wasn't even aware she was trembling until he gripped her knee, pulling it close to his thigh. "Hold on." She nodded, gripping him with her legs, her arms. If her cheek could have gripped, it would have grabbed hold of his jacket. She bit the inside of her lips, the bright pain pushing back the panic until they were moving again. A moment later Tater crossed a bridge where an open-topped boat was passing underneath. Bella saw party lights strung along the railings as carefree couples danced under the moonlight, music and laughter washing up and coasting over her, leaving a longing behind which she didn't know what to do with. Then Tater leaned the bike, and from long practice, she leaned with him, and they were up a ramp and onto a highway. Fewer vehicles, no more stopping, just the road and wind and the rumble of the engine. And the heat and strength of the man she pressed against.

Long before she was ready to stop, he slowed, moving over, exiting the highway and they were back on surface streets. Less traffic here in this residential section, but the buildings were stacked close beside each other, hardly enough room to walk between them. Suffocating. Driveways led to basement garages, homes soared three and four stories overhead, wires crisscrossed the space between structures. A turn, another, and they were on a road, not a street. A tiny oasis of space in a crowded neighborhood. A small house sat on the left-hand side of a driveway turned alley, lights shining through the large bay window in the nearest wall. Bella could see deeper shadows cast by tall trees behind the structure. On the other side of the alley was a sprawling single-story house. A three-bay garage and a tall fence extended off the back.

Tater pulled the bike up in front of the first garage bay, and Bella dismounted, letting him do the same. She watched as he gripped the handle, rolling the door up and out of the way overhead. The other two entrances each had a pair of swinging doors, simple latches locking the doors together. He rolled his bike into the darkness, coming back out to tug the door back into place. One hand extended to her, he waited, and she took the three steps to take it, gripping tightly.

Gate, patio, screen door. "Wait here." Bella stepped to one side as he pushed the inside door closed behind them, then light bloomed in the room. She was surprised because Mason's house was lovely. It looked lived in, and this room was very much like a farm kitchen. It was comfortable, meant to be used, meant for a family. Tater walked through an archway and into the darkness beyond. A moment later a light clicked, and she saw the back of a large couch. His footsteps retreated, and more light reflected off the inside of the windows. "Bella."

"Yes?"

"You're in Mason's room. It's the last one at the end of the hall." Tater's voice grew louder as he walked back to where she stood in the kitchen, still unmoving from where he'd placed her. He walked past her to the door and locked it, then flipped open the door to the security system, punching buttons. "Don't open any doors or windows, or it'll get noisy."

"Okay."

To the side, the refrigerator door opened, and Tater stepped back into her line of sight, holding a beer and a bottle of water. Handing her the water, he looked at her for a minute then shook his head. "You're pooped, Bella. Go on to bed. I'll be out here for a little bit." She looked at him for a moment, and he tipped his head to one side, muscles in his cheek popping. "You're safe."

"Okay." She let her feet take her into the next room, seeing a second couch, a couple of wide armchairs and a huge TV. Light streamed into the room from a hallway opposite, and she drifted that direction, seeing more light coming from the end of the narrow hallway. Two closed doors to the right which she didn't open, and one open to the left, a dim nightlight inside showing the sink and mirror of a bathroom. In the bedroom she looked around, immediately gravitating towards the pictures on the wall.

Aunt Loretta, she thought, staring at one of the pictures of a woman bent over a washtub, corded muscles standing out in her arms as she wrung the wet out of an article of clothing. Never having met the woman, but her daddy had pictures from Kentucky. A woman she didn't know stood in front of a truck, belly swollen in early pregnancy. Another picture of a group of men standing shoulder-to-shoulder in front of a gaping maw leading into the ground.

As a child, she'd listened one night as her father told the story of how his daddy died, and for weeks Bella had been afraid of dark, enclosed places. Afraid of being buried alive. Petrifying blackness swept up and over her at the thought, narrowing her vision to a pinpoint, and she crashed her teeth together on her bottom lip, grinding into the flesh, pushing the fear and terror back. *I'm alive. Alive. Alive.* Shaking her head to rattle the thought loose, she stared at the picture of the men again. The knowledge beat at her that she had suffered the same fate as her grandfather; had been buried alive, drowning in air that held no spark of life in it, and survived. *I didn't die.* The thought had a feeling of marvel in it, and she pulled it close, wrapping her arms around herself to hold it to her. *I didn't die.*

A noise behind her and she whirled to see Tater standing in the doorway. "You okay, Bella?"

She nodded. A chill hit her, and she shivered. Cold dampness against her skin and she looked down, finding the bottle of cold water cradled to her chest. The condensation from the bottle had soaked through her tee and thin bra, nipple standing at attention, areola plainly visible through the wet fabric. When she looked at Tater she saw his gaze was fixed on her chest, tiny flicking glances up to her face, her lips, back to her chest, that muscle jumping in his cheek again. He shifted and angled his hips away from her, but not before she saw the tight fabric defining the shape of his arousal. *He's interested in me?*

Testing her theory, she took a deep breath and watched, enthralled as his lips pursed and twitched as if he were sucking on something. Bella experienced the surprise of tightly coiled tension low in her belly, a welcome slickness between her legs. The gusset of her panties accepting the burden of wetness brought on by the sure knowledge that this man found her attractive. She wasn't a virgin, her prom date had successfully wooed her, and they'd left the dance early to go to a hotel where he'd arranged a room. He had been sweet and anxious to do everything right, and Bella thought he was her forever. Then right before graduation, he'd found another girl who was more forever, and once Bella found *that* out, she'd dumped him. Over the summer she'd had two more lovers. California had been good to her, and she'd discovered that while prom night had seemed perfect at the time, her boyfriend had lacked in both endowment and skills.

She wasn't afraid of being intimate. That at least was something Edwardo hadn't done. He had been far more interested in the pain he could give than anything to do with pleasure.

Something about Tater made her feel safe. The implied power in his hands, the strength of his legs. In the whole time she'd been here, he hadn't been more than thirty feet away from her, and he hadn't made any advances. Full on ignoring mode, which was safe, but rocked her self-confidence. Which had led to her studying his type. So Bella knew she wasn't anything he would normally go for, not generally. *I just want to be held*. Maybe he could be tempted.

Staring at him, she brought the bottle to her other breast, rolling it across the nipple, wetting the fabric on that side, too, feeling her skin draw taut as her nipple hardened into a peak. "*Jesus*," the word seemed forced from him and with a glower in her direction, he turned his back on her, taking up all the available space in the doorway. His voice was soft when he ordered, "Get ready for bed, baby."

She froze at his use of a pet name, and then looked down at the pair of pebbled nipples on her chest and barely managed to choke off a wry laugh before it escaped. *He likes me*.

***

Juanita

Spider sat on the couch and stared at the TV, but Juanita knew he wasn't seeing the comedy playing out on the screen. Tipping her head to the side, she studied him. He'd been off since Bella was rescued. In the years since Daena had died, Juanita and Spider had become friends. His three kids were all older than Bella, but once they added Mela to the mix, they had a stair-stepped population of children. Dean, the oldest, had finished community college last year but had opted to work instead of going on to school. He was in El Paso. Levi, Spider's other son, and Wanda, his youngest, had moved to California to be with Daena's family, leaving Spider on his own.

Spider had been staying with them for the past several months, and Juanita had been grateful for not only the help, but the feeling of security and companionship he gave her.

She startled now, when without looking away from the TV, he asked her, "Why you eyeballin' me, 'Nita?"

"Are you okay?" She chewed on the inside of her cheek. "You've been quiet for the past few weeks, and I just...is everything okay?" He turned to look at her and the ravaged expression on his face froze her breath in her lungs. Pain, raw and real, stared at her from his eyes. *Christos*. Her throat tightened around her question, "Spider?"

He moved fast, his hand reaching out to grab her wrist before she could pull back and he yanked her closer, pushing his face into hers as he said, "No, shit ain't okay." She fell against the back of the couch, pressing into the cushions as he loomed over her. "Ain't been okay for a long time, 'Nita. I see bad things comin', can't make the curve to bring them back right. Ain't gonna be okay, not unless things change."

As fast as it had happened, it was over, and he was on his end of the couch, again facing the TV. Juanita carefully eased back to a sitting position, watching him from the corner of her eye. His voice was a rasp when he told her, "Never hurt you. Don't gotta be afraid of me. Never hurt a woman. Men who do..." The laugh track from the TV filled the silence for a moment, then he continued, "oughtta be castrated and killed. In that order. Never understood a man like Lalo. Like Carlos. Never understood 'em."

Quivering with terror at something she didn't understand, Juanita stayed on the couch for a minute, then two. At the next commercial break, Spider leaned forwards, elbows on his knees as he reached for the remote and muted the TV. "Gettin' a beer. Want anything?"

"No," she responded instantly. "I have a headache."

"You should lay down, 'Nita."

"I will," she said, pushing up from the couch. Going down the hallway to the bedroom felt like a retreat, and she wondered if she should say anything to Watcher when he called tonight from wherever he wound up today. He and the other Soldiers were still hunting Lalo, and had followed a lead west. Closing the door behind her, she fought against the desire to lock the door. Fought and lost, the look on Spider's face that sprang to mind renewing the terror in her belly.

Best laid plans

Watcher

"Wanna say that again? I'm not sure I understood correctly. How many kids does Slate have now?" Watcher laughed as he asked the question, lifting a can of beer to his lips, leaning one elbow on the bar. He was in Fort Wayne at Marie's, one of the Rebel businesses. Surprised when Slate hadn't been on hand to greet him, Watcher had been shocked to find out he'd entirely missed hearing about Ruby's pregnancy.

"Too fuckin' many, you ask me." One of the men standing next to Mason spoke up, and the people nearby laughed. "Seriously, he's too fuckin' excited about this, man." The man tipped up a bottle, taking a deep pull at his beer, then lips to the bottle grinned. "Four kids in diapers. Man's a glutton for it."

"Too true." Watcher drained his beer, setting it near the inside rail on the bar as a signal for another, he then turned to face Mason. "How's your boy?"

The self-satisfied smirk on his friend's lips made Watcher laugh aloud. "He's good." Watcher shook his head, and Mason grinned broadly. "Strong as shit. Pulls up on everything." Mason cut his eyes to the top of the bar and back up to Watcher's face. Voice pitched for privacy, he told Watcher, "Willa wants another, right away. I'm all for attempting, and she's all in. Wears me out, brother."

"Good kinda exhausted." Watcher jumped when something brushed his hand, and he turned to see a new waitress setting a beer beside his hand. The blonde had trailed her fingers across the backs of his knuckles as she set it down. Scowling, he pinned her with a glare and flipped a bill onto the bar. "Close out my tab." She flinched and nodded, but he didn't care.

"Goin' somewhere?" Mason finished his glass of what looked like whiskey and set it down, shaking his head at a silent question from the bartender.

"See the newest additions to the Jones' crew." Watcher pushed the still-full beer away, gathering up his change and leaving a carefully calculated 20-percent tip on the bar. "Wanna ride?"

"I could roll," Mason told him, cutting his gaze around the room. Watcher didn't know what he was looking for, but he must have found it because without delaying further, Mason led him out of the bar. Ten minutes later, Watcher was hugging DeeDee, and grinning at an over-the-moon Slate cradling one of his infant daughters.

***

"Whadda you mean, you lost her?" Watcher pushed upright and swung his legs off the bed, sitting on the side and reaching out to flick on the light. Groggy, he shook his head, trying to chase the cobwebs away. Neck bent, he listened to the voice on the phone for a minute, then lifted one hand and pounded on the wall beside the headboard. A minute later his door opened, and Opie stuck his head in, hair sticking up on the side of his head.

Watcher pulled the phone away from his face and told him, "Boys lost Mela. She's alone, right now, in the wind somewhere in southern Illinois. Her design, she worked for it, but we need to roll, brother. Call Slate, get the info on the park."

"Jesus," Opie clipped, his face disappearing as he ran back to his room at the Rebel clubhouse in Fort Wayne. Watcher shoved his feet into his jeans, listening to Diamond tell him again that he didn't know what happened.

"What happened is you were fuckin' outmaneuvered by a damned girl. Raul called when she booked outta Chihuahua. We picked her up in Odessa. Shouldn't have been a hard job. Follow a slip of a girl on a motorcycle and keep her safe. You didn't do that." Watcher shook his head. "Lemme get folks rolling here. You keep looking. I'll call Raul."

DeeDee's fault. Mason's cousin, and Ruby's long-time mother figure, had wanted a last-of-the-season camping blowout with the girls. Ruby had jumped at the chance, as had some of the Rebel women from Chicago. Mela, cooped up at her daddy's compound down in Mexico, had gotten a wild hair that she needed to run cross-country to join the women for a two-night campout. Thirty-five hundred miles for two fuckin' nights. She knew what was going on, knew what had gone down with Bella, had nearly been taken herself, and she still rolled. Raul called Watcher, who had called Slate, who had said he would have men on the campsite and have it closed for casual visitors. Watcher had assigned four men to find and tail her, the intent to keep her safe between Texas and Indiana, and then back again.

The plan for his trip up here was to finalize things with Mason to disband the Southern Soldiers and migrate his men to the Rebels, writing a charter for chapters in Las Cruces, Lamesa, and El Paso. It would get Mason two states which were closer to California, a target that mattered to the man for some reason. It would also gain Watcher and his men breathing room as the landscape of the clubs in their corner of the world adjusted to an expanded dominant. No longer beating back the competition alone, but standing with the full force of the Rebel Wayfarers membership at their back.

Opie was for it, so was Diamond. Hell, all his officers save one were for it, drooling at the idea of being the big dicks in town. Spider was the sole dissenting vote, holding up Darrie's memory at every chance, his sullen attitude growing with each sitdown or meeting. This was one of the reasons Watcher hadn't argued when Spider opted to stay in Las Cruces this trip.

"Fucked sideways," he muttered, shoving his phone in his pocket, noting he had a missed call from Juanita. Resolving to call her back as soon as he could, Watcher walked out of the room and yelled, "Opie, you ready to roll?"

Time's a passing

"There's my baby girl," Watcher murmured softly, lips pressed to the side of her head. For her part, Bella had her arms wrapped tightly around his waist, cheek pressed to his shoulder. Watcher gave himself permission to just stand there, soaking up the moment and taking in the feel of her, absorbing the sure knowledge his daughter was whole and healthy. Far from the fearful woman who had to be threatened to drive her onto the back of Fury's bike for the trip up, she'd run to Watcher with shining eyes and a broad smile. *Praise God*, he thought. *My baby's okay.*

He gave her a squeeze, then another one and she read the signals, lifting her head and tipping it back to grin up into his face. Fingers brushed his jaw, scratching through his beard and she whispered, "Missed you, Daddy."

Nothing matters more. Safety and happiness of my girls. He cleared his throat once, found himself still unable to talk and tried again. "Missed you too, my Bella." *Get to see both my girls, same weekend, does my heart good.*

Mela had been somewhat less happy to see him, but then she'd been rollin' in the sack with a man at the time. Hurley, now a prospect for the Rebels, and the man had stood strong, pulling her back and stepping in front of her so she knew she wasn't facing the rage of her Papa alone. Watcher had nodded at the sight, even as DeeDee murmured from behind him about Mela's confessed fears and how this man had alleviated them. Mela had gotten over her annoyance quick when Watcher explained his intent of her helping stand guard on Juanita in Las Cruces instead of heading back to the Machos compound in Chihuahua. He'd grinned when she'd hesitated, cutting a glance to Hurley for approval who gave her a nod in response. Mela was on her way back to Las Cruces right now, with a strong escort consisting of several Soldiers and a lone Rebel.

Now to gather his other chick back to the nest. Watcher opened his mouth, trying to determine the best way to begin the conversation but stopped himself when he saw Bella's smile fade completely away. "Daddy," she said, her voice high and tight, "we need to talk."

He squeezed her tightly, held it until she squeaked a complaining, "Daddy," and then smiled and tipped his chin down, brushing a kiss across her forehead.

"So talk," he urged, pulling her close again. She tightened her arms around him and then moved so her palms were against his chest, and pushed, gaining a few inches. Reluctantly, he released her and watched as she walked halfway across the room from where they'd been standing, turning and resting her back against a wall. Whatever this was, she needed distance, and painful as it was, he had to give it to her.

They were standing in Mason's living room, the house where she'd been staying for the past few weeks. With Mason in Fort Wayne, it had been standing empty and was the perfect place for Bella and her security guards. Watcher tipped his head to glance around the room, glimpsing two men out the back window. They were standing near a fire pit on the back patio, one looking down at the cold bricks, one staring in the window at Bella. Watcher studied the look on the man's face for a moment and had a feeling he knew where this conversation would be going. He made an instant decision to give Bella what she needed. He didn't give a fuck whatever it was, or however it looked to the outside world. *I got her*, he heard Duck's voice in his head, *she's alive*. Watcher vowed again as he had that day, the man's efforts would always be honored by her living life to the fullest.

"About Las Cruces," she started, her tone wary and he didn't make her wonder, didn't make her wait. Gave her everything she needed, not making her work for it.

"You should stay here." Her chin jerked towards her neck and he saw the confused happiness spreading across her features. Watcher decided to take it a step farther, make his approval explicit. "And if you like that Rebel the way he likes you, you should absolutely stay here. Indefinitely." He tipped his head towards the window and her hair fanned out as she whipped to face that direction. Watcher saw a soft look come over her and shifted so he could better see the man outside, watched as his face sharpened, features taut with desire. "He got a name?" Watcher already knew the man, knew his name. Had mistaken the red hair for his cousin many a time over the past months, but Tater was night and day in terms of personality from Fury. He just wanted to hear Bella say it.

Bella whispered the name, her lips shaping the sounds carefully like she only had once chance to get it right. "Tater." *Jesus, give her a million chances*, he prayed. "I like him, Daddy."

"Glad to know he's not out there twistin' on his own." Watcher kept his voice soft as he offered her a joke to break the tension in the room, but she didn't take it, didn't let up giving him everything she was feeling.

"He thinks he is, but he's being stubborn. Thinks sixteen years is a mountain. I've been leveling that mountain, slow and steady." She took a deep breath, still holding Tater's gaze, and without turning, told Watcher what she needed. "Could use some help on that front, Daddy. If you could see your way clear to assist."

"Anything for you, baby girl." Her surprise was evident in the way she swung to face him, and from the corner of his eye, he saw Tater on the move, her startled actions pulling him inside to see what was going on. "Anything. Ever. You know it."

The kitchen door burst open, and in three swift strides Tater was beside Bella, hand cupped to her chin, pulling her around to face him. Protecting her from her own father. In a deep, gruff voice, Tater asked, "Everything okay, baby?"

At the question, Watcher relaxed. Tater didn't care who was in the room, and from his actions, whether Bella recognized it or not, she was claimed.

Watcher answered for both of them when he said, "Yeap, it's all good."

***

Mason

Mason pushed another pillow behind his back, rolling slightly to one side, arm firmly holding his welcome burden to his chest. A soft sound rose from the blue blankets he cradled, repeating but changing in tone, sliding up and then back down the scale. "Ba, ba, *ba*, ba, ba, *ba*..."

Tipping his chin down, he stared into the eyes of his son, Garrett. A sweet, clear blue, slowly changing to grey. Gar looked up at him, head wobbling back and forth on his whimsical neck. With a thud, the boy planted his face against his father's chest, rubbing back and forth, cheeks pinking from friction against the tee Mason wore. Coming to rest with his face turned to one side, Gar quietly started up the sounds again, chin bobbing up and down with each sweet rendition. Mason laughed softly as the boy wiggled, skootching his knees far underneath his belly. Butt hiked in the air, Gar's white diaper shone, Mason's palm securely cupping and holding him in place.

With a grunt, Gar picked his head up again, wavering wildly from side to side until the wobble was calmed by Mason's support. His head plopped down again, and then his knees slid out from underneath him, feet flailing wildly as the boy gave a short, frustrated cry.

"Y'all okay in there?" Willa's voice came from the kitchen where she had been ensconced for a while. She'd retreated there after amusingly rejecting Mason's persistent offers of help earlier when Gar was still asleep.

"You won't help," she told him, gripping both his hands in hers in an attempt to keep them away from her body. "You only want to get sexy frisky." He twisted his hands, quickly reversing the hold and shifting control from her to him, using her hands to pull her close, pinning them behind her back as he arched her into him, capturing her mouth in a demanding, deep, wet kiss.

"So?" he asked, grinning as he dropped hard kisses along her shoulder.

"So, then we won't have dinner. I want to make something special, and that means I have to focus." Her tone was half scolding and half irritated, making him grin.

Nibbling up the column of her neck, he told her between bites and kisses, "I could eat you, babe. Eat you right up. So fucking hungry for you, Willa." Her breath caught in her throat, and he thought for a moment he'd won the war, but she twisted out of his grip entirely, propelling herself across the room and managing to get the table between them.

"We have to eat, Mason." Gaze locked on him, she stood with her hands on the back of a chair, ready to dart either direction. "Food. Sup-

per. Dindin. Means you need to leave me alone, honey. Now, what do you want for your special dinner?" Today was Mason's birthday, and for at least a week she had asked him the same question. He had given her lots of options, laughing with her as she shot down each one.

"At this point in time, I'd like to point out I already told you what I want to eat, babe. More than once. And yeah, I'd eat that particular meal any day of the week. Gladly, babe. My favorite of all time." He feinted left, continuing a step or two until she was committed to the direction and then reversed, rounding the table to catch her and wrap her up in both arms.

"Mason," she yelled, twisting futilely, finding her struggles to escape wasted effort. As he leaned in, angling for a kiss, they both stopped still, mouths a fraction of an inch apart. From the baby monitor came a squawk, then a rustling noise and then they were listening to the crooning sounds of a baby waking. "Mason," she whisper-yelled. "You woke up Garrett." He gave her a squeeze, taking his kiss from her lips, sounds from the monitor increasing until the babbling came up the hallway as clearly as from the speaker.

"I got him, babe," he told her, tightening his arms a final time, squeezing a high-pitched and laughing squeak out of her that brought a smile to his lips. "You woke him, just sayin'. But, my boy needs some Daddy time."

That brought him to now, where he held their son to his chest, watching with a proud smile as Garrett struggled to figure out the whole scoot or crawl thing. He lifted his gaze to the doorway to find Willa leaning against the frame, head tilted to one side, wiping her hands on a towel as she watched him hold their son. "You're okay," she said, answering her own question and he nodded. "Love my boys," she whispered. She walked to the couch, crouching down so her head was level with Garrett's. Reaching out, she smoothed her palm over his head, back and forth and back again, and under his mother's touch, Mason felt their son relaxing into him.

"He likes that." He told her something she already knew, earning a one-sided smile. She reached up, trailing the backs of her knuckles across his cheek, pressing them against his pursed and demanding lips, giggling when he smacked a kiss against them. "Like father, like son. I love your hands on me, too, babe."

"Yeah." She breathed out the word, eyes fixed on his lips. Mason knew what she wanted so he reached out, cupped the back of her neck with one hand and pulled her close so he could kiss her again, mouths working against each other. Her breath came fast when they stopped, and he looked to see her arm had wrapped around Garrett, too, their boy held secure in the embrace of his parents who were so very much in love. Her eyes slowly opened, and she blinked, seeming to come out from under a spell.

The spell was broken by a loud beeping from the kitchen and she grinned. "Time to get back to slaving away over a hot stove for my man." She started to move, and then paused, biting her lip as she looked at him, whispering, "I love you, Davis Mason."

"And I love you, too, Willa Mason." He returned the sentiment easily, truthfully. He shifted to accommodate the movement on his chest, feeling Garrett beginning the squirming slide of his knees again.

"He looks more like you every day." This was also whispered, barely breathed, sounding as much a hope as a promise.

"He's a good lookin' boy." Mason teased, knowing the doubts still ate at her, the not knowing for sure. What she couldn't seem to understand was it didn't matter to him. Never would have, but when she finally got to a place where she was easy with it, he had papers to show her which would lay her fears to rest once and for all.

First, she needed to be in a place where she could believe it didn't matter. Needed to come to grips with it on her own to be stronger than the fear. "Looks just like his daddy." Which was the truth, because Garrett held a lot of Mason in his face. Eyes, nose, hard to tell for sure, but the hen's party consensus was the boy was a dead ringer. He had his momma's mouth, though, sweet and expressive. The happy baby had her disposition, too.

The beeping escalated, and Willa pushed up, leaning over to kiss their son's head. "Slave labor commencing."

Over the next hour, Mason lay on the couch with his boy, laughing at the running commentary from the kitchen. After the first few minutes, he identified a tell-tale clink of ice cubes and suspected Willa had started in on the lemon vodka, her newest thrill on the beverage side of things.

Then, music playing softly in the background, he listened as she muttered to herself, "Is it too early for happiness? Oh hell, no. Never."

"Why won't the bottle"—she grunted—"of vanilla"—she made guttural, straining noises—"open?" She yipped in pain. "Motherfucker, that was my thumb." He heard the water running in the sink, then she grunted again, laughing through the sounds. The water turned off, and he watched her shadow dance across the far wall, arms moving up and down in weightlifter poses as she provided different accented renditions of, "I have the powah!" Ice clinked again.

Whisking sounds, the metal tool scraping the sides of the plastic bowl. "Ugh," she muttered and then laughed. "Lumpy cream cheese looks like ghost turds." This time, she snorted a laugh before singing, "Ooohhh. Who ya gonna call?" The freezer door opened, and he heard more ice clinking, followed by the sound of liquid pouring.

Tilting his head to one side, he listened to cabinet doors opening and closing, drawers being pulled out and then returned to their closed positions. Those were the sounds of his woman moving through the home they were making together. Contented, he closed his eyes. "Finally." She had a tone of celebration in her voice. "Power mixer, coming up." Louder thumps followed by the sound of the mixer powering on, it ran for a minute, then two, before shutting off. Stark silence from the kitchen, followed by a loud, "What the..."

Rustling, thumping, angry-sounding thuds followed by water running in the sink. "I told you that bowl was too fucking small. Now you have a mess to clean up, girlie." Her voice fell to a mutter, his quiet laughter nearly drowning it out, but he heard, "Look at the whipped cream flung over all the canisters, counter, stove top, and my shirt." Water in the sink again, then, "I told you the bowl was too fucking small."

Mason's hand smoothed down Garrett's back, rounding his bottom and snuggling him up a little higher. He was surprised Gar didn't complain at the adjustment, and Mason looked down to find his boy had dozed off. Cheek resting on his daddy's chest, his little cupid bow lips were pursing and relaxing. Mason thought the boy might be practicing his babbling in his sleep, or perhaps thinking of the same breasts his daddy loved. They had been tender and sensitive the first time Willa nursed their newborn in the hospital, Mason cradling her in his arms, for once not thinking about bedding her. That had changed the first time he'd caught her in the shower at home, standing motionless in the stream of water, hoping the heat would ease her pain. His massaging had helped, she'd told him later. He laughed quietly at the thought. "Sure know it helped me."

She called from the kitchen, "Why am I making a fourth pie? Why? You'd literally be as happy with a box of popcorn, but no—" She stopped talking before he could answer, and then he heard her say, "Holy shit." She quickly corrected herself. "Oops, Nana wouldn't like that." She paused, then muttered softly, "Jesus Christ." A solid thump and she said, "Annnd, she'd like that even less. Thanks, Nana. Instant karma, knocking my head like that. Fucking shit. Damn shitty cocoa all over the crappy floor...sorry Nana."

A minute later the freezer opened again, ice tinkled into a glass and then the glugging sound of liquid being poured. Glancing at the clock, he marked the time, thinking he might be the one to salvage dinner in about an hour if she kept to this pace. His Willa was kinda a lightweight when it came to alcohol.

He pushed up from the couch, Garrett in his arms, and walked their boy to the nursery. Laying Gar on the crib mattress, he adjusted the boy's position, tucking the blanket securely around him. Making sure the monitor was on and in place, he moved back up the hallway to the living room, catching a glimpse of Willa through the kitchen door.

Beautiful. My God, she's so beautiful. I'm a lucky fucking bastard, he thought as he stalked towards her. Standing there in one of his ratty Support Your Local Rebel Wayfarers shirts, stained apron tied across her middle, she had her back to him. He tilted his head. She had a hand up by her face, the other propped on the edge of the cabinet holding a cheesecake batter-crusted beater from the electric mixer. With a laugh, he called across the space separating them, "Are you licking those beaters?"

She twisted, looking at him over her shoulder, then silently reached out and plunged one hand into the dishwater standing in the sink, still clutching one beater in her grip. "No," she said, a strip of batter smeared across one cheek. She shook her head, eyes wide as she modified her statement. "Not now."

"Willa, babe." At his words, she scrunched up her nose and stuck her tongue out at him. "Got something you can lick on, anytime you feel a need." Raising her chin defiantly, she lifted the remaining beater to her mouth, tongue coming out to swipe a big path through the remaining batter.

A moment later her chin came down, and she made a gagging sound. Lifting her wet hand to her mouth, she covered her lips, frantically looking side-to-side. "I think I just ate a cat hair."

"Wills," he got out, laughing harder. "We don't own a cat."

"And we never will," she vowed, gagging again. "Never, ever, ever. Pretty sure that was a cat h—" She gagged and dropped her hand. "I can't even say the word now. Just the word's gonna make me sick. I'll bleep myself. Wonder how many bleep bleeps I've eaten?" She gagged, and he laughed aloud. "Stop laughing at me. I'm never eating at a clubhouse party again. Half the guys have dogs. Look at Gunny, he's got two."

"Honey, a little cat hair..." He paused and waited as she gagged again lifting both hands to her mouth, then continued, "...ain't gonna kill you."

"Stop saying bleep bleeps," she whisper-yelled at him.

Wordlessly, he reached out and grabbed her glass, then lifted it to his mouth, intending to finish it off before pouring her another. The lemon-flavored water hit his tongue and, surprised, he lifted his gaze to hers. She smiled at him, looking like the cat that got the cream and his brows came together. Willa liked her beverages. She'd taken care when nursing Garrett, but once he'd refused to nurse last month, going on the bottle, he'd expected her to loosen back up.

He stared at her a moment more, taking in the way her eyes stuck on him, the curve of his tee across her chest and belly. Placing the glass on the counter, he flicked the rim with a finger, listening to it ring. *Beauty everywhere*. There was a wide fucking smile on her face that said so much. This was a woman with a secret.

Crossing the kitchen, he herded her into the corner, pressing against her as he ran a hand up her side, holding her in place. "Willa Mason, you got something to tell me?"

"Maybe." She drew the word out, turning the two syllables into a handful. "I don't know. I wanted to be sure before I said anything."

"You want to be sure?" He was already reaching for his keys, knowing from the bright look in her eyes that this mattered to her. Mattered just as much as their confirmation over a year ago sitting in the sunlight on a California beach. When she nodded, he dropped his head down and took her lips in a hard, demanding kiss, then without looking back—because he knew if he looked back to see her spellbound again, he would not be leaving the house anytime soon—he went out the door to the garage.

Ten minutes later he was back, angling the bike into his parking space within the structure. After the engine sounds trailed off, he could hear her, even through the door.

"That's the same fucking bowl, you stupid bitch!" she yelled, and then her voice dropped to the whisper-yell from before. "Look at the mashed potatoes flung all over. Fucking shit, and I don't care if Nana wouldn't like that, it's just the way my mouth is today." As he opened the door he heard her sigh. "You can't be taught, can you, Wills? Stupid for life."

Standing in the doorway, package in hand, he watched as she finished wiping down the cabinets and opened the refrigerator, a cheesecake balanced on one palm. Muttering, she swung the fridge door closed, still talking to herself. "Told you there wasn't any room." Her immediate rejoinder was, "Shut up." This time, he couldn't help himself lifting a hand to his face and laughing hard at her unintentionally hilarious behavior. "Shut up, you," she called across the kitchen at him. "You're gonna wake up the Gar boy again."

"I wake him, I got him," he told her, taking the half a dozen strides that separated them. "You're not stupid, Willa. Beautiful, I'll buy that. Sexy as hell? Yeah, you're all of that too. Gorgeous, babe. Gorgeous and hilarious."

"There's no room for the pies." She made a face and complained when he took the pan out of her hands. She looked down as he replaced it with the package from the pharmacy. "Oh," she whispered, lifting her gaze to his.

"I got the pies. You take care of that," he ordered, turning to the refrigerator and opening the freezer.

She called out over her shoulder, pausing in the doorway, "There's no room up there, either."

He pulled the vodka out of the freezer, there because she liked her drinks cold, and positioned the bottle on the countertop before placing the pie inside. That was his one concession to hoping the answer would be what he wanted. *No sense jinxing things*, he thought. "Now there is."

Her laughter chased up the hallway, and he turned to survey the damage wrought on the kitchen. Surprisingly clean, she had cleared tools and implements away as she'd finished with them, the only things left on the countertop were the empty bowl and a crock filled with mashed potatoes, ready for baking. Dosing them with a topping of cheese, he slid them into the oven, checked the temperature and smiled when he heard cooing over the baby monitor. Willa's voice, soft and low, "Who's Momma's big boy? Such a good boy, my Garrett. Baby boy, Momma's baby boy." He moved to the sink with the bowl, cleaning it with a quick swish of cloth.

Her voice caught, and it sounded like she swallowed a sob. "You ready to be a big brother?"

When he heard her, Mason tipped his head back, closing his eyes, letting the peace those words offered sweep through him. Something he wanted, and she needed. Their family, growing, a little bean-sized promise and hope inside her.

When she walked back into the kitchen, Garrett in her arms, it only took a glance for him to know for sure what he had heard was real. A smile wide as Texas stretched her lips, and she held their boy close, his cheek resting between her breasts. Breasts he had noticed this morning were fuller, more sensitive again, his prayers rising like the sun on the moans she'd given him as they'd moved together.

She tilted her chin, asking him softly, "Whatcha doin', Mason?"

He stretched his arm up, carrying the small bowl in his hand to the back of the top shelf in the corner cabinet. "Babe." That was all he gave her, and the single word caused peals of laughter to spill from her lips.

"I know, I know," she called, still amused, Garrett now giggling along with her, the sound of their mingled merriment swelling to fill his heart. "If I can't be taught, at least I can be inconvenienced."

He turned, resting against the countertop and holding out his arms. As she moved to him, he asked her, voice soft, hopeful, "Got something to tell me, babe?"

She turned Garrett in her arms, facing him towards Mason and waved his chubby little arm at him. "Daddy, Daddy," she called, her voice adorably high-pitched, imitating a four-month-old baby's cooing attempts. "I get to be a big brother!" In her normal voice, lips hovering over his, she breathed, "Surprise! Happy birthday, Mason."

***

Watcher

The door to the diner opened and shut a dozen times before Bones walked through, Watcher already on his third cup of coffee. He studied his friend, seeing a fatigue on Bones' face he hadn't noticed the last time they'd had a conversation. He then got lost trying to decide the last time he'd actually seen the man.

As Bones pulled out the chair on the other side of the table, movement across the street caught Watcher's eye, and he saw a small figure sidle along the wall towards where their bikes were parked. Not tall, not broad, it almost looked like a child. He stared warily, trying to determine if vandalism was the goal. Appearing to slide along the surface, whoever it was stopped about ten feet from the bikes and settled to the sidewalk.

"Do not worry about my shadow," Bones said in greeting, and Watcher twisted to look at him, accepting the hand extended across the table. A tight grip and release. "She will not bother things."

"She?" Watcher turned to look at her, still not seeing the gender markers he would expect. Then hands slipped out of the sleeves hanging from the figure's shoulders and shoved back the hood shadowing much of the face. Her face, now clearly distinguishable as female, a mass of hair escaping from the hoodie. "Who is she?"

"I only know a little," Bones admitted, staring across the street along with Watcher. "She is just...always around. She goes by Ester." His voice was wistful, musing, and Watcher looked at him, seeing a softness on Bones' features he'd never seen.

"She follows you?" The question of "and you let her" was on the tip of his tongue, but he restrained it, glad it remained unspoken when Bones responded.

"As she likes. At times"—he turned to face Watcher—"I follow her."

"You ever have an old lady?" Watcher couldn't honestly remember, couldn't recollect having ever seen the man with a woman for more than a few hours, and those party dolls, not someone who could stay the distance. Club relationships were one thing, family was another.

"I have not been blessed with a partner, no. Not yet." Bones turned to glance out the window, and then back at Watcher. "But this is not what we are here to discuss." He shook his head, flexing his hands around the cup the waitress had dropped off, not even having to put his order in. The ink on his skin danced with the movement of muscles and tendons under the surface. Tattoos on his neck and face helped hide many of Bones' reactions, a permanent solution Watcher always wondered about.

Watcher shook his head, shoving the thought aside. "No, I wanna talk about how you dealt with killin' your club." Even the tattoos didn't hide Bones' flinch at Watcher's word choice.

"Did you know they called Mason a club killer at one time?" Bones lifted his coffee, sipping noisily at the liquid. "It was a label he did not believe could be outlived. Resurrected when he burned the charter of the Outriders chapter in San Diego. One I tried very hard not to allow spoken when I merged my Skeptics with his club." Bones shook his head. "Now, calling them his Rebels feels wrong. I'd been part of them in many ways for a very long time. Always careful to keep the separation between me and mine, and his. Now, this patch—" He jerked one tattooed thumb over his shoulder, pointing towards his back. "—is mine and the club is mine and the man who I called president for a year before we made it official, is also mine. You will not regret this, Watcher."

"Who started the Skeptics?" That was one question that kept circling Watcher's head. *Darrie's club.* Everything Watcher had done since putting Darrie in the ground had been to keep his brother's dream alive. *Not everything,* he thought, trying to be honest with himself. Darrie wouldn't have taken a stand against flesh trade, and he knew it. *That was all me.*

"Patch brother, not blood." Bones cut straight to the heart of the matter. No surprise, because he was intuitive enough, and been around long enough to remember the why and when of Watcher leaving the Outriders to head west. "I did not have a personal stake other than years of blood and sweat poured into the Skeptics patch. The desire to be best, make the biggest mark, surround myself with righteous people. Unlike you, I came to my position at the top of the heap by more traditional methods."

"Blood," Watcher said, glancing back out at the girl leaning against the wall across the street. "Darrie wanted it, worked for it. Was steadily fucking it up, but the want was so strong for him." Watcher sighed, idly reaching out with one finger to push at the handle of his mug. Back and forth. "Then he died. For the patch. Died wearing it." Back and forth, the unglazed bottom of the cup producing a narrow skree sound as it twisted and glided on the tabletop. "Died and was buried in it. I do this..." He paused, stilling. "...it's the last thing he did on this earth. I do this, I throw that away." Back and forth. "It's like I'm throwing him away. Don't sit right."

A tattooed hand settled on top of his, forcing his fingers away from the mug. Watcher lifted his eyes, seeing Bones' steady gaze trained on him. They sat in silence for a moment, then Bones sighed and released his grip. "Danger died a long time ago."

"I know that," Watcher snapped, leaning back in his chair. "I know when he died, Bones."

"Life was different then. As different then as that time was from your youth in Kentucky. As different as that youth was from your cradle days, my friend. Life"—Bones gestured, indicating something only he understood—"moves on and changes. Things are different today from yesterday. That girl"—he poked two fingers at the glass, not looking, but drawing Watcher's gaze across the street to see her still seated in the same position—"will be different tomorrow than she is today. And you"—those same stiffened fingers were directed across the table towards Watcher's chest—"will make a thousand decisions in the next year you will never remember. Life was different, and who can say what Danger would guide you to do, or what he would do himself if put in the same position. You cannot falter based on what you think he would say or do, because he did not have time to gain the wisdom you have in the intervening years. He was not granted that grace. You were." Bones sat back, lifting his coffee and taking a drink. "You know what you need to do, and never needed permission for a single thing in your life before now. Why are you seeking approval now, Watcher? Ask yourself that question, because therein lies your confusion."

Spider's face swam up in front of Watcher, and he heard the unrelenting questions again. *Danger wouldn't have... Danger never wanted... Danger should have...* All the things Spider was convinced he knew, and yet Watcher, who knew Darrie better than anyone, didn't have the same convictions. Watcher already knew the answers, but needed to have the push Bones gave him.

"Smart little fucker, ain't ya? You're right." Watcher felt a grin curl the corners of his mouth. "But you can't tell anyone I said so."

"Our secret, my brother," Bones replied, his own grin crinkling the corners of his eyes. "When do you think you will phone Mason?"

"Now," Watcher said, digging in his front pocket for his phone. "No time like the present."

Changing of the guard

Hell yeah, Watcher thought, finger flicking his blinker on, guiding his bike smoothly into the left lane. Squinting against the setting sun, glancing in his mirrors, he saw the double column of motorcycles following, snaking left to pass the grouping of trucks and cars. It had been a good two weeks in the north, a very good couple of weeks. In the Texas panhandle now, he was headed west to Las Cruces with an honor escort, carrying new patches for each of his members in one of the bags strapped to his bike.

After passing the traffic, he signaled and changed lanes again, seeing Opie shift right behind him. Years and miles of experience bonded the two men, neither of them could make a move without the other anticipating it, all of which made for not only a tight formation but also a close friendship. Opie was all in on this change, as was Diamond, Pops, and nearly all the members Watcher had spoken to personally. He'd spent a significant amount of time on the phone in the last two days, setting plans in motion, pulling all his men to Las Cruces for the changeover.

That was what he and Mason agreed to call it, a changeover. Soldiers had been wearing an RWMC support patch for a long time now, and it wasn't a merger, not like they were trying to blend two families into some kind of a yours-mine-ours club. His men were already Rebels; they just lacked the official backing of the larger organization. This would alter their position, and the act of Watcher and his men dropping their center wouldn't be like some of the clubs in the past. It wasn't adversarial, not at all. This was a planned change, but not a shift in local structure or power.

Glancing in his mirrors again, he grinned at the sight of Mason riding to his right. Mason didn't have to give him this, could have mandated all the Soldiers come to Chicago for the changing of the patch. Didn't have to show this level of respect by riding at Watcher's side. From what Mason had confessed this morning, it might have slightly less to do with respect, and a little more about avoidance. Willa was pregnant again and grumpy as hell, so this would give Mason at least a week of peace. Watcher rolled his eyes. Not that the man seemed to want it, really, because every stop he was on the horn with the woman, demanding updates on Garrett and her condition. Like things would change in ninety miles. Or *every* ninety miles.

He looked at the bike's odometer and shook his head. *Speaking of that...*

Watcher lifted a fist, then pointed to his tank, checking his mirrors to see the motions repeated down the line of bikes. Next exit saw the entire column stopped on the lot of a small truck stop, lining up at six pumps for fuel, each member respectful of the citizens around as well as each other's time. Backing into a parking spot near the front doors after his turn, Watcher tipped his chin at Mason as the man settled his bike to its kickstand, sharing the space with him.

"Brother," Watcher called, seeing Mason looking down at his phone. "She doin' okay?"

"What?" Looking uncharacteristically distracted, Mason glanced up at him. "Willa? Yeah, she's good. Got a text from her. Layin' down for a nap while Gar sleeps." Mason stared down at his phone again, poking the screen with his finger, then glancing up and across the lot. Watcher suppressed his shiver as a trickle of tension rippled down his spine. This wasn't normal attentiveness. Not for Mason.

"Trouble?" Watcher sat up straight on his bike, unconsciously mimicking Mason's posture and alertness. "Whatcha got, Mason?"

"Not sure, brother." Head down, staring again at the phone, Mason seemed to be waiting for something. A moment later he got it in the form of a text and at the chime. Watcher heard his groan. "Diamante."

"Where?" Now Watcher put both feet on the ground, standing upright, ass just off his seat, still straddling the bike. He kept a steady watch, head sweeping left to right, glancing over his shoulders at the end of every arc. The same kind of watchfulness that had earned him his name.

Mason looked up, reacting to the tension in Watcher's tone. "On the Interstate, they're about fifty miles west of us. We'll pass 'em on the road, man. No worries." He looked at the people still fueling, and said, "Soon as the brothers are ready, we'll roll. Go ahead and stage out there so they know to put a hustle on it." Mason tipped his head towards the drive and Watcher nodded.

Finger to the button, he started his bike and rolled forwards, calling Opie to him with a chin lift. "Diamante rolling," he said, gesturing towards the holster strapped to Opie's handlebars. "We'll pass 'em in probably twenty minutes. We need to head out soon as we can, brother." Opie nodded, lifting a hand to stick his fingers in his mouth, producing a piercing whistle that gained the attention of nearly every rider. Hand in the air, he whirled a finger to urge speed and got a dozen nods in response.

Mason pulled up beside Watcher and put his bike in neutral, still bent over the phone in his hand. He got another update and looked to Watcher, the expression on his face conflicted. "Lalo's leading."

Shouts and dust followed Watcher out of the lot as he punched through the gears, hitting eighty before he settled into the shadows covering the westbound lanes. Looking straight ahead, he didn't flinch when a bike came up on either side of him, the only thing he could see was Bella's limp body cradled in Duck's arms. *I went south, and if it weren't for Duck, she'd have been dead. Lalo's gotta pay. He's gonna pay in blood.*

Thirty miles later, he saw a doubled column of bike headlights approaching and knew it had to be at least another ten miles to the next exit. There was a rough crossover ahead. He could just make out the strip of dirt in the dimness cast by an overpass.

Without signaling his intent, he leaned left, dogging the rear brakes hard, his back wheel chattering and chirping as it slid sideways, his downshifts locking the rubber for seconds at a time. The squeal of tires surrounded him as men struggled to accommodate the accordion effect his actions had on their speeding column, but he didn't care. As long as they didn't hit him, didn't take his chance for vengeance away, they could ride past and leave him standing alone.

He didn't care.

Lalo mattered.

Bella's face as he'd last seen her flashed in front of Watcher and he winced. Bright eyes, a carefree smile curling her lips as her hand curved around the bicep of the man standing next to her. That man's hand lifting to cover hers, protection evident in every line of his body. Bella leaning into Tater's side, sighing with happiness when he wrapped his arm around her shoulders, pulling her close. A man promising with everything in him that his woman would be healthy and happy. *Always.*

Mela facing him down, standing shoulders back, strong, even as he shouted at her. The shocked pleasure in her expression when Hurley stepped between them, pulling Watcher's ire in his direction. Deflecting and protecting her in one movement, making it clear he had a claim on her. Hurley would not let anything hurt her. *Never again.*

Juanita's voice last night, listening as she whispered naughty secrets to him, hearing the breathy catch in her voice that meant she was close, measuring his strokes so they came together. Laughing at their solo cleanup tasks, him promising to be home today. She'd been happy with all the news he'd offered, glad things were settling out so well with the girls. His Juanita had come back from so much in her life, and knowing this, knowing she'd come to the other side, he knew she was finally— *God, finally*—okay.

Gravel tried to slip away from his wheels, and he had to yank and lean to keep the bike upright, heard the click of a downshift and crunch of stones behind him and knew at least one brother made the turn. But Watcher focused ahead. Not behind. Never again. Bones had taught him that. *Things change*, he thought as he saw the shocked expression on Lalo's face.

Still fighting the bike for control, Watcher found a solid piece of ground and with that traction, gunned his engine, arrowing straight at the bastard who took his baby girl. Nearly took her from him. *Been hunting you for months*, he thought, bike wheels finally back on the pavement. Watcher reached behind him, pulled out his pistol and brought it up level, hand steady. Left-handed practice paying off, he remembered Mason's long-ago story about Roadkill's death. Knees clamped tightly on the tank, Watcher squeezed the trigger, feeling instant satisfaction when he saw the crater appear in Lalo's neck, blood filling the air in a fog around the lead riders, knowing there was no way the man could survive that wound. *Dead man. Fuckin' finally.*

Then he was among the oncoming riders, no time for avoidance. None for terror, either. His bike jolted sideways from a hit. Keeping it upright, he rode that one out. Then another bike smashed into him, turned him entirely around, and he was sailing, legs screaming as they unwrapped from where they'd bent the wrong way around the handlebars. His shoulder was the first thing to hit. He tried to tuck away from the piercing pain, failing as his limbs whirled through the air. Ragdolling through the sand and brush as his body bled off speed, leaving skin and flesh in his wake.

Gunfire sounded nearby. Shouting, the words unintelligible.

An explosion rocked the ground underneath him, drowning out all external sounds. He thought he heard Ma's voice, "Mikey, see to Tabby." *I did, Mama.*

He'd come to rest face down, mouth full of sand and grit he couldn't dislodge, blinking to expel the darkness creeping around the edges of his vision. *Bella*, he thought, remembering the weight of her tiny body in his hands. *My miracle.*

Darkness closed in, the pounding in his head slowing, his body heavy, held immobile under the mass of a mountain.

Love you. Knowing what was coming, he projected the thought as hard as he could, praying Juanita would feel him loving her. Honor. Club.

Family.

What comes after

Fury

Fury folded in half and sagged to the bench behind him, forehead supported in one hand while the other held the phone to his ear. Shouts and curses sounded in the background, but silence otherwise filled the call as he struggled to pull in a breath that didn't break, making his chest hitch. He cleared his throat and swallowed, then swallowed again before he could speak. "Brother," was all he got out before he had to stop, throat tight around the words he wanted to say. Something tickled his top lip, and he flicked at it with his tongue, tasting bitter salt trickling through his mustache.

Clearing his throat again, he held his breath, letting his emotions settle a moment. Even to his ears, his sigh sounded painful, but he bulled through, beginning again. "Brother. Tell me what happened."

"Lalo. Fuck man, I knew I shouldn't tell him, but I didn't—" Mason stopped speaking, not trailing off, but interrupting himself and Fury heard the inrush of breath which wasn't weeping, but rode the blade of grief, and knew it felt very much like pain. "Didn't expect him to go off the reservation, Fury."

"And Lalo?"

"Very dead." That response was quick and definite. "Watch took care of that."

Sirens sounded in the distance, and Mason cursed. Fury knew what it meant. "In the wind?"

"No." This was firm, definite. Mason's next words were pained. "Won't leave him behind, man. Can't. I'll get him settled and then get to Las Cruces. Juanita deserves to hear it from me."

Gooseflesh raised on Fury's arms at the emotion held in check. "You want me to make some calls?"

"Yeah, start the tree. This ain't a text message notification. Chapters need to get a call. We do this like he'd already changed his patches. All respect, brother." Silence, then Mason finished with, "Talk soon."

***

Bones

With careful, precise movements, he laid the phone flat on the table in front of him, and reached to pick up his beer only to find he lacked the strength to lift the glass. Bones remained in this position for a long time, chill fingers wrapped around the glass slick with condensation, beer slowly warming, the ring of wet collecting underneath spreading. A body entered his view, and he slowly lifted his gaze, taking in the questions bubbling underneath the surface of the man's features.

Without moving, Bones asked, "Did you also receive a phone call?" Road Runner, someone he'd known a long time, one who'd worn a Rebel patch long before he did, nodded. There was a honed anger on his face, warring with grief. Bones released his grip on the glass and sat up. "You received more than a phone call, didn't you?" Mouth twisting to one side, Road nodded again.

"Gunny called, right after Mason."

"And what information did Gunny have to impart?" Bones was still reeling from the call to tell him Watcher had died on the side of the road in Texas. Only seven hours from his beloved Juanita. *He went fast, Bones.* Mason's words ran through his head again. *Nothing anyone could do.* They'd all seen it before. He knew. Every rider knew the odds. It's not if you go down, it's when. Mangled bodies from crashes, riders more vulnerable than they appeared. Bodies subjected to impacts which destroyed them. Every person had a lifeline, and when the fates decreed an ending, it would come. Whether peacefully in bed, or in a crumpled pile on blood-crusted sand.

Road made a noise and Bones looked up, realizing he hadn't listened to the answer he'd requested. "My apologizes." He swallowed and corrected himself. "Apologies. What did Gunny say?"

"You were good friends with Watcher," Road Runner commented, and Bones tipped his head to one side, nodding slowly. "Did you know his sister?" A headshake, because he hadn't met Watcher until after he'd left the military, back when he was in the Outriders. Back before the world changed. "Fury has Gunny looking into some odd accidents in Kentucky, and turns out Watcher's sister was one of the oddnesses. She died in a single car accident. Everyone thought it was suicide, because of...shit that happened to her when she was little."

Road's pause was odd, and Bones noted that so he could question it in a moment. For now, he allowed the man to continue speaking unimpeded.

"Now it's looking like it wasn't what they thought. Duck's woman, Brenda, her parents were killed in a single car accident. She survived, but the circumstances around her survival are murky. Gunny's finding it harder to zero in on that one, there's some mystery about how she even lived. But there's a pattern of deaths in that area of the country that does not feel right."

"Why are you...?" Bones took a breath. "What does this mean to you?"

Road took a breath, and Bones braced for his next words. "Things line up with Morgan's time in that part of the country, boss."

Bones shook his head, still not sure what this meant. "Shooter's been in and out of Kentucky for decades. I'm not sure—"

"Not Shooter," Road Runner interrupted him. "Justice Morgan. Mason's step-dad."

***

Juanita

Juanita stared up into the darkness. She'd been awake for hours, knew from the glow slipping in around the curtains the sun would be rising soon. One of their roosters shared her knowledge, and crowed, his cracked voice pulling a weak smile to her tear-smeared face. Watcher insisted they have chickens, claimed he enjoyed the noisy things. The door to the bedroom opened silently, letting in light from the hallway, and she held her position. *I refuse.* Soft footfalls against the floor signaled the entrance she'd been dreading. Spider.

She'd been napping when she felt it, a pain in her chest that pulled her awake, sweating and gasping for breath. Heart pounding, she'd listened, but there was nothing more than the TV in the living room. As she sat upright, the ache spread, becoming agony swarming along her bones and she'd instinctively crawled to Watcher's side of the bed, pulling his pillow to her body to help blunt the pain. His scent on the soft surface of the pillow had soothed her, a forest musk which never left him, melding with the metallic smell of a thousand road trips, musky and male, and *him*.

Throat tight, she'd been trying to fight tears, wanting to call out to Spider to pull him away from the television show, desperate for anything to distract her from the pain, when she'd heard his phone ring. The bright sound cut off quickly, and she'd strained for anything that would tell her what was going on. Bending to bury her face in the pillow when her hands lifted to cover her ears, trying and failing to block out the sounds of his grief. Sobs and cries that tore at her, leaving furrows of anguish behind.

Coward, she'd taunted herself, and still remained behind her closed door. Feigning sleep the dozen times he'd checked on her, leaving them to each fight their demons alone. The hour came and went when she would have expected Watcher to return, the clock on the nightstand uncaring of the order she tried to impose on it with her mind.

Now her time was up, gone was the solitary space she'd carved out by her refusal to admit what she already knew. The edge of the mattress depressed near her hip, and she slowly turned to face Spider, seeing news on his features she didn't know she could survive. Outside a rumble grew and grew until she could pick out individual exhausts from the mix of what sounded like hundreds of motorcycles. Not the one she needed, though. No matter how she listened, how she searched, that belling rumble her ears were tuned to failed to appear.

And still

"How many did we lose?" The question came through the phone and he sucked in a steadying breath, not surprised when the question was snapped again, the man on the phone impatient for knowledge he didn't want to impart. "How many, dammit?"

"Too many."

The end (of this story)

THANK YOU FOR READING *Watcher*!

This is Book #9 in a series. Throughout this series we've been introduced to so many wonderful characters. People who live in my head in a way that makes them seem real in many aspects. I hope you fell in love with Watcher and his Juanita, and will continue in this saga along with me. Next up will be Bones' story, fraught with love and loss, and love.

MUSIC PLAYLISTS

I put together playlists of music both mentioned in the book, and used during writing and editing. Want a peek into the mind of me? Be sure of your decision, it's not always normal here!

Playlist: bit.ly/watcher-playlist

ABOUT THE AUTHOR

Raised in the south, MariaLisa learned about the magic of books at an early age. Every summer, she would spend hours in the local library, devouring books of every genre. Self-described as a book-a-holic, she says "I've always loved to read, but then I discovered writing, and found I adored that, too. For reading...if nothing else is available, I've been known to read the back of the cereal box."

Also by MariaLisa deMora

Alace Sweets

A dark thriller, this book is not a light read. Filled with edge-of-your-seat suspense, this intense story commands the reader's attention as it drives towards the explosive ending. Alace Sweets is a vigilante serial killer, with everything that implies and is sure to trip all your triggers. Be ready.

At seventeen, Alace Sweets turned a corner in her life, taking the wrong shortcut home from school.

Resisting the harsh knowledge her attackers will never be made to pay for their actions, Alace takes a stand. Justice must be served, and if fate's scales are out of balance, she's determined to set things right as best she can.

When the laws of men fail, the rules of Alace prevail.

5-Star Reviews for Alace Sweets

"deMora has a superb story-line and exceptional character development. All of her characters have such depth that will intrigue the reader..."
~Turning Another Page

"Hot, sweet, dark thriller."
~Beth D

"It will keep you on the edge of your seat and give you chills."
~Escape Reality Book Blog

"Disturbing, haunting, sickly; yet hot, sexy and heart racing!"
~Amanda L

"From the first page [deMora] pulls you into the world she has created and you do not even try to escape..."
~Little Shop of Readers Blog

"A must read for all those dark, gritty romance fans out there."
~Sweet & Spicy Reads

"You will find yourself so drawn into the story that the outside world is blocked out and your locking the doors and turning on all the lights."
~Danena F

"Don't judge me for bonding with a vigilante serial killer, she's more than what she does."
~iScream Books

"Thrilling...chilling...full of suspense, nail biting edge of your seat excitement."
~Tracey H

"Every time MariaLisa deMora picks up her pen (or opens her computer), she creates characters you want to believe in."
~Gail S

"Intriguing dark storyline, beautiful love story and nail-biting conclusion, what more could a reader ask for?"
~Manda M

"This book takes you a dark and twisted ride that is gripping..."
~Renee Entress' Blog

"This book is dark and gritty and I literally had to take a day off from reading it because it's that intense."
~My Girlfriend's Couch

"This is my favourite book so far from this author ... I recommend this book if you enjoy dark romantic thrillers."
~Cheekypee Reads and Reviews

"There's not enough stars to give this book and 5 just doesn't really do it justice!"
~DeLane C

"I couldn't put this book down from page one! Tried to stop & go to bed but couldn't sleep thinking about Alace and got up & finished the book."
~Debbie M

"MariaLisa DeMora, wordsmith that she is, made this a story of the enlightenment of a woman and finding love in a life where she has had none."
~Kat W

"Whatever deep dark trench [deMora] pulled a character like Alace from should be revisited again and often."
~Confessions of a Serial Reader

ADDITIONAL SERIES AND BOOKS

Please note that books in a series frequently feature characters from additional books within that series. If series books are read out of order, readers will twig to spoilers for the other books, so going back to read the skipped titles won't have the same angsty reveals.

Rebel Wayfarers MC series:

Mica, #1
A Sweet & Merry Christmas, short story #1.5
Slate, #2
Bear, #3
Jase, #4
Gunny, #5
Mason, #6
Hoss, #7
Harddrive Holidays, short story #7.5
Duck, #8
Biker Chick Campout, short story #8.5
Watcher, #9

A Kiss to Keep You, novella #9.25
Gun Totin' Annie, short story #9.5
Secret Santa, short story #9.75
Bones, #10
Gunny's Pups, novella #10.25
Never Settle, short story #10.5
Not Even A Mouse, short story #10.75
Fury, #11
Christmas Doings, #11.25
Gypsy's Lady, #11.5
Cassie, #12
Road Runner's Ride, novella #12.5

Occupy Yourself band series:

Born Into Trouble, #1
Grace In Motion, #2 (TBD)
What They Say, #3 (TBD)

Neither This, Nor That series:

This Is the Route Of Twisted Pain, #1
Treading the Traitor's Path: Out Bad, #2
Trapped by Fate on Reckless Roads, #3 (TBD)

Other Books:

With My Whole Heart
Alace Sweets
Hard Focus

More information available at mldemora.com.

www.ingramcontent.com/pod-product-compliance
Lightning Source LLC
Chambersburg PA
CBHW050023030726
47506CB00001B/84